I Loved Thy Creation

A collection of short fiction
by Maya Kaathryn Bohnhoff

O SON OF MAN!
I loved thy creation, hence I created thee.

Bahá'u'lláh

Contents

Foreword

The short fiction contained in this collection was originally published in the United States and the United Kingdom in such magazines as *Analog Science Fiction, Amazing Stories, Century,* and *Interzone.* All the stories are speculative in nature, and range from science fiction to fantasy to magic realism. They are bound together by the fact that they contain references to the Faith of Bahá'u'lláh in the form of inspiration, characters, and/or themes. They are grouped, in these pages, by genre and subject matter.

The title of the collection derives from a verse in *The Hidden Words of Bahá'u'lláh:*

> *O SON OF MAN!*
> *I loved thy creation, hence I created thee...*

The idea that creation is driven by a pre-existing love of the creature and of the very act of creation itself, is something I believe is understood by most artists whether they be writers, painters, sculptors, or musicians. It certainly describes my feelings about the worlds and people I created in these stories.

> *O SON OF MAN!*
> *Veiled in My immemorial being and in the ancient eternity of My essence, I knew My love for thee; therefore I created thee, have engraved on thee Mine image and revealed to thee My beauty.*

Hand-Me-Down Town

A story of speculative fiction

Hand-Me-Down Town was originally published in *Analog Science Fiction Magazine* in 1989 and was my first published work of fiction. I wrote it in reaction to the criminalization of homelessness by a California town trying to protect its tourist industry. The name of the town in this novella is fictionalized. Bahá'u'lláh, in His voluminous writings, refers to the poor as *"the trust of God in your midst,"* and further writes:

> *Be generous in prosperity, and thankful in adversity. Be worthy of the trust of thy neighbor, and look upon him with a bright and friendly face. Be a treasure to the poor, an admonisher to the rich, an answerer of the cry of the needy, a preserver of the sanctity of thy pledge.*
>
> *Gleanings from the Writings of Bahá'u'lláh,* p 285

These are the principles on which my hand-me-down town was built.

-1-

Stu Williams pulled his jacket across his chest and zipped it all the way up to his chin. It was damned cold for February. He dug his hand into his left coat pocket and counted the change there without taking it out to look. About $4.00 in quarters; enough to buy a decent breakfast at Caroline's or a not-so-decent breakfast and a newspaper. He decided in favor of a decent breakfast and a trip to the Sears electronics department around noon to catch the news on the tube. Of course, TV's didn't have tubes anymore, he reflected. Old habits die hard.

Mike Hanrahan fell in with him on the way down Hennessy, grumbling about how difficult it was to make it on recycling these days. "Problem is," he complained, plucking burrs off the front of his disreputable Rob-Roy, "everybody's doin' it now. *Everybody!* And his Aunt on top o't. Th'only place the market's not jam packed is the freeways."

"Freeways, Mike?" Stu wrinkled his nose. "Naw, you don't want to get into freeways."

"Damn right! But a man's gotta eat, doon't he?"

Caroline's was warm and smelling of coffee and baked stuff and bacon cooking. They ordered breakfast and sat back to enjoy a discarded newspaper. Stu disappeared behind the sports page.

"Well, damn it all to hell!"

Stu lowered the paper and peered at Mike over its edge. "Excuse me?"

"Those blue-suited bureaucrats an' their idiot measures an' bills! Good Lord, they think they can legislate the world away. Do you know what they're proposin' to vote on today at noon?"

"I have no idea."

"That damn Bag Lady bill."

Stu dropped the sports section. "Let me see that."

Mike flipped the paper across the table.

Stu fielded it and found the offending column easily without the aid of Mike's out-thrust finger. There it was in black and white—"City Council Votes on Criminalizing Vagrancy." Noon today.

"We should pick up every transient on the Boulevard and go picket city hall," Mike decided.

"What, and provide them with 'Exhibit A?'" Stu shook his head.

Mike stared at him thoughtfully. "I suppose a college man like yerself's got a better idea?"

Stu laughed. "Mike, if I'd had a better idea, I wouldn't be sitting here with seventeen cents in my pocket worrying about being 'criminalized.'" He glanced down at the column again. "But I might be picketing city hall, anyway."

-2-

Annie Lee Paice stepped off the curb almost into the path of an oncoming truck. The air horn shoved her back a step and the truck rumbled harmlessly by.

Too bad, she thought. *Might've been for the best.*

A wash of cold guilt followed immediately. Her eyes found the dilapidated old Chevy wagon in the shaded lot across the street and misted when she saw Sammie waving at her from the roof. The guilt curled in the pit of her stomach and moved upward toward her throat. She swallowed it again—pacified it by walking to the corner and crossing with the light.

"Did you get it, Mom?" Sammie bounced off the hood of the car and met her nearly eye to eye. So tall for his age—going to be just like his Dad.

She shook her head, glancing over her shoulder at the HEW building. "She didn't even have new forms for me to fill out. She said I oughta see a lawyer."

"What the hell's a lawyer gonna do for us?" Her oldest son, David, had hauled his lanky frame out of the passenger seat and hung on the roof of the car, chin propped on his crossed arms.

"Pry some money out of your Dad, I s'pose."

"Huh! They'd have to find him, first. Did you tell her that?"

She grimaced. "I mentioned it. She said that wasn't their line of work. So we were back to the lawyer again."

David's expression didn't change. "Okay, so what's next?"

He was trying so hard, she thought. Trying to act like everything was going to be just fine. It was just a matter of *what's next?*

She fought a through a wave of cold panic before drawing some sanity out of his dark, resolute eyes. He was right. That's what it was—*what's next?* Small steps. She silently thanked God for him and prayed that by the time he turned fifteen he could go back to being a normal teenager.

She smiled brightly and ruffled Sammie's hair. "Next, I look for a job."

"Me too," David said.

"Who's gonna take care of Sammie and Trudy?"

"I can!" Sammie protested loudly enough to wake Trudy up. In the back of the wagon, she stretched and blinked.

David ignored him, his eyes kindling. "Make you a deal, Mom. We both look for work and the one who gets the best money works while the other one stays home with the kids."

"I said, *I* can!" Sammie repeated. "I can take care of us. I'm not a kid."

"Yeah, you are."

"If I'm a kid then you're a kid!"

"You're a kid, Sammie," David repeated.

"I'm twelve years old, dammit!"

"You're eleven," David corrected, "and watch your mouth."

"You watch my mouth!" Sammie's tongue made a rude appearance.

"In the car." Annie gave the younger boy a gentle shove.

"Let's go find a newspaper."

-3-

Loucette Doucette rocked gently back and forth on the park bench, eyes on nothing in particular. The sun felt warm on her face despite the near freezing temperature, but then her face was the only part of her body not swaddled in layers of warm flannel and wool.

She was indulging in her favorite pass-time just now —'membering. She was very good at it—excelled at pulling faded bits of sepia-tone out of dark hiding and colorizing them. No high-tech movie magic could do what Loucette Doucette's memory could do.

God, it was all there today, too. New Orleans greens and blues, hot whitewashed walls, cool shadows, bright smiles in chocolate faces. And over all, the sun whispering a warm, loving benediction.

Her full lips curved as the smells began to emerge. New Orleans smells—hot, spicy, sizzling smells; dark red smells in her Daddy's restaurant. And she sat on the stairs that led up to their flat, rocking back and forth to New Orleans sounds, eyes on nothing in particular, with that knowing smile her Daddy said'd get her in trouble some day.

It'd done that.

She stopped 'membering and got up, hungry, longing for Creole food. They didn't know Creole cookin' at the Mission. Not like she did. Maybe Nancy'd let her putter in the kitchen today. She liked that.

Behind her shopping cart, headed across park, she started 'membering again. Old, flat, crepe-soled sturdies grew sleek and high-heeled. Her steps tapped with the rhythmic authority of youth, hips swayed.

This time the memories carried her for three blocks—all the way to the front door of the Mission. She swept in like she owned the place, feeling that powerful flush of warmth that only came when many pairs of eyes were on you. Then many pairs of lips would whisper your name—"Loucette Doucette."

"Lucy-Ducy! How you doin', hon?"

Memories fled before the grizzled smile. Loucette parked her shopping cart by the door and returned the smile with one of her own. She still had good teeth that were still dazzling against her ageless café-noire skin.

"Allo, Guillaume," she said and sat next to him at the long table, pulling off elbow-length fingerless gloves.

His smile deepened. He loved the way she always called him 'Guillaume.' Everybody else called him 'Billy,' thought of him as a gin-soaked old rodeo bum. Not Lucy—not Loucette. She was a class act and she thought of him as a class act—made him feel like one. Guillaume.

"Breakfast, Lucy?"

She nodded, shrugging off a few layers of unnecessary warmth, and smiled when Billy came around and took her elbow.

"Why, *merci*, Guillaume," she exclaimed, as if he didn't perform the same ritual almost daily. But she always acted out her surprised pleasure, always let him escort her to the chow line, take her down a tray and help her select her breakfast—*putee dayjunay*, she called it.

But today there was a surprise after all—the usually sunny group of faces behind the steaming trays seemed pinched and grim. Behind them, beyond the racks of fresh-baked rolls and kitchen utensils, angry voices carried over the hiss of running water.

"Inhuman, fratricidal, cold-blooded *bastards!*"

Billy paused in the act of handing his tray to the uncomfortable-looking black girl just that side of the scrambled eggs and peered past her, eyes seeking the source of the argument. He'd never heard Nancy Yee being angry before.

Wouldn't have thought she had it in her.

The guy behind him in line poked a finger at the kitchen. "What the hell's that noise about?"

The black girl (Delores, that was her name—he could never remember it because she didn't look like a 'Delores') shifted from one foot to the other and cast a chocolaty glance over her shoulder.

"*Don't* tell me to calm down!" yelled Nancy Yee's voice. "I don't *want* to calm down!"

A male voice mumbled something unintelligible in return.

Delores leaned over the scrambled eggs. "Nancy's pretty steamed about that new bill."

On cue, Nancy's voice shot from the back of the kitchen. "Dammit, Leon, stop *patronizing* me!" She was obviously steamed about something.

"What bill's that?" asked Billy.

"The city council is voting on a bill that would make transients criminals."

"Transients?" Billy frowned. "You mean-"

"She means you guys." Nancy Yee appeared between a couple of bread racks, her dark eyes back-lit with anger. Her assistant, Leon Squires, lurked behind her, hangdog. "They want to make bad luck illegal."

Loucette set the dish of peach halves on her tray and turned to look at the young woman. "Theah must be somethin' we can do," she said. There was always something one could do.

"You can pray," said Nancy Yee, and left the kitchen.

"Oui." Loucette nodded thoughtfully. "One can always pray, because God will always listen."

"Funny," said the guy behind Billy, "I never noticed her havin' a Chi-nee accent."

"Vietnamese," Loucette corrected him. "Nancy is Vietnamese. From a very old, very fine family. She speaks French very good, too," she told Billy, and went to eat her *petite déjeuner*.

-4-

There'd been little on the noon news from the official contingent about the Vagrancy Measure as it was politely referred to. On the street, it was the "Bag Lady Bill" and no one referred to it politely.

What the news did show were man-on-the-street interviews (ironic, Stu thought) and a healthy uproar from religious groups and community service organizations. The men and women in the street were divided over the issue. Comments ranged from: "It sucks!" to what was shaping up to be a long-winded diatribe against the evils of laziness before the tele-journalist put a cork in it.

"I think it's about time," said a thirty-ish woman with an armful of toddler. "I mean, my kids gotta walk down the streets an' see them people lyin' there—pushin' their little carts around an' all that. I mean, I don't know who those people are or where they been or what's goin' on in their heads."

I wish I knew what was going on in yours, Stu thought.

Mike snorted. "Lovely woman," he said.

The reporter next tried to flag down a young collegiate type who was in an obvious hurry. He afforded the discamera a second of anger. "It's f___ed," he commented, before the censor could react.

Mike laughed. "Ain't it," he said.

The next woman interviewee agreed, if more politely. "I think it's an obscenity. I don't believe we have the right to legislate people out of our cities just because they're homeless.

They need help, not a drop kick out of town. I don't understand this bill at all. It's not solving a problem, it's just hiding it...or hiding from it. It's morally reprehensible."

"It's absurd," said a middle-aged businessman. "I wouldn't be surprised if Santa Theresa was consumed by a ball of fire. Maybe we ought to rename the place—Santa Adolpho after Adolph Hitler."

"Human litter," said the next Santa Adolphan, shrugging. "You find litter lying around, you pick it up and throw it away. Same difference."

An interview with members of the Inter-faith Council followed which went a long way toward reviving Stu's faith in his fellow men and women. A graying Catholic priest and a young female Bahá'í with matching expressions of deep concern, represented the organization against the backdrop of city hall and picket signs.

"This bill will do nothing to address the problem of homeless people," said the girl, earnestly. "We're dealing with an age-old disease here, and this bill is only aimed at masking the symptoms."

"So, you're saying this is just a band-aid measure?" asked the TJ.

"It's worse than a band-aid measure. It's like putting a dirty dressing on an already infected wound. And it's as much a tragedy for the people responsible for this cruelty as it is for the homeless. They can't possibly understand the reality of what they're doing."

"There have been rumors that the churches and organizations of the Inter-faith Council will offer sanctuary to the homeless if the bill passes. Could you comment on that, Father?" The TJ poked her bright blue microphone at the priest.

"The member organizations of the Inter-faith Council are planning to offer shelter and sanctuary to as many homeless people as their facilities can legally contain. If this bill passes, and we're praying it won't, we'll publish a list of centers that will be open for that purpose."

"But, Father, won't you be aiding and abetting criminals?"

"No. We're simply taking them off the street. If they're not on the street, they're not vagrant. If they're not vagrant, they're not criminals."

The newswoman swung to face the discamera, adopting that serious 'on-the-beat-reporter' look. "So, surrounded by a show of solidarity from the religious community, the Santa Theresa city council deliberates over this highly controversial issue. We'll be on hand to report on their decision as soon as it's made. This is Karen Culver for Channel Seven News."

Stu shivered and shrugged his shoulders deeper into his jacket.

Mike made a rude noise and turned to go. "Better gi' back to work."

"Yeah." Stu followed him out of the over-heated department store and out onto the sidewalk. They went their separate ways there—Mike returned to scavenging for aluminum cans, and Stu headed for the Murphy Street Mission for an afternoon's gainful employment.

Nancy Yee must be climbing the walls, he thought.

A chipped kitchen counter and three broken chairs later, he ate dinner, listening to Lucy-Ducy talk in her smoky N'awleans *patois* about singing in her Daddy's restaurant. He hadn't seen Nancy all day. A frustrated Leon told him she'd disappeared right after breakfast, probably to join the picketers at city hall.

At six o'clock, Leon disappeared into the Salvation Army store next to the Mission and reappeared with a portable TV. He set it up in a corner of the dining hall and turned on the evening news. Everyone stopped talking, chewing or washing dishes to watch and listen.

The decision had come in at 5:30 and was written in the angry faces of the crowd in front of city hall. There was a futile confrontation on the steps of the building between exiting councilmen and picketers, then the list of religious centers open for sanctuary rolled slowly up the flat screen.

"There's Nancy!" someone yelled, and they all watched her shout soundlessly into the face of an equally furious councilman while names and addresses slid over her tear-stained face.

Stu helped the Mission staff and evening regulars set up cots in case they had a lot of sleepers. Nancy showed up as they were finishing, eyes red from crying, voice hoarse from shouting. She paid Stu for his work and offered him a place to stay. He declined, pocketed his money, and headed for the 'Y.'

He had to pass in front of city hall, skirted it quickly, the way a man hustles past an open grave, and hurried across the adjoining park. He slowed a little to enjoy the moonlit-lamplit beauty, watch milky tendrils of steam rise like wraiths from the damp sidewalk. He short-cutted across the frosty grass and came out on the parking pad, near its lone occupant—a battered station wagon with frosted-over windows.

He was about three feet from it when a flashlight beam lit up the inside of the car, throwing the shadows of two people into relief against the semi-opaque glass. He was in the act of slipping quietly away when a third, smaller shadow popped into sight and a plaintive voice wailed, "Mom, Sammie's kicking me!"

His appreciation of the situation did an Immelman loop. The next thing he knew, he was tapping on the driver's side back window. There was a moment of total silence inside the wagon, then the window rolled slowly down.

"Oh," said a woman's voice, in obvious relief. "I thought you were a cop."

"You're lucky I'm not. A cop would have to arrest you. I'm just going to warn you that you'd better move your car."

"Can't. We're outta gas. Or just about, anyway. That station down the block is about as far as this old junker's gonna get."

"Well, ma'am, I don't know if you've heard any news today, but there is a new law on the books that says if you're caught loitering in this parking lot after midnight tonight, you'll be committing a punishable offense."

There was another silence.

"We're not hurting anybody here," she said.

"No, you're not."

"And we can't move the car. We don't have money for gas."

"I do," Stu offered.

"We can't take your money, mister." The adolescent voice was defensive.

"Yes, you can. Look, ma'am, I know you don't want these kids to spend the night in protective custody, but I'm afraid that's just what might happen if you don't move this car someplace less conspicuous."

Stu waited out the whispered conference, his eyes fixed on the halo of gold around a traffic signal at the corner of San Pablo and Main. A long, low car glided to a stop as the halo flared to crimson.

Stu leaned down to the window. "Ma'am, I'd suggest you come to a quick decision. There's a police car at the corner."

"Go around to the passenger side," said the woman. The car rocked with the flurried rearrangement of its occupants.

Stu rounded the Chevy's nose, keeping his eyes on the police car, which still sat at the intersection. They had to exit the parking lot practically in front of it and sidle past on their way to the filling station. It executed a wide u-turn and followed them, pulling up beside the mini-mart when they stopped at the pumps.

"Geez!" whispered Sammie. He watched the cops watch Stu pump gasohol while they bought and sipped hot coffee from biofoam cups. The steam looked wonderfully hot and delicious. A rap at the back window made him all but jump out of his skin. He rolled the window down viciously.

Stu peered in at him. "Let's go get some hot chocolate for everybody, okay?"

Sammie forgot his anger at being scared and grinned. "Okay!"

His mother started to put a damper on his enthusiasm. "Mister, we can't-"

"Yes, you can. It's my money. I'll spend it any way I want. And the name's Stuart—Stuart Williams. Now, you want coffee, tea or cocoa?"

Annie relented. "Coffee... Thank you, Stuart."

"I'll have coffee, thanks." David asserted his adulthood matter-of-factly.

"Chocolate!" cried Trudy, unconcerned with asserting anything.

"Okay. Two coffees, one chocolate. Coming?" He looked at Sammie.

"Sure!" Sammie catapulted out of the car. "You can call me 'Sam,'" he stage-whispered, eyeing the police officer near the door of the mini-mart.

"Thanks, Sam. You can call me 'Stu.'"

"Thanks, Stu."

They smiled at the cop on their way in, collected their coffees and cocoas, paid with most of Stu's meager earnings and smiled at the cop again on their way out. He managed a half-hearted response, then returned to his partner and his squad car.

Stu took over the driver's seat and did some quick thinking about where they were headed. He decided the Mission was the best place, but realized halfway there that the police car was still tailing them. He felt a deep reluctance to let the cops know they were shopping for a place to crash. It would mark that old gold Chevy for future suspicion.

He silently cursed the situation. Part of him understood their curiosity—he could've kidnapped these people for all they knew. But most of him was angry. Angry that a quirk of fate— the loss of a job or, in this family's case, he suspected, a husband and father—could transform a person from citizen-in-good- standing to suspicious character.

He was the same man he'd been two years ago, before all this—sure, a lot poorer and a little more cynical, but that didn't mean he'd come unhinged. Maybe the members of the city council or whoever was in that squad car simply judged other people by what they thought they'd do under the same circumstances. Sort of an upside-down, inside-out Golden Rule: Do unto others as you suspect they'd to unto to you if they had the chance.

In the end, he took them to the Bahá'í Center, intending to see them settled in, then leave. But the place was over-run and under-staffed and he found himself useful as a distributor of blankets and pillows. When that was over, it was easier just to find a free corner to curl up in before he fell asleep on his feet.

-5-

At 7:00 a.m. the next morning, Stu quietly consumed a breakfast provided by the local Bahá'ís and Quakers before wishing the Paices good luck and heading for Murphy Street. He felt guilty about accepting charity. He may be out a job and a home, but he wasn't drunk, disabled or destitute. Not like Billy or Annie Paice or-

He stopped, staring at the gleaming squad car parked boldly in front of the Mission. Two cops sat in it, watching the comings and goings of its 'patrons.'

He watched as Loucette Doucette made her way out onto the sidewalk on Billy McGuire's gnarled arm. She was without her shopping cart today—for obvious reasons. Billy shot the officers a sassy grin and touched the brim of his stained Stetson.

One of the officers flipped open a voice-activated compad and began mumbling notes to it. He was still mumbling when Stu passed by and entered the Mission. Nancy Yee was just inside, glaring out the big front window.

"Friends of yours?" Stu asked dryly.

"Not funny, Stuart." She turned from the window, glossy, black pageboy fanning with the movement.

They walked side-by-side toward the kitchen.

"Got a lot of customers today," Stu noted.

Nancy glanced at the crowded dining hall and nodded. Cots and mattresses and sleeping bags were propped or stacked or rolled against the walls. "Yeah. I don't know how long we can handle this many people, though. We're meeting with the Goodwill and Inter-Faith people tonight about forming an organized cooperative. You eaten?"

Stu nodded. "Nancy, you wouldn't happen to need some extra kitchen help, would you?"

"Oh, I *need* it, alright. I just can't afford it. I can barely keep what I've got. Why?"

He shrugged. "I ran across a family living in their station wagon. The mother and oldest boy could use some employment."

"Sorry, Stuart. But I will keep my ears open." She punched his arm and smiled. "I've got plenty for you to do, though."

He smiled back. "I was hoping you'd say that."

The news became the focus of the day's activities. At noon the little portable flat-screen in the dining hall provided the Mission lunch crowd with some rousing entertainment.

The Mayor of Santa Theresa wasn't the most popular celebrity in town, but he was easily the most controversial. He had everyone's full attention the minute his face appeared on the screen. He got more than their attention when they heard what he had to say.

The anchorwoman did the warm-up in neutral tones: "It's been less than twenty-four hours since the vagrancy ordinance came into effect, but there are already problems with enforcement. According to Mayor John Eastwick, a lack of cooperation from certain civic and religious organizations has impeded the ordinance's effectiveness. Mayor Eastwick, what, exactly, are these organizations doing?"

The mayor's very angry face appeared on the screen. "They're subverting the law. The entire point of the ordinance was to safeguard the tourist trade that Santa Theresa depends on. Because of this gross interference on the part of a group of well-intentioned but misguided organizations, we are seeing only the minutest drop in the number of vagrants wandering our streets. I seriously doubt these people realize the impact this can have on our tourist trade."

"But isn't the incidence of actual vagrancy—by that, I mean people sleeping and pan-handling on street corners—significantly down even this early on?"

"Yes, it is. And those vagrants who were in violation of the ordinance were dealt with. Last night, the streets of Santa Theresa were conspicuously clean. The problem is that our sanctuary groups turned their charges back out onto the street at first daylight. That means the people we don't catch will just wander the streets all day, then hole up in their missions and churches and halfway houses at night."

"But if they're off the streets at night, hasn't the ordinance accomplished its purpose?"

"No, it has not. The intent of the ordinance was to drive indigents out of Santa Theresa, not force them underground."

A loud hiss rippled around the dining hall and a wad of paper napkin sailed at the screen.

"What does the City Council propose to do about the situation?"

"We do have some legal recourse, but I'm not free to reveal what action we'll take first."

"Then you do intend to take action?"

"Only if these groups continue in this flagrant attempt to circumvent the law. I don't imagine they can afford to offer this level of support for very long, but if they persist, we certainly will take legal action."

"Mayor, it sounds as if you're prepared to challenge the entire concept of sanctuary."

The mayor looked momentarily uncomfortable. "Let's say I'm prepared to question it."

Whatever recap the anchor made was lost in the general outrage from the Mission audience. A flurry of napkins fell around the TV, prompting Leon to rush protectively to its rescue.

Stu Williams spent the day suspended in unease—and with good reason. The first legal action the City Council took when the "well-intentioned but misguided" civic groups revealed no sign of capitulation was to become unbendingly strict in its enforcement of the building capacity ordinances.

The sanctuaries reacted by shuffling their occupants from one room to another whenever the suddenly ubiquitous police force put in an appearance. The police counter-reacted by

making surprise inspections at twelve midnight on a Sunday. By
four a.m. the first group of indigents was transported to the
Juvenile Authority to await final transport out of town. Mike
Hanrahan was among them.

Stuart Williams didn't know that until nearly two p.m. the
next day. By that time, he'd found Annie Lee Paice's oldest boy
part-time work and helped several more single-parent families
settle into the annex of the local Bahá'í Center. Like the Paices,
they had to share single rooms, but it beat the hell out of air
mattresses at the Mission or the underside of a staircase.

"What were you, Stu? Before, I mean." Annie Lee pulled
him out of a half-anxious/half-aimless stare across a park that
was, for once, empty of everything but early tourists taking
advantage of a warming in Santa Theresa's ambivalent weather.

He shifted slightly on the faux-adobe bench, squinting at a
pair of tourists who squinted back as if at a museum display—
Theresan Couple at Lunch in Natural Habitat.

"An urban planner," he said. "You know, one of those guys
who're paid to look at your orange groves and see shopping
malls."

Annie gave him a surprised glance. "I'd think you'd make a
good living at that."

"If you're good at it. I wasn't good at it. I looked at shopping
malls and saw orange groves."

"That why you're doin' odd jobs at the Mission an' sleepin'
at the Y?"

He tilted his head, considering his own particular set of
whys and wherefores. "My wife died," he said. "We had all
these plans that... Well, they were the kind of plans that only
work for two people. So I found myself suddenly..."

"No place to go?" guessed Annie. "In here, I mean." She
tapped her chest.

"Yeah," he agreed. "I got sad and drank too much. Then I got sober and mad and picked fights with everybody I knew—my boss included. And somewhere in there I realized I didn't want to be good at turning orange groves into shopping malls."

"You quit?"

"I got fired." He shrugged. "I *deserved* to be fired, I have to admit. So, I sold my house and drifted around. 'Going on sabbatical,' I called it. I wanted to look at architecture, get some direction, some inspiration. Those were all my good reasons for not getting into counseling instead. I dropped out. Then, I ran out of money in Santa Theresa."

"No, kids then, huh?"

He shook his head. "We were going to wait another year, till Beth finished her Master's degree. She was younger than I am."

He was depressed, suddenly, remembering that. He hadn't thought about it much since he'd washed up under Mike Hanrahan's staircase in a chilling rain almost a year ago.

Annie looked at her five year old Adidas and empathized. "My old man went on sabbatical, too," she said. "Took his secretary with him. She was a *temp.*"

"Shouldn't last too long, then," said Stu.

Annie gave him a sideways look. He was looking back, face ultra-serious...all but his eyes. She laughed.

"How does a man do that?" Stu asked, as they made their way back to the Mission, later. "How does a man leave his family—his *children,* for God's sake!"

"I dunno. I guess he couldn't take *me* anymore. Showin' a cute li'l Georgia peach off t'your National Guard buddies is a lot different than bringin' your boss home to a high school drop-out who doesn't even know what it is you do for a livin'."

"What did he do for a living?"

"Something to do with micro-circuits. Hell, I thought it was something 'lectrical. You know, like house wiring. I called him an electrician. Made an ass of myself. Never knew what was goin' to pop out of my mouth. His friends at work thought I was cute. *He* didn't think I was cute. He thought I was dumb."

Stu glanced at Annie Lee, assessing her. She still looked like a cute li'l Georgia peach to him—a harried, hassled and worried peach, but peach none-the-less.

"You're not dumb, Annie," he said. "Don't ever let anyone tell you you're dumb."

-6-

The Mission was a madhouse this afternoon. People jostled each other for a place at the rear of the main hall—a place where a policeman entering the room might not see them and single them out. Children milled and squealed under foot. Somehow through it all, Stu saw Nancy Yee gesturing at them from the kitchen door and steered Annie in that direction.

Nancy pounced on Annie first. "Delores is sick and this place is a zoo. Could you *possibly* help out in the kitchen? I can pay you five dollars an hour."

Annie glanced at Stu and shrugged. "Where do I start?"

Nancy flashed a relieved grin. "Thanks. Just go on in. Leon will put you to work."

When she turned back to Stu, the grin was gone. He had the impression that it still hung in the air on the other side of her head, waiting for her to step back into it.

"Stuart," she said, and he knew something serious had to follow. "Stuart, the police picked up Mike. They caught him scavenging for returnables along the Main Street off-ramp."

Stu stared at her, suddenly chilled to the marrow. "Where do they... Do you know where he is? Jail?"

Nancy shook her head with a swish of gleaming black silk.

"Not jail. They don't want to be responsible for these people, Stu. They were to be detained in an annex to Juvenile Hall until there are enough for a busload. Then they get bussed out to the interstate."

"To do what?" Stu asked, heat rising into his face. "To starve or get run over or hitch-hike into oblivion?"

Nancy shrugged. "Who cares, right? They're no longer Santa Theresa's problem... Where are you going? You can't bail him out, Stu."

He stared at the small brown hand gripping his sleeve.

"I've already tried," she said. "Only next of kin can get them out, and then only if they can produce proof of residence somewhere."

"Proof," Stu repeated. "Everywhere you go these days— everything you do—you've got to prove something to somebody. Prove you have credit, prove you've got a degree, prove who you are, prove you really exist...prove you even have a *right* to exist. And then, some god-forsaken place like Santa Theresa questions that right-" Tears of exasperation made him pinch his eyes shut. "Damn," he finished.

"There's nothing we can do," Nancy murmured.

Even before she'd finished the cliché, Stu could see her challenging it. Her eyes kindled. "Yes, dammit! *Yes!*" She tugged at his sleeve. "My office," she told him, and struggled toward it, sidestepping floor-sitters, side-jumping kids.

He followed.

Forty-five minutes and half as many phone calls later, Nancy was fading, but triumphant.

"So, let's say you can really mobilize these people," said Stu carefully. "Then, what? You get all this stuff together and take it where?"

"We'll have to find a place."

"*Find* a place?"

Nancy was already on her feet, already sifting through a file drawer. "I've got an old map here somewhere..."

She came up with it instantly. Stu didn't doubt that her files were as well organized as the rest of the Mission...under normal circumstances.

She plopped the map down in front of him—"SANTA THERESA CHAMBER OF COMMERCE," it said, and "SANTA THERESA AND OUTLYING AREAS." She tossed her credit card on top of it.

"Do you think Annie would let us use her car? I get followed everywhere in mine. I'll pay for gas." She pointed at the card.

"Newspaper?"

She nodded. "*And* police. Would you ask Annie about the car?"

✦ ✦ ✦

"Turn left here." Nancy pointed at the faded sign. It proclaimed, to anyone who cared, the junction of Santa Theresa's modest I-80 Business Loop and State Highway 19.

Stu turned onto the tree-lined washboard, grimacing at the tattered patriotism of a once-upon-a-time red, white and blue gas station. Fifty yards later, he had brought the car nearly to a crawl, staring out the window.

"What *is* this?"

Nancy folded the map neatly across her knees. "This is—or should I say, this *was* Serendipity Springs. You won't find it on your GPS and it's a little the worse for wear, but still worthy of the name."

Stu turned his stare to Nancy. "Meaning, it still has springs?"

She slapped his leg with the map. "Yes! And it's still lucky, lucky, *lucky!* Pull over."

It was a mess—a disaster. The buildings were aging recluses; smothered with vines, over-shadowed by monster oaks, hemmed in by tree-sized rhododendrons and choked with dust. Three out of four roofs had accidental skylights and several front porches featured a direct path to the root cellar. There was a drug store-cum-grocery (a "Mercantile," according to the drooping sign), a boarded-up café—replete with warped lunch counter, a post office, a drive-in of indeterminate age and another building of indeterminate use. There was also a church, a peeling, weed-choked motel with tiny, square cabins, and a quintet of houses that the most entrenched realist would declare haunted.

Stu stood tentatively on the porch of one of the almost-certainly-haunted houses and surveyed the street. The opposing house surveyed him in turn, its empty windows passive and benign. He felt a tickle of something like excitement struggle up from the pit of his stomach.

Nancy was watching his face. "Well?"

He shrugged, attempting to appear uncommitted.

Nancy stamped her feet. "This-is-it, this-is-it, *this-is-it!*" she said. "It's perfect!"

He shook his head. "Nancy...I don't know..."

She sobered suddenly, dousing the smile. She could do that. It was like having a deep hole appear in the sidewalk right where you were about to step. It always scared the stuffing out of Leon.

"Would you rather starve? Do you think *they'd* rather starve? Right this minute, there could be a bus loading up at Juvenile Hall. Your friend Mike could be on it. It's going to take him to a place without roofs or walls or food or drink. This looks pretty good next to that."

It did look pretty good next to that. "It'll take a lot of work," he said.

"Anything that's worth anything takes a lot of work," Nancy countered. Then she punched his arm. "Come *on,* Stu. What do you *really* think?"

He grimaced. "If I told you, you'd think I was out to lunch." He slapped his thigh. "Let's get this show on the road."

On the way back into town, Nancy made copious lists of tools, supplies, sundries and urgent phone calls to make. Meanwhile, Stu paged through imaginary architectural renderings of red, white and blue gas stations and drive-ins of indeterminate age.

As a result, he nearly missed the scene that was unfolding in the parking lot north of the town square—nearly, but not quite. Nobody could fail to notice the trio of black-and-whites converged in one corner. Stu swore and pulled the car into the curb.

Nancy looked up from her lists. "What-? Lucy!" She was out the door before Stu could even think of dissuasion, clipboard forgotten on the empty seat. He sat there in uncertainty for a moment, then got out of the car and followed, cautiously.

Nancy was already involved in the standoff, putting herself directly between the cops and their quarry. She was gesturing wildly, her voice creating hot punctuation marks in the cool, crisp air. Behind her, the old woman sat cross-legged on the grass, her little piles of goods—pilfered from the dumpsters of the rich and famous—spread about her on colorful scarves.

Her head was tilted stubbornly, arrogant chin thrust upward. Dark eyes spat a tirade of steamy Creole invectives at the four young city soldiers, who were clearly not sure what to do. They eyed the small crowd of tourists and natives that had gathered to watch.

A fifth officer manned the radio in his squad car, no doubt seeking guidance from higher up. Apparently, he received it—he left the car and issued a report to his teammates that took all of two seconds.

Stu stook helplessly by and watched as both Lucy and Nancy were escorted to a squad car and ducked inside. Lucy's goods ended up in the trunk of the same car. Her shopping cart —a late model Raleys—was left in the care of two blue suited boys who peered uncomfortably at the crowd. They peered back — interested, angry, uncertain.

That was when Stu saw the discams topped with station call letters; saw the TJs in their ersatz-wool blazers with matching microphone wind filters. One camerawoman zeroed in on the shopping cart. He followed the movement with his eyes and stared at the cart for a full minute before he could tear them away. When he did, it was to see Billy McGuire standing not five feet away, his colorless eyes squinted into desperate, miserable slits.

Stu moved quickly, pulling the old cowboy away from the scene, listening silently to husky whimpers of desolation.

"My Lucy...why'd they hafta find Lucy? Oh, damn that girl! Why'd she hafta go out peddlin' her crap? Didn't she know this'd happen? My Lucy..." And it started all over again.

Stu drove Billy back to the Mission, where someone would have to stand between him and that suddenly irresistible bottle of booze. A peculiar feeling that was neither shock nor anxiety nor good red anger roiled behind his solar plexus. He was calm telling Leon what had happened. Calm, because Leon could be counted on to panic and make his voice squeak incoherently. He was calm driving Leon to the police station, where it took over two hours to get Nancy released.

He didn't know what he was saving his anger for until the three of them were back in Annie's station wagon.

Nancy slammed the passenger side door and looked at Stu with eyes that had "mutiny" etched across each iris. "Now, we mobilize," she said.

Stu nodded, gritting his teeth so hard his jaw ached. He gunned the engine viciously and jerked the car into reverse, checking to make sure that no one had wandered into the path of their backward plunge. In the rear view mirror, Leon's face had gone suspiciously white.

-7-

David Paice wriggled in his seat and adjusted his baseball cap. The street looked the same as it had half and hour ago—dark, misty and quiet, except for the comings and goings of dart-like prowl cars. The garage doors he watched disgorged them it regular intervals.

He glanced at Stu. "Maybe they won't do it tonight," he said.

"Unless they want to have to feed these people another meal and put them up for the night, they have to move them pretty soon."

"How about now?" David pointed across the street.

The sharp nose of a police van had appeared in the exit of the station parking lot. It rolled down the ramp that sloped to street level and turned left onto Darlington Avenue. Stu and David watched it glide past their side street observation post, streetlights flickering on the faces of its passengers.

"That's it," said Stu. After a discreet pause, he started the car, flicked on the lights and pulled out onto Darlington.

The van's taillights glowed ahead of them at a traffic signal. They caught up before the light changed and rode the van's trail out of town.

It was the proverbial piece of cake. The only problem was that the drop site was on the opposite side of town from Serendipity Springs. It was a grove of trees near an overpass. Chosen, Stu imagined, for its proximity to the freeway and a major county road. It was a broad hint to the indigents to take a hike—literally.

He by-passed the grove and pulled the station wagon onto a rutted dirt track.

David flipped off his seat belt. "I'll bet I can see from the roof," he said, fumbling for the door handle.

"Whoa!" Stu's hand clamped on his shoulder.

"What's the matter?"

Stu pointed at the roof of the car, then twisted the dome light to an off position. *"Now go."*

David grinned. "Sorry, I forgot." He was out the door and clambering onto the roof.

The car rocked briefly, then settled as David found a comfortable position. There was a bare five minutes of calm before the car began rocking again. The door popped open and David deposited himself inside.

"All done," he said. "The van's on its way home."

The pitiful group of transients was still standing in a confused huddle when Stu caught them in the cold glare of his headlights. They all turned and blinked warily, then one stocky, glaring, red plaid figure separated itself from the group, assuming a defiant posture.

Stu grinned and brought the car to a halt. "Mike!"

Within fifteen minutes of their hurried conference, Stu was transporting a car full of indigents to Serendipity Springs.

Nancy had set up her command post in one of the creaking houses and was ready for an army of homeless. The nine that arrived were overwhelmed by the warmth and hospitality of their greeting.

Stu was overwhelmed, too—with the complete
transformation Nancy's team had worked on the dilapidated
building in a mere six hours. The interior had been scrubbed
within an inch of its life and smelled, not of disinfectant, but
cedar and spice. Oil lamps were scattered about everywhere,
illuminating piles of blankets and goods. It was like Christmas at
Aunt Mary's or a scene from *It's a Wonderful Life.*

Stu told Nancy where she could find the remainder of her
lost sheep and accepted an invitation to a hot dinner. He slept in
Serendipity that night and dreamed of drive-ins and malts and
carhops on roller skates.

There were twenty-five homeless in Serendipity by
morning. They were clothed, fed and the mostly sober put to
work on Nancy's scrub team. Stu spent the morning running
errands for "The Committee"— the unofficial title of the ad hoc
steering group of which Nancy Yee was the nominal head.

By the time Stu and his companions stopped erranding,
another group had an unofficial title. The homeless had begun
calling themselves the "Down & Outer Club," and Billy McGuire
solemnized the appellation with some boards and paint. Stu
held the ladder while the old cowboy mounted the "Club"
shingle from the porch of the shabby Victorian that served as
relief center. The "Down & Outers" broke into spontaneous
applause—the probably haunted house was theirs.

"Who owns this property?" Stu asked Nancy after the
impromptu "ceremony."

"I don't know. State of California, probably."

"Aren't they likely to want it returned to them at some
point?"

"Why? So it can continue to rot in peace?" Nancy's dark eyes flashed. "I've seen you snooping around the foundations and poking your nose into the attics. These buildings are salvageable, and you know it."

"*Marginally* salvageable."

"*Salvageable,*" repeated Nancy. "Why are you trying so hard to be a wet blanket, Stu? This sort of thing should be right up your alley."

"Stealing towns?"

"No, urban renewal. And we're not stealing. Borrowing, maybe... Scavenging. These people are professional scavengers, aren't they?"

When he didn't reply, she gave him a sly glance. "You didn't answer me. How come you're being such a drip?"

Stu barely managed to keep from laughing outright. "I didn't know I was being a drip. I thought I was being a realist."

"Realist-shmealist. You're being a drip." Nancy got suddenly and disconcertingly earnest, scooting sideways on the porch step to face him. The step groaned in protest. "Stuart, Serendipity is no place for realists. It's a place for dreamers."

"You evicting me?"

"I'm exposing you. You're no realist. A realist would still be in Chicago planning lucrative suburbs, not nursemaiding the refuse of Santa Theresa."

The word "refuse" raised his hackles. He started to rise to the bait, then accidentally let his eyes get tangled with hers.

"*Dream,* dammit," she said.

He sighed deeply and gazed around him. "It's salvageable, Nancy. Every building but that old barn next to this place. That should come down."

"Okay. What about this place?" She nodded back over her shoulder.

Stu grinned. "I was thinking it'd make a great Bed &
Breakfast for the Down & Outer Club."

Nancy's answering smile was dazzling. "Then Bed &
Breakfast it shall be. How many able-bodied souls do you need
for your construction crew?"

Stu shook his head. God, but her mind moved like a cat. "Six
or seven."

"You got 'em."

Nancy was up and away, leaving Stu feeling as if he'd just
visited Oz... Or the Twilight Zone, he thought, surveying the
tree-shrouded street. Just beginning to bud, the half-naked trees
looked benignly sinister. Their skeletal branches dangled like the
arms of lonely wraiths, wearing nothing but bracelets and rings
of peridot and emerald.

He shook his head. Definately Oz.

By three p.m. that afternoon, he found himself at the head of
a team of out-sized Munchkins. Billy McGuire and David Paice
were among them, as well as an out-of-work carpenter and an
aging bricklayer. The remainder of the eight-person crew was
young and inexperienced, but eager.

Stu put a group of four to work cataloguing areas that were
merely unsightly, while he checked more thoroughly for
structural problems. Annie Lee set about tearing down
crumbling wallpaper, while her sons tagged obediently behind
Billy, scavenging for usable wood. There wasn't much, although
a search of the ramshackle barn revealed a stack of warped but
recyclable two by fours under a rotting tarp. Nancy Yee added
wood to one of her ubiquitous lists.

The donations of food, clothing and supplies were
astounding. Members of the Committee's various civic groups
would visit Serendipity with eyes wide open. "You could use
'this' or 'that,'" they'd say, and disappear, to reappear later with
the aforementioned 'this' or 'that.'

By the end of their first week in Serendipity, the Down &
Outer Club's growing membership had lawn mowers, hand
tools, power tools, wood, some odd lots of brick and cinder
blocks and one small semi-quiet generator. They also received
old furniture, rugs, and even a couple of wood stoves.

Nor were their less tangible needs ignored. There was no
alcohol in Serendipity Springs, but there were a number of
alcoholics. There were no drugs, but there were those who
considered them essential to their existence. Nancy's contacts
with AA were immediately on the scene setting up meetings,
recruiting people to attend them.

"Only seven?" Nancy asked, looking over the list of
volunteers. "Only seven people signed up?"

Shelley Forbes shook her head. "Don't let it worry you, Nan.
These are just the ones who are ready to admit they have a
problem. There'll be more coming as soon as it sinks in that
they're cut off. The only way for them to get booze or drugs is to
go back into Santa Theresa, and if they do that, they'll just get
kicked right back out again. A word of warning, though. They
could cause problems for you in the meantime."

Nancy nodded in resignation. Problems. There always
would be problems. Somehow she'd hoped Serendipity would
make them all go away.

Stu's work crew expanded, so he expanded his renovations
to the old mercantile. As it happened, that was a stroke of good
timing—thanks to a few carefully placed suggestions, there was
a sudden influx of day-old baked goods and other perishables
from the supermarkets and bakeries of Santa Theresa.

"We need a refrigerator for all this," someone said, and
several old butcher cases and freezer chests appeared. Some of
them were broken, but between the four members of the "D&O
Electrical Group," two meat cases and three freezers were soon
restored to a semblance of functionality.

"I could can this stuff, if I had mason jars," Annie said, eying the perishables, and jars appeared. Annie Lee and Loucette became the hub of the food preparation team—"The Cookery." They turned questionable materials into stews and goulashes and broths.

If it was old, or new but not working just right, if it was perishable, unwanted, or not worth selling, it showed up in Serendipity. Which was not to say that many nice, new, shiny things didn't also show up in Serendipity, but used things appeared in much greater abundance.

"Hand-me-down things for hand-me-down people," muttered Mike Hanrahan acerbically, appraising a truckload of gnawed looking furniture. "This whole damn town is a hand-me-down."

"Now, y'old mule-head," returned Billy McGuire. "This stuff'd be great if it was refinished proper."

"Hmmm. And I s'pose yer just the fella t'restore't?"

"It'd be a job," Billy admitted, "but if I had some varnish remover and sand paper..."

"Beautiful job, Billy!" Nancy admired his handiwork from the open front door of the D&O Club. The little Queen Anne table glowed with the warm sheen of wood oil from beside the half refinished staircase. "Who did the doily?"

"That's tattin', deah," Loucette informed her, entering the hallway from the front parlor. "That dahlin' old girl, Mrs. Etterly done it. Lahd, when she come heah, she'd a whole bag o' tattin'." She chuckled. "Totin' that big ole bag, an' not one stitch a' clothin' in it, jus' lace an' thread an' them little crochet hooks." She said something in French and laughed.

Nancy stared at her. "Lucy, *where* did you get that wonderful outfit?"

Lucy smiled her glorious smile and made a piquantly tottering pivot. "Isn't it *grand*, though?"

"I certainly is *you*," Nancy said, and meant it.

The old red dress with its padded shoulders and tiny waist almost made her see the elderly woman as she no doubt saw herself—a Creole Queen, eternally youthful. To add to the quality of agelessness, Loucette's hair was sprayed and netted into a style that fit the dress perfectly. The whole effect was underpinned with a pair of worn black velvet pumps, complete with round toes and tiny, crooked red bows.

"A very kind lady from the Salvation Army gave me these," said Lucy. "Can't see why anybody'd throw out such a fine dress. Annie did my hair," she added, patting the sleek, black coil.

"You look like a model-doll, Lucy," Billy enthused.

Lucy's black face glowed with delight. "An' your table is *trés belle,* Guillaume."

Nancy looked at the little table speculatively. "Billy, didn't I see about three more of these little guys in the cellar?"

"Yeah, I got one for th'other house in the works."

"Will they all look as good as this one, do you think?"

Billy scratched the snowy carpet of stubble on his jaw. "Don't see why not. One's got a cracked leg, but I think I can wood putty that just fine."

Nancy crossed the hallway and brushed her fingertips across the warm grain. "Hmmm," she said, and smiled. "What's cooking? Smells Creole."

It *was* Creole. Everything, from the potatoes to the plentiful zucchini to the fish, tasted of Louisiana kitchens.

Two rooms had been set up for dining, making use of the various shapes and sizes of second-hand tables and junkyard chairs that had found their way into Serendipity.

Nancy stayed to dinner, sitting at table with the Paices and Stu. She was tending toward moody silence until David's "Pass the zucchini" became "Pass-the-zucchini-you-should-see-what-Phil-Kroeger-and-I-found-out-behind-that-old-filling-station!"

"David, where're your manners?" asked Annie Lee reflexively. "Didn't I teach you to say 'please?'"

"Sorry, mom. Please. It was the neatest thing—this whole barn full of old junkers."

"Junkers?" asked Nancy.

"You know, old cars. *Really* old cars. Antiques."

Nancy's eyes took on a speculative gleam. "Hmmm. I wonder if we could sell them to a junk yard or car mechanic?"

"*Sell* 'em?" David laughed. "Over Phil's dead body! He wants to—um, re—um, refur—um, fix 'em up. You should've seen the way he drooled over this old Buick. *Gag* me! It was really pukey."

"Yeah, pukey," echoed Sammie, rolling his eyes.

Annie Lee bristled. "David Andrew Paice, you watch your tongue! You're not too old to have your mouth washed out with soap."

"Just to big, huh, mom?" David quirked a grin at Stu, who failed to return it. The grin faltered. "Uh, sorry, mom."

"Me too," said Sammie, not to be outdone, even in contrition.

Nancy picked up her half-empty plate and headed for the kitchen. "See ya," she said.

Stu watched her go, suspecting that a new list had just sprung into being.

-8-

The truck arrived bearing a jumble of auto parts. It left carrying several pieces of Billy McGuire's refinished furniture, a crate of The Cookery's canned goods, and a bag of Pearl Etterly's tatting.

Phil Kroeger was ecstatic, and closeted himself and David Paice in the rundown garage with a decrepit Buick and the parts. They were seen only at mealtime, looking like they'd been bathing in thirty-weight. Annie Lee quickly despaired of getting her oldest son washed up for dinner.

A bare week after the arrival of the auto parts, Phil stood sheepishly outside Nancy's office at the Mission, looking as if he'd committed some heinous offense.

Nancy glanced up and saw him there—lumberjack cap in hands stained even darker than their normal mahogany. "Good grief, Phil! What's wrong?"

Phil shuffled. "Well, Miss Yee, it's like this... It's my cars."

She didn't even help him along with so much as an 'Oh?' so he was forced to clear his throat and look even more sheepish and shuffle again.

"I finished one of 'em."

Nancy's face lit up like Mrs. O'Leary's barn. "That's *wonderful!* You'll have to take me out for a spin."

"Well, Miss Yee, that's just it." Phil's voice, soft as his over-sized black eyes, grew even more muted. He saw that Nancy was about to ask him to speak up (everybody did), and cleared his throat again. "I can't take anybody for a spin. I don't got gas."

"Gas," echoed Nancy weakly.

"Um...yes, ma'am. *Real* gas...gaso*line*. I managed to get a gallon here'n there to test the engine, but not enough to *drive* anyplace. Stuff's hard to come by these days."

Nancy flipped open a notebook and scribbled something. "Gas-o-line," she said, then reached for the phone and her Rolodex simultaneously.

Phil boggled, watching her move—flipping through the Rolodex with one hand, picking up the receiver and punching out the prefix with the other. The Rolodex hand stopped and the phone hand completed the number.

"Hi! Is Mr. Garvey in? ...Nancy Yee. Thanks!" She winked at Phil and picked up a pencil. "Hi, Mr. Garvey, Nancy here... What..? Oh, yes, the car parts were a *God*-send. We really appreciate- ...Oh, no, thank *you*, Mr. Garvey... All right, Jim... Actually, that's what I'm calling about. Phil's got one of the cars in running condition, but it doesn't have a converter and we don't have any gasoline for it and... Well, that'd be nice... Well, I'm sure Phil would be happy to show it to you... Sure!"

She glanced at her watch. "How about one o'clock? You could have lunch out there with us... Nonsense, Jim. There's plenty. All our friends have been just as generous as you have... Great. You like Creole? ...Fantastic! See you at one, then? ...Oh, it's that old red-white-and-blue filling station on A19 at 80... Uh-huh. Just turn in there... Wonderful. We'll meet you there, then."

She hung up with a smile of satisfaction. "You shall have fifteen gallons of gas at one o'clock this afternoon. That ought to enough for a good spin."

Phil's slow smile was crooked and full of holes. Nancy thought it was one of the best smiles she'd ever seen.

Jim Garvey was as good as his word, showing up at 12:50 in front of the old filling station with three five-gallon cans of gasoline.

"What a gasser!" he chortled, ogling the faded red-white-and-blue pumps. "Little pun, there," he informed Nancy.

She smiled and nodded. Phil shuffled.

It took ten minutes to pull Garvey away from the battered garage, but he finally followed them to where Phil's pride and joy awaited what was probably its first square meal in forty years.

"Fifty-two Buick!" Jim Garvey breathed awfully. "Not bad shape. Little dinged up, though."

"Haven't got the stuff t'do much body work," said Phil defensively.

Garvey waved that aside. "Pretty is as pretty does," he said. "Let's see how she runs."

"She" ran like an Olympic marathoner—steady and smooth. Phil took Nancy, David and Jim Garvey on the inaugural spin and was toothily beaming from ear to ear when they pulled up again twenty minutes later in front of the gas station.

Stu was there, examining the underground gas tanks, when they drove up. He rose and waved, unable to resist answering Phil Kroeger's infectious, lopsided grin.

"Sounds great, Phil! Good work."

"Thank you, Mr. Williams."

"Stu," Stu corrected him (for about the fiftieth time).

Phil smiled and nodded.

Jim Garvey had gotten out of the Buick and was peering into the gas tanks. "Y'know these tanks look like they're still good."

Stu joined him. "I was wondering about that. Is there anyway to tell for sure?"

Garvey chuckled. "You thinking of setting up business?"

"No, just idle wondering."

Nancy squatted down opposite them, staring at the stygian hole. "Of course, we could use some gasohol for all the relief vehicles, and gasoline for Phil's projects." She wrinkled her nose. "Pretty silly idea, huh? It'd take a fortune to fill these."

Jim Garvey's eyes fell on the Buick, returning only reluctantly to Nancy's face. "I imagine it'd be real handy for you folks to have working pumps out here... Especially if Phil here is planning any more renovations. Wouldn't hurt to check it out."

Nancy smiled.

Jim Garvey was mightily impressed with the Cookery's Creole cuisine. He was also impressed with the amount of work the Down & Outers had done on their new quarters.

"This is great, Nancy," he congratulated her after a lunch of filé gumbo and hot, sweet French bread. "You folks have done a bang-up job on this place. That little motel is looking real cute. Y'know, it kind of reminds me of the little town I grew up in. ...Truelove. Truelove, Idaho."

He smiled reminiscently, stomach and heart both apparently full. "I remember we had one of those drive-ins, too. You know, the ones that looked like a giant mug of root beer? Sat out by the highway...such as it was."

He chuckled, then stretched and stood up. "Well, I got work to do this afternoon." He rolled comfortably to the dining room door, then glanced back at Phil Kroeger. "You do body work, Phil?"

"Yessir."

"Hmmm." Jim waved a hand in farewell and left.

The double tanker truck showed up five days later with a big, red ribbon around its curved flanks. A huge banner across the nose of the truck announced it as a gift "From the Petroco owners of Santa Theresa." It rolled into Serendipity at noon on a

Saturday, escorted by Jim Garvey and a TJ from the local PBS station.

Nancy was immediately wary. "Jim, you *know* we don't want any publicity."

Garvey had the good graces to look embarrassed. "It wasn't me, Nancy. One of the other owners happened to mention to his wife that we were doing this charity bit and she works for KETV. Next thing I know..." He shrugged and glanced at the journalist —an earnest-looking young Hispanic woman with glossy black curls that were bobbing vigorously as she tapped her first notes into a pocket compad.

Nancy scowled and opened her mouth to say something thwarting, when the young woman looked up and gave her a smile no less dazzling than her own.

"Hi. I'm Pepper Delgado." She held out her hand. "You must be Nancy Yee."

Nancy smiled weakly and took the hand. It had a very firm grip. "Pepper, I... We're really not in the market for publicity. Could I convince you to...to leave?"

"*Why?* I'd think publicity would be exactly what you *did* want. You could be drawing support from statewide—even nationwide."

"We could also be drawing unwelcome attention from statewide, Pepper. This little town may have owners somewhere who might suddenly decide their worthless property is worth something after all. Or at least that they don't want it in the hands of a bunch of reprobates. I don't want this to end up in the courts—we'd lose."

Pepper was shaking her head. "Do you have any idea how much weight popular opinion carries in situations like this?"

"Actually, I do. But popular opinion didn't save these people from being dropkicked out of Santa Theresa. I doubt it'd save them from a charge of 'grand theft, town,' either."

"I'd be willing to bet you're wrong. If the media took an advocacy role-"

Nancy's eyebrows twitched. "*Can* the media take an advocacy role?"

Pepper had the honesty to blush slightly. "Not strictly speaking. But a journalist can. Please, Nancy. This is the most important story Santa Theresa has ever produced. This isn't just tourist pap, it's-it's an epic. It's-"

"It's the lives of about fifty homeless people at the moment."

Pepper nodded, soberly. "I *know* that. But if this fifty people are successful, if they can survive, if I can get *other* people interested in their survival—get them to *care* about it... Nancy, that's worth something, isn't it?"

Nancy Yee sighed. "It's worth a lot, if it would really work that way. But what if the wrong people get interested in Serendipity, Pepper? What then? You look at these folks and see heroes—so do I. But a lot of other people look at them and see drunks and junkies and derelicts and juvenile delinquents. If we show Serendipity off to the wrong people..."

"Then it becomes a media battle. It already *is* a media battle. I don't think you realize what a stir this has caused. We still get calls asking what's happened to these people. That's why I'm here—because people still care. Out of sight isn't always out of mind."

Nancy considered that. "And who are these people? The callers, I mean."

"Some are just concerned and curious. A few expressed a great deal of interest in helping."

"Did you get their names and addresses?"

"They're on file."

"Can I have them?"

"Can I have a story?"

Nancy looked at Pepper speculatively. "How'd you like to do a documentary?"

"A documentary?"

"Yeah. Instead of just popping a human interest story, why not a feature: The Resurrection of Serendipity Springs?"

Pepper answered the other woman's slow smile. "Something to air around the Fourth of July, huh?"

"I like the way your mind works, Ms. Delagado."

"I have a cameraman whose mind works the same way. I'll need him."

"Can you trust him?"

"With my life. He's my fiancé."

Nancy tapped the top of her clipboard thoughtfully. "How soon can you have him here?"

Pepper's fiancé, Georg "Sunny" Durande, was an amiable young man with glossy black dreadlocks and skin the color of bittersweet chocolate. He spoke with a tease of Jamaica and moved with a thin whisper of music.

"Don't those give you audio problems?" asked Nancy, fascinated by the sheer number of tiny silver bells entwined in his hair.

He smiled blindingly and drew a soft, black hat out of his jacket pocket. "Part of my recording equipment." He pulled the hat over his head, effectively silencing the bells, and hefted his Lasex PortAVee to one shoulder.

Nancy was quickly impressed with the way Pepper and Sunny worked. They were ubiquitous but unobtrusive—filming everything and everyone, but staying out of the way. The ceremonial filling of the gas tanks, attended by the entire population of Serendipity, was covered in full. Afterward,

Pepper interviewed a few of the residents and took a tour of the inhabited buildings.

"You've done an amazing piece of work here," she told Nancy over a cup of hot coffee. "This is a legitimate miracle."

Nancy shot Stu a conspiratorial glance. "We're just getting started. As soon as the motel renovation bears some fruit, we'll be able to house more residents."

"How are you housing what you've got now?" asked Sunny. "Fifty-seven, I make it."

"It's not easy," Stu admitted. "We've got three houses livable. This one, moderately so, the others just barely. We've got running well water. We manage to get it hot once a day to allow bathing. There's electricity for the kitchen and work sites only. No flush toilets yet, but we're working on it. We had to dig outhouses," he replied to Sunny's raised brows. "Two of these old Victorians have five bedrooms. The other one has four. Plus, we've converted a couple of downstairs sitting rooms into bedrooms. Everybody has at least one roommate. Actually, we've got room for more. As far as feeding everybody...well, right now we do it in shifts, the cantina here only holds about thirty people."

Pepper nodded, following his gaze around the cozy suite of the two converted parlors, which even now held about fifteen occupants. "This is a real cute place," she complimented them. "Sort of faded Americana. I'll bet it's good for morale to have a place like this to hang out."

"My patrons seem to be happy." Nancy surveyed the Down & Outers in the "café" and felt a moment of intense satisfaction.

"So what's next?" asked Sunny. "I'm sure your population is growing."

"You bet! Especially since we're literally soliciting citizens. These are just the folks that haven't been able to get off the street in time, or who volunteered to come out here and put their supposedly useless talents to work."

Stu smiled at his coffee cup. "When we hit one hundred, Billy wants to erect a population sign out on the Loop."

"Billy McGuire is our master carpenter," explained Nancy.

"We've sold some of his work in Santa Theresa."

Pepper's ears perked almost visibly. "They're self-sufficient?"

Stu and Nancy both laughed.

"Not by half!" said Nancy. "But, we're trying. It's like digging for buried treasure—discovering half-remembered or never-developed skills, putting them to work. Sometimes the hardest part is getting these folks past the idea that they're useless or worthless. They're far from it. If we could just convince people of that, get them to invest in Serendipity..."

"One of our biggest material problems," said Stu, "is power. We've got three little Honda generators and four full propane tanks. But to get this place fully modernized..." He shrugged.

"What about alternative power sources?" asked Sunny.

Stu nodded. "We're looking into both wind and solar. But we need materials and expertise."

Pepper looked thoughtful and tapped on her compad, while Stu wondered if she generated as many lists as Nancy did. He felt a niggle of something like guilt and cleared his throat. "Of course, those are just the material problems. We have human problems too. Some of these folks are alcoholics, some of them have other problems, some of them are just trouble."

"Or troubled," said Nancy.

Stu nodded. "Or troubled. A couple of them have the DT's pretty bad. One guy's coming off heroin... We've got people from AA out here all the time. "

"I heard you had some runaways," observed Pepper quietly. "Can you tell me about that?"

Nancy glanced at Stu and shrugged. "They wanted coke. They wanted it bad enough to hike all the way back into Santa Theresa for it. One of them is in jail on a possession charge. The other one is still missing."

"They were kids," said Stu, and was angry but didn't know who to be angry at.

"Sounds like you could use a full-time counseling staff," Sunny said.

Nancy smiled faintly. "We can dream."

Pepper's compad squealed at the speed of her note taking. She wanted to do more than dream.

"I like them," said Stu, after Pepper and Sunny had packed up notes and PortAVee and left. "I think they'll help."

Nancy sighed. "Me too. But they made me realize just how much help we need. I mean, this place is reclaimable, but at what cost?" She shook her head, looking, for the first time since Stu had known her, almost defeated.

"Is it the place or the people you're thinking about?"

"Both."

"Are we doing badly?"

"No. No, we're not. Not right now. But Stu, it can't go on indefinitely—all this largesse. People can't keep pouring funds and materials and energy into Serendipity forever. At some point, we've got to become self-subsistent. And we've got to solve our own problems. Maybe we can give these people a place to start over—big 'maybe.' But we can't make them *want* to start over. What if we get somebody who just doesn't want to do it? What do we do? Kick them out? And if we did that, wouldn't we be just as guilty as the society that rejected them in the first place?"

"Some people don't want to be helped, Nancy. That's just the way it is."

"But what do we do with them? What do we do with Stark Benson if he won't go to the AA meetings and he won't work and he won't even talk to the counselor?"

"I don't know. I don't have an answer to that. But I do have an answer to the other problem. I think we can be self-subsistent. Hell, I *know* we can." He got suddenly to his feet. "Come on. I want to show you something."

He took her hand and led her out through the kitchen, past the coy looks of its staff, across the half-groomed back yard and through a recently re-hung gate in the unkempt hedge.

Nancy sidestepped the pair of shears lying near the gate and stopped, her eyes wide. In front of her, within the huge rectangle formed by the hedge, neat rows of tilled and furrowed soil stretched in a crazy-quilt pattern. On stakes marking each section, seed packets proclaimed what was planted between the furrows. In one corner, a monstrous growth of squash sprawled, a pile of clippings lying next to it on the earth. Other, less primordial-looking plants dotted the large plot.

"When did all this happen?"

Stu laughed at the expression on her face. "Not over night, I assure you. Some of our Club members found the plot and decided to try their hands at gardening. Seeds are cheap, so we approached a local nursery..." He shrugged. "We'll know if any of us have green thumbs in a week or two."

"But those great big...whatevers..." Nancy waggled a hand at the squash.

"Remnants of the previous residents. It was pretty wild, but I think we've trimmed it back enough to see some produce in season. And this isn't the only plot. There's another one in about the same condition behind the pink stucco. Plus, there's the orchard on the other side of the motel. Peaches, cherries, apples.

It's pretty overgrown, but the trees all seem healthy enough. Some of them are starting to blossom already."

Nancy smiled. "Just like the Down & Outers, huh?"

"Feel better?"

She laughed outright. "Can this be Stuart Williams, the realist?"

"Realist-shmealist," Stu grinned. "Serendipity is no place for realists. We ran 'em all out of town." There was a definite dream-gleam in his eye.

Nancy saw it and nodded. "Yes, I feel much better."

-9-

The rains came in early April and, with them, enough indigents to more than double the population of Serendipity Springs. Billy McGuire chose a piece of wood for his population sign.

Three units of the motel were finished and pressed into service and work started on the interior of the little church.

Glorying in the equipment lent by Jim Garvey's Petroco, Phil Kroeger finished the bodywork on the '52 Buick and unveiled her during a break in the weather. Jim Garvey immediately handed him a check for $40,000.

Phil, who had never seen so much as a fifty-dollar bill, could only stare at it.

"She's a classic car, Phil," said Garvey. "And you did a classic job on her."

"But, Mr. Garvey," stammered Phil, still staring at the check, "you can't drive her out on the road. She's illegal—she burns gasoline. You need to get 'er converted."

"No, sir." Jim patted the Buick's gargantuan nose. "What I need is a classic car permit and I have one of those. She's worth more than forty thou', of course, but if I leave you the equipment you've been borrowing, we should be even up."

Phil's big, dark eyes filled with tears. "Thank you, Mr. Garvey. Thank you."

"My pleasure," said Jim. "Literally." He studied Phil's face for a moment, then said, "D'you mind if I ask sort of a personal question?"

"No, sir."

"How'd you come to be a-a-"

"Hobo, sir. Tha's what I call myself. Jus' a hobo."

"What I mean is, how come you're not doing this kind of work for a living? You're damn good at it, you know."

Phil glanced at the check again. "Well sir, I used to do this sorta work. Then I got real sick. Didn't have no bennie-fits. Y'know, hospital—that sorta thing. When I was well enough to work again, I was sorta broke up lookin'. An' *broke,* too. Hadta go on welfare. Nobody seemed to want an old, broke up dude with no schoolin'. Nobody believed I could do what I said I could do."

Garvey nodded. "Well, I believe you, Phil. You've got a touch with old cars."

Phil smiled his slow, holey smile. "Tha's 'cause I love 'em, I s'pose."

"Yeah, and I bet they love you, too." He patted Phil's shoulder and headed off to take possession of his old new prize.

"Don't spend that all in one place."

The check was spent in many places, but the Committee made certain some of it went toward turning Phil's ramshackle auto shop inside out and putting it back together in much better condition. He even got an old Coke machine to stand invitingly against the front of the building.

Billy McGuire painted his population sign red-white-and-blue and used the same colors on a sign for Phil's garage. Both signs were reared the same day with all Serendipitans in attendance.

One sign said: "Serendipity Springs—Population 137." The other said: "Phil's Klassic Korner." The news team of Delgado and Durande recorded the event for posterity.

They also recorded the return to Serendipity of several runaways. There was an angry and tearful welcome. There was a fight. Two stayed and entered the rehab program, one left and never returned.

When a couple of residents were found smuggling booze into Serendipity, Delgado and Durande recorded that as well. And when Billy McGuire, suffering from the lingering effects of their smuggling, went into DT's, he insisted they be there to disc his agony.

"I want to remember," he said. "An' I want them kids to remember. This is what hell's like. It ain't no burnin' place. It's a damn drunk tank."

His Lucy cried and that went down on disc, too.

They also recorded the ongoing restoration work. There were four crews, now. Two handled destruction and construction, two handled interior finishing. While one crew tackled further clearing and cleaning of the motel with inexpert gusto, the more experienced took over work on the two half-finished Victorians.

The finishing crews followed them around cleaning, painting, and wallpapering. "Granny wallpaper," Annie Lee dubbed it. It was leftover stuff, mostly; dignified patterns in muted "granny" colors. It fit the aging houses to a "T". So did the truckload of antique furniture and carpets driven into town by two smiling representatives of the local Catholic Relief Association. Nancy and Pepper, chopping weeds in the front yard of the Down & Outer Bed & Breakfast (or the D&O/B&B as it was affectionately called), ogled the rich assortment with unabashed lust.

"What's this?" Nancy asked the beaming driver.

The woman looked as if she was fighting a raging case of giggles. "This," she said, "is from the estate of Dorothy Calderon. She died two days ago and bequeathed all of her furniture and some of her cash assets to Serendipity Springs."

After five seconds of silent amazement, Pepper giggled. So did the Catholic Relief ladies.

"This is just great!" sighed Pepper finally. "I'll get Sunny and the discam-"

"Right behind you, and recording," said Sunny's voice.

"Nancy, are you going to open your present?"

Nancy laughed, eyes dancing. "Wow, you betcha!"

It was Christmas in April. There was a literal houseful of antiques, every one of them breathtakingly beautiful. The Down & Outers unloaded each piece with awful care, ooh-ing and ah-ing.

"I ain't never, *never* had anything like this!" exclaimed one middle-aged woman cradling a Tiffany lamp in her arms as if it were a baby.

The riches were distributed between the restored Victorians, finding places of honor in parlors, front halls and bedrooms. All three of the late Mrs. Calderon's fine dining tables went to The Cookery dining parlors. Those, with a few additional appointments and some of Pearl Etterly's tatting, gave the establishment a breath of fading class—like a dried orchid pressed between the pages of a first edition of *Jane Eyre*.

Annie Lee laughed delightedly at the stunning effect of polished wood reflecting the dancing flames of a dozen oil lamps and candles. "This is fantastic! Lord, I wish we could open up for business. Can you imagine, Lucy?" She draped an arm

around the older woman's thin shoulders. "Now all we need is a
piano so you can sing for our supper."

"We do have a piano," said Nancy. "A baby grand. That is,
it's ours if we want it. Or we can sell it for what it'll bring at
auction. They left it in town because it needs to be moved by
pros. Do we want it?" She looked to Lucy for an answer.

"It'd prob'ly bring a lot at auction..."

Nancy shook her head. "Not important. The question is, do
you want it?"

Lucy's eyes glowed. "Oh, Miss Nancy, I would jus' love to
have a piano."

They installed the baby grand in one corner of the larger
dining parlor. Pearl Etterly draped it in lace and Lucy sat down
to test the keyboard. It was well tuned and Lucy's experienced
but rusty playing filled both rooms with sweet, blue sounds. She
played and sang for the diners that night, accepting their
requests (when she knew them) with smiles, and their praise
with flushed modesty. Her voice, deep and smokey, was seamed
with the hairline cracks of age, but still had the power to
enchant.

After dinner, Nancy called a town assembly. All adult Down
& Outers and several of the older kids crowded into the twin
dining rooms to hear what was up. The Delgado/Durande news
team put the gathering on videodisc.

Nancy stood at the head of the front dining parlor on the
raised flooring of the big bay window embrasure and addressed
the assemblage.

"By now, you've all seen the beautiful furniture that's been
moved into the houses. It's ours because a very sweet lady
changed her will three weeks ago and made us—Serendipity—
heir to her house furnishings and about $80,000 of her cash
estate."

A murmur of stunned appreciation circled the room, followed by enthusiastic cheers.

"I believe she knows how grateful we all are for her wonderful generosity," Nancy continued, when the good-humored roar abated. "But I still wish she could be here tonight so we could throw a party for her. However, we've got lots of friends who are still very much alive, and I think it would be a nice gesture to throw a party for *them.*"

The idea went over like fireworks on the Fourth of July. Plans for the May Gala began immediately. Nancy compiled the invitation list and Jules Trevor, secretary of the Committee, printed the invitations and recruited a detachment of couriers to hand carry them to the recipients. Annie and her kitchen staff planned a sumptuous but thrifty buffet and Lucy practiced her repertoire of silky, sultry tunes.

The Construction and Interiors crews put in extra hours, exhausting themselves in an orgy of cleaning and finishing. They converted the remaining parlor of the D&O Club into yet another intimate and homely dining room, and turned the old house into a Victorian showplace.

Pepper Delgado surveyed the finished product thoughtfully, then hiked down to Phil's Klassic Korner to use the pay phone. She returned to town looking like a cat backstroking through heavy cream just about the time Sunny was introducing Stu and Nancy to a gentleman with white hair, wire-rim glasses and a PhD in solar engineering.

The gentleman, Paul Walker by name, spent the afternoon in conference with Stu, either closeted in Stu's office or wandering about Serendipity. Pepper, meanwhile, spent the afternoon softening Nancy up to receive one of her brainstorms. After chatting at length about the wonderful progress the D&O Club had made and how many new friends they had enlisted among the more influential citizens of neighboring Santa Theresa, she finally made an approach.

"That," she declared, nodding at the D&O/B&B, "is a major accomplishment. I mean, it looks like it was done up by some hot-shot architect/designer."

Nancy beamed at the old house. "It does look great doesn't it? These are pretty exceptional people."

"I kid you not, Nance. This place would look right at home on the cover of *Home & Garden* or *California Life*... It's a shame it has to be hidden from the world."

"What do you have in mind, Pepper?" Nancy glanced at the other woman's face. "Or maybe I should have said, 'Pepper, what have you done?'"

"Nothing reprehensible. It's just that I have connections with a couple of magazine publishers. I called them in."

"Called them in?"

"Favors. I share research with people, do some interviews, special interest stuff."

"And what did you tell these connections?"

"That I had a special interest scoop—a unique restoration project."

"Pepper..."

"I didn't reveal anything important. Laid it out like kind of a 'Mystery Spot.' They *love* that kind of stuff. Whets their appetites. More to the point, it whets the readers' appetites."

She watched the expressions chasing each other across Nancy's face for a moment, then said, "By the way, I've found us another benefactor... Can Sunny disc the Gala?"

Nancy choked on a laugh, then scowled with mock severity. "Sunny had better disc the Gala, or he'll be the last course of the evening. And who's this mystery benefactor?"

Pepper pulled a business card out of her pocket and handed it to Nancy, suspecting for a moment that she had wasted her trump card.

"Hey! This guy owns a lot of real estate. And isn't he involved with civil liberties stuff?"

"He's an attorney. A very wealthy, very nice, very generous attorney. He's represented homeless people in court a number of times."

"No kidding?" Nancy tucked the card into her shirt pocket and headed for the house, wielding her trowel. She stopped halfway up the porch steps. "By the way, wish the readership of *Home & Garden 'bon appetit.'* I hope they like Serendipity Surprise."

Pepper whooped and ran all the way to Phil's.

-10-

The May Gala promised to be bigger and better than anyone imagined. The guests begged to bring guests of their own, and started a new flood of giving. The "thank you" banquet turned into a fund-raiser with no prompting whatsoever from Nancy or her cohorts.

Offers of assistance poured in. Area high schools formed support groups and volunteered after-school and weekend help to speed the renovation process along. They dug and planted, scraped and painted, polished and waxed. And they took their orders in all of this from people who bare months or weeks before had been considered worthless by nearly everyone, including themselves.

Wherever they went, they left a gleaming trail. Everything gleamed. Everything from the finish on Loucette's piano to the finish on Phil's two newly refurbished cars. Even the four more barely finished units of the "Lucky Lullabye Motel" gleamed—

with fresh spring green and white paint. And if the row of fresh Cypress trees along its sweeping gravel circle didn't gleam, at least they looked "damn fine," in the opinion of Mike Hanrahan, who engineered their planting. The motel units were immediately inhabited by three families and four young women late of Santa Theresa's blossoming red-light district.

The night of the Gala, Phil's two new antiques took places of honor flanking the Down & Outer Club's white picket gate. Jim Garvey added a third vintage vehicle to the line up; his two invited guests brought the tally up to five. By 7:30 the main street of Serendipity was lined with limos, compacts, beat up station wagons—even a school bus.

It was a barely clouded night with a slight, balmy breeze. Japanese lanterns bobbed down the walkway on a silver cord, swayed under the eves of the B&B's wide verandah and dotted the yard with little pools of golden light.

Nancy decided she couldn't have begged for a better night. In the light of Serendipity's four honest-to-God propane fueled street lamps, the place really looked like a living, breathing town.

"Pretty, isn't it?" asked Annie Lee Paice from beside her on the verandah.

Nancy nodded and glanced at her. "Wow! So're you! Has Stuart seen this get-up?"

Annie blushed. "It's just an old square dance rig I altered, that's all." She stroked the lacy shoulders.

"Ah! Do I detect the fine hand of Pearl Etterly in this so-called 'old square dance rig?'"

Annie nodded. "You really think it's pretty? I mean, it doesn't seem...silly or old-fashioned?"

Nancy studied Annie again. The verandah, with its lanterns and old white-washed porch swing, was a suitable frame for a pretty Southern belle at a garden party; her guests coming and going behind her, their conversations mingling with the breeze, music floating from her open parlor windows.

"It fits the night, Annie," said Stu William's voice from behind Nancy. "It fits the town. Old-fashioned...that's just right here."

Nancy grinned. "Took the words right out of my mouth," she said. "S'cuse me. I've got to check up on the seating arrangements."

Annie watched her duck into the house, glanced at Stu, then smiled shyly at the porch railing.

"I hope you're not planning on hiding that pretty dress in the kitchen all evening," Stu said.

She quirked an eyebrow at him. "Why, you got something in mind?"

"Dinner and dancing. That is a dancing dress, isn't it?"

"I guess it's got a few dances left in it."

"Then we'll make sure they get put to good use."

"Look at them kids!" snorted Mike Hanrahan. "They look like somethin' out an old High School year book! White socks 'n' duck-tail do's."

"You complainin' again, Irish?" asked Billy, handing him a large tray of vegetables and dip. "I like the way they look—takes me back, y'know?"

"Somebody oughta take you back, Cowboy, an' see if they can't fix yeh."

"Guillaume *est parfaitement*," Loucette informed him. She pointed at the kitchen door. "Now, you jus' take that tray out to dining room one. Dining room one, you heah?"

"Yes, madam. I ain't deaf, just-"

"Stubborn," Lucy finished for him. "That's what's wrong with you, old man. You're stubborn. You jus' can't *stand* to have any fun."

"Fun? Pffft! You call this *fun?* House full o' noisome strangers...laughin', carryin' on... Hmph! Fun won't start, Miss Lucy, until you start singin'!" And he wheeled out of the kitchen with his laden tray.

"Old crocodile..." muttered Lucy, shaking her head. "Scowl at you, an' then pay you a compliment."

Billy shrugged affably. "Guess that's the way he has fun, Sugar."

"Um, Mr. Garvey?" David Paice's fourteen year-old face looked as if it belonged to somebody caught tee-peeing the mayor's house.

"Yessir, what's the trouble?"

"Well, it's this, sir." David fumbled forty dollars and some change out of his jeans pocket and held it out. "Um, I think it belongs to you. It's from gasohol. Well, some of it, anyway. Some's for gasoline."

Garvey put down his fork. "You had customers?"

"Well...yessir. I was helping Phil in the shop and this car pulled up and they wanted gas. They were real desperate—they were nearly out... Then, a couple more people came in and... Was I wrong to sell it?"

Jim snorted. "What else could you do, son? *Give* it away?"

"Coulda, I guess."

"Hmm. And the gasoline?"

"Some guy with an antique car. He had a license for it—he showed me." David grinned. "You shoulda seen the way he looked at that '72 T-Bird Phil's doing for you. Nearly popped his eyeballs out."

Jim Garvey looked thoughtfully at the handful of money. "How'd you and Phil like to manage a franchise for me?"

"Sir?"

The media was not blind, deaf or dumb. Nancy knew that. And she knew that whatever else it was, the Gala was a media event. It was a calculated risk, and today she hoped they were ready for the onslaught of attention. They had to be ready. They had something to fight for—and there were more of them to fight for it every day.

Billy's little population sign featured a replaceable placard which tracked the rise of that statistic in increments of twenty-five. Just that morning, it had been amended to read: "Serendipity Springs, Population: 225."

That same morning, Sunny's plaid PhD friend had begun spec'ing alternative energy sources for Serendipity. And that morning, Stu had conscripted a crew of twenty to start work on his drive-in, while Annie Lee, Billy, and Lucy fielded a similar team to give the old café a thorough scrubbing down. And that morning, another group of Down & Outers had begun finishing work on the church.

And that morning, Stark Benson had stolen his roommate's pitiful savings and some of his clothes, snatched a loaf of bread and some fruit from the kitchen of the B&B and taken off for parts unknown. A failure. *Another* failure. As many times as Nancy Yee told herself the failure was not hers, she still racked her brains for something she could have done—something she could do for the next Stark Benson.

She would still be pondering it that evening while she was being interviewed on national TV. And she would probably still be pondering it the following week when, a bit short of the Fourth of July, Sunny and Pepper aired their documentary.

When maybe all hell would break loose.

-11-

What broke loose was more like purgatory... No, Stu decided, that wasn't quite right. It was just life to the power of ten. There were flashes of hell, bursts of heaven, and a very earthly sense of waiting in between.

The media was a pain and a pleasure. It was suddenly and constantly under foot, in the way, and generally obnoxious, but the influx of media resulted in the influx of something else that Stu was sure Serendipity Springs had never expected to see-- tourists. And with the tourists came money.

MacDonald's Mercantile, set up for the limited needs of the Down & Outers, found its supplies decimated in a weekend. But —wonder of wonders—there was *money* to buy more goods. Bea MacDonald's staff started canvassing local farms for assistance and came up with enough response to open a produce section. Two farm owners even lent their skills to help the Down & Outers growing group of would-be farmers with their garden plots.

Phil's Petroco station, with its fortuitous location, was doing land office business and so was his auto shop. Antique car buffs wandered in from far and wide, bringing their special-license machinery with them. The beat up red barn behind Phil's Klassic Korner became a clubhouse for Jim Garvey's Antique Auto Club —the "Great Gatsbys"—as they liked to be known.

"This place is a damn zoo!" muttered Mike Hanrahan murderously, glaring out the window of the Mercantile. "And we're the damn specimens!"

"Nonsense, Michael," Bea MacDonald had retorted. "We are *not* a zoo. In a zoo, the specimens don't get to keep the proceeds."

It was that, along with the genuine caring exhibited by most of their visitors that kept the residents of Serendipity from feeling like they were living in a literal zoo. It was the hell side of the equation that kept them from feeling like they were living in a literal heaven.

Some of the TJ's were from the Tabloids. They weren't so much interested in the progress made by a group of rehabbed street people. They wanted dirt. They wanted to hear about the runaways, asked if the "shady ladies" at the Lullabye were still practicing their trade, imagined secret murders and drug caches.

Several of them disrupted an AA meeting and had to be removed. Nancy simply called the state police. It was an irony, and the police were reluctant to respond at first, but they did come and they did get the Tabloid TJs off the premises.

No hell is complete without it's arch-demon, and in this somewhat homespun version of Dante's Inferno, it was Santa Theresa's mayor, John Eastwick, who assumed the role of Old Nick.

When he had contemplated the possible results of the "Bag Lady Bill," the appearance next door of a thrift-store township was not one of them. Outraged and embarrassed, he called on the police and had Nancy Yee and several other members of Serendipity's guiding Committee arrested. Since he had no grounds to hold them, he was forced to order their release almost immediately. All he got for his pains was bad press and a headache to match.

He appealed to the county supervisor and sheriff, but they were both unsure of their jurisdiction. Serendipity Springs had been an incorporated township and that status had never been changed on the books.

Frustrated, Eastwick telephoned the Governor and was informed that Serendipity was rather far down on a long "to do" list. The mayor swallowed his impatience, and ordered his staff to find any landowners who might have soil underlying the upstart town. They found two—both irritatingly sympathetic to Serendipity's populace. One said that for a dollar a month, he'd rent the place. The other made a family dinner once a week at the D&O/B&B the fee.

More frustrated, Eastwick contemplated ways in which he could use the press against Serendipity. His one and only attempt ended in a sharp focus on his own role in the town's rebirth. He quickly realized that any meddling on that front would spread his own name across every tabloid teaser on every rack in every supermarket and convenience store in the country.

John Eastwick could do nothing but dodge reporters and wait for the Governor's office to act.

"So, we're still an incorporated township," Stu repeated thoughtfully.

"I hate to sound dumb," said Annie Lee, "but what does that mean, exactly?"

"It means that we can elect a city government. *Should* elect one."

"Stuart's right," agreed Nancy decisively, pencil bouncing on her steno pad. "A city government could solidify Serendipity's legal status, which right now is just a paper fact.

According to expert opinion, it would give us a clear legal identity."

"What would we need?" asked someone from the packed audience in the half-finished church. "What kind of government?"

"Do we get to have elections?" asked someone else.

"Sure. We'd elect a mayor, a town council..." Nancy looked to Stu.

He shrugged. "A police chief might be a good idea." He chuckled at the "boos" that elicited. "Come on, folks! Not all policemen are bad guys, you know."

"I think Mr. Williams is right," said Phil Kroeger tentatively. "We need a police chief. I mean, after all, we got crime jus' like anyplace else. Seems like it's gettin' better, but I still gets my tools took sometimes."

"We need a school board," said a forty-ish woman with a shock of red hair. "We've got enough kids here to warrant starting a school. Right now, our kids are truant. Or at least they have been. The last thing we want is for the state to take our kids away from us."

There was a ripple of "amens" and sundry mumbles to that.

Annie was nodding vigorously. "I agree with Sharon a hun'ert percent. And we *could* start a school, too. Right here in the church building."

"You used to teach, didn't you, Sharon?" Nancy asked, her pencil suddenly active.

"Yes, I did. Junior high school level. I had a drinking problem," she added. "That's what got me fired. I've handled that. But, if it bothers anybody..."

"It don't bother me," was the general response.

"Just means you understand the rest of us," said one of the ex-prostitutes. "Maybe you can pass that along to the kids."

"So, we want a mayor, a town council, police chief or sheriff or something, school board, principal..." Nancy stopped scribbling and bounced her pencil a few times. "Most of these are elected positions...heck, we ought to just make them all elected."

"So let's have elections," said Annie. "We all know each other pretty well. Let's go for it."

That night, Serendipity Springs elected itself a mayor, a town council, a police chief, and a school principal. The school board was gotten on a volunteer basis and made up almost exclusively of parents. There were no nominations, no time for campaigns, just names written anonymously on little pieces of paper and counted dutifully by Sharon Vandeman (Principle of Serendipity School) and Annie Lee Paice (a member of the school board).

The first action of Mayor Stuart Williams and his Council was to set aside the still vacant building of indeterminate use as the town library. The four young out-of-work ladies from the Lucky Lullabye immediately volunteered to stock the proposed shelves with the used books that had been flooding Serendipity since its revival.

The first action of Police Chief Michael F. Hanrahan was to consult with the town council about the fines and disciplines for various offenses. There was no holding tank, no jailhouse, just an office an old hat and a pair of handcuffs for the incumbent.

Most of the discipline revolved around work crews. It was unanimously decided that repeat offenders of the worst offenses be punished by deportation from Serendipity's safe haven. You could get deported for drug abuse or violence, but little else.

The Down & Outers became their own police force—pushing and pulling at each other's problems. Pleading, threatening, and hollering a lot as they struggled for order and self-esteem. A number of people got to see the inside of Mike's office, whether they wanted to or not. Young most of them, angry most of them. Mike would give them the kind of talking to only Mike could give and find them something to do with their anger.

The Library opened on the Fourth of July amid great celebration. Also being celebrated: The debut of the Main Street Malt Shoppe—a gleaming bit of chrome and vinyl nostalgia replete with jukebox and endless counter. The tourists, many of whom attended the fête in the styles of the 50's and 60's, loved it. And they loved the barbeque held all along Main Street and the fireworks display that capped the evening.

Santa Theresa's mayor, John Eastwick, did not love it. He loved even less that the Governor, as the guest of honor, was given the key to the "city" by Mayor Stuart Williams, and had more or less officially commended the re-founders of Serendipity Springs for their "courage, vision, and outstanding effort."

He loved less than that the opinion of the governor's office that there was nothing illegal about Serendipity's inhabitants. They had settled with the landowners who had interest in the town and they had incorporated status and a city government. Their inhabited buildings were up to code, and they had been most cooperative with the county regarding health and safety regulations. Their business licenses were in order—their attorney had seen to that. They had a licensed nurse living in the pink stucco Municipal Building, and a licensed counselor in their Rehab Center.

So, Mayor Eastwick was forced to smile plastically into discam lenses and say, "I'm pleased at their success," and "No comment," through clenched teeth.

That July was a hot month for Serendipity could be measured by more than just the giant thermometer outside Police Chief Michael Hanrahan's office. After the Fourth of July fête, the tourists came rolling in like the ground support forces in a benign war.

The multi-Faith church was opened for worship; its one large stained-glass window, designed by a local artist, dedicated to Nancy Yee, "who's impulsive vision made Serendipity possible."

"What should we call this place?" Annie Lee asked, staring at the window. Her eyes reflected the pantheon of color in the stained-glass replica of Earth displayed against sun and moon and star field. "I mean, it's going to be a Synagogue and a Church and a Mosque and-" She shrugged. "Church just seems like too small a word for all that."

"And My house shall be called a House of Prayer," quoted Loucette, softly. "Book of Isaiah."

And so it was. And it witnessed the prayers of Hindus, Jews, Buddhists, Christians, Moslems, Bahá'ís and Native Americans. It also witnessed two weddings: Sunny Durande married Pepper Delgado beneath the multi-hued glow of Nancy's window; and Billy McGuire took his Lucy to the altar, and from there to a cottage across from "Fortune's Fruit Farm."

In August, Stu and Annie Lee gave the House of Prayer its third wedding and opened the little drive-in caddy corner to Phil's Klassics. Which institution provided Serendipity with enough converted antiques to clutter Main Street quite cheerfully. Each residence had its own vehicle parked out front, the keys assigned to a peg by each front door. Main Street was a portrait of "faded Americana."

The August issue of *California Life* carried that portrait in a full color spread. So did the August issue of *Time*. The D&O/B&B displayed both in a big marquee, on the front hall —"foyer," insisted Lucy.

"Hometown USA," read the *Time* article. "If you didn't grow up there, you'll wish you had."

The tourists seemed to agree. They kept all three of Serendipity's eateries bustling, and crowded the new units of the Lucky Lullabye. The Down & Outers opened a gift shop and a clothing store, which carried only fashions of the 50's, 60's, and '70's. It was established that when one went to Serendipity, one dressed for it. It was a weekend's fun: Put on your hand-me-downs (or your Hometown designer fashions), get into your classic car and drive to Hometown USA for a pleasant, carefree stay in the Lucky Lullabye Motel. Dine on classic Malt Shoppe faire, drive-in delicacies (delivered by real carhops with ponytails and roller skates), or Creole cuisine. Go to sock hops and hayrides and barbeques.

More homeless found their way to Serendipity. They became instant citizens, built homes and learned how to till the soil, pick fruit, raise windmills, adjust solar panels and greet visitors. They, too, wore second and third-hand clothes and didn't seem to mind living in a place that looked as if time had abandoned it somewhere in the middle of a past century.

Most new residents learned quickly how to stay out of Mike Hanrahan's office. Those that didn't saw a lot of Mike. A few saw their way out of town. One or two saw the inside of the county jail. They weren't the rule, but the exception to it.

People now came to Serendipity because they wanted to be there. It was a fresh start place on its way to becoming a legend.

Billy McGuire built a new population sign in the woodshop behind his furniture store and emblazoned the title "Hometown USA" across the top in bold red-white-and-blue letters. "Serendipity Springs," read the royal blue letters beneath. "Population: 450."

"Hometown, my aunt's bunions," groused Mike Hanrahan.

"It's nostalgia, you old coot," said Bea MacDonald, and dumped a bagful of fresh-picked pippins into an apple barrel.

"It's nostalgia's worst nightmare," corrected Mike. "Claptrap, rundown, hand-me-down town. Don't they remember what we've been. Derelicts!"

"It is *not* run down!" objected Sammie Paice-Williams, around a mouthful of green apple. "It's neat! All the tourist kids wish *they* could live here."

"Hmph!" Mike eyed the boy skeptically. "An' I suppose yer gonna tell me you'd rather be here than some nice neighborhood with a baseball diamond an' a shoppin' mall an' a McDonald's an' all, eh?"

"Sure! Anyway, we're gonna have a baseball diamond next spring and, well...we already *got* a MacDonald's." Sammie cast a squinty glance at Bea, who chortled.

"And who promised you a baseball diamond, may I ask?" asked Mike.

"Dad did. And Mr. Walker even said we could have *lights.*"

"Hmph! Typical politician. Promise you the moon!"

Sammie bristled. "Dad's not a politician. He's the *mayor.*"

"Speaking of your Dad," said Bea, "isn't that him outside shouting for you?"

Sammie's head swiveled so he could see out the front window of the Mercantile. "Wow!" he yelled. "He's got a *bicycle!*" He was gone like a shot.

"Noisome brat," groused Mike, blinking.

"Stodgy coot," said Bea. "You love it here. You can't tell me you'd rather be someplace else."

Mike's exaggerated gray eyebrows scooted up his forehead. "I could tell you that, old woman, but it'd do no good at all. Listenin' to drunks howlin' an goin' through hell in the night. Watchin' poor old gits like Gunnar dyin' of Aids or poor young gits like Alice dyin' of crack."

Bea glared at him, exasperated. "At least there's someone here that *cares* about those 'poor gits,' Michael Hanrahan. *You* care, too, but you won't admit it. Won't admit you care and won't admit how happy you are here."

"Happy? Pfft! What I *will* admit is that on a scale from scroungin' in dumpsters to livin' at the Ritz, Serendip falls somewhere in the middle."

"Coot," Bea repeated, and left him sitting among the vegetables.

-12-

It was a good year for Hometown USA. Thanksgiving was celebrated with a Harvest Festival that included a special service in the House of Prayer followed by a banquet in the new school building, and a Pumpkin Patch Hop in the open field behind the Fortune orchard.

December brought a week long Winter Fair in celebration of Christmas and the Solstice. There was no snow, but both of Serendipity's streets were lit up with a riot of twinkling color. Even the windmills that powered the decorations were festooned with them. Four hot pretzel and apple cider stands kept natives, guests, and visitors warm outside, carolers and wandering street performers kept them warm inside.

On the Loop, Serendipity's floodlit signboard, flanked by a shimmering, thirty-foot Douglas fir, charted the growth of the native population: 500 on Christmas day.

"We're in the black," Nancy Yee announced at the January Town Meeting. "The Harvest and Solstice Festivals actually gave us a jump on our budget for the first quarter. Folks, I can't believe I'm saying this, but we have extra money."

The meeting hall erupted in cheers.

"And since we have extra money," Nancy continued when the cheer mellowed, "the Town Council unanimously decided that everyone should have a vote in what we do with it. But, before we start collecting ideas, Stu has an announcement to make."

Nancy yielded the stage to Mayor Williams, who smiled at the hall full of citizens before speaking. He smoothed the much-folded piece of paper and cleared his throat. "This came this morning, and I've got to say, it's been hell waiting for the chance to tell you about it. Ladies and gentlemen, a group of about thirty homeless people have taken up residence in an abandoned mining town east of Barstow."

A wave of electricity swept the room, bringing in its wake a slew of questions. There were no further suggestions as to where Serendipity's extra money might be spent. Serendipity sent seventy-five percent of its "extra" money and a team of volunteers to Sage, California. Hometown II was born.

By April, Sage had amassed a population of over 200 and strong support from its neighboring communities. By May, Sage was not alone. A ghost town in Kansas, an abandoned riverfront community in Ohio, an old resort town in Missouri, a played-out gold camp in Northern California—all across the United States, the sleeping awoke and the dead resurrected.

The homeless began to flee the cities, flocking instead to the Serendipitys and Sages and Middleforks and Ahanus. And the media followed; and where the media went, so too went the tourists.

"It says here this new Hometown in Arkansas' doing kind of a hillbilly thing," said Bea MacDonald, perusing the Serendipity Sunday Herald. "That'd be something to see."

"Hmph! Oughta send the ol' Cowboy doon there," groused Mike Hanrahan, fanning himself with his Police Chief hat. He groused as often as ever, but with much less acid these days.

Sometimes, as now, the grousing was even accompanied by a smile.

Bea ignored him. "Well, I like our Hometown just fine. It reminds me a little of where I grew up. I remember my family had a red and white Mercury wagon—just like that one." She nodded at the automobile in question, parked at the curb just below their shared seat on one of the benches that lined the Mercantile's wide, shaded porch.

"Just like home, eh?"

"No, Michael. Not 'just like it.' This *is* home. It's got all the things home's supposed to have. Old folks, kids, dogs, cats, cat fights...a ballpark, a graveyard." She nodded, acknowledging the rightness of that and thought of old Gunnar. "A graveyard with fresh graves," she added. "And a place to pray for the dead— and the living. Old drunks and old houses, old cars...and old *coots*." She glanced sideways at Mike.

"Gullible old biddy," he snorted enthusiastically. "Gettin' all misty-eyed over some ol' hunk o'tin. Serendipity always was an' always will be a hand-me-down town."

"Coot," said Bea disparagingly.

They were both silent for a moment, eyes going back to the street. On the curbing below, a couple of antique car buffs argued the relative merits of Mercuries and Fords while a gaggle of teenagers in worn denim and sneakers drank cola and watched and giggled. Across the street, three little girls roller-skated up and down the sidewalk, scooting and weaving through roving groups of people who laughingly accepted them as part of the scenery.

Up the block, against a backdrop of greenery, a dozen or so gyrating splashes of color dotted the ballpark between the House of Prayer and the new Rehab Center. An upbeat selection from the Malt Shoppe jukebox accompanied the wild ballet, punctuated by the squeals and shouts of the dancers, and underscored by the buzzing of summer lawn mowers.

Mike took a deep breath of the too-warm July air and stretched and slouched, making the old bench creak in protest.

"Biddy," he said, with no acid at all.

The Devil His Due

A story of magical realism

The Devil His Due was originally published in *Amazing Stories* in 1992. It was inspired by the Bahá'í concept that knowledge must be accompanied by volition and action. An idea expressed in the Gospels and the writings of Bahá'u'lláh alike is that while Evil cannot produce good effects, Good *must* produce them.

> *It is incumbent upon every man of insight and understanding to strive to translate that which hath been written into reality and action...*
>
> Gleanings from the
> Writings of Bahá'u'lláh,
>
> p. 250

Herbert G. (Bert) Wells stared at the dog-eared manila envelope numbly. This was the fifth time—*the fifth time*—OF BLOOD DARK SKIES had ricocheted off New York City like a badly aimed bullet and ended up buried deep in his mailbox. Gut shot, he shambled down the hallway of his Boston brownstone apartment building, his face wearing the same blank look of despair and puzzlement he'd seen on the homeless wrecks he usually stepped over on the way upstairs.

Down the battered corridor a door opened. Bert froze. Jack Baddely (aka, The Jackass) stepped out into the hall, then swung back to lock his door. Bert thrust the misshapen package under the lapel of his coat and tacked a garish grin to his face.

"Hi, Jack," he said, his voice as bright as the paisleys on his tie.

"Oh, hi, Bertie. How's the writing life? Any news on your block buster no-vel?" He always said "novel" as if it was some bastardized French word. (It was actually bastardized Italian).

Bert flattered himself that his smile did not slip an inch. "No news is good news," he said, hurrying past.

"Yeah. Or it could mean the editor ran out of kindling."

His back to The Jackass, Bert's face went into a litany of rude expressions.

"Or maybe he needed a door stop."

Bert kept walking.

"A paper weight?"

Bert made his apartment door and opened it, trying, unsuccessfully, to ignore the raspy chuckle digging, stiletto sharp, into his unguarded back.

"Jackass," he muttered and hurled the door open. He slammed it shut again behind him and threw the manuscript onto the sofa.

The frayed, stressed manila split at the seams, spilling its contents from the sofa cushions onto the bare wood floor. Snide chuckles sprayed from the ruptured package and scurried to find hiding places in the room. They would emerge later to scoff at him. He'd hear them as he labored at his second-hand laptop —sneaking out from nook and cranny, scuffling among the dust-bunnies, tittering at the man who would be King.

He ignored the litter on the sofa long enough to brew an industrial strength pot of coffee, climb into his sweats and sit down, cup in hand, to assess the mess. After three sips, he was able to pick up the rejection letter and read it. It was a form job, but the editor had scrawled a hand-written message beneath the neatly printed kiss-off.

"Nice, tight style," it said, "but has no one told you that horror with a social conscience is a dead art form? Not even The King could sell this stuff in this day and age. Can the metaphysical crap. Give the market what it wants—try cyber-shock."

A dead art form, indeed. It matched, Bert thought, the social conscience of the age. Deader than a doornail—whatever the heck a doornail was. Cyber-shock! An AI droid could write cyber-shock: Tales of senseless carnage perpetrated by mindless machines or crazed cyber-men. Luddite rubbish! The publishing industry was clearly in the hands of idiots.

Great, he thought. *Right,* he thought. Distract us with tales of impossible evils so we'll forget about the possible ones—the *real* ones. Exorcising imaginary demons was always so much more gratifying than facing the real ones: Greed, corruption, injustice, excess. He could go on and on.

He checked his watch. Five-fifteen. Writer's Group wasn't for another two and a half hours—a long time to wait to get this off his chest.

He sighed, supposing he could just go hang out at the coffee house and hope another of the undiscovered *literati* would wander by in need of a *kvetch*-mate. But if he did that, he'd have to drink more coffee and between the cup he'd just had and the two pots he'd consumed at work today, he was already in a caffeinated time warp. The High-flight Zone, the Group called it. He'd only seen one or two of his literary buddies when they weren't cranking along on a full charge of caffeine-induced adrenaline—it wasn't a pretty sight.

For about the two billionth time Bert considered "giving the market what it wanted." He knew he could do it...well, at least, he was pretty sure he could. After all, he had it on good authority that he possessed a "nice, tight style." He had every confidence—well, at least a sneaking suspicion, that if he sent that *bourgeoisie* establishment pig-dog editor a cyber-shock novel, he'd woof it down like steak tartar—killer 'bots and all.

Luddite.

The anger peaked, sending him on a slow glide toward the abyss of despair. Who was he kidding? He couldn't write that crap. All that gore and sexual carnage—he just didn't have it in him.

Sure you do, said a scoffing voice from left of center. *All human beings have it in 'em. You think you're an exception? Are you sure you wanna be? Look at the prize—PUBLICATION. MONEY. AUTONOMY. CELEBRITY. You got the tools, bwana. You can exploit the unreasonable fears of your fellow men and women right up there with the best of 'em.*

Exploit? His brain braked in mid-meander. *My God,* he thought. *What are you thinking?* Exploit? Sell out? Pander to those antiquarian anarchists? This was a New Age. The publishing industry just hadn't caught up yet. If he just hung in there, stuck it out-

Bull hockey.

He put down the cup of coffee. *Need to get out,* he told himself. *Need to get out and take a walk; clear the chuckling dust-bunnies out of my head.*

He pulled on his coat, boots and a muffler, grabbed his portfolio and went out. Four aimless blocks later, he found himself wandering the River Charles. It was a much cleaner river than it had been last year at this same time and Bert tried to make that cause for celebration. A group of musicians had started that campaign, he recalled—a brigade of world-class rockers who had descended on New England like a plague of leather-clad locusts and bent the ears of every living thing in the Thirteen Colonies.

Rock musicians were not inclined to beat around the bush; the message was blunt and to the point: Man was out of tune with the environment. If he didn't get in tune instantly, the consequences would be devastating: Global warming, a new ice age, pollution toxemia—all frightening, but mere bagatelles compared to the real threat rammed home via synthesizer and power chord by the heroes of a new generation.

TEEN REVOLT.

The rock slogan "Tune It Or Die" took on a whole new meaning when emblazoned across the chest of your fifteen-year-old's green globe-and-crossbones T-shirt.

Bert stared at the water. A month ago that had been one of his fondest recollections—a story he loved to tell whenever some formaldehyde guzzling nerdle elevated his snoot and opined that the arts were sheer frivol. Now, it only made him feel worse about his own inability to make any difference to the planet. In the two years since he'd left university, all he'd managed to contribute to society was a mountain of waste paper and enough shredded manila to fill the Prud up to the thirty-first floor.

Face it, he told himself, *you're a wimp. A noodle. A wet rag. Couldn't write your way out of a recycled paper bag...in the driving rain, even. If you could write—really write—they'd publish OF BLOOD DARK SKIES if it was a multi-generational pot boiler. You, Herbert George Wells, are no credit to your namesake. You, sir, are a fake—a failure.*

He stared down at the swiftly moving Charles, chin quivering, eyes moist, anger shriveling. Despair and gloom perched on his sagging shoulders like the Twin Ravens of Doom —foul-smelling, heavy-toed birds with smug, knowing faces. They reminded him of two of his college professors, Bernhardt Brecht and Madlyn Carrey, who had both told him his propensity for crusading would ruin him as a writer of fiction, if (and it was a BIG IF) he could ever contrive to WRITE WELL.

The not-so-muddy river beckoned, singing the bawdy refrain of a song he was half a generation too young to remember. "Love that dirty water..."

Come on in, the water's fine.

He sniffled, tucked his portfolio under one arm and swung a leg over the low stone parapet. Then he swung the other one over. He sat for a moment, facing the water, making his peace with the Universe.

Sorry, God, he apologized. *I'm a wimp. But then, You already know that.*

He contemplated the next morning's headlines: UNKNOWN SCHLOCK HORROR WRITER TAKES OWN LIFE.

What headline, beef brain? asked a disparaging voice from right of center. *You'll be lucky to make the obits. Give us a break, here. Nobody knows who you are but those self-centered quease-in-arts you hang out with at the Espress-O. And they'll think you're some kind of idiot saint. Saint Herbert, Patron of Pansy-asses. Your mother didn't raise you right.*

Herbert became highly offended at the disrespectful tenor of his thoughts. *Leave my mother out of this!*

He paused in mid-rage. Mother. Someone would have to tell his mother that her only son had kissed his ass goodbye and taken a header into the River Charles. She might even have to identify his body. What would she think? What would she do? He knew exactly what she'd think. She'd think she was a BAD MOTHER—a failure. She'd get depressed, maybe even...

That, Bert decided, would never do. He swung one leg back over the wall onto tarmac firma.

Dufus, said the left-hand voice. *Can't even do suicide right. I'm sure your mom loves having a zombie for a son. What does your boy do, Dr. Wells, Ph.D. in astrophysics, hmmm? Oh, my little Herbie, he recycles paper...lots of paper. Great, kid. Really great.*

Bert wobbled, straddling the wall. A peculiar *whoosh-clickety-clickety* sound filled his brain and he thought for a moment he was headed for a psychotic Walter Mitty episode. He raised terrified eyes and met the curious ones of a kid speeding toward him on a powered skateboard. The kid and the *whoosh-clickety-clickety* both stopped right beside him.

"Geez, mon," the kid said, looking sincerely concerned, "You look like your Mom just died. What could be that bad?"

Bert blinked. "I can't write," he said, shocked into total honesty. "I'm a failure because I can't write cyber-shock."

The kid looked at him; he looked at the kid. A little globe and crossbones dangled from one earlobe and the letters "IT OR" were clearly visible on the patch of green T-shirt that peeked between the lapels of his black leathyl jacket.

"You know," the kid said finally, "there's an exceptionally good literacy program at the library."

Bert coughed. "Thanks."

The kid smiled. "Sure." He *whoosh-clickety'd* off, leaving Bert miserably alone.

The right-side voice was back, popping in like a fritzy channel on a bunged stereo. *Some people,* it said, *can't even read.*

Bert swung the other leg over into the walkway. *Yeah,* he thought, *and even I can do that. Maybe I could even teach other people to do that.*

"Yeah? And where'll it get ya?"

Bert was trying to think of a comeback when he realized the voice had not come from inside his head. He looked up. Standing before him on the river walk was a short man in a fur-collared stressed leather coat, matching Gucci shoes, gloves and burgundy sharkskin pants. His hair was fashionably cut—a straight, glossy, lobe-length pageboy, black, obviously natural, center parted. He was handsome in an oily sort of way, and was smoking a red, spice-scented cigarette.

Bert found his eyes hypnotized by the glowing tip. Cigarettes were highly illegal. He only knew one person who smoked them—a beefy, middle-aged fictioneer who had been a correspondent during the last known war (years ago in Swaziland or someplace) and who thought he was the reincarnation of Ernest Hemingway.

"Want one?" asked the Smoker and held out a little ebony box. The cigarettes lay inside on black velvet.

"No. No, thanks."

The box disappeared.

"I asked a question, Jack," the guy said. "What'll it get ya, this literacy bunk?"

"I...I...I want to do something. Help somebody. Make a difference."

The Smoker laughed. It was an acrid sound. "And teachin' a bunch of snot-nosed ghetto geckoes how to read is gonna make a difference? Great. Yeah. They'll be able to read those little signs that say 'shoplifting will be prosecuted.' That way they'll know what they're bein' busted for. Get real, bwana. These guys are gonna be doin' their reading in a cage."

Bert stood. "Well, I'm going to do something with my life, dammit. I don't care if I have to write copy for the Salvation Army."

A gloved hand shot out and patted his arm, pushing him back onto the parapet. "Cool your thrusters, Jack. I'm not saying you can't do nothin'. I'm sayin' I think you can do better."

"Do better? Look, who the hell are you, anyway, and where do you get off interrupting my private thoughts?" He glared fiercely at the little man, then felt the glare slip. Those really had been his private thoughts. His *silent*, private thoughts.

The Smoker rocked back on his well-heeled heels and grinned. "I wondered when you'd tumble to that. You're not a very quick study, Jack."

"My name isn't Jack, it's-"

"Yeah, yeah. I know. It's Herbert. Herbert G. Wells, named after the famous sci-fi writer. Your Mom is a big fan."

"Well, then why-"

He spread his hands. "It's just an expression."

"How do you know who I am? How do you know so much about me? Are you-?" Hope leapt in his breast. "Are you from the FBI—the CIA? Is that it? Is my writing too incendiary? Too dangerous?"

The man guffawed. "Dangerous? Criminy, kid! If you had *talent,* you'd be dangerous! As it is, you got nothin' but good intentions and a lot of gall. Dangerous, Saint Chris's keester! That's a yuck, bwana-san. A real yodel. Dangerous!" He chuckled, wiped tears from the corner of his eyes and wheezed down to silence.

Bert glared at him. "Get to the point. I have a meeting to go to."

"Oh, yeah, right. The Literary Group. Yodel number two."

"The point?"

"The point is—I'm here to help you."

"*You're* here to help *me.*"

"I thought I just said that. Is there an-"

"Oh, please."

"Okay, okay. Look. You wanna save the world, right?"

"Not the whole world. Only a little of it. Just a tiny piece will do. I...I just want to write well—really well. Convincingly. Startlingly. I want to horrify and edify. Make people see that real horror is in the way they waste time and life and money and resources and-"

The Smoker raised his hands to stem the rush of words. "Whoa, whoa, *whoa!* Writing well? That's your answer to the world's problems: World hunger, political corruption, spiritual decay? Kid, you got a lot to learn. Writing is nothing. Money, now, that's something."

"Money?"

"Money, celebrity, status—that's how you change the world. Just think of it: You got money—you can give it away. You got celebrity—you can be visible. You got status—you can throw it around."

"Yeah?"

"Yeah. Believe me, as a good writer—even a great writer— you're nowhere. You got zip. You appeal to the so-called intelligentsia and what have you got? A bunch of smug, self-righteous 'admirers,' that's what you got. Know what that is? Zip. They read your books, then sit around on their Bistros agreein' with your insights and sayin' how brill you are and how brill they are for recognizing how brill you are. That's crap. But if you got money, celebrity, status—we-ell, then you put on one of those crummy T-shirts you're so stiff over and people will notice. You hear what I'm sayin', Jack? You got to be visible before anything you do or say means a damn."

"Yeah, so what? I don't stand a snowball's chance in Hell of that happening."

The Smoker scratched his nose. "Funny you should say that, kid, 'cause, in point of fact, you got a chance."

"I do?"

"You do."

Bert nodded. "Sure. Right. And you're going to give it to me."

"I am."

"How?"

The Smoker took a long drag on his illegal cigarette (which seemed not to have gotten any shorter during their conversation) and smiled. "The mechanics are my problem. All you gotta do is wait. You know what they say: All things come to those who wait."

"*They* do, huh?"

The Smoker scratched his ear. "Yeah. You know, the famous They. Wha'd'ya say, kid?"

"What do you mean—what do I say?"

"To the deal."

"The deal?"

The little guy sighed. "Holy Christmas, kid. You are truly dense. Look. You go home, see. Hang out. Do your own thing—whatever the jargon is these days—and I do the rest."

Bert pursed his entire face. "Fame? Fortune? Status?"

"The works."

He felt a tiny hope springing eternal in his breast. "You mean, I can go home and keep writing what I've been writing and it'll sell? I'll become famous and-"

The gloved hands were up again. "Hold your fire, bwana. Gimme a little help here. You do that and the deal is off. No way even I can do that big a miracle."

Bert scowled, then shook his head. "Wait a minute. What am I thinking? This is crazy. Nobody can do that kind of a miracle except God and up to now He hasn't seen fit."

His companion smiled and nodded, puffing vigorously on his smoke. "And so it devolves upon yours truly."

"Oh? And who are you—the Archangel Gabriel?"

The smile deepened. "Not exactly."

"Oh, oh, wait! I see. You're the Devil, right, and you're offering me all this in return for my immortal soul, right?"

"Your immortal soul is already spoken for, Jack. Besides, I wouldn't know what to do with it if you gave it to me."

Bert gaped. "You expect me to believe you're really the Devil?"

The man spread his arms. "In the flesh."

"Oh, come on!"

"Hey! Who knew what you were thinkin', here, huh? Who knew all about you?"

"You could've seen me around. Or—or someone might have put you up to this. Like my jackass neighbor. That's it, isn't it-- Jack the Ass sent you! You followed me here-"

"And just happened to overhear all your innermost thoughts?"

Bert was silent.

"You have a birthmark next to your navel. You love Peking Duck, hate pizza, and think Hemingway was overrated. You haven't had a steady girlfriend since your junior year in college. You're a virgin. You wanna hear more?"

"I-"

"Oh, yeah—your most embarrassing moment was during high school when your English teacher found this poem-"

"Stop! Stop! Okay. I believe you're...something... So, where do I sign?"

"You don't sign. Remember, I'm Satan-the-Devil." He said it fast, like one of those televangelists, as if it was all one word. "I'll know if you've been living up to your part of the bargain. All that contracts-in-blood stuff was just bad press. A strong verbal and a shake are good enough for me."

"Okay. How do I know you're living up to your part of the bargain?"

"Easy. You'll become rich and famous."

"Uh-huh." Bert gave the little man a hard look. "Oh, what the Hell—you'll pardon the expression. Okay, sure. I'll bite." He held out his hand for the guy to take and was embarrassed to realize he expected it to be hot. It wasn't, of course.

The guy chuckled. "Everybody expects me to burn 'em. More bad press. You could give me a little help in that department, if you're so inclined."

"Oh...sure."

"Well, nice doin' business with ya, bwana." He gave a mocking salute and turned to go.

"Hey, wait a minute. Can I ask you something?"

"Sure."

"Why do you have a Brooklyn accent?"

"Damned research department. I asked for Brook*line*." He shook his head and moved off into the dark. *"Putzes."*

Herbert skipped Writer's Group that night. He went home and read part of a cyber-shock novel. Then he started to write one. He skipped the Group for the next two months, too, busy working on the novel.

He finished the book and sent it off to an agent he knew was hot into the genre, then missed the next month with the Writer's Group because he was a little ashamed of what he was doing.

At the end of the month, the agent sent Bert contracts. The novel gave him dry heaves, he said. It was great. Bert started writing short stories. He was too busy to go to any Writer's meetings and felt it was better to write than to merely talk about writing.

Within two weeks, the agent called and told Bert his novel, *Night of Steel Death,* was going up for auction between three major houses. Bert dropped by the Espress-O just long enough to tell his old cronies he had a bid war going for one of his books (he neglected to mention the title or genre), then took himself out for dinner.

In the time before the auction, Bert finished four cyber-shock stories and mailed them off. The novel sold for a seven-figure advance. The stories went for $3,000 apiece. Bert quit his job and began his second cyber-shocker, throwing in a twisted version of the love story from *Of Blood Dark Skies.*

He didn't see the Writer's Group again; by now he considered them a bunch of hopelessly self-involved losers. He was surprised to find he didn't even miss them.

He bought a house in Marblehead, started an investment portfolio and got a girlfriend and a dog. He gave a substantial amount to charity and wore his "Tune It Or Die" T-shirt proudly. He did the workshop circuit, TV talk shows, book tours, Horror fiction conventions. After a few tries, he gave up attempting to weave his philosophy of life into these endeavors and talked shock-shop to the delight of his ardent fans. After a while, the philosophy seemed pretty sophomoric. He was visible —that was what really mattered.

His career was long and successful by almost any standards. Only his ex-writing buddies spoke of selling out. He didn't know that, of course, he never saw them.

He was ninety-five when it began to occur to him that his time might soon be running out. He began to expect to look up one day and see the Devil—in more traditional garb—beckoning him through the fiery gates. By his ninety-sixth birthday it had become an obsession. It colored his work, showing up as a fixation on the mortality of all flesh, but that seemed only to increase his popularity. He realized that, at this point in his career, he could say anything he wanted, but found, perversely, that he had very little to say.

One crisp winter evening he took a nostalgic stroll by the crystal waters of the River Charles and waxed retrospective. He had gone through his collection of thick scrapbooks that evening, ensconced in the artfully lit recesses of his "trophy room." It occurred to him then that, while his reviewers raved about his novels, using words like *terse, horrific, paralyzing, disturbing, electrifying,* not one had ever said his work was *thought-provoking* or *illuminating* or even *passionate.*

Still, he was earning millions every year, while the most successful member of his old Writer's Group was pulling down a paltry 90k per annum as a college professor of creative writing and turning out thick, thoughtful science fiction tomes.

He watched the lights from the shoreline promenade cavort among the ripples of the Charles and wondered what life would have been like if he'd kept writing books like *Of Blood Dark Skies* —books with heart and soul and relevance.

"Hell," said a voice behind him. "It would've been pure hell, kid."

He spun around as fast as his ninety-six year old body would allow and propped his butt against the parapet. "You."

It was the Devil, of course—taller, younger, more handsome than before and dressed in this year's latest fashion, but undeniably the same. He was smoking one of the red cigarettes (it could have been the same one, for all Bert knew), but had dropped the Brooklyn accent.

"So," said Bert, nodding.

"So," said the Devil.

"So, it's pay-off time."

"Well, accounting time, anyway."

"So, this is where I hand over my immortal soul and go to Hell."

"Nope. I told you, kid, I wouldn't know what to do with your soul if you gave it to me. And I'll let you in on a secret-- there is no Hell. He made it up to scare the sinners."

"You don't want my soul?"

"No."

"Really?"

"Really."

"You're not joking with me?"

The Devil pointed up at his lean, good-looking face. "Does this look like the face of a joker?"

"No."

"Then, trust me—I'm not joking."

"But we had a contract—an agreement."

"We did."

"Well, when do you collect?"

"I already did, kid. I did what you expected; you did what I expected. Good business, all the way around."

Bert shook his head. "But I don't understand. What the hell did I do? I didn't do *anything*."

The Devil smiled. His teeth were perfect and even and very white. "Just what you said, kid. Nothing. You didn't do a damn thing. You wrote uninspired novels that didn't do anything but scare people. You never wrote anything even remotely important, never challenged yourself, never challenged anyone else. Except for a few handouts—most of which were eaten up by the overhead those charity organizations lug around—you never did a damn thing to better the world around you. Hell, you even turned into a recluse there for a while. That was great. You might as well have gone to Tibet."

"I did go to Tibet."

The Devil shrugged. "Well, see. Even *I* lost track of you. In short, bwana, you never set forth one original, inspiring, illumined, or impassioned thought. I couldn't have asked for better than that. I'll tell you, kid, I wish I had ten billion more just like you." He clapped Bert on the shoulder and smiled into his ninety-six year old face. "Nice doing business with you, kid."

He turned then, and stepped briskly away down the promenade, his patent leather Guccis clicking contentedly against the gleaming lightstone of the walk.

Several yards away, he turned back for a last glance at the stoop-shouldered old man perched, like a stranded albatross, on the parapet. He chuckled, appreciating the scene. "By the way, kid—have a nice forever."

Sons of the Fathers

A story of speculative fiction

Sons of the Fathers was originally published in the 3rd issue of *Century* magazine in 1995. It is an exploration of the Bahá'í principle of the equality of women and men set in a religious fable. It is also a commentary on mankind's tendency toward selective deafness.

> *The world of humanity has two wings—one is women and the other men. Not until both wings are equally developed can the bird fly.*
>
> Selections from the
Writings of `Abdu'l-Bahá,
p. 302

Gilad considered himself the most unfortunate man on the face of the earth. He left his tent with the look of doom on his face and made certain everyone saw it as he moped his way down the sandy swathe to the council tent. The Uncles would be there, and he could show them his long face and get some sympathy.

It was cool and dark in the council tent. The Uncles were sitting in a circle on a pillowed carpet, drinking cold mint tea. They all looked up as he entered, then looked away again when they saw the expression on his face.

He sat down next to Dovev, the youngest, accepting a cup of the tea. He took a sip and nodded. "It's very good, Abran," he complimented the Father of the Tribe. "Refreshing."

"Buried for two days beneath this very tent," said Mahir. "Perfect for coolness and flavor." Mahir was an expert on the preparation of tea.

There was silence but for the gentle flapping of the tent around them. Gilad sighed.

"We grieve with you, brother," said Chanoch, the High Priest, "and will pray your misfortune not be repeated."

Avidor laid a consoling hand on his arm. "I know better than anyone how deep is your sorrow at this moment. Have I not been visited with the same tragedy *seven times?*"

The others nodded and clicked and crooned. All but Dovev, who simply stared with thoughtful eyes into his teacup.

Gilad took another painful swallow of tea and sighed again. "Assuredly, God despises me," he said.

"Nay, Brother," Chanoch remonstrated. "He is only testing your faith. Pray that you not be found lacking in that."

These words did nothing to comfort Gilad. He felt tears pressing the back of his eyes. Ashamed, he put down his teacup and got wearily to his feet.

Dovev reached up and touched the sleeve of his *jalabba*. "Is your wife well?" he asked softly.

"My wife?" asked Gilad, numbly. "My wife is fine."

"And your child lives?"

Gilad nodded, preparing to lose himself in profound misery.

"Then, you are not so unfortunate."

Gilad shook his head again, wondering why Dovev was so insensitive. He sighed a third time. "A *girl*," he said.

The others clicked and crooned and shook their heads.

"*Another* girl," he said and went out into the bright sun, where he at least had an excuse for the watering of his eyes.

"Poor Camel Hump," sighed Avidor. "I believe his heart is broken. Two girls in a row! God favored me with a son the second time."

"A testimony to your faith, Brother," Chanoch informed him.

Abran, the Elder, stirred himself. "Dovev, why did you torture the poor man so?"

"I simply thought it might lift his spirit if he looked at the positive side of things."

"What positive side?" asked Mahir.

"Why, that his lovely wife, Adiella, and their daughter are alive and well."

"If they had died," Mahir told him, "he would have had one less daughter and could have taken a new wife that might bear him sons. Now, Adiella must give birth to yet another girl before poor Gilad may take a second wife."

Avidor chuckled. "There is something to be said for having more than one wife." He had three, himself. "Ah, variety!" he breathed, raising his cup to Heaven.

"Avidor brings to our attention an important matter, Brother Dovev," said Abran. "Your wife, Jaffa, has failed these three years of your marriage, to give you any issue. You are entitled to select another wife."

Dovev looked extremely uncomfortable. "Yes, I know."

"When do you propose to do this?"

"I hadn't really thought about it," said Dovev to his teacup.

"Perhaps you should. The sooner you get another wife, the sooner you can produce a son."

"My daughter, Tirza, is of marriageable age," offered Avidor eagerly. "And she often expresses admiration for you, Dovev."

Abran nodded. "Tirza would be a perfect choice, Dovev."

"Yes," agreed Dovev. "She would make a lovely wife, if I were in need of one. But I'm not. I have a wife."

These words did not please Father Abran. "You have a wife who has borne you no sons, Dovev. Your duty to the Tribe goes unfulfilled."

"Your duty to *God*," interjected Chanoch.

Dovev gazed at him. "But surely it is God's will that Jaffa has borne no children. And if I am to have children, then, by His will, Jaffa will bear them." And with that pronouncement, he rose and left the tent.

Chanoch shook his head. "I never realized what a stubborn man Dovev is. His soft-spokeness blinds one to the fault."

Avidor shrugged. "He will come to see the light of reason. When another season passes and Jaffa continues to be worthless, he will see that he must choose another wife." He sniffed. "I cannot imagine why he persists in his loyalty to this barren creature. She is not particularly desirable—passingly pretty, maybe. Certainly not the beauty my Tirza is."

"It is not so much loyalty to Jaffa," explained Mahir, "but loyalty to her family. Their fathers were like blood kin. Jaffa's father, Omra, saved Dovev's family during the Great Windstorm. You remember, don't you Avidor?"

He nodded. "Indeed. That was the year we moved to the Oasis of the Sweet Spring. Twenty years ago, now. You are correct. Dovev surely feels a debt of gratitude to the family of Omra. He could not, in good conscience, turn Jaffa out."

"He doesn't have to turn her out," reminded Chanoch. "He can keep her. So it is written in the Tablet of Sala. She may be barren, but if she pleases him in other ways..." He shrugged eloquently. "Young men are, after all, closer to the Earth than to Heaven."

"You must speak to him, Chanoch," said Abran, scowling. "You must teach him the Law and make him see his duty." He tugged at his beard, the scowl deepening. "Gilad's tragedy has disturbed me deeply, Brothers. Twenty women have given birth so far this spring. Of those, fourteen have given birth to girls, and of those, seven have borne girls for the second time."

Chanoch clucked sadly. "That a man should be forced to endure the indignity of fathering a girl-child twice! Surely it is a great test of faith." Chanoch knew all about tests of faith. His own first wife, after giving him one boy, had borne two stillborn sons and a daughter before he could marry again.

"Test of faith or no, it is demoralizing the Tribe and causing strife in the families," said Abran. His white, bird-wing brows settled over the bridge of his nose. "Amira has brought complaints from among the women of husbands who will no longer speak to them or who are threatening to disown them."

Mahir snorted. "I suppose she thinks these threats are unwarranted?"

"My wife offered no commentary. Though she did mention that several of the younger women are chafing under such threats. One referred to them as 'camel dung.'"

Mahir snorted again. "Sabra's the only one who would dare to speak so! She should be packed off into the desert! Little would she understand a man's feelings!"

"The implication was that we didn't understand a *woman's* feelings."

Mahir shrugged. "What's to understand? Does a man bother himself to understand the feelings of his dog or his camel? He feeds them and cares for their needs. What is to understand?"

All the Uncles clicked and crooned at this wisdom.

"Camel dung," said Sabra. "That is what our men use for brains. And as to their hearts—I doubt they have any."

Amira sent her a disapproving glance and returned Adiella's infant daughter to her arms, cleaned and wrapped in soft swaddling.

Adiella sniffled and clutched her baby protectively. "Oh, I can understand how they must feel, Amira. How poor Gilad must feel. Two daughters in as many years! He must feel accursed!"

"Do *you* feel accursed?" asked Sabra. "Look into that baby's eyes and tell me you feel accursed. Better yet, tell *her*."

"Oh, I can't!" sighed Adiella, looking into her daughter's tiny red face. "You know I can't. I probably should."

"According to the men," retorted Sabra scornfully.

"According to Emuna, too," reminded Amira.

"Emuna is a fly on a heap of camel dung!" opined Sabra. "She'll believe anything they tell her. If Chanoch said, 'Emuna, you are a she-camel', Emuna would tie on bells and a muzzle and offer to carry his pack-saddle."

Adiella blushed prettily and tried not to giggle at the thought of the High Priest's wife so attired.

"Well," said Amira wearily, "if the next three births are boys, perhaps they will calm down a bit."

"And if they are *not* boys?" asked Sabra. Her brows bobbed exaggeratedly.

Amira frowned in contemplation, following the movement absently. Even in the dim interior of Adiella's tent Sabra's eyebrows were ridiculously red. Her *burnoose* had slipped (it had always slipped) and bright strands of copper hair were escaping it. Amira was saved from having to answer Sabra's question by the return of Dovev's wife, Jaffa.

Sabra pounced on her the moment she entered the tent. "Well, did you talk to the Uncles?"

Jaffa shook her head, her huge, dark, soulful eyes looking bottomless in the half-light. "They were busy."

"Busy?" snorted Sabra. "What were they doing?"

"Praying."

"Praying?"

"They were praying for sons," said Jaffa quietly. "And for an end to the Curse."

"You *listened?*" breathed Adiella, aghast. "You listened to their prayers?"

"I'm sure she only heard one side of the conversation," said Sabra dryly.

"Sabra," warned Amira, "control your tongue. Your heated words do nothing but incite contention. Still..." The matriarch gazed out through the tent flap, squinting against the blaze of sun on sand. "I wish they might understand how we feel. It's hard enough to face their disappointment, but when they behave as if we do it on purpose—who'd have a daughter on purpose?"

"I would," said Sabra. "And the problem goes deeper than understanding our feelings, Amira. They refuse to believe we have any feelings worth understanding."

"Dovev isn't that way," murmured Jaffa.

"Dovev!" snorted Sabra, tossing her head and losing her *burnoose* altogether. "If all men were Dovev, all women would die of bliss!"

"They are the Uncles," reminded Amira patiently. "They have the entire tribe to consider in all things. The complaints of a handful of women..."

"The tears of *all* women..." interrupted Sabra.

"Are seen and measured by God," Amira finished. "We shall receive our recompense. *If,*" —and she looked pointedly at Sabra— "we are obedient in the Lord's path."

"Dovev is an Uncle," Jaffa reminded them. "Perhaps he can make the others understand that we *do* have feelings."

"Ah. Here comes the Camel Hump," warned Sabra, peeking through the tent flap.

"Oh, I wish you wouldn't call him that," begged Adiella. Her eyes got very big. "How does he look?"

"Miserable, of course."

"Angry? Does he still look angry?"

"Yes."

"O-o-oh!" Adiella began to cry, clutching her daughter, who also began to cry.

Gilad pushed his way into the tent, his face longer, if anything, than Adiella had last seen it. She cried harder.

"So what are *you* crying about?" Gilad asked. "*I'm* the one who's cursed! *I'm* the one God hates! I'm-I'm-"

"I'm-I'm-" echoed Adiella. On the third "I'm", she finally managed to continue. "I'm sorry you're so miserable."

"As you should be. Now I have to wait another year to either have a son or take a new wife! If you had been stupid enough to have twin girls, at least I would have been eligible to pick a new wife, but no-o-o! You have to prolong my agony!"

"I didn't do it on purpose," mumbled Adiella.

"What? *What?*"

Sabra came to her feet, dark red hair spilling over her shoulders in an angry cloud. "She said she didn't do it on purpose."

Gilad looked at her down a nose of patriarchal proportions, mentally disparaging her brazen tresses. "It hardly matters whether she did it on purpose or not—she did it."

"Gilad," said Jaffa's fleece-soft voice from the semi-dark at his shoulder, "who forms the child in the womb of its mother?"

Gilad jumped and squinted at the dark spot until he saw Jaffa's darker eyes gazing at him so directly. "God does, of course."

"And is it possible that God has formed something imperfect?"

"To think so would be blasphemy! God is the sum of all perfections." He hastily made the sign of the Circle-star with his forefinger.

"Then would God perform an act that was counter to His own will?"

"Absurd!"

"Well, then," Jaffa concluded, "your daughter must be a perfect creation whose birth is certainly the will of our perfect God. Are we not taught to accept the will of God with radiant acquiescence?"

Gilad gaped.

"A-a-h!" breathed Sabra to the silence. "Elegant!"

Hedya had awakened that morning in nervous anticipation. She performed her ablutions, said her prayers, started a pot of water and some wheat cakes over the fire and put her nose outside the tent flap to sniff the air. It was cool this morning and there was a sweetness like the coming of rain, but it would not rain. She knew that without knowing how she knew it.

She prepared breakfast for herself and her father. As always, he smelled it cooking and came shuffling out of his closet to sit by the fire.

"Near time to set up the cook fire outside," he said. "Warmer these mornings."

"It's too early in the season to count on the weather being stable," Hedya returned. "We'll have another frost."

"Rain, do you think?"

Hedya frowned. "No, not rain. Something else."

Through breakfast Hedya was distracted and her father had to repeat himself occasionally. They spoke of their goats and the number of kids they expected this year; they discussed Scripture and the Temple's new altar with its twin golden angels.

After breakfast, Father Kedem wandered off to visit with his cronies while Hedya followed the call of her uneasiness to the Temple. She rarely received guidance there (she never thought of it as revelation), but a brief contemplation always put her in the right frame of mind to receive it. The only time she'd been visited by guidance in the Sanctuary itself was the Year of the Flood.

They'd settled in a river valley that year. Her warning had saved most of the Tribe from disaster. Only Chanoch had kept his family along the riverbank, insisting that any major revelation to the Tribe would come through him. He and Emuna had lost half their goats and most of their sheep. Chanoch's tent and personal belongings were washed completely away.

Chanoch's wives and children had shown much respect for Hedya after that. Chanoch, himself, showed her nothing but contempt. He begrudged her visits to the Temple, but there wasn't much he could do to stop them. Instead, he contented himself with requesting that she limit their duration, so as not to interfere with his priestly duties.

This particular day Chanoch was not about. His eldest son, Leor, was involved in the task of refilling the altar braziers with incense when Hedya entered the Sanctuary.

"Hedya!" He smiled a greeting and bowed deferentially. "This is a pleasant surprise. What brings you here today?"

She smiled shyly in return. "A...a need to be here."

His eyebrows rose at the implication of her words. "Are you preparing to receive revelation, then?"

Now Hedya blushed, her dark skin suffusing with color. "Please, Leor. I can't think of it as revelation. Revelation is reserved for the Apostles of God—may my life be a sacrifice to

Them. I receive only guidance. A very small thing compared to revelation."

"Hedya," —his voice was kind but stern— "what you receive is no small thing. You've saved lives and property many times." He was suddenly grinning, his dark eyes glinting maliciously in the smoky light of the altar. "You would have saved my father a fortune if he hadn't been so puffed up with himself."

Hedya's blush deepened. "Leor, please! I did nothing. I merely repeat what I...what I see—what I'm told. And to say such a thing of your father—!" She broke off in a giggle at the mental image of a puffed-up Chanoch.

Leor laughed aloud.

"S-shh!" Hedya put a finger to her lips. "Your father will hear you and accuse me of profaning his Temple."

"*His* Temple? This is God's Temple, Hedya, not Chanoch's— although I suspect he sometimes thinks it is his. And on what grounds could he accuse you of profanity? Because you made me laugh? God *loves* laughter!" Leor's eyes glinted wickedly again. "Can you imagine the laugh He must have had when the river Nibis overflowed its banks?"

He glanced furtively about the empty sanctuary, eyes rolling like those of an old man with a great secret to tell. "The hour is midnight. The rains have ceased and Chanoch lies blissfully asleep—safe in his tent. His second wife, Emuna, lies trustingly at his side. The sound of thunder rolls across the high mountain passes. Lightning twitches through the clouds. While Chanoch sleeps, his first wife, Keturah, and her son pack their belongings and put them into a cart. As they free their camels, the camels of Emuna begin to flee the rising river. And as they free their sheep, the sheep of the trusting Emuna begin to swim."

He made paddling motions and Hedya stifled a giggle. "As they remove their belongings to higher ground, Chanoch's

belongings begin to swim. And as the faithful Keturah races to
her husband's tent to warn him, *he* begins to swim." Now Leor's
eyes opened as wide as they could and he made a fish face,
paddling frantically.

Hedya shook uncontrollably. "S-s-stop!" she giggled.
"P-please, s-s-stop!"

Leor stopped paddling and laughed. "I would love to have
seen the look on my father's face when he first realized he was
awash. I know God saw it. I could hear His laughter above the
mountains...before Emuna's squealing drowned it out. Father
should have listened to you, Hedya. He shouldn't treat you the
way he does."

She shrugged. "I understand how he feels. He is the High
Priest. Prophecy is his province. It must be very hard for him to
understand how the Gift can be given to a woman. Especially
one who is not of the prophetic line. I don't understand it
myself."

"God speaks to whomever He wills, Hedya, and none may
ask of His doings—not even His High Priest." He put a hand on
her shoulder and gave it a gentle squeeze. "Now, I think I
should leave you to your contemplation. I shouldn't like you to
keep God waiting." He withdrew his hand and moved to the
doors of the sanctuary, pausing there to look back at her. "You
could be of the prophetic line, if you wished it," he said. "By
marriage." He slipped out through the tent flap.

Marriage! That could only mean... Her cheeks flamed. Only
the Priest-class were of the prophetic line, and the only way she
could join the Priest-class was to marry one of Chanoch's sons,
and the only one of Chanoch's sons who was both unmarried
and of age was Leor.

As a result of this train of thought, Hedya found it difficult
to be contemplative, but finally she got her mind off Leor and
onto her favorite passage of Scripture.

She knelt before the altar and sang it softly to herself: "I sing praise to Thee, O mighty God. I give thanks for all Thy wonderful works. Where is sorrow when Thy Joy fills my heart? Where is death when Thy Life fills my soul? I dedicate myself to Thee, O God."

She opened her eyes and drank in the quiet, scented, warm half-light. The two new altar angels gleamed, golden as sun-drenched sheaves of harvest wheat, from their niches at each side of the Seat of Oration where the Scripture was read. Dovev had fashioned them and they seemed almost to breathe. These were Dovev's children—these beautiful, golden twins.

Hedya smiled, absorbed in admiration. Then she blinked. Then she rubbed her eyes. The smoke from the braziers behind the angels must have gotten thicker, for there seemed to be a golden mist rising about the altar. And the lamps must have suddenly flared, because the Sanctuary seemed brighter. And the angels...

She rubbed her eyes again. The angel on the left—a female angel in Jaffa's likeness—seemed to be the source of the light. Hedya stared at it. It was. The Jaffa angel was glowing.

She wasn't afraid. Not even when the angel's shimmering outline began to waver and change. Not even when it began to move. Not even when the radiant thing rose slowly from its kneeling position to stand majestically over her.

She took a deep breath and waited.

The Angel smiled down at her through silvery eyes and said, "Hedya, daughter of Kedem, the Lord is with you. Blessed are you, for He has chosen you to be His Prophetess."

Hedya only half-heard the words, but the voice she would never forget. It was a reed flute played in the river canyon, it was water spilling over rocks, it was wind rustling a thousand leaves. It was both warm and distant; it came from inside her and it came from everywhere around her.

"The Lord requires you to give two messages," the radiant Being continued. "To the women of the Tribe, say: Take comfort, daughters of the Living God; your forbearance is known. It is manifest to the One Who is Himself the Most Manifest. He has conferred upon you the stations of servitude and stewardship. You have made a glory of the first and have had the second stripped from you. Your Lord will no longer wait in silence. Your reward is coming.

"To the men of the Tribe, say: Take heed, sons of Disappointment; your arrogance is known. It is not hidden from the One Who is, Himself, the Most Hidden. He has conferred upon you the stations of servitude and stewardship. You have abdicated the first and abused the second. Your Lord will no longer wait in silence. Your reward is coming.

"Say: You boast of your superior strength. Verily, it dies with your body and, in My kingdom, counts for nothing. It is your spirit I judge, not your wealth or your strength or the number of your sons.

"Say: We gave to you daughters as a gift of joy, yet you mourn them. We made woman your equal, yet you count her inferior. Treat her as I made her.

"Say: We hear you cry for sons. If you are superior, bear them yourselves.

"Say: Here is the Law of Marriage, which you have abused: Take one wife. If she bears sons, love her and make of your sons heirs. If she bears daughters, love her and make of your daughters heirs. If she bears neither sons nor daughters, love her. Take to yourselves orphans or appoint yourselves heirs from among your kin. But appoint no male heirs from among kin or orphans if you have daughters.

"Cease whining to Me and perform what I have commanded you. Hedya, My anointed, is My prophetess to you, My daughter, and My priestess."

The Angel paused, her words ringing like camel bells from everywhere and from nowhere. Hedya was awestruck—His prophetess, His priestess, His *daughter!* Had the Angel really said those things?

"The Most High God has spoken," the Angel said, and reached out a blazing finger to touch Hedya's brow. "I anoint you by the power of God. Arise and give the message."

Give the message!

The enormity of that settled on her shoulders, driving the breath from her body. This message the Angel so calmly spoke of ran counter to everything upon which tribal relationships were based. This message seemed to contradict what the Elders had taught as Scripture for centuries. Perhaps she had misheard it. She dared to speak.

"Could you—ah—repeat the message, Angel? I fear I may not have heard it right."

The Angel did repeat it, but the words were the same, each one falling to the sandy floor like a bolt of lightning.

Hedya quaked. "M-must I tell them...all those things? Must I *call* myself...those things?"

"Your humility is well-beloved," said the Angel. "But you must deliver the entire message, and the hearers must know who speaks to them and by Whose authority."

"But these are such hard words. How shall they be heard?"

"They may not be pleasing," the Angel acknowledged. "Still, they must be heard. The Lord has willed it."

Hedya could only nod, feeling the Angel's touch like a cool, tingling flame in her head. "I do my Lord's will," she said. "But...they won't believe me. They'll say that our God would never say such things: That daughters are a joy, that women should be equal in stewardship, that girls might inherit..."

The Angel's smile offered comfort and rebuke at once. "These things are in the Lord's hands."

Hedya bowed her head. "When...when shall I speak and where?"

"Stand and turn around, daughter of the Living God," the Angel instructed.

Hedya obeyed and found herself facing the empty Sanctuary.

"Sabbath day, after the Scripture has been read, you will stand here and speak to the assembled Tribe."

"To the-the whole Tribe?"

"God wills it."

"Then I must obey."

"His blessings are upon you, Hedya," said the Angel, and was gone, warmth, glow, and incense.

Hedya turned back to the altar. Dovev's two angels knelt, golden, by the Seat of Oration, each guarding its brazier of incense. The Temple was silent but for the tiny sputter of embers in their bowls and the hammering of her heart.

She knelt again, sent a brief, heartfelt prayer for inner calm and left the Sanctuary.

She told only her Father she had received guidance. He merely smiled and nodded at her with a look of fatherly pride. She knew that by Sabbath the whole Tribe would hear of it— Kedem's daughter had received a revelation from God. The prospect of transmitting that revelation filled her with quaking dread.

Sabbath came at last, and Hedya, though she had fasted and prayed and meditated, was still trembling at the prospect of delivering her message. She had caught herself wishing she might forget the Angel's words, and thus be saved from having to repeat them. But she did not forget; they were burned into her memory, and her guilt at having wished them away only made them burn brighter. They were God's words, and as hard as they would be to hear, they must be heard.

That conviction did not keep her heart from pounding, or her mouth from going as dry as the sands beneath her feet as her father escorted her to Temple. The doors and walls of the huge tent had been rolled up so that the entire Tribe might attend. Banners waved high up on the massive poles that marked the outer court and the fabric roof of the Sanctuary rolled like a crimson ocean above the worshippers.

The very sight of it made Hedya want to run and hide, but she could not hide from the Lord and He had given her a task to perform.

Hedya and her father were near the front of the crowd as worship began, and she tried futilely to concentrate on it. But her mind could be no more still than her galloping heart, and she could only whisper prayers to God that He would grant her the strength of His will.

At last, Chanoch was reading the Scripture. He chose a passage from the Ninth Chapter of the Book of Musa: "O sons of the Living God! Religion is surrender to My guidance. Those who formerly received the Scripture argued as to its meaning. They have made it a source of conflict. For this reason shall they receive guidance.

"O My Anointed! If they argue with thee, say: 'I have surrendered myself to God. Have ye surrendered?' If they surrender, they are rightly guided, and if they turn away, it is thy duty to warn them of the God who reads their hearts.

"O my Anointed! Those who disbelieve My revelations and scorn the prophets and slay those who enjoin equity: Promise them a painful doom. But to those who surrender, promise a sure reward. Say to My people: If you love God and follow His guidance, He will love you and forgive your sins. God is the Forgiver, the Merciful."

Hedya shivered. By no coincidence did Chanoch select that particular passage.

Oh, he doubtless believed he had chosen it for its relevance to the rash of female babies—his commentary about the sins of the fathers (and mothers) being visited upon successive generations seemed to confirm that. The birth of girls undoubtedly meant that someone was sinning, he expounded. His guidance: Stop sinning. No more sin, no more girl babies.

Suddenly, it seemed, Chanoch's commentary ended and the crowd of worshippers began to jostle with conversation. Chanoch stepped down from the altar. Hedya fought down her fears and took his place.

"Wait!" she cried, her voice strong and clear. "Hear me, people of Musa!"

Her voice carried well and silence came swiftly—they had been expecting this. She stood for a moment with all eyes on her, banners snapping overhead, counterpoint to the rippling of the roof.

Chanoch, scowling, was moving toward her when a sudden, sharp gust of wind pulled the bindings on the section of roof above the altar and flung it back. The altar was struck with a blaze of sunlight—the angels became giant torches and Hedya, in her virginal white robes, gleamed like a full moon.

She glanced at the Jaffa Angel and felt her fear evaporate like dew from morning sands. Then she turned her gaze to the crowd of gaping people, saw her father's eager, near toothless grin, felt Leor's intense scrutiny and his father's fury, and began to speak.

She delivered every word of the Angel's message, her voice like an alarum horn. She looked every inch a prophetess. Wild-eyed and pale-faced, her black hair a cluster of flying banners, her robes a cloud of glory, she made her announcement. And when she was finished, there was a profound silence.

Predictably, it was Chanoch who broke it. "Blasphemy!" he cried. "How dare you blaspheme in the Temple of the Most High God?"

"I speak at His bidding," Hedya returned.

Chanoch moved toward the altar, shoving aside those in his way. "You dare proclaim this the word of God? How came you by it?"

"I was in the Temple," said Hedya, "and an Angel of the Lord appeared and gave me this message. I have only obeyed."

"An Angel?" scoffed Chanoch over the murmuring of his flock. "Describe it."

Hedya pointed to the kneeling statue beside her. "This Angel. The Lord caused it to glow with light and rise and speak to me."

The noise of the wagging of many tongues swept through the congregation.

"You are a-a madwoman!" proclaimed Chanoch.

"'I have surrendered myself to God.'" she quoted. "'Have ye surrendered?'"

Chanoch's lips curled. "Who are you to throw scripture in the face of your own priest?"

"I am the Anointed of the Lord and His Priestess," said Hedya. All diffidence had vanished.

"PRIESTESS?" Chanoch flung himself at her, but it was his son, Leor, he faced when he reached the altar.

"Will you commit violence against her in the Temple, Father?" Leor asked.

Chanoch glared past him at Hedya. "She is a demon!"

"Demon, Father? Because she delivers a message that doesn't tickle our ears?" Leor's eyes found Father Abran among the people. "Will you listen to her, Father Abran?"

Abran shook his head, dazedly. "How shall I listen to such words, Leor?"

"You've listened to her before."

"These words are hard to hear."

"That does not make them blasphemous words, Father Abran. Hasn't Hedya prophesied before?"

"You know it."

"And haven't her words always been true?"

Abran nodded. "Yes."

"And hasn't she always been rightly guided?"

"So it seemed."

Chanoch exploded. "This is a matter of more import than spring rains or accidents or-or-"

"Or invasions of enemies or...floods, Father?" asked Leor. "You disbelieved Hedya once before...or have you forgotten?"

The muted laughter that rippled beneath the tent roof proved that no one else had forgotten.

Chanoch flushed. "I am High Priest! God speaks through me, not through this—this *woman!*"

"If God speaks through you, Chanoch," called old Kedem, "then how is it your goats came to be floating down the Nibis? My stock was safe. So was anyone's who heeded my daughter's warning. Your own son and wife heeded her and saved their stock. Only you lost, because you wouldn't listen."

"It's true!" shouted someone else. "Hedya has always been true. She's the one who warned us the Leamites were encamped in the pass to Yathrib, not Chanoch. She has always been true."

"Not this time!" roared Chanoch. "Her words are the words of the Evil One. They make a lie of our Law."

"Our Law, Father?" asked Leor. "What of *God's* Law? Doesn't the Book say a man shall have one wife?"

"Yes, but it says nothing about what a man shall do if that wife is barren. It devolved upon the Apostle Sala to give us the Law of Remarriage."

"That isn't the point. Doesn't the Book of Musa say a man may put aside his wife only for infidelity?"

"You say this because of your mother," Chanoch accused.

"What does the Book say?"

"The first wife is not put away. She is kept."

"But then, doesn't she cease to be a wife? In the Book of Musa isn't it written that a man may only have one wife?"

"Yes, but-"

"But then, is not the man with multiple wives committing adultery?"

"Now, how can a man commit adultery with his own wives? The Tablet of Sala specifically enjoins that a man may not visit more than one wife in the same month."

"The Book of Musa calls it adultery if he visits more than one wife in the same *lifetime,* unless he divorces one of them first. It is clear from Hedya's message that we are breaking God's Law."

Chanoch spluttered. "A man must not die without male issue!"

"Is that written in the Book of Musa? I don't recall having read it."

"It is in the Tablet of Sala. And it was the way of the Tribe before Musa came to us."

Leor nodded. "Yes, before Musa. But Musa made provision for heirs. Hedya has reminded us. A childless man may adopt sons. He may assign a male heir from among his kin, if he so desires. Or a man may allot his portion to a daughter."

"Shameful!"

"Scriptural," countered Leor. "Does God ask us to do shameful things?"

"Viper!"

"Because I quote the Scripture to you?"

"Because you wrest it to your own purposes! You are in league with this consort of demons!"

Leor turned his eyes to Hedya, who was peering watchfully around his shoulder. "She is no demon's consort, Father, but if she is willing, she will soon be mine."

Hedya's eyes widened, but she kept them on Chanoch, who was now beyond mere rage. He might have physically attacked his own son, but Father Abran raised his hands and mounted the altar.

"Peace! Peace!" he cried. "It is unseemly for violence to enter our Holy Place. You, Hedya, claim you are a Priestess of the Most High God and you, Chanoch, say she is demon-possessed. Clearly, we must have a sign. Hedya, if what you say is truth, prove it. Give us a sign from God."

Hedya paled. The Angel hadn't discussed this eventuality. She closed her eyes and cleared her mind, aware only of Leor squeezing her hand. Suddenly, the conviction came—a sign would be given; she knew it beyond a doubt.

Her eyes opened. "Let Chanoch name the sign."

Chanoch smiled maliciously. "You say Dovev's angel came to life before your eyes. Let it now do so before ours."

"Then will you believe and obey?" asked Hedya.

"Produce the sign," snarled Chanoch.

Hedya stepped away from the Seat of Oration and turned to face the congregation. Her hands raised toward the sky, she opened her mouth and cried, "Angels of the Lord, I beseech you —attend your earthly sister!"

There was a long moment when it seemed the whole camp had been turned to stone. Silence fell. Then a cry came up from the crowd. A woman screamed. People stared and pointed.

Hedya wished she could see what they saw and suddenly, in her mind's eye, she did. Both golden Angels glowed with a great light. Both rose from their places and kept rising until they hovered nearly twenty feet above the altar. Their eyes were silver orbs of flame and they cried out together in the voices of a man and a woman: "Glorified is our God, the Most High, and blessed is Hedya, His Anointed."

They hung above the altar on massive, slow-moving wings —hung there long enough to leave no doubt in anyone's mind that they had witnessed a miracle. Then they floated slowly downward, golden feathers rippling. Once in their places, they closed their fearsome eyes, folded their great wings and knelt, their heads bowed toward Hedya.

The Prophetess lowered her arms and looked at Chanoch. So did everyone else.

"Well, Chanoch," said Abran weakly. "Produce a sign for Hedya."

Hedya declined. "Let him decide his own sign."

Chanoch mounted the Seat of Oration. On each side of him were the bowls of Holy Fire, their low flames sending trails of scented smoke into the air. Hedya knew immediately what he was going to do. It was one of his stock "signs", performed regularly at the festival celebrating the Revelation of Musa.

He bowed his head for a moment, holding the pious pose until anyone holding their breath would have swooned. Then he threw back his head and called in a loud voice: "Vindicate me, O my God!" In a swirl of robes, his hands flew up and outward and, from the braziers, came a mighty roar and a great flash of flame. Two balls of green fire shot skyward and two pillars of smoke loomed, glowing with orange light.

The crowd was only mildly impressed. They waited for more. More came, but not at Chanoch's bidding.

A peal of thunder rocked the Temple and the sky turned dark so quickly, some thought they had been blinded. Just as Chanoch's face began to sprout a look of satisfaction, the clouds opened and rain fell in a torrent—on the two bowls of incense and on Chanoch and nowhere else. The two angelic guardians of the streaming braziers were not even splashed.

It was over in a moment and Chanoch stood, dripping, while his congregation roared with laughter.

It took Abran a long time to gather the Council of Elders to his side and draw them away from the Temple for an emergency conference. The congregation rushed forward to touch Hedya and congratulate her. When it looked as if the flood of well-wishers would inundate them, Leor took Hedya and her father away to their tent.

When they had gone, the congregation swarmed about the altar, examining every inch of it, touching the dry angels and the wet Seat of Oration, collecting sooty water from the slopping braziers. Children danced and made up songs about the event. Women nodded to each other and murmured about how things would change. Men frowned and whispered in huddled groups and snuck glances at the women.

All waited to hear what the Council of Elders would say.

Father Abran sat among the pillows in the council tent looking very old and withered. "What now? How must we respond to Hedya's message?"

"Hedya's message?" asked Dovev. "It's *God's* message. Hedya is only the messenger."

"Hedya is a demon," insisted Chanoch. "Or she is possessed by one. I say we must destroy her."

"And make ourselves guilty of the very thing the Scriptures warn against?" asked Dovev. "You read the words yourself, Chanoch: 'Those who disbelieve My revelations and scorn the prophets and slay those who enjoin equity: Promise them a painful doom.' Do you desire a painful doom?"

"Painful doom!" spluttered Chanoch.

"Do you disbelieve God's warnings?"

Chanoch dropped to his knees before Dovev and thrust his face close. "I disbelieve," he said, "in Hedya's demonic ravings."

Dovev met his eyes, unblinking. "God gave her a sign, Chanoch. She even let you choose what it would be. The angels came to life—we all saw it. You saw it."

"A demon can produce signs, too, Dovev."

"Then what is the point of asking for them?"

"To prove that she was being directed by the Evil One," said Chanoch. "Only he has that kind of power."

The others crooned in agreement.

Dovev gazed at Chanoch for a moment then said, "When the Prophet Musa went before Firon, he was asked to produce a sign, was he not?"

Chanoch nodded, suspiciously.

"Tell us of it."

"You know the story."

"Tell it anyway. It bears on our consultation."

Chanoch complied. "The priests of Firon threw rods upon the ground and the rods became serpents."

"How were they able to do this?" interrupted Dovev.

"Magic. They were aided by demons."

"Then what did Musa do?"

"He threw a branch upon the ground and it became a fiery, winged serpent and ate the serpents of the priests of Firon."

"And how was he able to do this?"

"Through the power of God, of course."

"Of course. But why did not the priests of Firon produce yet a greater sign than the Prophet Musa?"

"They couldn't. God is all-powerful. He wouldn't let the priests of a false god best His Prophet."

"Ah," said Dovev. "I see." He caught a drip from the folds of the High Priest's sleeve.

Mahir began to chuckle. Avidor guffawed. Even Abran was having difficulty keeping a straight face. Gilad just looked glum.

Chanoch turned his back on them all.

"Dovev makes a good point," admitted Abran reluctantly. "Chanoch was powerless against Hedya."

"But what she requires of us!" exclaimed Avidor.

"What God requires of us," corrected Dovev.

"That has not been proven," snapped Chanoch.

"What more proof do you want?"

"It would be safest to do whatever Hedya says we must," mused Abran.

"Hah!" snorted Avidor. "That's easy for you to say! You have but one wife. What am I to do with my three, or Chanoch with his two? Or Gilad, who now has two daughters?"

"Why don't we ask Hedya?" suggested Dovev. "Meanwhile, we can start by treating our women with more equity."

"Don't any of you see what's going on here?" asked Chanoch, turning to face them in a dramatic swirl of soggy robes. "The women are behind this. No doubt Sabra is their ringleader. They have gotten the assistance of a powerful demon and are attempting to subvert the Religion to their own gain. It was our ancestor, Father Sala, who sanctified multiple marriages. He was an Apostle of God. Haven't we all read how he, a pagan, was converted to the Religion of Musa by direct revelation? If we believe Hedya, then we make Sala a liar."

Gilad was nodding eagerly. "Now that you mention it, I've caught a group of women meeting in my wife's tent a number of times. And Hedya was among them!"

"'And even if one were to rise from the dead, they would not believe,'" Dovev softly quoted Scripture.

"What would you suggest we do, Chanoch?" asked Abran.

Dovev got to his feet, his patience exhausted. "Why will you listen to him, Father Abran? He's all wet!"

"He's our High Priest."

"Then why didn't God speak to *him*?"

Abran gazed at Dovev for a moment, then turned his eyes to Chanoch. "Our High Priest must be heard. What is your counsel, Chanoch?"

Dovev turned away and went to stare from the tent flap. A crowd of people was gathering around the council tent.

"I say we put this message to the test. First of all, we ask Hedya to undergo exorcism. If she refuses, we'll know the message is false. If she agrees and the demon leaves her, we'll know it is false. If the demon won't come out, then we must wait and watch to see what happens next. If her message is demon-inspired—and it must be to violate our Scripture—"

"When did the writing of the Apostle Sala become Scripture?" asked Dovev, still gazing from the tent flap.

"You know that as well as I do," snapped Chanoch, annoyed at the interruption. "Our Fathers—blessed be they—agreed it should be so in the Year of the Great Questioning."

"The question was rhetorical," murmured Dovev. "I merely wondered if God was consulted in the matter."

Chanoch ignored him. "If her message is demonic in origin, God will deal with her. If it is His message, she'll be vindicated. Simple."

"What say you?" asked Abran, looking to Avidor.

"Test her as Chanoch says. Exorcise the demon."

"Mahir?"

"The Law indicates this is the correct procedure."

"Gilad?"

"As Chanoch says."

"Dovev?"

He turned to look at them. "I believe Hedya's words are true and that they are of God. You are misled by your own selfish desires. Your reward is with God. As for me, I will do as Hedya says. My wife is my equal, and together we shall find an heir among the orphans of the Tribe. Perhaps even a female heir."

He disappeared through the tent flap, leaving the Council to arrange their exorcism without him.

When news of the exorcism reached the female members of the Tribe, it provoked complete outrage. A group of women, led by Abran's own usually obedient wife, Amira, descended on the Tribal Elder and cornered him in his tent. When the interview proved unsatisfactory, the women adjourned to Amira's tent for a strategy meeting. As a result of this meeting the women took to their tents and denied their menfolk access—unless, of course, their menfolk were willing to see things from their perspective. Those women who shared tents with their husbands immediately packed up—hoof, horn, and bleat—and moved in with a fellow suffragette.

By the end of one dark day, the only men on speaking terms with their wives were those astute enough to register a complaint with Abran regarding Hedya's forthcoming exorcism. Those who didn't went unfed, unmended, and otherwise uncomfortable.

This did not deter Chanoch from going forward with his plans to exorcise Hedya's demon. He was stunned when she consented to it, but determined it would be his best exorcism ever. This was quite a step up from driving demons out of recalcitrant camels or capricious children.

It took place in the Temple with the Elders looking on and a quietly enraged Leor assisting. Hedya, dressed in dazzling white, was patient throughout the absurd ordeal. Chanoch chanted and capered, intoned and incanted. He shook staves of gold at her, swung censers around her, and sprinkled Holy Water over her.

Nothing happened. No demon struggled to free itself or threw Hedya to the floor or spoke through her mouth. All that came from Hedya's mouth was a giggle, in response to which Chanoch wanted to apply a hot coal to her tongue.

Abran stopped him. "It is the demon we wish to injure, Chanoch, not Hedya," he said irritably.

Ego wounded, Chanoch resorted to praying. He burned some of Hedya's hair in the censer, he doused her with Holy Water, he whispered the Greatest Name of God in her ear. He even made her say the Name aloud. She said It nine times.

Nothing happened.

Finally, sweating and exhausted, Chanoch dropped mutely to the steps of the altar, and glared at the patient Prophetess.

After a long silence, Leor asked, "Father Abran, are you now convinced that Hedya has no demon? Surely no demon could utter the Greatest Name."

"I didn't think so," said Abran wearily.

"Well, then?"

"If a clear sign could be had..." grumbled Gilad.

Leor's eyes widened. "Angels hovering over the altar aren't clear enough?" The expression on Gilad's face said they were not.

"A sign, Lord!" begged Chanoch loudly. He pointed at Hedya. "Decide between us!"

A delicate flapping was heard and through the open Temple doors flew a dove every bit as white as Hedya's robes. It fluttered directly to her and perched on her right shoulder. With it came a fragrance like a garden full of summer roses.

"Hah!" cried Chanoch, jumping to his feet. "She's not possessed! She's a witch! See? This must be her familiar!"

Before anyone could comment, the sound of wings was heard again. Through the Temple doors flew a crow so great and black, even old Avidor had never seen its like. It flapped its way straight to Chanoch and perched on his left shoulder. And with it came an odor of indescribable foulness.

Chanoch shrieked once and sat stone still, transfixed by the bird's beady black eyes. Everyone else leapt back and covered their noses. They gathered around Hedya, whose aura of scent overpowered the stench of Chanoch's crow.

Leor laughed aloud. "And is this your familiar, Father?"

Chanoch shrieked a second time and ran from the Temple. The crow followed at a leisurely pace.

Word spread quickly that the exorcism had failed to produce a demon. A crowd gathered, again, outside the council tent, waiting to see what the Elders would do next. What they did first was mope. When Dovev prodded them for some sort of decision, they grumbled.

Finally Mahir said, "I say we wait to see what happens."

"We could pretend to go along," suggested Avidor. "Then maybe Hedya will be satisfied."

"You keep forgetting," said Dovev, "that Hedya is only the messenger. Do you think pretending will satisfy God?"

"We need more particulars," said Avidor. "We need to know how far this equity business is supposed to go. And what are we supposed to do with our extra wives and their children? Surely God can't expect us to disown them. How do we decide which wife to keep? And what of our Scripture—do we rewrite it or just add to it the Tablet of Hedya?" He looked to Abran, who could only shrug helplessly.

"We've already added the Tablet of Sala," observed Dovev quietly. "What's another tablet more or less?"

"Brothers," sighed the Father of the Tribe, ignoring him, "we can but wait."

While they waited, the Prophetess Hedya received another revelation. At its conclusion, she sent Leor to invite the Elders to the Temple. They arrived quite promptly to find the Prophetess seated on a sack chair before the Seat of Oration, flanked by Dovev's angels, which were now standing. Any pride and fury Chanoch had been able to pump up deflated immediately upon seeing them. He was sure those horrible silver eyes were looking right at him.

"The Lord has heard your deliberations," said Hedya in the strong, clear voice of a Prophetess. "He has instructed me thus: Say, O Hedya, to the Sons of Indecision: Know that in all things but the strength of the body, I have made woman your equal. This is the balance—that she can bear life. Yet, for that life, man and woman must have union. This is My wisdom. As the bird must have its two wings to fly, so the Tribe must have the strength of both man and woman. Hear Me: The women shall have a Council even as the men, that their voices be heard. And the men shall listen to their voices.

"Your duty is to your first wife. If she has borne you children, upon them is your inheritance; if not, then your other wives' children may be heirs. Settle on the additional wives a portion, but hear this: they are no longer lawful consorts—do not trespass on them. It is lawful for them to marry again so that the duty may pass from you to their lawful husbands.

"As to the Scripture: Sala was no Prophet of Mine, nor was he an Apostle. He spoke from his own desires and you were misled by yours. You call the Tablet of Sala Scripture—I call it

Corruption. Strike it from the Book. I, the Lord, know what is in every heart."

The message was at an end. The stunned Elders removed themselves from the Temple and shuffled back to the council tent. The waiting crowd followed them. When Dovev left the tent some time later, he told them they might as well go home. It appeared the Elders had no comment to make.

The Tribe waited. When two days had passed and the council tent produced no response, the women of the Tribe elected a Council of Matriarchs. The first action the Matriarchs took was to move the tents of all the women who believed in Hedya's Message away from the rest of the camp. They were joined by a number of men, including Dovev and Leor, who either believed or had no desire to be caught in the retribution of an angry God.

So the camp remained divided for some time—split nearly in half by Hedya's revelation. When no fiery doom followed immediately, angry and desperate men from the Patriarchal camp began to kidnap their wives and children back from the Matriarchal camp. A few women exerted their newfound autonomy and returned, but most, who were uncertain the word "autonomy" even belonged in their vocabulary, stayed with their men.

By the end of three moons, the Matriarch's camp was down to a small but solid core of fifteen families and about a dozen autonomous women. Hedya continued to receive revelation for the guidance of the Matriarchs; across the swathe of sand that separated them, Abran and the remaining Uncles continued to pray for sons.

By the end of six moons, they knew their prayers had been answered. While in Hedya's camp, babies continued to be born in the usual ratio of male to female, the Great Separation brought to the Tribe of Abran precious sons.

"It's a miracle!"

"It's more than a miracle, Mahir," said Chanoch. "It is my vindication. In answering our prayers, God is displaying to all eyes the utter falsity of this 'Prophetess'."

Mahir nodded, gazing across the valley at the Hedyite encampment. "Not a girl-child born to the Tribe since Hedya and her followers departed. Obviously, it was Hedya's presence among us that caused God to ignore our pleas. Now that we have proved faithful to Him, He blesses us."

"Hedya must be a powerful sorceress to have produced such signs and wonders," said Abran almost wistfully. "I nearly believed." He caught Chanoch's disgruntled expression and added, "Now, of course, it's plain she was a sorceress—a very great one to have thwarted you, Chanoch—but obviously false."

Chanoch preened his beard and smiled. "Not so great, Father Abran. Our faith defeated her. The Curse is past. We are receiving sons from God...while the women of *her* tribe yet give birth to girls!"

And so they did. About two-thirds of the babies born to the Tribe of Hedya were female. Hedya, herself, had a daughter a year after her first revelation. She and Leor named their daughter Matana—meaning "a gift."

The summer after Matana's birth, the Tribe of Abran moved. He chose a valley along the broad, slow-moving Nibis. The Tribe of Hedya moved also, settling at the far end of the same valley in a grove of trees. Only when the trees lost their leaves did Abran realize the Hedyites were so near. He sent a messenger to Hedya asking for a meeting, and they convened with their respective Councils on the banks of the river.

"Why do you follow us?" Abran asked Hedya nervously.

The Prophetess demurred. "Please, speak to our Matriarch, Father Abran. I am a Priestess, not the tribal elder."

Abran colored and cleared his throat. The "Matriarch" of the Hedyite Tribe was his own wife, Amira. He hadn't anticipated having to face Amira. He was a little surprised at how strong his feelings for her were still. She was a handsome woman, his Amira.

"Abran," she said brusquely, and nodded as if to a peer.

He sighed. His no longer—she was Amira the Matriarch, now.

"To answer your question," she said, "we are following you, because God has so instructed us. He has said there must be no more than a valley or a hill between us."

Chanoch harumphed. "God does not speak to witches. You mean Hedya has commanded you to trail us. There is no answer to that but battle."

Amira glanced briefly at Hedya, then said, "We won't fight."

"If you won't fight and you don't wish to die, then you'd best go. We will attack."

Abran cleared his throat and glared at Chanoch. "You are making our people nervous," he told Amira. "If you could take yourselves out of sight..."

"Consider it accomplished," said Amira. "You will see us no more unless you desire it." She departed with her Council.

The next morning the grove of trees was empty. Abran, gazing at it from the door of his tent, sighed deeply. He truly missed Amira and the family members that had defected with her. Here, he had only his youngest son, Hod, and a family that included a growing number of grandsons.

Gilad put on a long face and made sure everyone saw it as he picked his way over the rocky clearing to the council tent. The Uncles would be there and would see the look of doom on his face, but there would be little sympathy. Everyone had the look of doom these days.

It was cool and dark in the council tent. The Uncles were sitting in a circle of pillows, drinking cold mint tea. They all looked up when he entered, then looked away again when they saw the expression on his face.

He sat down next to Hod and accepted a cup of the tea. It tasted bitter on his tongue, but he drank it anyway. "A son," he said. "Another son. A-a-a-ah!"

"A-a-a-ah, yourself," grumbled Chanoch. "This is only your fourth. Emuna has born me six more sons—that's eight, altogether. *Eight!*"

"Huh!" exploded Mahir. "My son, Jubal, is of marriageable age this year, but there is no one to marry him. No one! Every woman in the Tribe is either married, promised, or too old to bear children." He turned a baleful eye on Chanoch. "Well, High Priest, this is your doing. What do we do now—*share* wives?"

"That is forbidden," said Abran sternly, and wheezed.

"Abran is right," said Chanoch, avoiding Mahir's pointed gaze. "To share wives would be... Well, it *is* forbidden, isn't it? However, we could possibly negotiate with another tribe for some of their daughters—we are near the Elamites this season."

A flash of spring lightning flooded the tent with white light, making them all jump. It was followed by a nerve-biting crack of thunder that rolled in a low growl above the hilltops.

"Damn," said Mahir. "More rain. This is bad for the crops. The seed will wash clean away."

"Other tribes?" repeated Abran. "But, that's also forbidden."

Chanoch shrugged. "Let us say, it is discouraged."

"Will God countenance the taking of pagan wives?"

"Have we a choice?" asked Chanoch. "The alternative is our extinction. Will God countenance that? We are His people!"

The Uncles all admitted that it was unlikely God would countenance their extinction.

Hod had an idea. He had a lot of ideas—at least, he had more than old Avidor, whom he'd replaced on the Council. "Let's pray about this dilemma," he suggested. "Surely, if we pray, God will send us a sign."

And so they prayed. First, they asked if marrying to other tribes might be permitted. Then, they begged for a sign. Chanoch broached the idea of sharing their remaining women. When Hod objected, he reasoned that God would certainly perceive this as a lesser sin than bringing heathens into the camp. Last of all, they pleaded for daughters.

The answer to their prayers was swift and unexpected. Just at sunset, the flap of the council tent flew aside, and in stepped a tall, imposing girl of perhaps fifteen with dark, flaming eyes and hair to match. The light from the firepot danced on her face and scattered sparks in the red cloud that fell wildly from her *burnoose*.

She let the Elders sit in shocked silence for a moment then said, "I am Nirel—the Fire of God. Hear me! The Lord says: You cried to Us for sons and We gave you sons. You counted yourselves fortunate, but you are of the cursed."

"Cursed?" squeaked Gilad. "God has *cursed* us? Why?"

"You cursed yourselves by your own perversity. I gave you children—male and female—that you might continue upon the earth. I made them of equal value, yet you count My daughters of little worth. So, We have taken from you the daughters you despise and given you sons. Still, you are not pleased. Surely, you are contrary creatures.

"As to your question regarding women of other tribes: Shall I allow the Religion of Musa to become dead among you? Already you fail to listen when I speak. I show you signs and you heed them not. You are deaf. Hear Me now: You shall marry within the Tribe, that your faith may not be diluted yet further. The daughters of other peoples are unlawful to you.

"As to your question regarding the sharing of women: Truly, Chanoch the High Priest has uttered an abomination. His reward is with Me. Do not listen to him.

"As to your plea for daughters: You have set your own course. Sons you begged of Me—sons you receive from Me."

Nirel paused dreadfully and swept them with her fiery gaze. "This is the message of the Lord God of all Tribes. He who has ears, let him hear it." She disappeared in a swirl of robes, fanning the sparks from the firepot. They seemed to follow her from the tent.

At some length Mahir said, "There is but one thing we can do."

"And what is that?" asked Chanoch irritably.

"Surely it's obvious," said Mahir. "God doesn't want us to marry pagans. But if we bring these women into the Tribe with the appropriate ritual—a few animal sacrifices, perhaps—adopt them as daughters and, most important of all, convert them to the Faith of God..." He shrugged. "They will no longer be pagan, will they?"

Chanoch smiled. "That, Mahir, is an excellent idea! It certainly answers any objections of a religious nature."

Abran scowled. "I'm not certain-" he began.

"Well, I *am* certain!" exclaimed Hod, rising to his feet. "If converting or adopting these women was pleasing to God, He would have said so. This is a false path, Brothers."

Chanoch concealed the irritation he felt at having a young pup like Hod address him as "Brother" and spoke soothingly. "Now, dear Hod, calm yourself. You know God doesn't always provide a set course for His children. He defines boundaries and intends us to find a path within those boundaries. Our cleverness will be well-rewarded, I'm certain."

Hod jumped as another crack of thunder slapped at the camp. Chanoch's words did not comfort him.

The Elamite girls that were ushered into the Tribe called God "Shahbahra." Among the things they learned from their new Elders was that His name was more properly "Jah" and that, if the golden effigies in their Tabernacle were any indication, their adoptive Tribe worshipped birds. The language differences made it difficult for them to discuss any of these issues or to disabuse anyone of the idea that their own religion (or ex-religion) deified a Fish. They suffered their lot in silence and went, one and all, to worthy, desperate husbands.

Hope was high at first, but as months went by, it became apparent that the curse of Hedya was still in effect. The ex-Elamites bore no daughters. Neither did they bear sons. None of them even became pregnant.

Nirel appeared at Abran's tent flap precisely one year to the day and hour of her first visit. The old Patriarch admitted her eagerly.

"Thank God, you have finally come! Tell us! What must we do to please the Lord? What does He want?"

"You have pleased Him simply by asking what He wants instead of telling Him what *you* want," answered Nirel. "Gather the Elders and you shall hear the word of the Lord."

With the Council mustered in the Temple, Nirel took a place on the steps of the altar—right where Hedya had stood so many years before.

"So, speak to us, Prophetess," growled Chanoch, uncomfortably reminded of that previous confrontation.

Abran paled and shuffled forward. "Please, Nirel—Prophetess of the One True God—Chanoch intended no disrespect. Speak to us, we beseech you."

Nirel smiled. "He intended every disrespect, Father Abran. But because of your attentiveness to His messenger, God will forgive him that. You have asked concerning the current curse."

"Yes!" cried Abran eagerly. "Tell us how to break it!"

"You are sincere in your desire?"

"Oh, yes!"

"And you are prepared to obey the Lord?"

"With open ears and humble hearts!"

"If We give you daughters, how shall you regard them?"

Abran nearly wept. "As gems! As pearls! As angels!"

"And their rights and privileges?"

"Guarded jealously—as those of our sons."

"And their education?"

"Abundant!"

"And their voice?"

"Shall be heard in the council tent! Oh, good Nirel, please, please, reveal to us the word of the Lord!"

"In a moment. First, the matter of the Elamite wives. You will return those that desire it to their own tribe where they may find husbands and bear children."

"But they no longer follow the Elamitish ways," protested Chanoch. "They've converted to the Religion of God."

"Their inner beliefs have not changed, High Priest. Only the form of their worship is different. They have kept their faith and for this, God is pleased with them."

"Pleased? But they're pagan—heathen! We converted them to the Truth."

"You forced them to accept what is true for the Tribe of Abran. Their worship was no more displeasing to God than your own. In due time, both will change. Now, as to the Elamite women..."

"It shall be as the Lord commands," said Abran before Chanoch could express further outrage. "Please, Prophetess—the word of God?"

"But it's been revealed to you already. All you lacked was obedience."

Abran looked confused. "But...good Nirel, what word was it in—ah—particular? We've had so many words revealed to us."

"And listened to so few of them," murmured Hod.

Nirel turned her flaming eyes to him. "True, Brother Hod. But you seem to have ears—perhaps you remember the word of the Lord with regard to marriage."

"The Lord said..." Hod knit his brow and puzzled for a moment. "...that we must have only one wife and that we must marry within the Tribe."

"Now, how can we do that?" asked Chanoch. "There are no marriageable women left. The Lord must give us daughters some other way."

"Hear me!" said Nirel, her face like a storm cloud. "Do not set limits on the Lord your God! This is His message: You shall have daughters only when you marry women of your own Tribe. When I hear the prayers of those women from your tents, then shall the curse be lifted." She strode from the altar and out the front doors of the Temple.

"We're doomed," said Gilad.

Hod, the look of revelation on his face, smote his moping brother between the shoulder blades. "No, we're not! Oh, of *course!* Why didn't we *see* it?"

Chanoch turned a bleary, baleful eye upon him. "Oh, please, dear Brother Hod, do enlighten us. Wherein have we been blind?"

"Wherein have we *not* been blind, Brother Chanoch?" He turned to Abran. "Father, it's a riddle. Where may we find women who are of the Tribe, yet not of it?"

Abran smote his brow. "Hedya!"

"Hedya?" repeated Mahir dazedly.

"No!" shouted Chanoch. "You can't! You cannot possibly think of taking that vicious, scheming, heretical rabble back into the tribe. We really would be doomed!"

"We're doomed already," observed Hod. "And the only way to find out if marrying the women of Hedya's Tribe will break the curse is to marry them."

"It's a trick!" ranted Chanoch. "Can't you see? Don't you recognize this Nirel? She's the image of that prickly Sabra. She must be Sabra's daughter. She's a Hedyite!"

"Well, at least we know their daughters are attractive," said Mahir dryly. "Hod is right. What worse fate could possibly befall us than extinction?"

"Women in the Council!" raved Chanoch. "Aunts as well as Uncles at tea! Matriarchs running the Tribe! Women in the Priesthood! In the Temple! In-"

"Chanoch," said Abran, "shut up." Then he smiled. Then he laughed. That felt good. He decided he'd have to tell Chanoch to shut up more often.

He thought of Amira. Sixteen years was a long time to go without a wife. He'd be pleased to see her again—more than pleased. If she was still alive. His smile vanished under the wrinkled folds of anxiety.

"We haven't seen the Hedyites for years," he fretted as they made their way back to the council tent. "Where shall we find them?"

Hod stopped at the end of the tent city's rocky main avenue. "I believe they've found us."

Indeed, they had. The entire Council of the Tribe of Hedya stood before the council tent, along with the Prophetesses Hedya and Nirel and—

"Amira!" Abran capered down the rough path like a young kid.

The Matriarch turned and smiled. "Greetings, old man," she said. "I believe we have some weddings to plan...beginning with our own."

Gilad strolled down the grassy sward to the council tent. There was a spring in his step and an absurd grin on his long, camelid face.

The Aunts and Uncles were gathered before the tent drinking tea and enjoying the sunset. They all glanced up at him when he approached and smiled and nodded at him.

"So, Gilad," said Dovev, "what good news today?"

"Ah, a girl!" he sighed ecstatically, "*And* a boy! Twins! I am blessed."

"And how is your wife?"

"She is well and happy. A wonderful mother, my Adiella. Oh, and my eldest son is promised to a daughter of Hedya and Leor." He bowed his head deferentially to that couple. "And my eldest daughter has just given birth to a girl. I am blessed," he repeated, and accepted a cup of tea.

"Speaking of blessings," said Abran, "how is your father, Leor? Settled into his cave all right?"

"He seems quite content," mused the new High Priest. "Since he lost his sense of smell, he doesn't even mind the crows that share his shade tree. I think he finds their antics amusing."

Abran nodded, glad that particular loose end had tied itself up by going into religious seclusion. He turned to his beloved Amira. "Dear wife, I shall be forever grateful that you returned to us and prayed God to lift the Curse from our shoulders."

"But, husband, we didn't pray God to lift any curse," said Amira.

"Well, prayed for daughters, then."

"We didn't pray for daughters either," said High Priestess Hedya.

Abran puzzled. "Well, then, what did you pray for?"

"We prayed that whatever God did, we'd have the sense to be content with it."

"Elegantly put, Hedya," said Councilwoman Sabra, and the Aunts and Uncles all crooned and clicked in agreement while above the hills, God's laughter rolled like distant thunder.

Content With the Mysterious

A story of speculative fiction

Content With the Mysterious was originally published in *Analog Science Fiction Magazine* in 1998 and placed on the 1998 Preliminary ballot for the Nebula Award given by the Science Fiction and Fantasy Writers of America. The story explores Bahá'u'lláh's principle of the harmony of science and religion and applies the lens of scientific inquiry to subjects considered by many to be supernatural.

The story poses a simple question: What is the nature of true skepticism?

> *As to thy question concerning the worlds of God.*
> *Know thou of a truth that the worlds of God are*
> *countless in their number, and infinite in their*
> *range. None can reckon or comprehend them except*
> *God, the All-Knowing, the All-Wise. Consider thy*
> *state when asleep. ...Behold how the thing which*
> *thou hast seen in thy dream is, after a considerable*
> *lapse of time, fully realized.*
>
> Gleanings from the
> Writings of Bahá'u'lláh,
> p. 152

Ken Shaw stared at the manuscript without really seeing it. The lines were gray blurs, a pattern of irregular stripes. He knew what it said, though; he'd read the march of words beneath his wife's byline.

"You'll love it," she said. "It's brilliant," she said. And he'd had no reason not to believe her. Most of what Lissa wrote, if not brilliant, was at least, very good; sharp, cogent, witty. This, however—he grimaced—this was arrogant, self-congratulatory and sarcastic.

He imagined telling her that. Not pretty. He'd critiqued her before, of course, edited her prose. That was his job. But, at the moment, he didn't feel like editing, he felt like doing a hatchet job.

Sighing, Ken rolled his chair across the anti-static carpet and over to the office window. He was people-watching and contemplating taking a walk down the Embarcadero when he saw her charging through the manicured courtyard four stories below.

She moved like a tornado with a fix on a trailer park. She always did. It was one of the things he loved about her. She researched her articles the same way, flying in, shredding, and reducing the subject to match sticks that could be easily vacuumed up—neat, tidy, and looking nothing like the original item.

Ken rolled himself back to his desk and tried to collect his thoughts. They refused to coagulate. *Fear of the storm,* he thought wryly, and slipped the article under the October issue cover layout. Maybe she'd grant him a reprieve. Let *him* bring up the article.

A moment later, she was breezing into his office, notebook computer over one shoulder, trendy but dilapidated safari jacket open over a black silk jump suit.

"Well?" she said. "Have you read it?"

So much for a reprieve. Ken pulled the manuscript out from under the cover art and nodded.

"And?" She perched on the corner of his desk.

"It's well-written."

Pale brows shot up under a thatch of strawberry blonde hair. "Well-written? Oh, Mr. Shaw, that's editorspeak for 'I hated every word of it.' What's wrong with it?" She got up, leaving her notebook on the desk, and began to pace. "I did good research. I conducted searching interviews. I collected solid evidence, evaluated it objectively-" She stopped in the middle of ticking off her processes and turned to stare at him bemusedly. "What? What's that sour expression for, my puckered pal? You look like you just swallowed some Vilex."

"You weren't objective."

The stare turned into a glare. "What do you mean, I wasn't objective?"

He shrugged. "You weren't objective."

"About what?"

"About anything in here."

Her hands were on her hips, he noticed. A bad sign.

"Give me an example."

"Okay. The meditation class."

She shrugged. *What about it?* her eyes asked.

He rubbed the bridge of his nose—a habit dating from when he had had to wear glasses. "Lissa, you were rude."

"Rude? Ken, the woman was having a room full of people meditate on a crystal that *didn't exist*. They took turns *holding* the damned thing."

"Did that give you the right to humiliate her?"

"Oh, please."

"Admit it, Liss. You didn't research this article, you went on a witch hunt. You didn't interview people, you played Inquisitor."

"I simply asked them to produce proof of their outrageous claims. I asked a woman who said she could read auras to read

me a few. And that clairvoyant character, Dreyfus—all I asked
him to do was foretell the outcome of a simple test."

"Did you hear yourself? 'That clairvoyant character?' He
was 'that clairvoyant character' before you even met him, wasn't
he?"

She glowered, arms folded.

"Well, wasn't he?"

"So?"

He flipped the first page of the manuscript over and read,
"'Your job is not to debunk—leave that to the vice squad. As a
scientist, you are not out to disprove or reject any claims out of
hand, but to discover positive evidence in favor of them.'" He
flipped the page back. "Despite that noble disclaimer, this article
is prejudiced, Lissa. It's arrogant. Worst of all, it's not scientific
inquiry."

Now she was gawping at him. "I don't believe my ears!
You're *defending* this crap!"

"No. I am defending objective analysis, which is absent from
this article, despite your claim to the contrary."

"Come *on*, Kenny. These people are fakes. They may be well
meaning, or misled, but they are fakes, nonetheless. If I can
disabuse even one person of their irrational, puerile—"

"Fine, but don't try to pass your crusading off as objective,
scientific inquiry. Above all, don't try to do it in my magazine."

"I don't believe this!" She turned her back on him and
stalked across the room to fume in front of an oriental print. "So,
I suppose you want me to soften it, or some such nonsense." She
raised a warning finger. "I don't believe in that. And I didn't
think you did either; call pseudo-science pseudo-science--that
was the *Skeptical Review's* ideal."

"This is beyond softening, Lissa. Your methods, the tactics
you espouse..."

She spun to face him. "What's wrong with my tactics?"

He covered his face, rubbing at a headache that was trying to gain a foothold in his brainpan. He groaned.

"What do you mean, 'they're low?'"

"I didn't say that, I just...groaned. I've got a headache."

"Which I'm responsible for, no doubt. And I heard you, clear as a bell. You accused me of using low tactics."

"You heard what you expected to hear. I *groaned*. But you're right. They *were* low." He pulled his hands away from his face and tapped the manuscript. "Infiltrating their ranks, attending their meetings, even offering to give seminars or work on the newsletter, passing yourself off as a 'true believer'—all so you can debunk them. You advocate lying-"

"Ken, everything they stand for is a lie."

He opened his mouth.

"And don't you *dare* say 'two wrongs don't make a right.'"

"I guess I don't need to—you just took the words right out of my mouth. And you're right. It's tantamount to lying on behalf of the truth. I find that hypocritical. I certainly can't advocate a debunking agenda in the pages of the *Skeptical Review.*"

"Debunking is too strong a term. I was investigating."

Ken picked up the manuscript, flipped to the last page. "'Once you've gained yourself a reputation as a true believer, it may be a while before the locals tumble to the fact they've invited a hat pin onto the Hindenberg.'"

She smiled. "Clever, isn't it?"

He shook his head. "Clever debunking, Lissa. You were intentionally setting out to explode myths—having already decided they *were* myths. That's bias. It's prejudice. It is not good scientific investigation."

"You want me to rewrite it."

"Are you willing to lose the smug tone? Are you willing to ask questions without supplying the answers?"

"Wait a minute. Are you telling me to re-conduct my interviews, my tests?"

"Not all of them. Several of them would stand up just fine, if you reported the results more objectively. Although..."

"Although, what?" she asked warily.

"You did seem to go out of your way to make your participants...uncomfortable."

"I used a scientific facility."

"You subjected a woman with a verified formaldehyde allergy to the chemicals in a lab. She was, in your words, 'demonstrably uncomfortable.' You cite fear of failure. Maybe it was because her mucous membranes were swelling up and her stomach was turning over. She still did better than fifty percent on the aura readings."

"I will *not* redo my research. And as for the interviews and confrontations—I can't just throw them out. They're what gives the article punch. I will not rewrite it."

"Fine. Then sell it to a cult-basher. I won't print it." He tossed the manuscript to the edge of his desk.

"Fine. Someone else will."

"I've no doubt. As I said, it's well-written."

She snatched up the article and her notebook and tucked both under one arm. "Sometimes I wonder if you're suited to editing a skeptical journal. Maybe the *National Tattler* would be more your style. Or maybe the *UFO Times*." She turned and headed for the door.

Oh, great, he thought. *This ought to be good for about three days of silence.*

"I'll talk to you again in about a week...if you're lucky," she said, and was gone.

(August 20—Interview: Dr. Petra Genoa, Ph.D. conducted by Kenneth Shaw of the *Skeptical Review*, Subject: precognitive experiences.)

SR: Would you call yourself a true believer?

PG: A true believer? In what?

SR: In psychic phenomena.

PG: That's an awfully broad area. Could you be more specific?

SR: Alright. Extra-sensory perception.

PG: If by that you mean do I believe there are more than five senses—yes.

SR: Would you call yourself a psychic?

PG: Would you call yourself a dreamer?

SR: Excuse me?

PG: Sometimes you dream. Does that mean you define yourself as a dreamer?

SR: I see your point; but do you believe you have psychic powers?

PG: Now there's a loaded term: *powers*. I believe I have experienced extra-sensory awareness. I don't know if I can lay claim to *powers*.

SR: What sort of experiences are we talking about?

PG: Knowing something was going to happen in advance, for
        example.

SR: Precognition?

PG: (nodding) Yes, that's a fairly precise term.

SR: And you've experienced this often?

PG: More often than most people I've interviewed, yes. I have
        maybe, oh, one or two episodes per month. (laughing) I
        seem to have them most often when I'm ovulating.

SR: Seriously?

PG: Seriously.

SR: Describe a precognitive episode for me.

PG: The first one that really got my attention was the day of
        my high-school graduation. I was sitting there, during the
        ceremony, when I had this sudden conviction that the girl
        sitting next to me—a close friend—was going to lose her
        father that night.

SR: It just came out of the blue, then? You weren't thinking
        about your friend?

PG: No, I wasn't. And I felt horribly guilty. I mean, what a
        thought to have about a friend's father! I almost said
        something, but—good God—what do you say? 'Gosh,
        Rose, I just had the weirdest thought...'"

SR: What happened?

PG: Her father was killed in a car wreck on the way to the
        graduation. I remember the look on her face when she

realized he was late. She kept glancing out the door, while I sat there and just about peed my pants in anguish.

SR: And that was the first time you had that awareness?

PG: No. That was when I realized...*suspected* I had some sort of...sensitivity. You see, before, it was always positive. I'd get the sudden feeling that I'd win a tennis match or an essay contest or receive an unexpected present or get a call from someone I hadn't heard from for a long time. That was the first time I couldn't explain it away as wishful thinking.

SR: The dark side of ESP.

PG: You could say that.

SR: Doesn't your belief in ESP conflict with your position as a professor of psychology?

PG: Now, I happen to know that you're a philosophical theist. Doesn't your belief in a Deity conflict with your position as the editor of the *Skeptical Review?*

SR: I'm not against belief, just *ignorant* belief.

PG: Can't argue with that.

SR: To what do you attribute your precognitive experiences?

PG: I don't know. I tend to think it's a sense we have, or a talent, maybe, that develops or fails to develop just like any other.

SR: Why don't I have it?

PG: Can you sing?

SR: What? Not really.

PG: Me neither. But I know many people who can. If they can sing...

SR: Okay. But isn't it more like sight or smell?

PG: I don't know. Is it? Or is it like the ability to make music or write...or conduct interviews? What makes one person a brilliant performer and another totally graceless? People ask me to explain my awareness. But how do you explain that sort of thing? How do you explain Mozart's musicality? The man pulled symphonies right out of his head and put them on paper—every note right the first time. You suggest it's like sight. Fine. We can explain blindness, even if we can't always cure it. We've yet to explain Mozart.

SR: Would you be willing to have your abilities tested under controlled scientific conditions?

PG: Willing, certainly. But you see, I'm a skeptic, too. I'm skeptical about the ability to be precognitive on demand—mine or anyone else's. I've never been able to sit down and meditate my way to precognition. It's like trying to pull in my favorite radio station; sometimes it comes in clear as a bell—sometimes it's pure static. And it's subjective as hell. *I* don't believe it when someone walks up to me and says, 'I see auras.' I've personally never seen one.

SR: But you *have* foretold the future.

PG: Don't put words in my mouth. I've had brief, uncontrollable precognitive episodes. Like...like sneezes. Can you sneeze on command?

SR: If someone waved ragweed under my nose, maybe. So, you don't believe ESP can be scientifically verified?

PG: I'm not sure. Maybe someday we'll be able to set up the right conditions or ask the right questions or take the right measurements. So far, we haven't been able to. No psychic ragweed, I guess.

SR: Some people are of the opinion that if you can't measure something scientifically, it doesn't exist.

PG: But doesn't that call into question the existence of a lot of things we take for granted? Things that are critical to the functioning of our society?

SR: Such as?

PG: Well, at the risk of sounding smarmy—love, truth, trust, honor, loyalty—that sort of thing. Even musical or artistic talent.

SR: Some people might say that's not the same thing.

PG: How do they know? If the thing's not measurable, if it's as subjective as love or loyalty, how can anyone say what it is or isn't if they haven't experienced it? I've *experienced* it and I don't know what it is. I only know it *is*. I can't convince the scientific community it is, because they can't measure it. They can't convince me it *isn't*, because I've experienced it.

SR: What about evidence, though? Mozart provided evidence of his talent. He composed symphonies that orchestras worldwide are still playing. What evidence can you adduce that you really have had these experiences?

PG: Good question. I'm conducting an ongoing project
      wherein subjects, such as myself, record their precognitive
      impressions. Altogether, I've gathered a study sample of
      fifteen other people who share this, um, little affliction.
      We have a co-monitoring system in place. When someone
      in the program has an episode, they call their assigned
      monitor and describe it. The description is recorded and
      logged and we wait and see what happens. If the event
      occurs, the monitor signs an affidavit and we attach any
      corroborating evidence to the file. It's the best we can do
      for now.

SR: Measuring the Mozart factor.

PG: Measuring the Mozart factor. I like that. Can I use it?

Ken flicked the notebook from play mode to record and
added some voice notes, watching the words march across the
flat display.

"Be it noted that I did look over Dr. Genoa's documentation
and interviewed two project monitors. Neither of them had ever
experienced any of the phenomena under study. In fact, they
viewed themselves as being originally skeptical or, at best,
neutral to the subject of ESP. One of the 'sensitives' had an
eighty-two percent accuracy rate over thirty-two recorded
events; however, I must note that some of the predictions are
vague enough as to be unfalsifiable. And, of course, this still
amounts to hearsay evidence and necessitates trust in the
perceptions and scruples of the group monitors."

Ken pondered that. Is that what it would always come down
to—having to trust the word of a go-between? And, reluctant to
do that, would he only trust what he, himself, perceived or
observed?

He had keyed the phone program before he thought about
what he was going to say and gave the computer Dr. Genoa's

number. To his surprise, she answered her own phone, her dark face appearing immediately on his display.

"Doctor! I'm surprised to catch you in your office."

She smiled—a flash of brilliantly white teeth. "I suppose I should say I had a feeling you'd call."

"Did you?"

"No."

He returned the smile. "I have an offer for you. I'd like to serve as a monitor for your project."

"Really. Are you from Missouri, by any chance?"

"Close—Alaska. And yes, I *do* want to be shown. I'd like to take on a couple of your most accurate people. Victor Chin, I think, and you, if you'd be willing."

She nodded. "All right. You've got yourself a deal."

"Great. Now, I noticed that your episodes tend to be cyclic-"

She laughed, dreadlock bells jingling against her earrings. "Cyclic psychics, huh? I sure hope the media doesn't get hold of that."

"I *am* the media, remember?"

"No. You are a respectable scientific journal. *The Tattler* is media."

"Thanks." He appreciated her making the distinction. "Now, as I was saying, I was wondering if you'd thought of setting up some sort of brain activity scan during your most susceptible periods."

She seemed immediately open to the idea. "Brain Pattern Monitoring? I'd thought of that, actually. U.C. Davis has a new remote BPM that can be worn away from the hospital while it relays brain activity back to the facility. They've been using it to monitor seizure-prone patients, looking for an early-warning signal. Unfortunately, they're reluctant to let it out of the house. Especially for—oh, shall we say—frivolous projects."

"But, you'd be willing to wear a scanner?"

"You bet."

"Fine. I'll see if I can call in some favors."

The expression on her face changed. "Ken, are you ready to start your job as monitor?"

"Sure...I guess. Why?"

"Your wife is going to experience some sort of trauma."

"What?" The tone of quiet certainty at once chilled him and raised his suspicions. "Emotional or physical?"

"Emotional... Art gallery. I had a sudden impression of an art gallery or museum or exhibition maybe."

"When?"

She shook her head with a sibilant clash of bells and earrings. "I don't know. I rarely know, exactly. Usually my range tops out at about three months. Can you save this conversation to a file?"

Ken nodded, righting himself emotionally. "Can you be any more specific about the nature of the trauma?"

"Fear. I know she'll be frightened. I don't know why."

Later, when he viewed the conversation log file, Ken couldn't help but wonder if Petra Genoa's prediction was entirely coincidental. Could she be playing on his emotions?

He went back to the case histories he'd gotten from her, in search of some sort of proximity effect. He found it; the precognitive episodes for the three subjects he studied related preponderantly to people they were in close contact with either physically or emotionally.

He had to smile at himself. His skeptic's sensibilities told him he should welcome evidence that he was being manipulated, but he knew such evidence would only disappoint. In some peculiar way he preferred being disturbed by Dr. Genoa's prediction to being disappointed by her duplicity.

"What did you say?"

Ken peered up at Lissa. She was gazing at him distractedly across the width of the coffee table, the display of her own notebook casting odd light-shadows across her face.

"I didn't say anything...I don't think. I thought I just cleared my throat."

"You muttered something about predictions. What are you working on?"

"Oh, I interviewed Professor Genoa Tuesday."

"Petra Genoa, the psychic psychologist? They should revoke that woman's Ph.d."

"She graduated at the top of her class."

"What good is that when she ends up retiring her brain to New Age mumbo-jumbo?"

"How do you know that's what she's done? Have you talked to her?"

"I read an article on her in one of those true believer magazines."

Ken failed to muzzle his laughter. "And you trusted their journalism? C'mon, Liss. Normally, you wouldn't believe a word they printed. Why don't you read *my* interview?"

"Maybe I will." She eyed him suspiciously. "You don't think she's legit?"

"I'm reserving judgment until I've finished my own study. I'm monitoring the project she's conducting in precognitive episodes."

"You're kidding."

"Not at all. Who better to monitor alleged psychic activity than a skeptic?"

She smiled. "Right, as always. You were right about my article, too."

He raised startled brows at that most un-Lissa-like admission. "I was?"

The smile broadened to a cat-eat-cream grin. "I *did* sell it somewhere else. Elaine Dehaut bought it for *Aware*." She bent back to her work.

He didn't remind her that *Aware* had a reputation as a forum for a fanatical ultra-skeptical fringe. Ken hated to admit the existence of that element within the skeptical community, but they were there—those who had ceased pursuing the truth in favor of pursuing agreement with their own personal worldview. Of course, everyone did that to one degree or another. Everyone made assumptions, betrayed bias, and struggled with prejudice.

For some reason, that conjured the Biblical story of Jacob struggling with the angel. Jacob, he recalled, was Hebrew for "deceiver." Prejudice was certainly that; it could make an unwitting fanatic of anyone.

She hated dreams like that. She'd had mercifully few of them. They disoriented her, made her feel ill-at-ease in the waking world. "Night-ponies," she called them. Dark dreams, but not black enough to qualify as nightmares. They were usually murky, leaving nothing behind but a smudgy residue studded with tiny pockets of lucid detail.

Lissa could still vividly recall one such moment when she hung above her bed, looking down on her own sleeping form, Kenny snuggled beside her beneath the covers. She remembered thinking there should be hair in her eyes, but there wasn't. Nor was there a hand to wipe it away with.

She'd had the impression that she was rising; the figures below stirred slightly, growing smaller. She had feared a collision with the ceiling, but a "glance" upward revealed only an endless, star-studded sky. She looked down again and saw her own rooftop.

Funny, she thought, *I've never seen it from this angle before.*

Bright orange fabric fluttered against the chimney. She remembered seeing the next-door neighbor's boy flying a kite that color the weekend before.

She began to move upward again, the rooftop receding too quickly. Terror lanced through her and she fell—no, was sucked down an invisible funnel through the rooftop into bed. She woke with an electric jolt, sitting, sweating, cold and clammy, heart haring.

She *hated* dreams like that. Associated them with stress. She associated this one with the stress over her most recent article.

She grimaced, close to admitting to herself that Ken was right about more than its salability. She hadn't meant to assume such a cynical tone. She really had set out to be objective, but the very thought of anyone granting credibility to that supernatural twaddle set up her hackles. The thought of people like Ken and Petra Genoa—educated people, *bright* people--buying into it made her want to rage.

And there was no relief from that rage in her morning schedule. She had two interviews lined up—an NDE and a Chinese healer.

The Chinese healer was first; a whimsical diversion. Professor Lin Wen was a scholarly gentleman who conversed as comfortably about Tantric Buddhism as he did about chemistry —a subject in which he held one of his two doctoral degrees. He discussed how the spiritual essence, or *qi,* possessed by an individual could be read to predict fortune, and channeled to change it.

Lissa asked how he, a man of science, could accept and even promote something of which he had no scientific proof. He smiled and asked if she had scientific proof for everything she believed to be true.

"No," she said, "but someone has."

"Ah," Wen responded. "Then you depend upon the science of others."

"Most of us do, largely because scientific ideas are falsifiable. *Qi* isn't."

"Ah," he said and looked inscrutably archetypal. He parted from her with avuncular concern, prompted, he claimed, by the lack of balance in her *qi*.

Great, she thought wryly. *No more PMS. Now I can just say my* qi *is out of balance.*

Her second interview took her to a pleasant neighborhood of neat, older homes where she expected to hear of Julie Pascale's near-death experience. The case was particularly interesting to her because of the media coverage it had received eight years before. It was still a high profile case—high impact, if she could break it. But when Pascale's husband met her at the door, she knew she was going to be disappointed.

"I'm sorry," he said, "but my wife has changed her mind."

"About the near-death experience?" The sarcasm was born of frustration.

He frowned. "No. About the interview. She's not feeling well."

"I can reschedule."

"I'll tell Julie that. I'm sure she has your number."

And I'll bet I have hers, Lissa thought irritably. She ought to congratulate herself, really; another true believer ducking the hard gaze of rationality. But she didn't feel congratulatory. Julie Pascale had a particularly well-documented set of NDE experiences and Lissa had been looking forward to a one-on-one confrontation. She drove home accompanied by acute disappointment.

She was pulling into the driveway when a momentary recollection of last night's odd dream drew her eyes to the chimney. A splash of orange caught her eye. She hit the brakes too hard and the Saab's tires yelped in protest.

Nestled against her chimney was the neighbor boy's orange kite.

She was fascinated. This was exactly the sort of thing that a 'true believer' would take as a psychic experience, yet she knew she had merely dreamed, spinning off stress and the events of the previous day. Though she didn't consciously recall having seen the kite on the roof, she certainly *could* have caught a glimpse of it, and she definitely recalled seeing it in flight.

She was in bed, asleep, before Ken got home. She half-dreamed him entering the room in a reptilian slough of textile, kissing her cheek, brushing his teeth, slipping into bed beside her. She dreamed it from above—spider's eye view—and he was no more than settled in when she was out on the lawn watching a peculiar ritual.

A car pulled up across the street and several young men, black-clad, got out. Whispering and laughing, they darted among the neighbor's trees and shrubs, trailing gauzy webs of white.

Amusement bubbled. They were teepee-ing the Rathman's house! Feeling as if she were afloat, Lissa drew nearer to the car —a dark green Saturn Electra.

A light went on inside the house and the boys fled with a slamming of car doors. Voices distracted. Not, oddly, the shouting of irate neighbors. She had expected that. She did not expect the well-modulated tones of conversation.

A woman's voice: "Photography has always been a passion of mine. Since I was a child, really. Now, it's my way of observing and absorbing the world."

Lissa's dream faded to black in a wild sensation of sucking speed—Alice down the rabbit-hole. The voice in the black changed: "Recently, you absorbed the sights of Tannu Tuva and showed Westerners what must surely be a lost world—a Shambala. What is remarkable about these photos is the contradictory senses of alieness and familiarity they evoke. I am looking at a photo of a group of standing stones. Near them is a circular tent-"

"That's called a *yurt*."

(Striped fabric, sheepskin, an odd wooden door.)

"A *yurt*. Before the *yurt* are a couple of young men in loin cloths doing a dance that looks like, well, like the funky chicken."

(Stocky, muscular bodies, arms akimbo, grins the sole adornment save for skillfully tied, fringed cloth. Nearby, an audience laughs and applauds, dark eyes glinting.)

"It's called the Dance of the Eagle and it's done to honor the patron spirit. They're preparing to wrestle. The quality of their dance will determine which opponent they're paired with."

"I'm out of the shower, Liss."

She stirred. Black faded to gray.

"Describe the next one for me."

"C'mon, Liss, up-getting time."

(Semi-dark gallery. Black and white photo, struggling toward color. A man clad in a combination of feathers, fiber, and colorful wood clutches a painted drum.)

"Chakar O is equal parts shaman and Buddhist bhikku. The drum is used not only to accompany the dancers, but to please the spirits and call down the bounties of the spiritual realm."

(Dancers; they are frozen in mid-step, feathered headdresses in mid-bob. They could be Cheyenne or Sioux instead of...)

Where the hell is Tannu Tuva?

"Lissa!" The radio snicked off.

She came fully awake.

Ken smiled at her. "Welcome to the land of the living. Where were you?"

Lissa stretched and yawned. "At a photo exhibit... What? What's that look?"

He shook his head. "Nothing. Just...nothing." He scurried downstairs.

He left before she did and so she sat, vagrant, over breakfast, nursing a second cup of coffee. She was rinsing her cup and regretting the loss of the Pascale interview when the phone rang. She was both surprised and smug when the other woman's new-age-gentle voice came over the line.

"Ms. Shaw, I've thought this over and—and I do want to talk to you."

Lissa made an immediate appointment, hurrying to gather her notebook and scramble out the door. She had backed down the driveway and turned the car when she caught sight of the Rathman's house. Slung between their mimosa trees, toilet paper fluttered festively in the breeze. Several rolls of the stuff littered the lawn.

Her mind did a double take. *Oh, God, I've started sleep-walking!*

She groaned. Which meant she had wandered out into the street in nothing but an oversized t-shirt. She hoped she had only gone as far as her bedroom window.

Behind her, someone honked. She unstuck herself and drove to Tiburon.

The first thing she noticed about Julie Pascale was the vulnerable expression in her over-sized brown eyes. The second thing she noticed was that, in crisp linen pants and a silk shirt,

she did not look the least bit New Age-y. The third thing she
noticed was that she walked with a cane. It was the result, Lissa
learned, of the same experience that had gifted her with the NDE
—in this case a near drowning.

The story was typical in its major points: There was a great
Light which the subject was drawn toward ("I was drawn to It
on a—a raft of love. It was the Beloved. Just that."), other souls
who milled about between heaven and earth ("They were so
confused...so lost. They didn't know where they were."),
deceased relatives about whom she learned volumes at a touch
("I'd never met my grandfather before, but now, I felt I'd always
known him.")

It was, perhaps, atypical in the angel's-eye view of Earth
Julie described—a view that encompassed all people, in all ages,
working their way toward ever-advancing levels of unity. Yet,
typically, she was nearly touching the Light when she was sent
back to Earth/Life in the company of what she described as
"two souls." ("They had the most amazing sense of humor.")

According to Julie, she came upon herself in the Emergency
Room at U.C. Davis. ("I was on a gurney, and a doctor—a heart
specialist named Mead—had been giving me injections of
adrenaline. He pronounced me dead and started to walk away
when my GP—Dr. Harris—came in and asked what he was
doing. He said, 'I've done all I can.' And Dr. Harris said, 'Like
hell you have.'")

Dr. Harris pounded on her chest and gave her further
injections. ("I wanted to shout at him to stop. But he couldn't
hear me.")

Forty-five minutes after she had drowned, twenty minutes
after the heart specialist had pronounced her dead, Julie Pascale
came back to conscious life.

"It was like being sucked down a drain," she said.

Lissa shook off the chill of a dream memory and readied her questions.

LS: I would think, after forty-five minutes of death, you'd have sustained some brain damage.

JP: I did. I had to learn to write again and speak in coherent sentences. The left side of my body is still weak. Poor Dr. Harris. When he came into my hospital room later and found me crying, I'm sure he expected some thanks or praise. Instead, I showered him with incoherent abuse. I wondered how he could dare bring me back. I almost hated him for it.

LS: What you say you saw in the ER—how close is it to what other people recall?

JP: You mean how close is it to what really happened? Ask my psychologist. Ask Dr. Harris. There was a nurse, too—a Mrs. Yamaguchi. I have their signed statements, of course, but you might want to talk to them directly.

LS: Your psychiatrist—do you still see him?

JP: Her, and she's a psychologist. Yes, I still see her from time to time. As friend, not as patient. I have copies of her statements as well, if you'd like to see them.

LS: You were very thorough.

JP: No, Dr. Genoa was.

LS: Dr. Genoa? *Petra* Genoa, the parapsychologist?

JP: I don't think she considers herself that. She certainly didn't when I met her in the hospital. I had a terrible time convincing her what happened to me really happened. I'll never forget her parting volley the day I was released. 'Take my advice,' she said, 'don't mention this NDE stuff to anyone else. Don't talk about it; don't even *think* about it. People will think you're crazy, documentation notwithstanding.' She was right, of course.

LS: But you didn't take her advice.

JP: No. I couldn't not think about it. It changed my life. I had to talk about it and wonder at it and pray about it. And I had to use it to help other people.

LS: How so?

JP: I work for a Youth Hotline. We deal with drug abuse, domestic violence, suicide prevention—any and all self-destructive behavior. I try to use my experience to keep other young people from ending their lives prematurely.

LS: I find that contradictory. If you know what it's going to be like in the next world, if you find it so wonderful, why would you want to keep others from experiencing it? In fact, why didn't you contrive to return there yourself?

JP: I learned many things through my experience, Ms. Shaw. One of them was that the next world isn't wonderful for everyone. Those spiritually confused souls were just that. They were unprepared for death—for *life* in that...realm. I also learned that life really *is* sacred. It's sacred to the Beloved, and therefore, it's sacred to me. The key word is 'prematurely.' I want to go Home, but I'll wait till I'm called.

Listening to the playback, Lissa chuckled. *What marvelous furnishings decorate the houses of the true believer.* A "raft of love"—she made a note to call it the "love boat;" God in the persona of the Cosmic Lover; disembodied spirits who cracked jokes. Cosmic comedy.

As if the homely details could make it real.

Ken stared at the invitation in his hand as if he expected it to sprout fangs and bite him. In a sense, it had done just that; the graceful script contained a quartet of verbal teeth: Photographic Exhibition, Amsted Gallery.

"Think you two can make it?"

He looked up into the eager face of his editorial assistant, Terri Mendez.

"I hate to be pushy, but, well, Naomi is my cousin and I guess I'm proud of her. She does wonderful work."

"I'll, um, I'll talk to Lissa. I'm not sure what our plans are that weekend."

Lie. He knew exactly what their plans were--nothing. He'd change that, he decided. A romantic weekend up the coast was easy enough to arrange. Lissa need never see the invitation.

Guilt poked him in the forebrain. Lissa was an adult. An adult who hated, above all things, to have decisions made for her. That, and the realization that he was granting too much credence to something he had every reason to be skeptical of, kept him from throwing the invitation away, what made him lose track of it until he got home, unloaded his briefcase, spread his papers out on the sofa and heard Lissa's voice say, "Oh, what's this?"

Ken made his face blank and managed to sound nonchalant. "Terri Mendez's cousin, Naomi Whitehorse, is a photographer. That's an invitation to her exhibit."

Lissa's eyes widened slightly. "Really? I've heard of her...I think. Sounds interesting. Do you want to go?"

He tried not to look wary. "If you do."

"Sure. I'd hate to disappoint Terri."

She sat down on the arm of the sofa and circled his neck with her arms. "So, what's for dinner, O Domestic God?"

He shoulders sagged. "Oh, yeah, it's my night, isn't it?"

She looked at his face and laughed. "Never mind. I'll go stick a pin in the phonebook."

"Bad for the display," he said and she laughed again.

Bemusement tickled him. Lissa was going to an art gallery. He couldn't imagine how that could be a traumatic experience. The more he thought about it, the more he thought Petra Genoa must have over-reacted.

Still, he had to allow, he was impressed. He supposed Dr. Genoa could have discovered the connection between his editorial assistant and the photographer, could have assumed he would receive an invitation to the exhibition and would include his wife, could have made her prediction as a way of manipulating a potential detractor. But Occam's Razor cut against such Machiavellian intrigue where simple coincidence would suffice.

It was the week from hell. The weird dreams continued, leaving her tired and listless. Fatigue made her angry with herself and, habitually, she transformed her anger into zeal. She composed a sharply skeptical, tongue-in-cheek piece about the Chinese healer, but the Pascale NDE, though met with equal zeal, yielded only frustration. Her interviews with the doctors, nurses and medical attendants on duty during the eight-year-old episode corroborated Julie's account of the scene in the ER. All agreed that the girl could not have been physically aware of what was going on around her.

"How can you be so certain?" she'd asked Dr. Harris.

"She was *dead*, Ms. Shaw."

"Evidently not."

The old man had raised a mottled eyebrow. "Then perhaps we need to redefine death."

Julie's mother was the one to whom she had first described her experience. It was there Lissa expected to find her angle; she hoped to surprise a confession from Mrs. Joyce Delaney that she had relayed facts to her daughter rather than the other way around. She was disappointed.

Arms folded across her chest, looking uncomfortable in her own living room, the older woman insisted she recalled, vividly, the day of Julie's return to wakeful consciousness.

JD: She told *me*. The words that were said, the actions that were taken, the medications they gave, even the amounts.

LS: After eight years, you're still convinced of this?

JD: Ms. Shaw, I realize people like you—people in your line of work, I mean—have a vested interest in making people like Julie look foolish and weak-minded, but I *couldn't* have told her some of that stuff. I wasn't listening to dosages and chemical compositions; my daughter was dying right before my eyes. She *died* right before my eyes on that boat dock.

LS: I have no desire to make Julie look foolish or weak-minded, Mrs. Delaney, and the only thing I have a vested interest in is the truth. Isn't it more likely that you simply absorbed more of what you were hearing than you thought, and that Julie gleaned what she 'remembered' from the ER from you and other visitors?

JD: I did not put ideas into my daughter's head, Ms. Shaw.

LS: Yet, Julie told me she had some brain damage that
      necessitated her relearning how to write and speak. How
      could she have relayed so much information to you?

JD: She had trouble with some words, some sounds—like her
      tongue was uncoordinated—but she obviously knew what
      had happened to her, and she spoke well enough to
      communicate it.

LS: Were the two of you alone when she first told you her
      story?

JD: Yes. Does that make a difference?

The artless question made Lissa embarrassed and angry in
turns—embarrassed because it *did* make a difference, angry
because she hated embarrassment.

The ER nurse, Evelyn Yamaguchi, was Lissa's next
interview. The woman was nearly as quakingly amazed in
retrospect as she had been at the time of the incident.

LS: In your estimation, how accurate was Ms. Pascale's
      account of what happened in the ER while she
      was...unconscious?

EY: She wasn't unconscious, dear, she was *dead*. Accurate--oh,
      my, yes—she was accurate! (rubs her arms) It still gives
      me chills, just to think about it. The conversation between
      Dr. Mead and Dr. Harris was practically word for word;
      the instructions to the nurses (shakes her
      head)...unbelievable.

LS: Yes. You were one of the trauma nurses, then.

EY: (nodding vigorously) I was with Julie from the time she came into the ER until she left ICU.

LS: Think about this for a moment, Mrs. Yamaguchi. UCD is a teaching institution. Isn't it possible Julie Pascale overheard a team of doctors going over her case history as she was regaining consciousness in ICU?

EY: Her case history—very possibly. But not the conversations and arguments that took place in the ER. No, ma'am. Doctors don't hash over arguments on rounds. They discuss treatment, progress, prognosis.

LS: What about the nurses?

EY: I don't know if you've ever been in intensive care, Ms. Shaw, but nurses don't gossip in the patient's rooms. That only happens in soap operas.

There was only one other person Lissa could interview who might throw some light on the Pascale story—Dr. Petra Genoa. She resisted doing that interview for the simple reason that Petra Genoa was not a reliable witness. Her credentials as a psychologist, however good they might look on paper, were contaminated by her work in parapsychology. They would still be impressive to the average reader—if someone of that stature could believe in life after death, the logic went, then might it not be true?

Human beings were nothing if not enamored of possibilities.

That nagged Lissa as she attempted to compile her notes late on a Thursday evening. She knew the article wouldn't be complete without Genoa's input, but she couldn't bring herself to face another immersion into the true believer mentality. It helped not at all when Ken came home puzzling over the results of his tenure as Genoa's project monitor.

"I have to ask myself if there isn't something here, Liss," he said, half to himself. "Something more than can be attributed to chance and unfalsifiable predictions. With most of the subjects it's six of one, half-dozen of the other. But this Victor Chin—his predictions have been remarkably accurate. This is fascinating. I'm hoping that when Dr. Genoa's BPM is installed we'll get some idea of the brain activity involved when she receives precognitive impressions."

God, if he could only hear himself—'received precognitive impressions!' He was beginning to sound like he *believed* in this stuff.

"Coming to bed, Lips?"

"Huh?" She roused out of a tangle of thought and glanced at the staircase. "Uh, not just yet."

He sat down across from her on the coffee table, scooting her papers and notebook aside. "What's wrong, Lissa?"

"Why? Why should something be wrong?"

"Something shouldn't. But it *is*. You look so worn out. You toss and turn in your sleep... Maybe you should see a doctor."

She did not have a poker face. "I'm doing more than tossing and turning, I'm afraid. I'm sleepwalking."

"What? I haven't seen any evidence of it."

"How could you? You sleep like a hibernating bear."

"Okay, but what makes you think you're sleepwalking?"

"I've evidently wandered into the yard...on a number of nights and seen things going on in the neighborhood."

"Such as?"

"I saw the Rathman's house get tee-peed. I thought I was dreaming, but when I woke up the next morning, lo and behold, the Rathman's house was...well, you saw it."

"They didn't see you—the kids who tee-peed the house?"

Lissa nearly giggled. She must've been standing right out in the street...wearing only an extra-large t-shirt with the 49'ers quarterback on it. "I don't know."

Ken looked down at his hands, folded between his knees. "Well, I have to admit, log that I am, even I've noticed you've been had some pretty restless nights. You look exhausted. You *are* exhausted," he added and she realized he was afraid she might be physically ill.

She hastened to agree with him. "I'm pretty drained. I suppose I ought to see a doctor."

By morning she was convinced of it. Another night of vivid, aerial dreams left her wide awake by four AM, waiting for sunrise. But a complete physical revealed that, except for suffering sleep deprivation, she was perfectly healthy.

"What causes sleepwalking, doctor?" she asked. "I've never done it before. Or, at least, I don't remember doing it. Although, I've always had unusually vivid dreams."

"Actually, not remembering is a normal function of sleepwalking." Dr. Velasquez leaned back in his chair, looking cool, unruffled, and relaxed. "Retaining any memory of the events is highly unusual. As to what causes it—we don't precisely know. We *do* know it's a timing problem."

"Excuse me?"

"At times during non-REM sleep a dissociation can occur between cognition and behavior. What that means in neurological terms is that the upper brain is not responding to the signals from the lower brain. The lower brain signals for REM sleep; the upper brain doesn't respond. In the resulting confusion, the waking and sleeping 'worlds' become intertwined and the body begins to act out dreams."

Lissa shook her head. "But I'm not acting out dreams. I'm walking around seeing things that are actually happening."

Dr. Velasquez considered that. "All right. Could you be awake but groggy?"

"No. No, I'm not awake."

"Are you sure?"

"I'm *dreaming*. I don't...walk out through the door, doctor. I fly out through the roof."

"Which could certainly describe what it feels like as you pass from dreaming into partial awakening."

Lissa felt suddenly foolish. "That sounds reasonable."

Dr. Velasquez, consulting his computer screen, didn't seem to hear her. "You mentioned insomnia. Have you been depressed lately?"

Lissa laughed. "Only about my resistance to sleep—or at least to dreaming."

"Well, Lissa, there's nothing physically wrong with you, that I can see. Your MRI shows no abnormalities. We could try monitoring your sleep."

"You mean with electrodes and all that? Why bother? I think you're right. I'm sleepwalking and as I begin to wake up, I have...interesting dreams."

"Lissa, that's a symptom, not a cause."

"All right. What might cause something like this?"

"Often sleep disorders are caused by stress, which is something for which I often prescribe meditation."

Lissa, snatched from the verge of relief, ogled. "Meditation? You've got to be kidding."

"Not at all. Concentration on something other than your anxieties—whether it be a pretty scene or a pleasant memory or an actual spiritual mantra—"

"Please, doctor—this New Age stuff—"

"There's nothing New Age about it. Meditation is as old as man's desire for control and serenity in his life."

"I do not believe in meditation."

The doctor gave her a look he probably reserved for recalcitrant children who refused to take their meds. "Fine. Then I'll prescribe some relaxation exercises. Can you handle that?"

Can I handle that? Lissa stared at the prescription. It outlined a series of exercises (*Toe-clenches, for godsake!*), and recommended that she see a therapist if her insomnia and anxiety continued.

She held out against doing the exercises for two hours of what promised to be a sleepless night.

"What are you doing?" Ken asked drowsily.

"I'm meditating," she growled and rebelliously clenched and unclenched her toes.

She held out against the idea of seeing a therapist until the following Tuesday. The therapist, a moon-faced, smiling woman who put her instantly at ease, probed her stress levels and asked about recent traumas.

Lissa couldn't cite anything but the argument with Ken over the article. It hardly ranked as a trauma, but it still rankled.

"You've never argued with your husband over a piece of work before?"

Lissa shrugged. "Certainly. But he's never condemned anything I've done out-of-hand before."

"Is that what you feel he's done—condemned you out-of-hand?"

"Me? No, he wasn't condemning *me,* just the article."

"You said he called you a fanatic."

"He claims he didn't. He says he yawned or hiccupped something and I heard what I expected to hear."

"What do you think of that?"

"I think he called me a fanatic and then felt guilty about it."

"Do you think he was right?"

"You mean, am I a fanatic? No. Of course not. No more than he is. I'm just committed to the scientific paradigm."

The doctor made a few notes, then asked, "What about past traumas? Childhood traumas, for example?"

"Like what?"

"The death of a loved one. A terrifying personal experience."

Lissa shrugged, trying to relax suddenly tense shoulders. "No more than anyone else. I...fell out of a tree once and broke my arm. My father died when I was twelve."

The doctor was reading her face. "You attach no particular significance to these events?"

She did, as it happened, but shook her head. She had fallen out of the tree into the swirling waters of a rain-swollen river. She had been in the tree because the plane she was riding in crashed into the South Platte. Her father had died in that crash.

She wondered why she was withholding from Dr. Van Owen even the fact that the two events were related; but wondered only fleetingly. She was being contrary because it was her nature to be contrary. She didn't like people digging around inside her—resented the idea that a stranger might know things about her she did not know about herself. She was not convinced, she realized, that the beads and rattles used by modern psychiatrists worked any better than the ones used by their more primitive forebears.

Dr. Van Owen veered from the discussion of PTD onto a completely unexpected tack. "Your description of floating or soaring through the ceiling of your room, the vividness of the detail you remember, none of this is consistent with sleepwalking. It *is* consistent with lucid dreaming or a classic out-of-body experience."

"A-a what?"

Van Owen raised her hands. "Not that I'm advancing that as a diagnosis, but you might want to see someone who'll at least consider it within the realm of possibility. I have a colleague--a Dr. Genoa—"

"Oh, you've got to be kidding."

"You've heard of her?"

"Only too often. I'm sorry, Dr. Van Owen. I can't take the woman seriously."

"She's a brilliant therapist."

"And a promoter of pseudo-science."

Van Owen gave her a long, steady look. "Well, you may have a point. Obviously you're not comfortable with that approach. That's fine. If you're willing, we'll just continue on and see what we can do."

That wasn't much. Dr. Van Owen seemed to know Lissa was holding back and Lissa, knowing that to be true, was distracted to the point of impatience. She was relieved when the session was over, and did not make another appointment.

The weekend found Lissa high on relief. For whatever reason, after her visit to Dr. Van Owen, she ceased having the vivid dreams. After two nights of uninterrupted sleep, she was nearly giddy and ready for a night out on the town.

Saturday evening they dined at the Equinox and strolled the Embarcadero. Oddly, the visit to the Amsted Gallery took some urging on Lissa's part. Normally, Ken was eager to share his colleagues' moments of pride and triumph. This time he was noticeably reluctant.

They arrived at the Amsted and were met just inside by an effusive Terri Mendez. While she engaged Ken in conversation, Lissa wandered the gallery walls, gazing at her cousin's photographs. Pastorals and portraits, alike, centered on the people. The people had engaging eyes and shy smiles. They were old and young, radiant, callused. Their faces spoke volumes about the nature of life in places far from cosmopolitan San Francisco—places Lissa had never heard of.

She entered a cubicle dedicated to the photographer's excursion through the wilds of Mongolia and found herself face to face with a culture that was a curious mosaic of native American and Asian. Peculiar music accompanied the exhibit— drums, voices and eerie flutes.

Fascinated, Lissa moved from frame to frame, reading about the culture of an unknown people; women who worked from dawn to dusk at every task imaginable, men who trained their throats to whistle dual tones.

That's what I'm hearing, she realized, and paused to study a photograph of the choir. The only instruments were drums; all other music was performed with voice and the strange split tones the Tuvali men produced in their throats.

She shook her head in amazement and turned to view another photo. In it, a group of young men danced the funky chicken.

Lissa's heart clenched, cold, in her chest. She knew this picture. She knew each face—the young man with the bashful smile whose loin cloth was too small by half; the old woman with the gap-grin; the dignified village elder seated before his striped, multi-hued *yurt.* She knew each standing stone, too, and every carved design.

Her memory at once seized on a distant, waking dream, but reason denied that tenuous connection.

Deja vu.

Why then, the certainty that somewhere in this room was a photograph of a shamanist ritual—that amid the pounding of drums, feet, and hearts sat a man who was both shaman and Buddhist monk, a man whose face she knew to its last chiseled line?

The image conjured, she moved her eyes along the linen-covered walls until the picture in her mind's eyes found a match. A *perfect* match. Down to the last long feather in the crown of the shaman's ornate headdress; down to the gleaming gold cap in his upper row of teeth; down to the eagle's-head drum mallet with which he beat his painted drum.

Horse, said Lissa's insistent memory. *He call it a horse.*

Her heart steadied. "This is ridiculous."

"There you are!" Ken's voice sounded strained.

No, she just imagined it because *she* was strained.

"What's the matter, honey? You look like you've seen a non-existent earthbound spirit."

She didn't laugh at the joke. "These photos...I've seen them before."

"How could you? This is Naomi's first exhibit since she came back from the Russias."

"Well, I must have seen them on TV, then, or in a magazine."

Terri Mendez entered the cubicle in the company of a taller, dark-haired woman with a tanned face. Lissa all but leapt at her.

"You're the photographer?"

The tall woman smiled, nodding. "I'm Naomi Whitehorse, yes."

Lissa returned the smile, dry lips sticking to her teeth. "My husband and I were just debating what magazine we've seen these photos in."

Naomi glanced at her cousin. "None yet, I hope. I'm due to have a spread in *Smithsonian* next month, but nothing before that."

"Oh, well, I suppose it must have been on TV then."

Naomi shook her head. "I haven't had any television coverage...yet," she added, crossing her fingers. "I did do a radio interview several weeks ago, though."

Ken was nodding, "I remember that. It aired on Fresh Art—the morning show."

Lissa remembered too, then. *Really* remembered. The foggy dream voices, the vivid dream images. "I'm...positive it had to be a visual medium. I'd swear I've *seen* these photos before."

Naomi Whitehorse shrugged. "I'm sorry, but that's impossible. I've only done the one radio interview since I came home. There were some newspaper stories on the opening, but no photos were shown."

"She described the photographs though," Terri offered.

"Yes. Yes, between the moderator and I, we described these two in some detail." Naomi indicated the wrestlers and the shaman.

Lissa felt a surge of relief. "Oh, of course, I remember now. I was just waking up. You described them in such vivid detail—the-the images on the standing stones; the shaman with the gold tooth, drumming away on his horse." She was gabbling and she knew it, but the passing of that horrible moment of weirdness was worth the minor embarrassment.

Naomi's eyes lit up. "Oh, you know something about the Tannu Tuva culture, then. Most people would have called that a tom-tom."

Lissa was confused. "I've never heard of Tannu Tuva. *You* called it a horse during the interview."

Naomi gave her cousin another glance. *What's wrong with this woman?* it whispered. "No," she said, "I didn't. In fact, I didn't describe it at all. I described the dancers in great detail. But I *know* I never used that terminology to describe the shaman's drum."

"You did describe the shaman, though; his headdress, his gold tooth—"

Naomi Whitehorse was staring at her now. "Honestly, I *never* described him in that detail."

"But I *saw*—" Lissa swallowed. She sounded so desperate. Three pairs of eyes were on her like hot little spotlights. "I realize how silly this sounds."

Naomi shook her head. "Not at all. I'm a firm believer in the mysteries of the human spirit. You must have heard the broadcast and somehow visualized what I was seeing as I described the photos. Have you had that sort of psychic experience before?"

"Psychic experience?" Lissa tried to laugh and choked instead. "That's absurd."

"Is it?" countered Naomi. "Why?"

"I'm not allowed to have psychic experiences, I'm a skeptic."

"A skeptic?" Naomi echoed. "About what, exactly?"

"About all this: psychic experiences, magic, the mystical."

Naomi's expression went from warm to chill. "My Tuvali friends would argue the reasonableness of that skepticism. They live their lives surrounded by the mystical—as did my ancestors."

That observation ended the conversation. Terri Mendez swept her cousin away with nervous glances at Ken, while Lissa, hot-faced, made her way to the buffet table.

"You probably think I'm going nuts," she murmured to Ken over *hors-d'oevres*.

"No."

"It's just a vivid imagination coupled with exhaustion."

"Is that what Dr. Van Owen thought it was? Her office left a message for you at home, asking if you wanted to make another appointment. What's this all about, Lissa? Is it the sleepwalking?"

"That and some other stuff." She told him then, about the weird bouts of *dejá vu* that seemed to occur with increasing regularity. "I'm thinking someone is going to say something and in the next second, the words pop out of their mouths."

"Or not, as the case may be?" He was looking into his punch glass, not at her face.

"What?"

"You've always accused me of saying aloud what I was only thinking. But lately, it seems to happen all the time."

She stared at him, trying to peek beneath the veil of caution that covered his face. "Always? I've *always* done that?"

He nodded, a smile lifting the corner of his mouth. "When we met, I thought it was cute. Special; like we were on the same wavelength. I've always liked it. Sometimes I know what you're thinking, too. Proximity effect, I suppose."

"Ken, that's absurd. It's irrational and it's unscientific."

He shrugged. "So's human attraction. I'm not going to knock it, though. It brought a balding, nerdy guy together with a hot, young journalism major. I should argue?"

He was trying to jolly her. She appreciated and resented it simultaneously. "How can you joke about it? How can you...court such irrational beliefs?"

"What beliefs, Lissa? They're not beliefs, they're observations."

Lissa put her glass down before her shaking hands could spill its contents. "Maybe I'm going crazy."

"Nonsense. What did Dr. Van Owen say?"

"She was leaning toward post traumatic stress disorder, brought on by childhood trauma, I'm pretty sure."

"Your father's death? The plane crash?"

Bingo. "I...I didn't tell her about that."

"Why ever not?"

"Just being perverse, I guess. And private. She said my dreams sounded to her like a—quote: classic out-of-body experience—unquote. She wanted to refer me to—you're not going to believe this—your friend, Dr. Genoa."

"You could do worse. Maybe you *should* see her."

"Absolutely not. The woman stands for everything I despise--irrationality, pseudo-science, mysticism."

"Why do you despise it?"

She stared at him. "How can you ask that? I thought we were involved in the same crusade."

He set down his punch. "Do you hear yourself, Lissa? 'Despise,' 'crusade.' Those are words from a zealot's vocabulary. I'm not sure they should be in a skeptic's."

"What words do you recommend I replace them with?"

"'Doubt,' maybe. 'Question.' And I've always felt we were involved in more of a *quest* than a crusade. A search for reality, but a search in which we try not to indulge fond, superstitious fantasies about the outcome."

"I don't do that," Lissa denied. "I'm not superstitious and I don't indulge in fantasy."

"You don't? You had no foregone conclusions about what your NDE investigation would reveal? You had no prejudice about the veracity of Julie Pascale's experience?"

She could not swear to that, and knew it, but attempted to anyway. "No. I had no preconceptions about Julie Pascale. I didn't label her a fraud. She might have been the victim of hallucinations, or delusion; she might have experienced the perfectly explainable effects of what happens when a brain shuts down for 45 minutes then...reboots. Or she might have been dreaming."

"Like you've been doing?"

"I...I suppose."

"But she couldn't really have passed into the next world and returned."

"She was on a gurney in ER."

"Don't be obtuse. 'Her,' meaning her soul or spirit or whatever you want to call it. You don't believe a spiritual state after death is a possibility, hence you conclude, at the outset, that her story is false."

"Yes."

"That's prejudice, Lissa. You don't see her story as evidence for a possible reality that we simply haven't plumbed yet. You see it as a lie to be debunked. Prejudice."

"Rationality."

"Bull."

✦ ✦ ✦

She did not sleep well. The photographs returned to haunt her and came to vivid, waking life. At some point, she began to have another of the flotation dreams, but rode it only as far as the ridgepole before forcing the dream to suck her out of the ether and back to bed.

Sunday night was no better. Monday morning she called Petra Genoa's office.

"May I ask what this is in regard to?" asked the young man who answered her call.

"I, ah, it has to do with a case Dr. Genoa was involved in some years ago. A young woman named Julie Pascale had a near-death experience. Dr. Genoa was her therapist. Julie recommended I interview Dr. Genoa as part of my investigation."

Genoa surprised her by seeing her that afternoon. She surprised her further by being an attractive young woman in a dashiki suit and musically trimmed dreadlocks. The suit was topped with an open white lab coat.

"Are you a medical doctor too?" Lissa asked, shaking the other woman's strong, tapered hand. (Gold fingernails.)

"Oh, no. They just like their professors to look professorial. Since my taste in attire runs to the, ah, individual, they've asked that I retain the coat." She tilted her pocket nameplate up and glanced at it. "Well, at least I can't forget my own name."

Seated in Professor Genoa's sunny office, Lissa was caught up in the anticipatory tingle of journalistic nerves. She lived for that sensation. It peaked as she slipped her notebook into Record Audio mode and readied her first question.

If there was a heaven, Lissa thought, fleetingly, it was this moment—perpetual interview.

LS: How clear are your memories of the events surrounding Julie Pascale's near-drowning?

PG: Crystal clear.

LS: This was eight years ago. I have trouble recalling what happened eight *days* ago.

PG: This was an event that wrought major changes in my life. I'm not likely to forget it.

LS: Were you on duty when Julie Pascale was brought in?

PG: I was just coming off duty. I got waylaid in the hall and asked if I could counsel the family of a drowning victim. I was told they were still trying to revive the girl but that her chances were slim. I got to the Emergency Room just as Dr. Mead pronounced Julie dead.

LS: Then you overheard the altercation between Drs. Mead and Harris?

PG: Yes.

LS: And how close was Julie Pascale's recollection of the confrontation?

PG: Nearly perfect. You said you interviewed Dr. Harris; I'm
       sure he told you as much.

LS: Why is it necessary to attribute that to a supernatural
       cause? Couldn't Julie have overheard, say, a couple of
       nurses or interns discussing the events in ER as she was
       coming around in ICU?

PG: Ms. Shaw, we've all been party to conversations that
       attempted to describe other conversations. How often is
       the format of such a dialogue 'he said-she said'
       interspersed with verbatim quotes? One thing Julie
       Pascale demonstrably possesses is an eidetic memory. I
       have to at least entertain the idea that she heard an actual
       conversation, saw facial expressions, observed actions no
       second hand conversation would have detailed, even if it
       had been carried on within her hearing.

LS: Then she must have been conscious or semi-conscious in
       the ER.

PG: Well, her heart had stopped and her brain waves were nil;
       neither sight nor sound was getting through to her. She
       had, in fact, been declared dead by a highly respected
       cardiac specialist. Even if she had been capable of opening
       her eyes, she accurately described things her physical
       vantage point on the gurney would not have revealed.

LS: For example...

PG: The fact that the nurse attending Dr. Harris originally
       picked up the wrong IV, noticed it and returned it for the
       appropriate solution. The fact that her Brain Pattern
       Monitor was showing nothing but failing Beta waves.

LS: She might have overheard the nurse tell someone she almost brought the wrong solution; someone might have told her-

PG: But they *didn't* tell her. I interviewed that nurse—Evelyn Yamaguchi. When I told her what Julie claimed to have seen, she was shocked and ashamed. She'd never told anyone about the mix up. She was just thankful she caught her mistake before Julie was harmed. It wasn't something she was proud of.

LS: Then someone else must have seen her.

PG: Someone did; Julie Pascale.

LS: That's impossible.

PG: Is it? You're obviously convinced it is. A moment ago you asked why it was necessary to attribute this to supernatural causes. I don't think they *are* supernatural. I think, because these things happen, they must be completely natural. How can any of us—except maybe a Julie Pascale—claim to have even an inkling about what happens after death, or during sleep, or in any other altered state of consciousness? From the perspective of twins during the birth process, the firstborn is dead, gone, unreachable. Neither could realize, until they reach the outside world, that there's more to life than the womb.

LS: So this is a womb-world and we're all headed for Julie Pascale's raft of love?

PG: Let me ask you a question: Why do you so adamantly refute Julie's experience?

LS: I'm not refuting it. I'm investigating it.

PG: No, you're trying to attribute it to something *you* can comprehend. Maybe it's incomprehensible...for the time being.

LS: Oh, I see. It's what the Catholic Church refers to as a 'mystery.'

PG: I'm not Catholic, but it's what *I* refer to as a mystery. I'm not saying we'll *never* understand it, just that we don't *now* understand it. The child in the womb doesn't have a clue about why she needs eyes. She probably doesn't realize she has them. She certainly couldn't grasp the concept of *seeing*, let alone the reality of it.

LS: So you do believe this is a womb-world and that we're—— what—carrying eyes we don't know we have, couldn't know if we wanted to, and won't use until we die?

PG: Could be. Could be that rare individuals like Julie get their eyes opened a bit. It's an interesting mystery, don't you think?

LS: And you're content with that?

PG: (laughing) Do I have a choice? The science fiction writer, Philip K. Dick, said, "We should be content with the mysterious, the meaningless, the contradictory, the hostile and, most of all, the unexplainably warm and giving..."

LS: A lovely quote, but don't you want the mystery explained? Don't you want to be able to comprehend Julie Pascale's experiences...and your own?

PG: Certainly. But I don't have an agenda that demands it be explained in a particular way. I'm content with the mysterious, but that doesn't mean I don't want to clear up the mystery. Really, the whole process fascinates me.

LS: Hence, your involvement with parapsychology.

PG: The term "parapsychology" has a decidedly negative connotation. You'll understand if I avoid using it. I'd like to be able to coin a more accurate term, but I'm not much good at P.R.

LS: But you are good, I'm told, at studying unusual phenomena. Just out of curiosity, I'd like to see what you make of...some experiences I've had over the last couple of months.

PG: Okay. I'm game.

Lissa leaned forward to flip her notebook out of record mode. She wanted this completely off the record.

"I've been having dreams," she said. "Dreams wherein I seem to be floating out of my bedroom, out of my house, sometimes out of my neighborhood. Four or five times I've seen things happening outside my house that I later find out have actually occurred. For example, my across-the-street neighbor's house was tee-peed by a bunch of high-school kids. I saw it in my dream—right down to the faces of the kids who did it and the car they were driving. The next morning I saw the house had actually been tee-peed. What could that have been?"

Dr. Genoa's eyebrows raised delicately. "I'd say sleepwalking, but somnambulists rarely, if ever, recall their wanderings—let alone in that detail."

"Rarely. But not 'never?'"

Genoa nodded. "The sensation of floating..."

"Now that sounds similar to what Julie Pascale described, doesn't it?"

The dark brows scooted higher. "That was a near-death experience. You weren't dying."

"Exactly. I was merely asleep. But you don't think I'm sleepwalking."

Genoa shrugged. "It could be lucid dreaming."

"Could you define lucid dreaming for me? I want to make sure we're on the same page."

"Lucid dreaming takes place in the middle of REM sleep—it differs from sleepwalking in that major respect. Lucid dreams usually occur in the early morning and are marked by unusual lucidity, clarity of thought, the awareness that we are dreaming, an ability to direct the action in the dream."

Lissa considered that momentarily. "I *was* directing the action somewhat. I was amused that my neighbor's house was under attack by boys armed with toilet paper and I consciously moved in for a closer look."

"Then what happened?"

"The neighbors woke up, the boys drove off, I was sucked back...um, into another dream."

"Sounds like lucid dreaming, except for one important detail; what you saw *really happened*."

Lissa toyed with the strap of her notebook. "My...a psychiatrist I interviewed said it sounded like a classic out-of-body experience."

"Known in the vernacular as an OBE. Uh-huh. We don't know that OBE's and lucid dreams aren't related phenomena. In some people, they seem to be practically interchangeable."

"Yes, but lucid dreams are in the realm of accepted psychology. Out-of-body experiences are psychic supposition."

"As recently as 1990 lucid dreaming was lumped in with all that New Age jazz by skeptics and true believers alike. The 'give-me-a-break' fantasy of last week often becomes the 'gee-wow' science fiction of yesterday on its way to becoming established theory."

"I could have sleepwalked, gone to the window—or even out onto the lawn—then experienced the floating sensation as I woke up to see the boys tee-pee the house."

"I suppose. But you didn't wake up in the street, did you?"

"No. But I could have slipped back into sleep and sleepwalked myself back to bed...couldn't I?"

"I've never heard of that happening...which doesn't mean it couldn't or didn't happen to you."

"Alright. Let me describe another lucid dream. The morning radio show I wake up to was conducting an interview with a photographer who'd just come back from Tannu Tuva. She... described a couple of photos—generally, not much detail. My mind filled in the details; a gold cap on a shaman's tooth, the images on some standing-stones. I'd all but forgotten the dream when Ken and I went to her exhibition. The photographs I saw fit the details I dreamed right down to the pattern on the head of the shaman's drum. Needless to say, I was a little rattled."

"Yes, I know. Ken...told me about it.

Lissa dropped the notebook strap. Hair stood up on the back of her neck. "He what? Would you mind telling me why Ken was discussing me with you?"

"When he spoke to me about becoming a monitor for my project, I had a strong impression that you were headed for some sort of disturbing experience related to a visit to an art gallery."

"I don't believe you."

Genoa shrugged. "Your prerogative, certainly, but Ken did record my statement."

"How long ago?"

"Three weeks or thereabouts... That was really what you came here for, wasn't it? To try to understand what happened to you." She shook her head, dreadlocks singing. "I'm sorry, Lissa. But I don't fully understand, myself. If I did, I wouldn't feel impelled to seek out people like Julie Pascale. I wouldn't be up to my ears in this project. And I'd be able to give you answers. Instead, all I can do is invite you to join in asking the questions. Maybe we can work toward comprehension together."

She rejected the invitation (out-of-hand, Ken would have said). She went for a long drive up through Sausalito and Tiburon. She sat on Stinson's Beach and stared at the randomness of waves and thought about her father and plane crashes and endings.

Finally, she went home.

"I was worried," Ken said.

"So was I."

He gave her his patented over-the-ghost-glasses look.

"I saw Petra Genoa this afternoon. We talked about NDE's and lucid dreams and OBE's...and photo exhibits."

"Oh," he said. Just, "Oh."

"Can I hear what she said about the art gallery?"

"Are you sure?"

"No. Can I hear it?"

He got out his notebook and set it up on the coffee table. "Are you sure?" he asked again.

She took a deep breath. "Yes," this time.

He opened the file and fast-forwarded to a bookmark he'd set at Genoa's prediction. On the flat screen, Petra Genoa's attractive face wore an expression of bemused concern.

"Ken," she said, "are you ready to start your job as monitor?"

"Sure... I guess. Why?

"Your wife is going to experience some sort of trauma."

"What? Emotional or physical?"

"Emotional... Art gallery. I had a sudden impression of an art gallery. Paintings...no, photos."

"When?"

She shook her head, making music. "I don't know. I rarely know, exactly. Usually my range tops out at about three months. Can you save this conversation to a file?"

"Can you be more specific about the nature of the trauma?"

"Fear. I know she'll be frightened. I don't know why."

Lissa was nodding. "She does now."

"You were frightened because you saw the photographs in a dream before you saw them in reality."

"Yeah. I dream orange fabric on our roof; there's a kite stuck to the chimney. I dream the neighbor's house is tee-peed; it happens. I see a shaman with a gold tooth; Naomi Whitehorse has taken his picture. Dammit, Ken," she complained, "these *can't* be psychic experiences. I'm a skeptic."

"Fine. Be a skeptic. Look for answers."

"I've *been* looking. My psychiatrist doesn't have a clue. She wants me to meditate. Dr. Genoa doesn't have a clue either, and she wants me to help her look for one." She fidgeted. "She quoted some science fiction writer at me: Be content with the mysterious, he said."

"Philip K. Dick. Yeah."

"That's hard for me, Kenny." She thought of Julie Pascale. "It's even hard for me to be content with the 'unexplainably warm and giving.' How do you do it?"

He shrugged. "I just try to keep an open mind. Look for truth wherever it may rear its often peculiar head."

"Even in Petra Genoa's camp?"

"Yeah, even there."

"Okay. I'll think about it. Right now, I've got an article to rewrite."

"Oh? Which one?"

"The Pascale NDE. I'm not saying I believe she went beyond the Great Divide, but I realize I reported with bias. Okay, *prejudice.* My approach to her interview was skewed because of it. I wasn't looking for truth, I was trying to satisfy myself that there are no mysteries I can't personally unravel."

"So what approach, now?"

Lissa shrugged, trying for a grin. "It's a mystery."

Ken smiled, bending over to kiss her as he rose.

"Where are you going?"

"To remove the kite from our roof." He paused, giving her a cock-eyed look. "Is there anything in the rain gutters I should know about?"

"No, but there's a chubby old guy stuck in our chimney."

They both laughed. She felt—not light-hearted—but better. 'Content with the mysterious'...she would try to be that, hard as it was.

She heard Ken's footsteps overhead. A moment later, a wad of orange polyurethane sailed past the living room window.

Oh, Mr. Dick, you said a mouthful.

Doctor Dodge

A story of magical realism

Doctor Dodge was originally published in *Interzone* in 1997 and was on the *Locus Magazine* Recommended Reading list for 1997. Like *Content With the Mysterious,* it takes on the subject of experience beyond this life, but in a rather different way.

> *O SON OF THE SUPREME! I have made death a*
> *messenger of joy to thee. Wherefore dost thou grieve?*
> *I made the light to shed on thee its splendor. Why*
> *dost thou veil thyself therefrom?*
>
> -Bahá'u'lláh,
> *Hidden Words,*
> Arabic #32

When Reedy Watson was still a young man, he determined he must find a way to avoid Death. He came to this determination as a result of the death of his father, a very direct and uncomplicated man who, as the cliché goes, died young and left a good-looking corpse. He also left a sorrowing wife and perplexed child. His father's death impressed Reedy. Within a few years, Death dominated his thoughts.

Reedy watched Death carefully. He observed the myriad ways people met it. They drove into it at high speeds, they walked in front of it, they leapt to it, they ate or drank or smoked their way to it. They variously took their loved ones with them or left them behind to grieve as his father had done. It seemed to

Reedy that no one tried particularly hard to avoid it. Mostly, they were *non-compis mentis,* their minds on something else, not looking where they were going, not mindful of what or how much they were consuming. They were, Reedy thought, just asking for Death to pounce upon them in inattentive moments. He decided he would not *have* inattentive moments.

He did not. He lived every waking moment in the present, self-aware and self-possessed. This impressed everyone around him—his mother, who thought him an overly serious child; his teachers, who thought him incredibly bright; his fellow students, who thought him patently strange. He was aware of their regard, but it didn't affect him.

He was a remarkable student, with tremendous powers of observation. He favored the academic disciplines—the sciences rather than the arts—for music and prose and poetry tempted him to forget where he was and dwell somewhere other than the here and now. He excelled in "hard sciences," won honors and, by the time he graduated high school, was being courted by prestigious colleges.

At this point, it occurred to Reedy that, though he was attentive, he was also distinctive. If mere mortals marked his achievements, what might Death make of them? He turned down scholarships from Harvard, Stanford, and MIT to attend a tiny college in Maine.

Away from home, he determined he must do more to keep Death from locating him. Death, he theorized, might be muddled by misdirection. He changed his name from Reed to Richard and from Watson to Willis. He still signed letters to his mother "Reedy," but it worried him to have such a traceable point of access. He mailed those letters from a neighboring town. He also taught himself to write with his left hand as he thought that might confuse Death. His papers and local correspondence were written in the stand-up characters of the sinister hand; only his surreptitious letters home were written right-handed.

Reed/Richard was happy in Maine. His ageless little college town tempted him to forget that Death existed. The ivy on the walls of the town hall was older than the Constitution, and as he prepared to accept his Bachelor's degree, Reedy came to believe he might last indefinitely here. Then two impressive things happened upon the same day.

The first of these was a moment of inattentiveness such as he had never before allowed himself. He was crossing the tree-shaded cobbles before the college's main auditorium, enroute to his graduation ceremony. Late, his arms encumbered with a half-open briefcase and his graduation robe, he was focused entirely on juggling. Out of the corner of his eye, as he approached mid-street, he noticed a female student hurrying in the opposite direction, her hair a banner in the cool spring breeze.

He hesitated, clutching the briefcase, and allowed himself a single moment to admire her beauty. In that moment, he was nearly run down by a car.

The driver swerved and honked and pulled over while Reedy rode a tide of adrenaline to the curb. The driver apologized profusely.

"I'm so sorry!" he said. "You were in such a hurry, I thought you'd be across by the time I got to this spot. When you stopped..."

Reedy soothed the driver, knowing the event was his own fault. From the safety of the auditorium steps, he looked about for the young woman who'd unwittingly distracted him. She was nowhere in sun-dappled view. He went inside. It was in this seemingly protected place that the second thing occurred: Reedy saw Death.

He was on-stage when he saw it. He had just finished his valedictorian speech and gathered up his notes when he looked up toward the back of the auditorium and saw Death sitting by the front doors against the wall. It looked much as he had imagined—dark clothing not unlike the habit worn by an Orthodox priest, a long saturnine face of which he could see only the half lit by the sunlight flooding through the front doors.

Reedy thought the thin mouth smiled. He froze for a moment--another moment of gross inattention—and wondered about the mechanics of Death. Had the near accident brought Death here? Had that been Death's way of announcing himself? Or had Reedy dodged Death's earnest attempt to take him?

"Mister Willis!" An urgent whisper from the assistant dean brought him back to where he was.

The audience watched him, expectant, hushed. He slipped from the podium drenched in sweat and applause and carefully retook his seat. He could still see Death sitting by the doors. His heart tripped over itself and began to race. He calmed it by reasoning that Death was no threat to him as long as he could see it and keep it at a distance.

He only took his eyes from it once during the remainder of the ceremony—when he returned to the podium for his diploma. When he glanced again to the back of the hall, Death had gone.

Words are inadequate to describe the extreme care with which Reedy left the auditorium and crossed the campus to his fraternity house. He didn't hurry—hurrying was what had driven him to inattention in the first place—he was careful, methodical. He packed, he arranged to get his transcripts, he left Maine, praying that Death might be diverted by digression.

He took a serpentine course across the country, heading westward. In Pennsylvania, he bleached his hair. When he reached the Ozarks, he had grown a beard, which he also bleached. In Nebraska, he changed his name to John Smits, reasoning that while "John Smith" was distinctive by virtue of its very blandness, he would be stupid to continue to use names with the initials RW. Perhaps that had been his mistake earlier.

As John Smits, Reedy enrolled at the University of Nebraska at Lincoln, shifting his major subtly to one side—Cultural Anthropology rather than History.

He spent two years in Nebraska, his gray eyes made blue by contact lenses, his hair kept carefully blond. Here, too, he was content. But here, too, he distinguished himself as a student, and at the end of his second year, he saw Death again.

A brilliant essay on the culture of Tannu Tuva had won him honors, attention and an awards banquet. He stood at the buffet, basking in congratulatory chatter and flirting with a striking young lady who had caught his eye, when he glanced up and across the food-laden table.

At first, he wasn't sure it was Death looking back at him, for the clothing was different and the face was almost featureless, but when Reedy looked into the eyes, he had no doubt. They were frigid, colorless eyes and they filled him with such terror, he forgot about the girl. He forgot about anything but how close he was to Death. He put down his plate, fled the banquet and received his award by mail the day he left Nebraska.

He understood now that digression was not enough. He must also avoid distinguishing himself.

When he arrived in Berkeley, California, his eyes were brown, his hair and mustache were black, his skin was deeply tanned from days beneath ultraviolet lamps (tanning in real sunlight, he reasoned, was an open invitation to Death). His name was Vishnu Bhaktidas and he had cultivated a very slight, but very precise East Indian accent.

Though she lived less than one hundred miles away, he did not visit Reedy Watson's mother. He did not go to her wedding when she remarried in the winter of his second year at Berkeley.

He earned a master's degree in Archaeology and did not wait for Death to put in an appearance before relocating again, this time in New Mexico.

Paulo Martinez took his Master's degree into the field, working as a corporate archaeologist. During his sojourn there, he saw Death only in art—in paintings, on the walls of tombs, as tiny figurines in native shrines. He was not a superstitious man, so unearthing and handling these things didn't bother him in the least.

He had seen Death; these were harmless effigies.

Three years later, when he returned to school in Arizona as Steve Nederman, he applied his time in the corporate environment toward a doctorate in History. He pursued postdoctoral studies at UCLA, reasoning that the sheer mass of the student body would grant him anonymity.

He was content during that time, if not happy. He had few friends, for he must keep people at arm's length, but he had History, which had become a passion with him. He called himself Dr. Douglas Dodge and there was more than a hint of pride in that name; he hadn't seen Death for nearly a decade.

He taught several classes in his second year at UCLA— classes that were always full. It didn't occur to him that his popularity was putting him in jeopardy until he looked up from a lecture one morning to see Death sitting in the front row. It wore a black leather jacket, which struck Reedy as somewhat cliché, but the expression in its colorless eyes vacuum-froze Reedy's heart.

His surprise was only momentary, then he continued his lecture, keeping his eyes on Death. At the end of the hour, Death rose and left, giving him a wintry backwards glance. Reedy's heart skidded, then picked up speed again, thudding so loudly, he barely heard the students clustered around him imploring his attention.

"Excuse me, professor?" A soft-voiced young woman tugged at his thoughts. "Are you all right?"

Already planning his next digression, he begged off, pleading a headache. He tried not to meet the girl's eyes, but they caught him, reminding him achingly of things that could not be thrown into a suitcase and moved, dyed a new color, or changed through the DMV. He experienced, for the first time, a soul-deep twinge of longing for something he had just realized he could never have.

He doubled back to Maine, enrolling as a student in the Master's program of the very school from which he had earned his Bachelor's degree. *Let Death try to follow this,* he thought, and thanked Providence for a youthful and easily disguised face.

This time he made real efforts not to be distinctive. His appearance was average, his grades were average, his name was average, his life was average...except in one respect; he kept himself aloof from members of the opposite sex, knowing full well that involvement could bring untold difficulties.

This gave rise to the assumption that he was gay, which in turn gave rise to several embarrassing situations that ended in hurt feelings on both sides. His small circle of friends dwindled even further. He was earning a reputation as an odd duck, and could only pray this did not draw Death's attention to him again.

In the third year of his new Master's program, Reedy's mother fell ill. He packed up his life and returned to California as Dr. Reed Watson, finding his mother in a Sacramento hospital. She had AIDS, she told him, having evidently contracted it from a second husband disinclined to fidelity. Though he had protested he would stand by her, she had started divorce proceedings the day she was diagnosed.

Reedy was not comforted by that justice. In his own quest to elude Death, he had abandoned her. He could have been there when she remarried—*should* have been there. He could have taken one look at her husband-to-be and seen Death perched on his shoulder, he was certain of it.

The hospital made him nervous, and at first he watched for Death almost obsessively. When he didn't see it, he reasoned that Death might simply be too busy here to bother with him.

He mentioned none of this to his mother, of course; she wanted only to hear about his life and accomplishments. So he sat in her sunny, depressing hospital room and shared these things with her, omitting the fact that his name had changed half a dozen times since she had given birth to him.

Her nurse came and went, smiling at him when he made his mother smile. He was warmed by her approval, but she reminded him of all the smiling young women who had strolled in and out of his revolving-door life. Her presence depressed and uplifted at once, making Reedy suppose he knew what riding a roller coaster was like though, of course, he'd never been on one.

He spent two weeks in Sacramento, visiting his mother daily, keeping his eyes open for Death. Every time the door of her room swung open, he expected to see it standing there in the hall, but it never appeared. There would only be his mother's doctor with his kind detachment, or his mother's nurse with her sweet smile and cheerful words, and Reedy began to wonder if Death was only visible to those it was about to take.

He asked his mother, "Do you see anyone else in the room, Mom? Besides me?"

She looked at him oddly. "I see my doctors when they're here. I see my nurse."

He glanced at the nurse, who was sorting medications into a little cup. Her nametag said "Layli." An unusual name. A pang of something like grief struck Reedy's heart and he almost blurted aloud that she should change her name to something bland, something ordinary like Mary or Ellen or Ann, so that Death wouldn't be so quick to notice her.

She smiled at him. "It's Persian," she said, then when he couldn't reply, "My name. I saw you looking at my badge."

"It's...lovely. Unusual." He took a deep breath. Held it...and said nothing more.

His mother fell asleep as they chatted, and even Reedy dozed in his chair. He woke to find the nurse, Layli, standing over him. "It's time," she said.

"I'm sorry? I..." Reedy tried to rouse himself, but all that became aroused was his awareness of the girl. He could feel the warmth of her body, the warmth of her smile, the warmth of compassion in her eyes. She smelled sweet, like cinnamon. He'd expected antiseptic.

Once, he'd perched on a stool in a sunny kitchen while his mother pulled cinnamon cookies from the oven. She would hold them up for his bright inspection and he would applaud.

"Visiting hours are over, Dr. Watson."

He rose and left, feeling suddenly and overwhelmingly lonely. His father was gone. Now he would leave his mother behind...and Layli, or anyone like her.

In the lobby of the hospital, he made his way to the sliding glass doors, standing aside as a new mother was wheeled out hugging her baby to her breast. She smiled at him and, from behind her wheelchair, her husband smiled at him. They crossed the threshold and went out into the darkening parking lot.

The doors slid closed with a hushed sound and Reedy stared at his own reflection in the glass. He expected to see someone old and tired-looking, but the man who gazed back was young. Too young, most people would probably say, to have a Ph.D. at the end of his name.

Does your mommy know you're wearing that beard? he thought.

He was stepping into the beam that would part the doors when he saw another reflection behind his in the glass. He recognized it at once, despite the white doctor's coat. The doors parted, flinging the reflection to one side. Reedy turned, but it had gone.

His first thought was for his mother. He hurried back to the nurses' station and tried to get someone's attention. It seemed to take forever.

"Mrs. Watson," he said when he was finally face to face with a nurse. "No, no. I mean Mrs. Hammermill. Could you check her status for me?"

The woman seemed happy enough to help him; he watched her phone the nurses' station in his mother's ward. She spoke, she glanced at him, she turned away.

He knew. He knew before she faced him at last and he saw the expression on her face—eyes kind but sad, mouth uncertain.

"I'm sorry, sir. Mrs. Hammermill passed on about five minutes ago. Were you close?"

Yes? No? How did he answer that? Afterward, he vaguely remembered saying he was her son. Remembered receiving condolences. He hoped Layli had been with her. He hoped that if death ever did catch up with him, there would be a Layli for him, as well.

He finished his second Master's degree in Canada, then went to Florida where he taught at the University of Miami. Then he returned to school as a student, earning a doctorate in Language. He taught college level French in Indiana. He returned to Berkeley for his Anthropology doctorate; he went back into the field and from there into teaching again.

By the time he was sixty-five, digression had earned him five doctorates and two additional Master's degrees. He was in excellent physical condition, for he was careful about exercise, diet, and lifestyle.

He was also compulsive and lonely and discontent, and envious of people who were none of those things. He wondered if he might have struck a balance in his life. He wondered if it was too late to find one now. He wondered if there might be someone, somewhere who could understand how he lived, who would be willing to share his somewhat bizarre lifestyle with him.

He'd become very good at the Dodge. He hadn't seen Death since that evening in the lobby of a Sacramento hospital, and Death had not been there for him, then. It was clear that Death had either lost interest, or did not know where he was. Sometimes, he didn't know where he was either—was this Maine or Canada? Florida or California? Arizona or Mexico?

Boston, Massachusetts. That was where he was this particular evening. He was Dr. Joseph Parry, professor of History at Boston College. He was in his favorite restaurant, alone, staring at the lights of the city laid out beyond and below the windows. There was also reflected light in the windows, thrown from the myriad tabletop candles. It was hard to distinguish one from the other.

He was making a game of that when he saw Death reflected in the glass.

It was sitting in a booth across the room. It was watching him. Its black suit and shirt made the featureless face seem unnervingly pasty as if all the color had drained away into the kaleidoscopic tie.

Reedy sat, lump in his throat, wondering what to do and feeling suddenly and excruciatingly weary.

Perhaps, he thought, *I should just go over and introduce myself. Perhaps, I should just get this over with. And perhaps,* he thought, not for the first time, *I'm completely mad and that is just a curious stranger.*

Survival instinct clamored for him to leave, but he could only sit there and stare at Death and wait for his dinner to arrive. Fight or flight. Adrenaline surged, making his heart race. *Get up and leave,* the rhythm said. *Get up and leave.*

He was at the point of doing just that, when movement close at hand startled him. He looked up to see a young woman sliding into the booth across from him. She was a stranger, young, lovely. She smiled at him, and her face took on a strange familiarity.

"Hello, doctor," she said.

His heart pounded with a new awareness—Death had risen and was moving toward him. He saw it peripherally, for he couldn't take his eyes from the woman sitting across from him. In that moment, she was every woman he had ever gazed at longingly and left behind on his mad zigzag through life. If loneliness were his personal disease, she was the cure. He forgot about Death and focused his attention on her.

"Do I know you?" he asked.

"Yes and no. We've met before, but you don't remember me."

He returned her smile. "I'd like to rectify that." He held out his hand. "I'm Dr. Joseph Parry."

She took the hand. "You're Dr. Reed Watson."

No. It simply could not be. That was so many years ago. "Are you...Layli? You *can't* be Layli."

"It's a name I've used." She held his hand between her own, eyes soft, wistful.

It was an odd thing to say, and it struck him with forcible certainty that she, like him, was a fugitive from Death. He felt so strange. Light-headed, transfixed. Her eyes, direct, all-knowing, pulled words from him.

"You're like me, aren't you? You know what this life is like. I sensed that in the hospital." So long ago, now.

"I do know. I know that you've been wretched and lonely. That you've *made* yourself wretched and lonely."

"What else could I do? I've had to..." He peered at her, suddenly perplexed. "But you...you worked in a hospital, surrounded by Death's doings. How could you do that?" And then it him—the simple logic of it. She had been keeping Death in plain sight rather than offering it the opportunity to sneak up on her.

This reminded him that Death was yet trying to sneak up on *him*. He cursed his inattentiveness and jerked his eyes from the woman's. The table across the room was empty and Death was nowhere in sight.

He relaxed, feeling leaden with relief. "It's gone. Thank God, it's gone." He looked at his companion anew. "No. Thank *you*. I believe you frightened it away."

"What?"

"Death," he said, daring to be thought mad. "It was sitting right over there."

She laughed and he wished his life had been full of that sound. Perhaps it could be yet. He felt hopeful for the first time in decades. He smiled.

"You think I'm crazy. I don't blame you. But it's true. Death came here for me."

She nodded. "Yes. Death *did* come here for you." She leaned toward him, her scent like the remembered fragrance of cinnamon cookies baking in his mother's kitchen. "*I'm* Death, Reedy."

He shook his head, and the room turned slightly on its axis. "But you're...you're beautiful, warm. Death is stark and faceless. It has glaciers for eyes."

"That wasn't Death."

"Then what?"

"Loneliness. *I* am Death. Where I go, Loneliness flees. You never knew me, Reedy. Know me, and you will never meet Loneliness again."

His heart trip-hammered. The restaurant melted into an overly warm blur of shadow and light and muted sound. Reedy saw only her eyes, the eyes of Layli—twin lights that beckoned. He breathed a last breath and inhaled the sweet fragrance of cinnamon cookies.

Heroes

A story of science fiction

Heroes originally appeared in *Analog Science Fiction* in 1990. It is the first in a series of stories I wrote that involved a time travel technology called the Temporal Shift. The story explores the beating of swords into ploughshares and the concept of scientific neutrality. This was published on the eve of the end of the Cold War, the fall of the Berlin Wall, and the dissolution of the Soviet Union, but it was written well before that. One reader asked where I purchased my crystal ball.

> *When soldiers of the world draw their swords to kill,*
> *soldiers of God clasp each other's hands! So may all*
> *the savagery of man disappear by the Mercy of God,*
> *working through the pure in heart and the sincere of*
> *soul. Do not think the peace of the world an ideal*
> *impossible to attain! Nothing is impossible to the*
> *Divine Benevolence of God.*
>
> -`Abdu'l-Bahá,
> *Paris Talks,*
> p. 29

There was silence in the Operating Room except for Shiro Tsubaki's soft voice counting elapsed time. Behind the broad expanse of duo-glass that looked down on the Theatre the technicians' faces flickered with reflected data from their computer displays. The video monitors each showed the scene from the Theatre below—a static scene in which a small cylindrical robot sat in a shimmering field of dancing motes.

Trevor Haley watched the same scene through the window, waiting tensely for something to happen.

"Shifting," said Shiro's voice.

Trevor blinked, his eyes straining to see any change in the bot. There was a change, all right. The little machine's solid lines began to waver and bleed into the shimmer around it. Before he could blink again, it was gone. He pulled his attention back to his console.

"Shifting to Green minus one," said Shiro. The counter on her monitor ticked off a series of numbers that looked like seconds, but were not. "Shifting Aqua minus one..." Another silence followed. "Shifting Blue minus one...minus two. Stop Shift at...Blue minus six. That's negative 36."

Someone said, "Wow," and the entire Operating Room breathed a sigh of relief.

"Halfway there," murmured Magda Oslovski. "Five minutes, Shiro."

"Counting."

Oslovski shifted in her seat. "Video status?"

"Fully functional." George Wu shook his head, trying to clear the sense of unreality. "The video carousel is at 30 degrees. We ought to have some great footage."

"Let's hear Toto's stats, Trev."

Trevor stirred. "Temperature: 18 degrees Celsius; humidity: 60 percent—a little higher than normal for the time of year; attitude: five degrees from upright and adjusting."

Oslovski nodded. "It'd be nice if we could maintain video contact."

George Wu snorted. "Right. Maintain an optic link across a temporal spectrum. Piece of cake."

"There was a time," said Oslovski in her when-I-was-an-eager-young-scientist voice, "when an optic link between *cities* was science fiction. Now it's just science—*old* science. Mark my words, George, given enough time-"

"Movement," said Trevor. "Thirty degrees, three meters distance. Object reads...less than a meter in height, about a meter long. Damn, I wish we could see..." He peered at the shifting readings on his display. "This is weird. The object is moving and *part* of the object is moving independently. Closing to two meters. Independent movement is rhythmic, uh... It's like, uh-" He waved his hand back and forth.

"Someone waving?" suggested Shiro.

"One meter tall?"

"Not waving, *wagging*," suggested George. "It's a-it's a dog!" He shrugged when everybody turned to look at him. "Well, it *sounds* like a dog."

"Object at one meter."

"You know if that *is* a dog," said George, "it just might mistake Toto for a fire hydrant."

Oslovski grimaced. "Great. We may get to see how well he withstands precipitation."

"I don't think that's what the Techs had in mind," George murmured.

"Two minutes," announced Shiro.

They continued to spout data intermittently for another three minutes, watching the progress of the "dog-like object" carefully. At the end of a full five minutes, Oslovski gave the order to reverse the field.

"Reversing field," announced Shiro.

Trevor laughed. "Object radiating percussive audio vibration and receding rapidly at 30 degrees."

"Ah," said George. "What is the sound of one dog barking?"

"Shifting to Blue minus one," said Shiro. "Aqua minus ten... And Green minus ten, nine, eight, seven, six, five, four, three, two, one and zero."

Every eye in the room went to the monitor that displayed the contents of the Theatre. In the shimmering field, the bot appeared, looking no different than it had when it left.

"Welcome back to Oz, Toto," someone murmured.

The O.R. exploded in a spontaneous cheer. Hugs and laughter and silly dances followed in a ritual celebration of accomplishment so ancient it had probably marked the creation of the first successful Folsom point.

It lasted for all of thirty seconds. Then the backslaps dwindled to pats, the laughter died to throat clearing coughs, the flushed faces drained of color and hilarity. Six pairs of eyes swung to Magda Oslovski.

She read the questions in them and sighed, feeling suddenly and incongruously depressed. "Okay," she said. "We did it. Presumably we did it successfully. Now we gather up our data and study it. We write our lab reports and...and move on to Phase Five."

People looked at their shoes. People looked at their handcomps. People frowned.

"Magda," said Trevor Haley tentatively, "when are we going to report to the Chiefs? You've been holding them off for the better part of a year with 'steady progress is being made.' We've shown them disappearing orange tricks and talked about it being years before we dare Shift human subjects. At some point they've got to be brought up to date."

"I have *not* been holding them off. I've been...cautious. Do you think we should let them in on all Phases of the Project?"

"I didn't say that. I just...wondered..."

"When the axe was going to fall?" asked Shiro.

"Falling axes have to do with being fired," George reminded her. "I don't think for a moment the Chiefs are going to let us get off that easy."

"No, they're not." Oslovski scratched at the edge of her handcomp with a well-manicured thumbnail. "In fact, General Caldwell and company are due here next Monday to check in on us. I didn't tell you before," she added over a chorus of protests, "because I knew it would affect your work...and your health."

She looked up. Her eyes had that steely look she was famous for. "I haven't decided how much we're going to tell them yet. Gather up your goodies, people. Staff meeting in half an hour."

Thirty-five minutes later, a subdued group congregated in the Level 3 Conference Room and took their places around its large oval table. Magda Oslovski was the last to arrive. She seated herself at the head of the table and called the group to order.

"All right, folks. I'm going to turn this over to George and company for show and tell. George?"

George Wu popped a videodisc into the console set into the tabletop before him. He glanced at his assistant, Louis Manyfeather, then threw the rest of the group a nervous grin. "I've got to admit, we peeked," he said. "This is great!"

He started the playback. Around the table, video displays came to life. The title screen showed first: Project Hourglass—Phase Four—4/21/24. Then they saw a dewy sward of close-cropped grass from roughly the vantage point of a four-year-old child. About four meters distant, a border of evergreen shrubbery blocked their view of the trunks of a variety of trees. The video image panned slowly, showing more of the same.

Through the trees a building came into view—low and squat and square and composed predominantly of greenish tinted glass and strips of pink granite. The image panned along the building further. Then something else came into view. A chuckle rolled around the table.

"There's your 'dog-like object,' Trev," said Shiro. "I think it's an Airedale."

"Told you so," said George.

The Airedale disappeared as the video unit continued its sweep. They saw more grass, a metal sprinkler head, the roof of another building.

"Wait! Pause that!" said Oslovski. "That's the roof of the Library building, isn't it? You can't even see that from here, now."

Heads nodded absently. The slow pan continued and concluded, and the screens went dark. Toto's audio recorder let out a wild yelp and a short series of barks. There were a few chuckles.

"Now," said George, "Louis hit the archives and came up with this." He slid a second disc into the unit. The displays lit up again with a still shot of a very similar scene. "This is the Campus thirty-five years ago. The photo was taken from the steps of what was then the Psychology building. That lawn is now covered by this facility. The white 'x' in the grass marks the spot in the O.R. where Toto was Shifting." He paused, ran a hand through his thick, black hair. "Ladies and gentlemen, we just sent Toto back thirty-six years in time. Chances are we can just as easily send him into the future."

There was a moment of hushed appreciation while seven people tentatively explored the wonder of what they'd just done. Trevor Haley put a damper on the wonder.

"Our masters aren't interested in the future," he said dryly. "They're interested in the here and now."

Magda Oslovski sighed and took off her glasses, laying them on the table with a solid click. Most people considered her glasses a scientist's professional affectation. The state of medicine being what it was, there was no reason for anyone to ever have to suffer glasses again. They were, in fact, more expensive than the corrective surgeries available. Oslovski was hard put to make anyone with 20/20 vision understand the mental benefits of being able to make the "real world" go out of focus at will.

The faces of her team were just fuzzy enough that she couldn't read their expressions. That was good, considering what she was going to say.

"As I mentioned previously, General Caldwell and the Joint Chiefs will be here next Monday. What that means, folks, is that he's expecting a full report on our accomplishments to date and probably some sort of whiz-bang demonstration. He will, no doubt, be very pleased with today's progress. And, if the milestones continue to be met, we may have positive reports to offer on Phase Five as well."

"Oh, joy," said Shiro, with nothing like joy.

"Do I need to remind you that we are under contract to the Department of Defense and are bound, by that contract, to deliver the fruits of our research?" Oslovski eyed the fuzzy faces.

A combination of mumbles and groans circled the table.

"All right. We've penetrated Negative 36. We're going to march back into our Operating Room, recalibrate our equipment and repeat Phase 4. This time we'll turn the clock back a little further—see if we can't extend Toto's leash into the Violet range. And I want scrapings from his casing to go to analysis for any signs of fatigue." She glanced down at her wristwatch, grimaced, put on her glasses and glanced at it again. "Let's take a lunch break. Meet in O.R. in an hour and a half."

Shiro dug her fork viciously into the lettuce on her plate, got too much and worried the excess off the tines. "This whole situation stinks like yesterday's garbage," she said. "How can we just go merrily along with our research when we suspect it's going to be used to change history?"

"We're under contract." Trevor mimicked Oslovski.

"Huh! A contract with the *Devil*." Shiro bit into a radish.

"It's not that bad...is it?" asked George. "I mean, we don't know that they intend to use it for anything heinous. They said they wanted to go back to strategic points in time to-to-"

"Meddle," said Trevor. "Oh, I know, I know—that wasn't the official language. What was the wording they used? Oh, yes —'rectify and enhance.' As if there was a whole lot to enhance. There hasn't been a war anywhere on the globe for close to fifteen years. No Communists have slunk up the continent from South America, no petty dictators have reared their ugly heads —successfully, at any rate—and the so-called Super Powers are behaving like kissin' cousins. How the hell do you enhance that?"

"Ah," said Shiro, waggling her fork at him. "*That's* the whole point! One man's poison is another man's dessert. What is good for the world does not necessarily seem good to all the officers and gentlemen being put out of work by what is good for the world. Nor vice versa. For years there has been talk about combining the military branches and putting them under the control of the National Guard and the United Nations. More military bases are closed every year. You know they feel the squeeze."

"And you think," asked George, "that *that's* what they want to rectify? The shortage of wars?"

"They're soldiers, George," said Trevor. "Soldiers are trained to fight enemy soldiers. With enemies in such short supply, there's not a whole lot for them to do these days. And the money that used to buy them technological gadgets is now involved elsewhere."

"So, then the question arises: *Why* are they spending the last measly mega-bucks of their dwindling budgets on time travel?" Shiro asked.

"Maybe," suggested George, "they want to go back to a simpler time when being soldiering was considered glorious and patriotic—if underpaid."

"I wish that was it," said Trevor. "But I'm sure it isn't. If we hand them the past, we're handing them the future right along with it. *Our* future—*everybody's* future. It scares the hell out of me."

Shiro nodded, her mouth full of salad.

"Okay, me too," admitted George. "But what can we do about it? We're just the hired hands. And, as Magda pointed out, we're under contract. The reputation and survival of QuestLabs is riding on our fulfilling our obligation to the Defense Department."

Shiro grimaced and pushed her plate aside. "There's a heck of a lot more riding on it than that."

The sequel to the Phase Four experiment was as successful as the original. Oslovski's team sent Toto (Totable Temporal Oculus) back over four decades. With the exception of smaller trees and the presence of a gardener and a few dorm-dwelling students (which shortened Toto's planned stay of ten minutes), the scene was much the same as it would be nine years later.

There were no cheers this time upon Toto's successful return, although the team's junior members, Manyfeather, Khadivian and Walsh, did exchange a "high five."

Afterward, Magda Oslovski barricaded herself in her office, ostensibly to draft a report for the Joint Chiefs. What she did instead was sit in the glow of her computer terminal, staring at the data through unfocused eyes. She took her glasses off, finally, and rubbed her eyes, then swore when she realized she'd just turned her eye makeup into brown and black smudges.

She was almost relieved when her three senior researchers violated the "do not disturb" message she'd left on her hall monitor. They collected before her desk like recalcitrant kindergartners, managing to look defiant and apologetic all at once. George Wu sat, Shiro Tsubaki perched on the arm of his chair, and Trevor Haley stood behind them, hands buried deep in the pockets of his blue lab coat.

"Have you been crying?" asked Shiro.

Oslovski shook her head and put on her glasses. "No, not yet. Are you going to make me?"

They smiled with all the sincerity of the second runner-up at a beauty pageant.

"Come on people, let's hear it."

Now they exchanged nervous glances. Trevor cleared his throat. "Madga, we... We're in a real dilemma over this project. Or rather, over the use we're afraid the results of this project will be put to."

"Frankly, the language of the contract bothers us," said Shiro. "We're very concerned about the morality of our position."

Oslovski was nodding. "I can't say I wasn't expecting this. I can't say I wasn't dreading it, either."

"Don't you have any feelings about it?" asked Trevor. "Doesn't it scare you to think what a group of men facing the extinction of their way of life might do with time travel?"

Oslovski made a peaked roof with her fingers and studied the long, natural fingernails. "Before I say anything about my *feelings,* I have a duty to deliver the party line."

They groaned almost in harmony and she held up her hand. "Hear me out, please. I've got to say this. We are not the first scientists to be confronted with this dilemma. Psychologists even have a name for it—the Openheimer Syndrome. Science is neutral—neither good nor evil. Only the end uses of science can be viewed through a filter of moral principles or ethics. You know all this; I'm not telling you anything new."

She got up and began a deliberate stroll around her office. "Party line, folks, is: We are not culpable for the actions of the people who purchase our expertise or the fruits of our research. We make time travel possible and our responsibility ends there. We aren't accountable for what's done with it once it leaves this facility."

"But, dammit Maggie, it *doesn't* leave this facility!" Trevor moved to follow her. "Don't we have anything to say about that? Do we have to be associated with their...historic enhancements?"

She stopped to look at him. "Are you suggesting we cast them out into the world with our research notes and wash our hands of the technology? Give them the recipe and make them find their own cooks?"

"We could do that, couldn't we?" asked George hopefully.

Shiro shook her head. "We were talking about morality, George. Is that any more moral than doing the work ourselves? Given our research, they could find other people to do the work. The world would still be up the tree without a paddle."

"Creek," corrected George.

"Creek, then.... I feel we should keep the technology
in-house and exert some control over how it's used. Can't we do
that?"

Oslovski shook her head. "I don't see how."

"Okay, Magda," said Trevor. "You recited the party line.
Duty is done. Now, tell us how *you* feel about this."

"Very uneasy. Close to crappy, in fact." She circled back
toward her desk. "General Caldwell has been extremely
closed-mouthed about the reasons the military community has
targeted Temporal Research for support. I'm not terribly
comfortable with phrases like 'enhancing history' or 'rectifying
cultural aberrations.'" She was back at her desk now, and seated
herself behind it. "Fact is, folks, we are bound by contract to
deliver the 'fruits of our research,' as the papers say, to our
clients. Fact is, our administration will hold us to that contract
regardless of our moral inclinations. Let's say we default—refuse
to continue. Best case, they take the body of our research and use
it without our cooperation, maybe even ban us from further
work on time travel."

Shiro gasped. "Could they do something like that?"

"Read the contract, Shiro. It gives them the right to the
disposition of Temporal Shift technology."

"So what's worst case?" asked Trevor.

"Worst case is, they do all that and bury this whole institute
to the bargain."

"So we're powerless over our own creation, then. That's
what you're saying. We can't do a damned thing." Trevor's fists
threatened to rip through his pockets. "Jesus, Magda, can't we
do *something?*"

Oslovski took off her glasses and rubbed the bridge of her
nose. "You ever read Saint Francis of Assisi?"

Shiro nodded. George and Trevor shook their heads.

"Saint Francis wrote a prayer that went something like this: 'God grant me the courage to change the things I can, the serenity to accept the things I cannot change, and the wisdom to know the difference.'"

"That's an answer?"

She shook her head. "It's a...a yard stick. If we start with wisdom, maybe we'll be able to determine whether the situation calls for courage or serenity. Right now, my best advice is accept the situation as it stands and pray for a sign from God."

They weren't happy with the advice, she could tell that by their glum faces as they filed out of her office. She felt sorry for them. Hell, she felt sorry for *herself*. She couldn't even go holler on their administrator. She and Peter had already been around the proverbial rocket silo with her ethical objections to letting the military lead her research team around a blind curve. He'd reminded her about the sacred neutrality of science.

"Screw the sacred neutrality of science," she'd said. "Neutral is not a synonym for amoral."

"You're a professional," he'd said. "I know you understand that there are also business ethics involved. Make your people understand. And make them understand that their temporal research would have died on the vine if the Defense Department hadn't gotten interested in it."

"Screw business ethics," she snarled, as she threw herself onto her living room sofa that evening. "Since when are business ethics more important than human lives? Since when are they supposed to count for more with scientists than-than moral integrity?"

"Since businessmen started managing scientists?" Her husband poured her a cup of coffee and handed it to her.

She grimaced. "God, yes. Bottom line... Party line.
Contractual obligations and scientific neutrality. And I, dutiful
parrot that I am, read it right off the cue cards to my Team. You
should have heard me, Vance. I actually quoted Saint Francis of
Assisi to them." She sighed and sipped her coffee. "The poor
man is probably spinning in his grave."

Vance smiled. "I would have quoted Galata."

"Galata?"

"One of my ilk—a psychologist. He said that human beings
who fail to adjust their situation will be forced to adjust their
attitude toward that situation."

"Meaning?"

"Well, in the case of your crew, it may mean that they'll
adapt by developing a thicker skin. Maybe focus on the
technology itself, on the scientific esthetic as opposed to the
moral ethic."

"I smell an 'or' in there somewhere. Faced with an
unchangeable something they either adjust their attitude or what
—go crazy?"

He shrugged. "That has been the reaction of some minds to
unbendable obstacles."

Magda shook her head. "No! Dammit, Vance, my Team
should *not* be the ones to have to adjust their attitude! It's
precisely because the military won't accept and adapt to its
dwindling sphere of influence that we're working on this
project."

"Mm-hm. Precisely. Because of their inability to adapt,
they're funding your life's dream."

She glared at him, thinking that there was a definite dark
side to being married to the Team shrink. "That's it,
Mr. Psychologist. Make me feel like a self-centered, spiritually
bankrupt toad."

"Everyone's self-centered, Mags. It's a perception we learn to adjust as we realize the universe does not revolve around us."

"Only some of us don't adjust very well."

"Don't be too hard on yourself. At least you realize there's a dilemma."

That was not enough consolation to give Magda Oslovski a good night's sleep. She arrived at work feeling limp and run down. A glance at the faces of her senior staff revealed matching sets of dark circles under their eyes. Louis Manyfeather and Vahid Khadivian looked better rested, but they were unusually quiet as they went about readying Toto for his morning outing. Judy Walsh was almost surly.

Oslovski gathered Haley, Tsubaki and Wu for a review of the previous day's data. They were business-like (she was beginning to hate that word) and muted, answering questions in monosyllables and sharing sullen glances. They were on their way down to O.R. when she was paged to take a phone call from Washington. Three pairs of eyes assaulted her.

She held them off with a shake of her head. "I'll handle this," she said.

"Handle it, how?" asked Trevor.

She grimaced and crossed her fingers. "With wisdom, I hope."

It was Caldwell, of course, wanting an unofficial report in anticipation of the official one he'd receive along with the other Chiefs the next week.

Oslovski licked suddenly dry lips. "We're...we're doing very well here, General. In fact, we...we've successfully completed Phase Three of the project." She was glad she had the video link off and he couldn't see her face.

"Phase Three? Ah, yes! That would be the short jumps into the past."

"Yes. We sent Toto—the Temporal unit—back in time in increments from one hour to one year and successfully retrieved it, of course. After a thorough study of the data we included a compartmented cage containing several varieties of insects. They survived and we were then able to send mice."

"Which also survived?"

"Yes, General. Although we're still monitoring them for side effects. There did seem to be some disorientation. You can never be too careful with live animals."

"Oh." He sounded disappointed. "Then you haven't sent a human being anywhere yet."

"Of course not. That would be premature... Of course, it's only a matter of time."

"If you need a volunteer-"

"No, General. We do not. It's too early."

"Hmmm. So the next Phase, then—Phase Four—that's where you'll shoot for longer backward jumps?"

"Yes. We'll lengthen both our stay and our range. It should be...exciting." (*It would have been if you hadn't been footing the bill,* she thought.)

"How far back?"

"Uh, we, um, had plans to attempt a jump of several decades."

"That's excellent, Dr. Oslovski. That is precisely the time period we're interested in for our first experiment. We need to know as soon as you can send a man back thirty-two years *and* put him wherever we want him."

"Well, spatial displacement is part of the n- um, of Phase Five."

"Excellent. Is there any chance you'll be at that level by next Monday?"

"Uh, there is a slim possibility."

"Outstanding. Then I'm going to give you a target, Doctor. A time and a place to shoot for: April 21, 1992, New York City, World Convention Center, Main Hall, Upper Deck."

Oslovski frowned. "Is there a particular reason for that target? Or is that something I'm not permitted to know?"

"I can only reveal the general nature of the mission, Doctor. There was a major snafu in New York in '92. We want to...set it right."

"Sounds...earthshaking."

"Oh, it will be." There was more than a little pride in that statement.

Oslovski was online to the Data Library within seconds of breaking the connection with Caldwell. She instituted a search for significant events connected with the date he'd given, knowing full well what she was going to find.

"First World Congress," returned the computer in well-modulated tones.

"Location."

"World Convention Center, New York."

Oslovski rolled her eyes. "Just this once, I couldn't be wrong?"

The computer didn't respond.

"Um, detail, please. Significant occurrences connected with the World Congress."

"Admittance to Euro-Commonwealth of the Soviet Democratic Republic of the Russias, Poland, Hungary, Czechoslovakia and Rumania. Euro-American Alliance formed, including broad-based arms agreement and Demilitarization Pact. Continue?"

"Demilitarization Pact—didn't that have a huge impact on the military establishment?"

"Affirmative. The Pact formalized the removal of American forces from Northern Europe and was the beginning of the ongoing dismantling and consolidating of the super-powers' armed forces. The Pact was signed on the second day of the World Congress by the Presidents George Bush and Mikhail Gorbachev."

Was that the snafu? The signing of the Pact? "Library, were there any negative occurrences at the conference? Any... scandals, things of that nature?"

"Affirmative. On the first day of the Congress, an attempt was made to assassinate President Gorbachev. It was foiled by the United Nations Guard."

Oslovski felt a chilly fist grasp her stomach. "Detail," she ordered.

"The attempt was made during a televised speech. The assassin was discovered as he was preparing to fire. The shot went wild. No one was injured. The President was escorted to safety. However, the assassin was shot while trying to escape. Members of the U.N. Guard denied responsibility for the shooting and a cursory examination revealed that the bullet came from a variety of long-range weapon not used by the U.N. forces. The assassin's body was destroyed in a fire before a complete autopsy could be performed. Arson was suspected. Destruction was complete."

"No teeth?"

"Specify."

"Weren't the assassin's teeth found? Couldn't they check dental records?"

"Negative. The assassin was apparently wearing a dental plate made of plastic. Analysis of the residue yielded no information. Identification was never made."

Oslovski sat quietly, stunned. Was *that* it? Was that the General's "snafu?" Two possibilities occurred to her simultaneously. One was that the military meant to keep the assassin from being killed so the conspirators could be discovered. That was laudable. But since President Gorbachev had survived, what was the point at this stage in history?

The other possibility...

"Library. Ramifications of attempt on Gorbachev's life—analyze."

"The success of the U.N. Guard in protecting the President forestalled a major socio-political disaster. The United Nation's position in the Congress and subsequent conferences was strengthened and Soviet-American relations cemented. Both the U.S. and S.D.R.R. expressed outrage at the destruction of the assassin's body, which was in the custody of a Naval hospital.

The investigation that followed was a joint Russo-American effort."

"Further analysis: Impact of these events on the role of the U.S. military in the world sphere."

"The handling of the assassination attempt by the U.N. forces and the subsequent charges of negligence brought against certain Naval personnel was a factor in diminishing regard for the military establishment. The ineffectiveness of the military to handle the situation with Gorbachev made the accords signed by U.S. and Soviet leaders regarding military decommissions much more tolerable to the American people. Political figures who had stood behind a strong military abdicated that position faced with what was perceived as a scandal."

Oslovski frowned. "Question: At the time the assassination attempt was made, had either Gorbachev or Bush signed any agreements significantly affecting the military?"

"Negative. As previously stated, the attempt took place on the first day of the conference at precisely 11:00 a.m."

Oslovski had one last question—one she was more than a little afraid to ask. "Was...was the military in any way...implicated in the assassination attempt, or was it just a question of negligence?"

"There were no formal charges made, although there was some speculation that the situation involved more than negligence. The assignments for security were handled directly by a committee made up of high-ranking military officers."

Oslovski sank back into her chair. *This has to be wrong,* she thought. *I have to be wrong. This can't be what it looks like.* It was inconceivable that intelligent human beings could be capable of something so impossibly evil as attempting to kill, not just a man, not just a country's leader, but World Peace.

She got up and went down to O.R., her brain ticking like a jelly-filled time bomb. The Team was waiting—not very patiently—and nearly mugged her when she came through the door. She waved them down.

"Yes, it was Caldwell. We...we have things to discuss—after we start Phase Five."

Trevor made an exasperated sound. "Why? Why can't we talk now?"

"Because...because I need to launder my brain. I need to be a scientist for a while." (*And because I'm half hoping Phase Five will flat out fail and buy us some more time,* she thought.) "Places, everyone."

They went without argument, slid into their duties and performed them flawlessly. Toto was sent backward in time to several sets of spatial coordinates that had verifiable landmarks. The experiment was a complete success. That generated some excitement, but not nearly what it should have.

At 1:00 p.m., Magda Oslovski looked over the body of data, gritted her teeth and called a staff meeting.

"As some of you know, I talked with General Caldwell this morning," she told the assembled Team. He and the Joint Chiefs of Staff will be here in six days to see what progress we've made on Project Hourglass."

"We've made wonderful progress!" enthused Vahid Khadivian. "Did you tell him that?"

Everyone else glanced at Khadivian, glanced at Oslovsky, then studied their blank video displays.

Oslovski started to take off her glasses, then changed her mind. She had to be able to read them accurately now.

"First, I'll tell you what he told me. Then I'll tell you what I told him. He gave me a target time and location. New York City, 1992, April 21, World Conference Center."

"Oh! First World Congress," said Shiro. Everyone else nodded.

"Correct. The General informed me that a...snafu—a major mistake—had occurred at this time and location. One the Joint Chiefs wanted to rectify." She engaged the computer. "Library. Display headlines pertinent to the incident on the first day of World Congress."

The computer produced the front page of a New York newspaper with a banner headline: ASSASSINATION ATTEMPT AT WORLD CONGRESS— GORBACHEV UNHARMED.

"The assassin was shot and killed," said Oslovski. "His body was destroyed by a suspected arson fire while in the keeping of a Naval hospital and under a U.S. military guard."

"Was that the mistake?" asked George. "The assassin's death and the destruction of his body?"

Oslovski shook her head. "I don't know. Let's see what you think." She filled in the details then—slowly, carefully, using the computer as part of her presentation. When she was finished, there was a heavy, disbelieving silence.

Trevor Haley broke it. "Do you think they intend to make sure the assassination attempt is successful?"

Oslovski shrugged and spread her hands. "I hate to think it, but it looks that way to me. The other possibility doesn't make sense. Frankly, it sounds as if the assassin surviving his capture would *really* throw a spanner in the military machine."

"What did you tell Caldwell?" asked Shiro.

"I told him we'd successfully completed Phase Three."

Khadivian and Walsh both blanched.

"Phase Three?" repeated Vahid. "But that's not true. We've completed Phase Four."

Oslovski shook her head. "I did not lie to the man, Vahid. I merely under-xaggerated. We *have* completed Phase Three."

"But when they check our reports-" said Walsh.

Oslovski held up both hands. "Forgive me, Judy, Vahid, but that is simply not important right now. We have a major moral dilemma on our hands. I trust I'm not the only one who feels that way."

A chorus of negatives indicated she was not. "I know I read some of you the party line yesterday—all that about the neutrality of science. Well, folks, science may be neutral, but scientists can't afford to be. *Mankind* can't afford for us to be." She stood up and put both hands flat on the table. "All right, situation is this: I suspect that the Joint Chiefs intend to use our technology to go back to the First World Congress and attempt to create a situation that will also make it the *last* World Congress. Does anyone else share that suspicion?" She raised her left hand.

Haley, Tsubaki and Manyfeather followed suit immediately —George Wu with reluctance. Vahid kept both hands in his lap and looked miserable. Judy Walsh just stared at the tabletop, a fierce scowl on her face.

"Do you two disagree?" asked Trevor. "Do you think we're being paranoid? It seems to me we at least have reason to tread cautiously here."

Vahid shook his head. "I don't know what to think. They... they've paid so much for this research. Without them, we wouldn't even have gotten to this stage."

"We'll all be paying for this research with our lives if they use it the way it looks like they mean to."

Vahid just shook his head again.

Judy said, "I just can't believe it. My father's an Air Force non-com. I can't believe they'd-"

"We're not talking about the whole military here, Judy," said Oslovski. "Just a group of very powerful men who...who may be having difficulty facing reality. Unfortunately, this group is at the top of the chain of command. I can arrange for a transfer," she added gently. "If you want to opt out now, you can."

Judy took a deep breath. "No. No, this project has been my life for four years. I can't just get up and leave. And I don't want to see it used to kill. Besides, my father would be ashamed of me if I ran out in the middle of it all."

Oslovski nodded. "Vahid?"

"I'm scared," he said.

"We're all scared," said Oslovski. "The question is, do we stand around and shake and shiver, or do we do something about it?"

"I'd like to do something," admitted Vahid.

"Right." Oslovski let out a pent up breath. "Now, given the situation, what do we do?" She looked at the group around the table.

"We could send the General and his people back to the Cretaceous and leave them there," suggested Trevor.

"Be real," said Shiro. "We don't even know if *can* penetrate the Cretaceous."

"Seriously. Can't we strand them someplace—I mean, some time?"

Shiro shook her head. "That would be as immoral in its own way as what they might be planning. Besides, they might manage to change the course of evolution or something."

Louis Manyfeather sat forward in his seat. "What if *we* go back in time and make sure the assassin is captured?"

Oslovski grimaced. "Tempting, but none of us is exactly James Bond. Besides, that might change history just as effectively as a successful assassination. We need to make as little impact as possible on what's already happened. We need to-to change the present to protect the past. Keep them from going back at all, if possible."

"We could lock up our data," suggested George. "Tell them what they're asking is impossible."

Oslovski nodded. "I thought of that. But remember, we've already shifted back *past* their target. The computers know that. I know you're a talented programmer, George, but you'd have to be the king of hackers to destroy all that data without leaving a trail. Every activity log on every piece of equipment in O.R. will call us liars if anyone develops a sense of curiosity. Besides that, whose to say they won't just go elsewhere for the expertise?"

"But that would take years," said Louis.

"The net result would be the same, don't you see?" asked Oslovski. "Time is no object. No matter how long they wait, if they achieve their goal..."

He saw, and nodded glumly.

"If we can't get rid of them and we can't fool them," said Trevor, "then what can we do? Hypnotize them so they give up and go away? They're not going to change their minds just because we think they need an attitude adjustment."

Oslovski stared at him. "An attitude adjustment," she murmured.

"What?"

"Something Vance said last night about human nature. That presented with an unchangeable circumstance, the human mind adjusts its attitude to accept it...or goes mad, I suppose."

Shiro nodded. "In other words, it grows the serenity necessary to accept the inevitable. But how can we make the irresistible force *believe* that is has met an immovable object?"

Oslovski raised her eyebrows. "Maybe Trev has something there—hypnotism."

Trevor snorted. "I was being facetious, Magda. There's no way we can hypnotize the entire Defense Department."

"We wouldn't have to. The entire Defense Department isn't going to be time traveling. They'll send one or two men back—hell, *we* can control that much. We'll tell them the field won't allow more than that." She started pacing, thinking. "I want to change the script for the next Phase Five experiment. We're going to send Toto downstairs."

While the others ate lunch, Magda Oslovski went up to her husband's second floor office. He was munching on a tuna sandwich when she came in clutching her coffee cup in both hands.

"Hi," he said. "Have you had lunch?"

She shook her head and he handed her half of his sandwich. "You have 'that look.'"

"That 'lean and hungry look?'" she asked around a bite of tuna.

"No. The patented Magda Oslovski 'I've come to a definite decision and God help you if you try to change my mind' look. So, what's it going to be, Saint Mag of QuestLabs: Courage or Serenity?"

"Our courage, their serenity. Before I tell you what that means, answer a question: Can you hypnotize someone to make them *think* they've done something they haven't done?"

"Can I, personally?"

She nodded.

"Ye-es," he said slowly. "Given the right environment. It depends a lot on the magnitude of the suggestion and the natural resistance of the subject. Some individuals require a little help—sodium pentathol or Ephkal-A."

"Ephkal-A—that was developed here, wasn't it?"

"Yes."

"You've worked with it, then."

"Yes, I have. It's been very helpful in handling the endorphin imbalances that contribute to nasty conditions like schizophrenia."

"In other words, it helps you adjust someone's attitude."

Vance shook his head. "Not quite. It helps the body adjust its own attitude. There's a difference."

"Okay, distinction noted. But it makes this hypnosis thing do-able?"

"Oh, it's do-able. But it's also undo-able. The effects have been known to fade."

"Fade? Over how long a period?"

"Years, months. But real memories tend to do the same thing. Even things I did—oh, last night, say—tend to take on an aura of...fantasy." He gave her a provocative look.

"I love you too," she said. "But couldn't this fading be counteracted with a regular regimen of Ephkal-A?"

He sighed. "We put schizophrenics on Ephkal-A boosters. It keeps their moods balanced and helps them to retain positive memory associations. It can be taken orally... Where's all this leading, Mags?"

"I'll tell you. But I want you to be quiet until I've finished. Take notes if you have to. Then I want to hear what you think. *Then* I want to know if you'll help."

She was back in O.R. an hour and a half later, her face flushed and a mad gleam in her dark eyes. She called her Team away from their calibration routines into a pow-wow.

"Okay, here's the new Phase Five game plan. The object of the experiment is to send Toto back one day to another location here in the Emerald City. Specifically..." She tapped out something on her handcomp and handed the unit to Shiro. "These coordinates."

The younger woman glanced at them, then looked up puzzled. "These are right downstairs, aren't they?"

Oslovski nodded. "They are indeed. Directly below us, as a matter of fact."

"That facility is identical to this one, isn't it?"

"Right again. I just notified Admin that we're going to be making use of it for some very delicate and oh-so-top-secret work. Peter was ecstatic. It's one more thing he can add to the DOD tab. Phase Five now goes something like this. We send Toto down and back to ascertain we can hit the precise coordinates. Then, we're going to incorporate a little bit of Phase Six into the plan: We're going to bring in our animal friends. First, the mice, then, if they survive, we'll send Q-Bert with a full medical array. And if *he* makes it through all right, it's onward and upward."

"You mean we're going to go to a human subject?" asked Trevor.

She nodded. "Except that for the first round human Shift, we'll just send someone downstairs in the same temporal range, just to make sure they're okay."

"Teleportation?" George looked both eager and concerned.

"What about Temporal Spectrum Shift? We've never tried moving an object along the same wave band. Theoretically, I'm not sure it would work. We can't put someone through solid walls."

"But we can use the Temporal Spectrum to move them from one place to another," said Shiro. "We can shift back, change the location on the Spectrum, then shift forward again."

"Ah!" George nodded. "Ah, yes! Sort of like a knight in chess."

Shiro looked doubtful. "I guess so."

"And to what purpose to we do this?" asked Trevor.

The devil was back in Oslovski's eyes. "To the purpose of making the irresistible force think it's met an immovable object. Think, Trev. What might make our clients adjust their attitude?"

"Is this a quiz?"

"Think."

"Okay. Well, you said it. An immovable object."

"Yes!" Shiro nodded eagerly. "I see. Something they can't change. A-a *future* they can't change, perhaps."

"That's what I hope to show them, people," said Oslovski. "A future that their monkeying around didn't change to their liking."

"And what about the other thing?" asked Trevor. "What are we going to do about that?"

"We're going to stop them. Stations, people. Let's complete our calibrations."

Q-Bert weathered his flight with all the aplomb of a veteran time traveler. He complained only when his sensors were attached via a small cap that fitted tightly over his head and fastened under his jaw. Louis had added insult to injury by laughing at him, something the genteel terrier couldn't abide.

"You're the first person he's bitten since he was a puppy," said Trevor, as they reviewed Q-Bert's data.

Louis stared glumly at the bandage on his finger. "Should I take that as a compliment?"

"I think you should take it as a warning not to laugh at Q-Bert. He's a scientist, after all, just like the rest of us. Except, of course, that he has a wet nose."

"Yeah, and sharp teeth." Louis shook his finger. "How did he do?"

"Just great. Respiration fine. Brain activity, relaxed—except when he bit you. Heart rate, normal. Blood panels look good. He's a healthy, happy canine."

Louis bit his lip and tried not to look desperately excited. "That means the next step is sending one of us."

Trevor nodded. "Once Magda's seen this data, I think she'll agree to that." He gave Louis a sideways look. "Are you volunteering?"

"You bet, Kimosabe. Wild horses couldn't stop me. I can just see the headlines: Descendant of Sitting Bull First Man to Time Travel." He grinned. "My folks will be so proud."

Trevor looked skeptical. "Are you really a descendant of Chief Sitting Bull?"

"Bona fide, guaranteed." He twiddled the eagle feather that hung, solitary, from the braid at the back of his head.

"That's ironic."

Louis raised his eyebrows.

"Little Big Horn," said Trevor. "The Sequel."

Operation Little Big Horn proceeded the next morning with a careful, full-staff study of Q-Bert's data. Q-Bert himself was subjected to a thorough examination by Drs. Trevor Haley and Judy Walsh. When that was over, Magda Oslovski okayed the next phase.

Louis took Q-Bert's place on the Spectral Grid, watching nervously as Trevor set up his sensors for the trip. Downstairs in the other O.R., Vahid Khadivian waited for the materialization.

Psychologically, Louis didn't take the Shift as well as Q-Bert had. His heart raced as the Field was activated and he was unable to slow it down. The Field danced like a swirling patina of stars before his eyes. A tingling sensation cascaded down his back, then spiraled upward again to spin crazily, but not unpleasantly, in his head. He blinked rapidly several times--saw colors flash vividly.

My God, he thought, *it really is a spectrum.*

Then the trembling stars returned and melted and he was watching Vahid Khadivian blink back at him. They stared at each other for a moment, then Vahid grinned and said, "Welcome to the Underworld, my son."

Louis let out a whoop.

"Your heart rate got a little crazy there, Louis," said Oslovski. "All through the Shift."

"I just got a little excited, that's all. Really." He shrugged. "Adrenalin is a powerful drug, doctor."

"No discomfort?"

"No. No, it was...tingly. Exhilarating. And there really are visible color bands. I saw them flashing when the Field effect faded."

"Mmm." Oslovski looked at the computer display again. "And most important of all, you made it. You ended up right where you were supposed to." She gazed off into space for a moment.

"Okay. All right. Next phase."

In the week that followed, they sent Toto back to the target date. He recorded the entire assassination attempt, tucked neatly away behind a pillar on the upper deck of the Conference Center. Oslovski's Team reviewed the footage painstakingly.

They studied official accounts. They met far into the night, discussing, consulting, arguing, mentally rehearsing routines for Phase One of Operation Little Big Horn; running over a long list of "what-ifs." They also started laying the groundwork for Phase Two.

When the big Monday arrived, the Chiefs appeared in full military regalia. With them were two "special operatives"— Ferris and Hilyard by name. Oslovski adopted the immediate suspicion that these were the would-be assassins. They contributed nothing to the briefing, but merely sat in silence, watching and listening.

Magda Oslovski conducted the briefing flanked by Vance Keller and Trevor Haley. The other members of the LBH conspiracy were busily readying themselves for the inevitable demonstration.

"Since I talked to you last, General Caldwell," said Oslovski, "we've had several important break-throughs. But rather than tell you, we'll show you. Dr. Haley, the video please."

Around the oval table, video displays showed footage taken by Toto during his sortie in New York. The aborted assassination played out, followed by mass confusion, an explosion of golden motes and a sudden shift to aqua. The screens went black.

Oslovski's eyes were still on Caldwell as he turned to stare at her.

"That...that was the assassination attempt on-"

"Yes. The date you gave me was the opening day of the First World Congress. But, of course, you knew that. We just happened to get this rather spectacular footage of the attempt on President Gorbachev's life. That was the event you were targeting, was it not?"

Caldwell glanced at his clam-faced peers and nodded once. The corner of his mouth twitched.

"Forgive my curiosity, General," said Oslovski, "but what do you intend to accomplish?"

"The righting of a wrong, doctor," he said. "That's all you need to know. And that our work, our very lives, are dedicated to the best interests and the honor of this great nation."

"And the well-being of its people?"

He smiled. "Of course, doctor. The two things are inseparable."

"And what about the welfare of the world as a whole society?"

"The world is not a whole society, doctor. It's a mish-mosh of societies and cultures. My concern—*our* concern is with the strength of the American nation. The other nations only concern us insofar as they are either beneficial or dangerous to U.S. interests."

"I see." Oslovski nodded. "And may I guess what you hope to accomplish?"

"You may guess all you want. We will neither confirm nor deny."

She nodded again. "Naturally. Two possibilities present themselves. One is that you wish to make sure the assassin isn't, himself, assassinated so you can find out who hired him."

General Caldwell's smile didn't falter. "A reasonable assumption, I suppose," he said.

"The other possibility is that you intend to make certain he succeeds."

None of the faces at the nether end of the table altered expression, but there was an eloquent flurry of exchanged glances.

Caldwell merely quirked an eyebrow. "What an interesting mind you have, Dr. Oslovski. I'm glad you're not working for the other side."

Oslovski smiled as if accepting that as a compliment. "What other side, General?"

"You do realize, of course," Caldwell said, ignoring the question, "that you are contractually and ethically bound to bring this Project to a successful conclusion regardless of what we intend to do. So, you see, our intent is really irrelevant."

"Of course."

"And, of course, as scientists, you must observe a sort of code of non-intervention."

That was more order than commentary and Oslovski bristled. If one more person cited the "Scientific Code of Non-Intervention," or preached objectivity at her, she vowed she'd send them back to the eruption of Krakatoa.

"So, we've seen that you can send a robot back to the target time and place. What else have you got for us?"

She showed them the bio-data on Q-Bert and Louis, which included Louis' recorded account of his experience. She took them to O.R. next, explaining the function of each station.

"How soon?" asked Caldwell when they'd concluded the short tour and examined Toto and the Field Generator. "How soon can our operatives begin making time jumps?"

"We can make them part of a demonstration right now, if you'd like."

The Chiefs were more than eager to see a Temporal Shift in action. They watched as each operative was sent to places and times that were easily verifiable. Both men handled the experience as if they were veteran time travelers and consumed healthy amounts of lunch immediately after.

"They're *ice* men," said Shiro.

Oslovski's Team was reconnoitering in the O.R. after their own hasty lunch, while their clients privately debriefed.

"You'd think they were just taking a drive around the block."

"Conditioning," said Trevor. "Mental conditioning."

"Mm-hm. And we have to get around it somehow."

Oslovski blew steam from her coffee cup and grimaced. "This is where we try a little psychology. They've been wondering all morning why the Team shrink's been included in. They're about to find out."

They rejoined the Joint Chiefs in the Level 3 conference room for a final meeting to discuss any questions generated during the day and to set a timetable for the next Phase of the Project. Could delicate equipment go through the Spectrum, the Chiefs wanted to know. Could weapons?

Toto *was* delicate equipment, Trevor told them, the video rig and medical array, likewise. "For that matter," he added, "a human being is delicate equipment. And as for weapons..." He wanted to claim some magical Omniscient Guardian of the Time Spectrum caused all weapons to disintegrate on transit, but couldn't. "There's no reason why they shouldn't be fine."

"I'm satisfied," said General Caldwell when the question-and-answer session had wound down into nodding and note taking.

Oslovski raised her eyebrows. "General, you're overlooking a very important factor in all of this."

"Oh? And what might that be, doctor?"

"I think Dr. Keller is more qualified than I am to speak to that subject. Doctor, would you answer the General's question?"

Vance nodded, tapping a pen lightly on the tabletop. "The psychological ramifications of time travel are quite complex."

"For example?"

"Well, General, you're undertaking to change history. Have you considered how many events might hinge on the one you propose to change?"

"It has been considered."

"Then you are all prepared to face the changes in your personal lives that may result from your..." He'd been going to say "meddling," but smiled and finished, "editing of history?"

"We're counting on it," said Caldwell, and the others nodded.

Dr. Keller spread his hands, palms up, on the table. "I just wanted to be sure you were properly prepared. It could be quite a shock for your operatives to return and discover they've edited a loved one out of existence."

"What?"

They were all staring at him as if he'd just said: "There's a bomb under this table." Oslovski fought the urge to grin.

"Gentlemen," she said, "you must be prepared for any eventuality. You *yourselves* could be 'edited' out of existence by a change in history."

"My God, how can anyone be prepared for that?" The reserved, soft-spoken Naval Admiral Krenshaw was visibly stunned.

Vance Keller nodded sympathetically. "I know it's a terrifying prospect—to suddenly find your entire life rewritten-- wives married to someone else, children never born. And, of course, the guilt factor could be immense—the realization that you did it to yourselves."

Caldwell looked like he'd just swallowed a sour pill.

"And then," added Oslovski, "there is the possibility that your operatives could be stranded in the past."

"I thought you said the technology was reliable," said Caldwell sharply.

"Oh, it is. But it's entirely possible that with a change in history, the technology might never be developed."

"That's damn pretzel logic! If the technology is never developed then how could anyone go back in time to-to get trapped?"

"The technology is reliable," said Oslovski. "But the concepts behind it are sometimes dimly understood."

Caldwell's jaw was ticking. "And how do you propose we prepare for these eventualities?"

Oslovski met his chilly gaze with an equal amount of frost. "That's what we have a psychologist on staff for, General. I would recommend that your operatives spend some time with him during their orientation."

"Orientation?"

"We'll need to do a complete medical work up on anyone who's going to be sent that far back through the Spectrum and stay for any length of time," said Trevor. "We have to know the normal physiology so any abnormalities can be spotted."

Caldwell nodded, once. "When do you want them?"

"Right now. Barring unforeseen difficulties," said Oslovski, "we can be ready to send one of your men back to the target in a week, maybe two."

Caldwell frowned, puckering his mouth. "You're sure the field can't be expanded to take both men through at once?"

"That could lead to a dangerous instability in the Field. We might attempt to send two subjects through in single file, as it were. But until we've successfully retrieved two non-human subjects, we can't try a double passage with your men."

Caldwell looked like he wanted to say something else, but didn't. He took his Joint Chiefs and departed for Washington D.C., leaving Ferris and Hilyard in the capable hands of Oslovski and Keller.

Vance began "preventative therapy" sessions with his two subjects almost immediately. They discussed the ramifications of editing history in great detail. He encouraged them to talk about their fears. Then he worked hard at exploiting them—something that rubbed completely against his grain.

"Dammit, Mags, I can't help but feel like a traitor to my calling. I'm supposed to help people *overcome* their fears and anxieties, not feed them." Vance ran a hand roughly through his curly, black hair and grimaced.

"Sometimes fear is healthy, Vance. You know that. It keeps us from doing stupid, dangerous things like screw with history. People *should* be afraid to do that shouldn't they? Shouldn't they be afraid or ashamed to commit murder?"

He looked up at her out of the corner of his eye. "Okay, when you put it like that, it sounds almost noble. I guess I just need to be sure that it really *is*. That we're not just rationalizing. Because using psychology that way rubs me raw."

Magda folded her arms across her chest and studied his face. "Is it that bad? Do you want to opt out?"

He threw up his hands in exasperation. "No, it's *not* that bad, dammit, but this little voice in my head keeps telling me it *should* be. Frankly, knowing what I know, it's hard to be objective. Hell, it's *impossible* to be objective. Ferris has the most advanced case of tunnel vision I've ever seen when it comes to the activities of the military. To hear him talk, you'd think the Joint Chiefs should be canonized—or at least knighted. And Hilyard-" He shook his head. "Hilyard gives me the creeps. I got him talking about war and how he felt about it. He said he thought dropping the bomb on Hiroshima was beneficial."

Magda shrugged. "A lot of people feel we wouldn't have achieved peace without having stood face to face with that horror first. You have to admit, it made the whole world stop in its tracks and realize war was a no-op."

"I think he meant it was beneficial because it let the other nations know who was boss. It established the U.S. as a Super Power—'separated the men from the boys,' as he put it."

"Oh... So, how are they doing with the program?"

Vance's dark face brightened a little. "Pretty well, actually. Hilyard is just oozing with half-healed post adolescent wounds and a lot of resentment against his superiors. He doesn't like feeling expendable and he fears that's just what he is. Ferris is just a conscientious G.I. trying to do what he feels is his patriotic duty."

"Assassination?"

Vance shrugged. "I've had them both under hypnosis. Ferris seems to take to post-hypnotic suggestion just fine, but Hilyard's a little resistant. Oh, there's one thing I might be able to use against him, though." He made a face. "Dear God, did I just say that?"

Magda threw a paper clip at him. "Snap out of it, Doc."

"Anyway, he expressed belief in reincarnation and past life regression. I think there are some possibilities in that direction."

Magda nodded, looking thoughtful. "Vance, what's your assessment of the mental and emotional health of these two men?"

"That's a tough one. Judging from what they're planning to do..." He shook his head. "I'd have to say we were looking at two pretty sick little puppies. Oh, mentally, I'd have to give them a clean bill of health—based solely on the standard issue tests. But faced with this...mission of theirs, they've got to be buying their day-to-day sanity at the expense of their emotional stability."

Magda got up and moved to face him, locking her fingers at the back of his neck. "While you're busy feeling guilty about brainwashing them so they don't have to go through with their mission, ask yourself what would happen to them, mentally and emotionally, if they *did* go through with it. Hilyard is right, Vance. As far as Caldwell is concerned, they *are* expendable."

During the week and a half prior to their Time Shift, Hilyard and Ferris each established their own unique behavior patterns. Colonel Ferris spent most of his free time alone or, almost perversely, it seemed, in Vance Keller's company. He rarely interacted with any of the other team members. Hilyard, on the other hand, elected to shadow different members of Oslovki's Team insatiably asking questions about the Temporal Spectrum and its attendant technology.

"It's almost as if he doesn't believe it," said Trevor, "and he's asking all these questions trying to catch us out."

Shiro nodded. "I know just what you mean. And you know, he actually seems to understand what we tell him. It's eerie. I feel like he's watching us all the time. Listening to everything we say and taking notes."

"He *is* taking notes," averred Louis. "Every time I turn around, he's talking to that handcomp. I'd *love* to get my hands on that thing to hear what he's been saying about us behind our backs."

"Let's get serious, folks," said Oslovski from the head of the table. "He's very likely keeping reports for Caldwell. Let's just make sure he doesn't see or hear anything compromising. Now, tomorrow's the big day. We'll have one more procedural drill tonight. Are their any issues we need to discuss...Judy?"

"I'm a little concerned about the combined effects of Ephkal-A and the tranq they'll receive. The tranquillizer will inevitably create a condition that the Ephkal-A will counter-act. I'm wondering if we shouldn't delay the infusion of Ephkal-A until after the Shift. That way they won't be subjected to an endorphin double-whammy."

Oslovski nodded. "A valid concern. Trev? What's your opinion?"

"I can see a potential for metabolic confusion. There'll be a natural tendency toward rapid pulse and increased adrenal activity. The tranq will damp that and it will depress some neural functions, which Ephkal-A will then try to elevate. But, frankly, that could be to our advantage."

Judy Walsh flushed angrily. "What about *their* advantage? Or don't we care if we drive them into a seizure?"

"Of course we care, Judy," said Trevor. "I just don't see a clear danger. Q-Bert didn't have any problem with the compounds."

"Q-Bert's a dog, not a man. His heart didn't pound the way theirs did. His nervous system didn't go into overdrive. They may seem like icemen, but they're not. I'm afraid of what the combination of drugs and adrenalin might do."

"I think Judy has a valid concern," said Oslovski. "Vance, is there any way they can receive the Ephkal-A at your end?"

"I don't see why not. We'll have to get the timing right—wait until their attention is engaged elsewhere—but sure."

"All right. Trev, will you oversee that?"

He nodded, making a note on his handcomp. "Got it."

Oslovski glanced around the table again. "More issues?"

Vance raised a hand. "I've got a couple. Which do you want first, the good issue or the bad issue?"

"Oh, please. Let's hear the good one first."

"Well, as you no doubt noticed, Bert Ferris has been stuck to me all week. He's a nice guy, but sort of a bundle of contradictions. He's a very...religious man, I guess you'd say. Very active in his church. The doctrines of his particular sect include the idea that world peace is something that won't or can't or *shouldn't* come until the literal and physical return of Christ. The current peace is, ipso facto, false and evil. He more or less told me that he considers it his Christian duty to 'undo the Devil's work,' as he put it, in any way he could."

There was a moment of complete silence at the table. Judy Walsh's face was a deep red and Vahid's lips moved in a silent invocation.

"The good news is, that this predisposition to-um-"

"Crusader mentality?" offered Trevor acerbically.

"Trevor, please," Oslovski cautioned him.

"Sorry. I just don't understand that mind set. If God hadn't wanted peace on earth, how the hell could we have achieved it? Look at all the obstacles that had to be overcome. If the history of the last thirty-five years wasn't some sort of Divine miracle-"

Oslovski raised a hand to stop him. "No one here is arguing with you, Trev. But our understanding of Ferris' mind set isn't germane. What *is* germane is that that mind set might be an advantage to *our* crusade."

Trevor mumbled something under his breath.

"As I was saying," Vance continued, "Colonel Ferris has a predisposition, even a deep-seated drive, to correct what he sees as a cosmic evil. He's a man with a mission—to see this false peace brought to an end. Now, I grant you that on some level, he is very likely aware of the contradictions in that ideology. And on another level, there's every indication that because of that ideology, these many years of peace we've enjoyed pose an extreme test to his faith. The bottom line (if I may be so crass) is that he'll *want* to believe he's accomplished that mission. He's already proved to take post-hypnotic suggestion very readily."

"Good," said Oslovski. "So, what's the bad issue?"

"The bad issue is that both of these guys are thoroughly terrified by the idea that they might 'erase' someone as a by-product of their mission. I think Ferris' sectarian indoctrination will override that fear, but I'm not so sure about Hilyard. He's a cold-blooded S.O.B., but he's got a mom, a dad, two younger brothers and a younger sister in Omaha, Nebraska. Even if he doesn't erase them, in any nuclear engagement that would be one of the first places to go—it's within spittin' distance of SAC Headquarters. He has what I'd call a very strong subconscious imperative *not* to believe that his mission was a success."

Oslovski's brow knit. "Has be been resistant to hypnosis?"

"Moreso than Ferris. It's not insurmountable. I just wanted to warn you."

"Consider us warned. Anyone else?" When no one answered, Oslovski started to dismiss the meeting. "In that case we'll-"

"Excuse me." Judy Walsh's voice was barely audible.

Oslovski motioned for her to speak.

"I just...I just wanted you all to know we're not all like that. Christians, I mean. Some of us—maybe even most of us—believe peace is God's will."

"And I must be honest in admitting," said Vahid, "that there are some very devout Muslims who feel much as Colonel Ferris does. I trust their beliefs will not reflect on me." He glanced at Trevor who shook his head.

"Of course not. I'm sorry if I was out of line. I hate bigotry. Especially my own."

At 0900 hours they were calibrated and ready. On strict orders from Caldwell, Ferris would be the first to go, Hilyard following as immediately as possible.

Magda Oslovski found that significant. It implied that Ferris was the primary operative and that Hilyard was his backup.

She, Trevor and Vance briefed them just prior to the Shift, reminding them not to stray too far from the Temporal Field Grid lest they lose track of it and become stranded.

"Of course, one of you could heft it and carry it with you," said Oslovski. "It's portable enough, but the potential for damaging it is increased if you move it. The nearer to the materialization point you can accomplish your...mission, the better. We've positioned you behind a support column, well out of sight so you should be able to just leave the Grid in place."

She glanced at her handcomp, checking her notes. "Oh, yes. You'll be invisible as long as you're within about two meters of the Grid. That's part of the Field effect. Again, if you stay close to the Grid, you can use that for cover."

Trevor Haley bit the inside of his lip and peered studiously at his own handcomp.

"If there are any questions?" Oslovski glanced from one operative to the other. Both shook their heads. "All right, then. Colonel Ferris, if you'll follow Dr. Haley, he'll set you up on the Grid. Major Hilyard, you'll watch from the observation deck with General Caldwell."

Judy Walsh was nervous. Her hands shook slightly as she prepared an infusion of tranquillizer for Colonel Ferris. She breathed a sigh of relief that he wasn't the type that liked to watch shots being administered.

She was just preparing to infuse him when he sighed and said, "I don't suppose you could give me a *pill* to adjust my electrolytes?"

She blinked. There was a smile on his lips and it unnerved her. She glanced at George Wu, who was performing the last minute adjustments on Ferris' bio-monitor.

"Sorry, Colonel," said George, "but we've got to get this stuff into your blood stream pronto. Besides, Dr. Walsh likes to watch people squirm." He grinned conspiratorially. "We have to let our M.D.s have *some* fun or they get cranky."

Judy smiled nervously and pressed the infuser against Ferris' neck. He winced, then sighed again and looked at her.

"Pretty women are so often cruel. I've never understood that."

"Yeah," said George, his eyes on Judy's blanched face. "Uh, Dr. Walsh, we'd better hurry." He jerked his head toward the O.R.

She nodded, picked up her tray and let him steer her out of the Theatre. Once in the O.R., she set the tray down with a clatter and wrapped her arms around herself.

"Thanks, George," she mumbled, her teeth chattering. "I'm sorry, but this whole thing is just-"

"Shifting," said Shiro.

Judy glanced at her, then at the monitors. The Spectral Field glistened like a shower of diamonds. Within it, Colonel Ferris faded from sight.

"Station, Dr. Walsh!" ordered Oslovski.

Judy exhaled sharply and slid into her seat. The data on the Colonel's vital signs rippled across her screen. "Heart rate spiked briefly to 150. It's falling off now.... One twenty... one hundred. Stabilizing at...95. Respiration seems normal."

Oslovski leaned toward Shiro Tsubaki. "Where is he? Or should I say, when is he?"

"Green minus seven and Shifting towards Aqua."

"On the timer, Shiro. Give the tranq a few more seconds to work, then make the spatial shift and pull him in."

Shiro nodded and glanced at her timer. "Okay, I'm going to reset coordinates in 10, 9, 8, 7, 6, 5, 4, 3, 2, 1, 0. Resetting coordinates." She punched up the new location on her keyboard.

"Cue Trevor. Reversing Field...now."

Oslovski activated her headset and hailed Trevor, who was standing by in the lower level Theatre. "Shiro's reversing now. You'll have him in about twenty seconds."

"We're ready." Trevor hefted the infuser-full of Ephkal-A and waited, his eyes on the spot where Ferris and the Temporal Field Grid were slated to appear. Beside him, Vance Keller took a deep breath and counted.

Ferris re-materialized right on schedule, head lolling slightly, hands still clutching his compact weapon. He materialized face into a curving screen that all but engulfed him. His unfocused eyes saw the sweeping upper gallery of the Word Conference Center. He wobbled his head to the right. A pillar blocked his view.

Trevor moved quickly with his infuser, then nodded to Vance.

"He's all yours," he mouthed.

Ferris was troubled. The Time Shift had disoriented him and he felt slow and muzzy. He was glad the chosen location offered so much protection. He knew he was supposedly invisible, but he found that a little hard to believe. He chucked inwardly at his own skepticism. Here he'd just traveled through time and he was balking at the idea of invisibility.

He scanned the immediate area. It was completely clear.

According to their information, this part of the auditorium had been totally sealed off and was guarded at either end. There was no way in and no way out...except *their* way.

He could hear the sound of a myriad voices rising from below and checked his watch. It was 1045. He settled his shoulder against the pillar and waited for Hilyard, the "Battle Hymn of the Republic" playing softly in his head.

Dr. Judy Walsh was ready this time, or so she thought. She had a smile all ready for Major Hilyard as she prepared his infusion of tranquillizer. Then, he turned out to be a watcher.

She gritted her teeth and smiled more broadly.

"What's in that shot?" he asked unexpectedly.

The infuser wavered an inch from his neck. Judy's face paled then flamed. "Just...uh...vitamins and...uh...a compound to-to balance your electrolytes."

"Why is that necessary?"

She tried hard not to meet his eyes, but hers kept colliding with them. "The effects of the Field cause certain...uh... stresses on the-on the nervous system. This will counteract them."

He studied her intently for a moment, eyes narrowed, then asked, "Is there anything harmful in it?"

She stared at him, half relieved, half terrified. "Oh, *no!*"

He nodded. "Get on with it, then."

Judy blinked at George—who stared back, owl-eyed—then administered the tranquillizer.

Bert Ferris swiveled as Hilyard materialized behind him. He checked his watch. It was 1050. They checked their weapons— matte black rifles with scopes that were as long as the barrels— then moved stealthily to the steel and cement railing at the edge of the gallery.

Ferris looked back toward the Grid. He couldn't see it because of the pillar, but he gauged they were within the two meter invisibility range. He raised himself up slowly and peered over the edge of the gallery. He checked his watch again—less than a minute to go. He readied the rifle.

Below, Gorbachev was introduced in several languages. The audience cheered and applauded at length. Ferris' lip curled—a standing ovation for the Devil. He rose to his knees and lifted the rifle. He sighted.

A shot reverberated through the hall and the figure in the center of the stage froze. In that second, Ferris fired twice.

The figure crumpled beneath a spray of scarlet.

In the pandemonium after, Ferris sank back and gave Hilyard the thumbs up, then he crawled back to the Grid. After a swift peek over the railing, Hilyard followed. Ferris mounted first and waited for the Field to engage. A mere twenty seconds later, he was back in his own time.

Hilyard followed, coming out of the Field to see Ferris wobbling away toward the door. His own legs felt weak and he staggered against someone. He turned his head groggily to see Dr. Walsh blinking at him. She tried to smile.

"You made it," she said. "Welcome back." She gave him another infusion. "Something for the disorientation."

He nodded and let her lead him from the room.

"I don't understand it," fumed General Caldwell, "You said expect changes. And believe you me, we did. But nothing's changed—not a *damn* thing. Killing- Fulfilling our mission seems to have accomplished nothing. I called our contacts in Washington, Berlin, Moscow—everything is the same."

At the mention of his contacts, Magda Oslovski glanced across the table at her husband, her heart suddenly feeling like an ice cube in soda water. Did the contacts check their history books?

If they did... She berated herself mentally for such a glaring oversight. They'd been so wrapped up in the technological aspects of the situation, they'd ignored the most obvious logical ones.

"General," said Vance, "we never said things *would* change radically. Just that they *could*."

Out of the corner of her eye, Oslovski saw George Wu trying to attract her attention. He gestured, first, at his video unit, then at himself. She responded with a slight nod.

"Are you *sure* you killed him?" Caldwell was asking Ferris.

"Killed or vegetized," responded the Colonel emphatically. "No one survives two direct hits to the head with an AK-70."

"Hilyard, you corroborate?"

Hilyard nodded.

"How can we know for certain?" was Caldwell's next question.

Oslovski glanced at George Wu.

"History books," he said quickly. "Newspapers. We can have the Library Computer get a sampling."

"Do it."

George keyed in his request. Within seconds, they were looking at a front page spread: GORBACHEV VICTIM OF ASSASSINATION PLOT.

"Continue," George prompted. The page changed. WORLD STUNNED BY VICIOUS ATTACK ON GORBACHEV: DOCTORS HAVE LITTLE HOPE FOR SOVIET LEADER'S SURVIVAL.

"Hold that!" said Caldwell. "Let me read the copy."

"Amplify," said George.

The page enlarged, rendering the text beneath the caption readable.

"He wasn't killed," murmured Caldwell. Then frowned. "But it amounts to the same thing—severe brain damage, kept on life support in a Moscow hospital. He's a vegetable." He shook his head. "I don't get it. How come nothing's changed?"

"What were you expecting?" asked Oslovski as dispassionately as she could.

He ignored her, his eyes devouring the story on the monitor.

"I could find some history books," offered George.

Caldwell waved a hand at him. "No, don't bother. I caught the drift from this-" He flicked his fingers at the newspaper spread. "A lot of wimpy speeches about 'our brother's sacrifice not being in vain,' a lot of fancy political rationalization about the impossibility of going back. Weak willed-" He clenched his jaw.

"Maybe the effects are further in the future," suggested Ferris.

"That's a distinct possibility," said Oslovski thoughtfully. "Time travel is a frontier. What we know of the Temporal

Spectrum suggests that changing history—altering the pattern of the Spectrum—might cause an actual branching effect. This close to the bifurcation, we might not see its full effects. Although, heaven knows, we could even have created an anomaly—a parallel history, or a bubble in history."

"And we could be in the middle of this...bubble?" asked Caldwell.

Oslovski adjusted her glasses on her nose. "As I said—a distinct possibility. Then again, maybe Someone or Something just won't let us change history...retroactively."

Caldwell just stared at her blankly. Ferris gritted his teeth. Hilyard smiled.

"How far in the future—these effects?" demanded Caldwell.

Oslovski shrugged, enjoying his frustration. "Years, decades..."

"I want to see it," he said. "I want to see the future."

"All right, but it will take several days to recalibrate our equipment for a forward Shift. We could be ready to send your operatives into the future in as little as...say...four days."

"Not them, *me! I* want to see it! Hilyard, you'll come with me. In the mean time, I'll be having my contacts check their own Library computers." He jabbed the table with his forefinger, then pivoted on his heel and left the room with Ferris right behind. Hilyard watched them leave, then rose slowly and followed, still smiling.

Oslovski shivered. "I see what you mean about him," she told Vance. "He *is* creepy." She turned to George. "I could just kiss you! Where did you get that stuff you showed us?"

George shrugged. "Over the last couple of days I got to thinking about how Caldwell and his bunch would react to this, and it occurred to me that they'd want to see solid proof that what their operatives said happened actually *did* happen. There wasn't any time to discuss it with everyone, so I had the Library

Computer play 'what-if' with the assassination and come up
with some hypothetical headlines and political analyses. Then I
just got a little creative with the output and had the computer
assign well-known authors to the commentary. There's a front
page, lead story and follow-ups for every major U.S. and
European publication. Oh, and I had the computer draft some
hypothetical history texts, too."

"What made you decide Gorbachev didn't die?" asked
Vance.

"Well, it also occurred to me that Caldwell might very likely
do his verification somewhere that fell through my cracks, as it
were. If he did, he'd see that Gorbachev died of natural causes in
a private hospital outside Moscow about eight years ago. I had
to adjust my 'history' to that. I was able to get to his private
computer through the Library of Congress system. If he connects
through that system, he'll find that Gorbachev was taken to a
private facility where he eventually died—this is history
according to George, now. I also planted the idea that there was
an attempted cover-up. That a group of Soviet higher-ups tried
to make light of the President's injuries and claimed that he had
only been superficially wounded—so that people wouldn't lapse
into despair or renewed animosity."

"Why that?" asked Vance.

"Covering our tracks, Doc. There's still every chance that
Caldwell or his contacts could look in the wrong places and
come up with a Gorbachev who was not only alive, but lively.
Even with my noodling, that could still unravel our whole
fabric. Now, if I knew who Caldwell's contacts were, what data
bank they'd be likely to access and what nodes they'd be using, I
could make sure they all got matching information.
Unfortunately, I'm not a mind reader."

"You might not have to be," said Oslovski. She held up a
small, dark gray box. "Hilyard dropped his handcomp."

George ogled. "And it's displaying a list of contacts?"

"No, it's displaying an index." She held it out to him. "You're the hacker—have at it."

It was at once logical and beyond all possible miracles to suppose that the names and system addresses of Caldwell's contacts for Project Hourglass were amongst the data stored in Hilyard's handcomp, but they were. George and Louis went into high gear. They downloaded the information to their own handcomps and immediately set about using it to shunt any requests for information originating from the contact's terminals through to the QuestLabs' Library server. Hilyard's unit was returned to him post haste.

"But what if somebody just goes to a library terminal and requests information about Gorbachev's assassination?" asked Shiro.

George allowed himself a self-congratulatory grin. "I planted something in the nature of a glorified IF-THEN statement in the Library of Congress system. IF anyone requests information on the assassination attempt, THEN they get routed to our ersatz fact file. Since all libraries network to that system-" He shrugged.

"George, you're a marvel," Oslovski told him.

He blushed faintly at the praise. "Well, I couldn't cover *all* our tracks, but I did what I could. It's just..." He made a wry face.

"What?"

"Well, it seems too much of a fluke, I guess. Here we find ourselves in a position where we could use certain information and—*bingo!*—it falls onto our conference room floor."

"Miracles do happen," observed Vance.

George tilted his head. "I don't doubt it. But there's something a little odd about this miracle. For two weeks,

Hilyard's been taking notes on that handcomp. I didn't find a trace of them."

"Maybe it was encrypted," suggested Shiro.

"Even encrypted information takes up room in memory, my dear. The only data left in that unit, with the exception of the information we needed, was general stuff. There wasn't even a letter to mom."

Oslovski stiffened. "You're suggesting we've been set up."

George shrugged. "The nodes I accessed were operative and the addresses and passwords were real. Maybe I'm just being paranoid."

"And maybe not." Oslovski frowned thoughtfully. "Let's keep a close eye on Major Hilyard."

"What do we do if he does anything suspicious?" asked Louis.

Oslovski grimaced. "I haven't the foggiest idea. But we don't have any time to worry about it. We've got to get ready for Phase Two of Operation Little Big Horn. First order of business is helping General Caldwell decide where to go."

"It has to be someplace where I can ascertain military activity," said Caldwell. "In other words, a military installation."

"A...War Room, perhaps?" suggested Oslovski.

"You mean a Tactical Center," corrected Ferris. "We haven't called them War Rooms for years."

A rose by any other name, thought Oslovski. Aloud, she said, "Tactical Center, then. Would that be appropriate?"

Hilyard looked up from fiddling with his handcomp. "Begging your pardon, sir, but if a Tactical Center was in operation in the future, wouldn't that indicate something about the health of the military establishment?"

Caldwell nodded slowly. "Makes sense. All right. Send us to Offutt. If there's any activity at all, it'll be there."

Four days later they were ready for the Shift, their target, the year 2075, Offutt Air Force Base, Bellevue, Nebraska. Caldwell didn't ask what was in his shot, but accepted the electrolyte story at face value. This time it was closer to the truth. Instead of a powerful tranquillizer, the infusions contained only a mild neural damper and a dose of Ephkal-A.

Hilyard went onto the Grid first—a precautionary measure, Cladwell insisted. Caldwell himself was plainly nervous as he followed; only Hilyard's extreme calm persuaded him he was not going to merely evaporate into the shimmering void.

He re-materialized in semi-darkness and stiffened in apprehension. The wave of anxiety passed at the pressure of Hilyard's fingers on his arm.

They were standing on a narrow catwalk. What light there was in the vaulted room seemed to be coming from below. Figures moving about the room cast eerie, elongated shadows onto the curving ceiling. Caldwell and Hilyard moved in unison to the steel railing at the edge of the carpeted walk, Caldwell looking back to make certain the move left them inside the invisibility range.

Below and beneath was a large horseshoe-shaped chamber bathed in mellow gold light and populated by uniformed soldiers.

Computer generated maps alternated with video screens along the curving walls, while in the heart of the room were several computer stations. Directly at center was an odd piece of equipment that looked like a rectangular stalactite/stalagmite formation rendered in some sort of anodized, black metal.

Between the top and bottom of the unit, hung a shimmering curtain of colored light. Next to that mystery stood a figure with what appeared to be an admiral's insignia on its shoulders.

Caldwell frowned. The uniform was an unfamiliar silvery-blue unrecognizable as being from any branch of the military. The rank suggested Navy, but... He scanned the other figures.

Several, apparently officers, also wore the silver-blue; others wore a vivid shade between royal blue and midnight. From his high vantage point, he saw nothing of their faces; only the tops of heads covered with unfamiliar caps.

Before he could solve the puzzle, one of the blue-suited soldiers seated at a computer terminal turned and said, "Commander, we're receiving new data on the Northern Front. It looks like a much bigger push than we anticipated."

"On screen, Tech Newman."

Caldwell stiffened. It was a woman's voice. He'd never objected to women entering the service—but in a War Room? Still, that the War Room was here at all was- One of the wall maps came suddenly to life. Caldwell's eyes flew to it and ogled.

Across a green representation of the United States and Canada, swept a coruscating swathe of gold, orange and red, its southern edge pressing as far south as Montana. On the east, it reached greedy fingers of glowing hues toward the Great Lakes.

"My God," Caldwell breathed awfully.

Hilyard glanced at him and tapped his ear.

The General barely noticed him. What nation could field such a massive front, let alone push it all the way into the northern states? He licked his lips, wondering what they were fighting it with.

"Have all the warnings gone out?" the Admiral asked.

"Yes, sir. Forty-eight hours before the leading edge. Status reports are already coming in; everybody's battening down for the duration."

The Admiral nodded. "When will the leading edge reach Yosemite?"

The technician plied his keyboard for an instant, then consulted his monitor. "Approximately twenty-four hours, sir. They've been advised."

Twenty-four hours? Caldwell thought. *What army could move that fast?* Maybe it was a weapon of some sort. Nuclear? No, too widespread. Chemical? Biological? How could they remain so calm in the face of such vast destruction—as if it was everyday fare. This looked like...Armaggedon.

"Thank you, Newman," the Admiral was saying. "Mr. Mendez?"

"Yes, sir." Another technician glanced up from her console.

"Are you in communication with Yosemite Base?"

"Yes, sir."

"What is their status?"

"Heavily embattled, sir," answered the slightly accented voice. "Commander Li says the situation is barely under control."

"Visual reference," ordered the Admiral.

Next to the huge map, a video panel pulsed on. Nothing showed upon it but billowing smoke and flames. So faintly he wasn't certain he'd really seen them, Caldwell's eyes caught the movement of bodies plummeting through the fog-thick smoke. The observing camera eye panned. He saw uniformed soldiers scrambling through the blazing brush, flames patting at their passing legs like playful but deadly kittens.

Below, the Admiral made a clicking noise and said, "Visual off. Advise Commander Li that we will send reinforcements immediately. Then contact Colonel Darnell and have her dispatch a company of men and aerial support units. I believe the closest air squadrons are aboard the UNS Crazy Horse. Have the air support sent in from there."

"Yes, *sir*."

"When you've completed that, put me in touch with General Dreyfus in Juneau."

The Admiral turned as a second officer approached her carrying what appeared to be a handcomp. He made what Caldwell felt was a half-ass salute.

"So, Mr. Krasnik," said the Admiral, not bothering to return the gesture. "What new hot spots do you have for me today?"

"Actually, sir, it looks very much as if we're going to have an unusual situation in Florida. Cuba Station has already begun tracking."

The Admiral jerked a thumb at the odd machine to her right. "Show and tell, Mr. Krasnik," she said.

"I have General Dreyfus, Admiral," announced Technician Mendez.

The Admiral signaled Krasnik to go ahead. "On audio."

"Admiral Halleck, sir. Good to hear from you," said a disembodied voice.

"I noticed you were out from under. What's your status, Vinnie?"

"Pretty bad. We've been hemmed in for the better part of four days. Everything was grounded. Today...it's terrible. The sheer number of corpses, sir—it's devastating. The bio-med team has been doing its best, but we-we've had to put so many of them down."

Caldwell's mind froze and threatened to recoil. What in the name of all things holy had they come to in the last fifty years— putting the injured down? His lip curled in disgust. He supposed they called it euthanasia or some such nonsense. Murder—that's what he called it. Sheer brutal laziness. He glanced again at the map. Or had the enemy weaponry become so hideous-?

Beside Caldwell, Hilyard frowned thoughtfully, almost unconsciously resting his elbows on the catwalk's padded guardrail.

General Dreyfus finished his report, noting that he could use something larger than his present complement of destroyer, cruiser and corvette to help "mop up."

"More men would be appreciated too, Admiral. We've got our hands more than full disposing of the bodies. It's gonna take one helluva pit to bury all of them."

Caldwell almost puked. He gripped the guardrail, oblivious to Hilyard's bemused observation. It *couldn't* be that bad. It could never be so bad that you had to-

Officer Krasnik turned from his machine and whispered something in Admiral Halleck's ear.

"My tactical officer informs me that you have about 5 days to get your situation in hand. You're evidently going to be hit fairly hard from the northwest again."

Dreyfus swore.

"Sorry, Vin. We'll get your reinforcements to you on the double. The battleship Walesa is in Anadyr. I'll have her deployed to your waters. How many men do you need?"

"I could use a battalion," said Dreyfus.

Halleck snorted. "Take two, they're small."

"I wasn't joking."

"I didn't think you were... Casualties were that bad?"

"Thousands upon thousands, Admiral. Worst I've seen in a situation like this. The Apah Param couldn't have struck at a worse time of year. Hell, it's hard to believe one damn boat could do so much damage!"

One boat! *One!* Caldwell swallowed and found his throat too dry for the activity. And what the hell was an Apah Param? He had the sudden horrible thought that perhaps the Enemy wasn't even human.

"They will insist on year-round activity," said Halleck.

"*We've* certainly advised them against their bad weather jaunts, but who can reason with them? It'd take another Gorbi, God bless him."

Caldwell's mouth popped open. *Gorbi?*

"Well, do your best, Vinnie," urged the Admiral. "Of course, you always do. Then, when this is all over, why don't you take a nice vacation somewhere sunny and warm?"

"Oh, sure. So I can come back and do it all over again next year!"

"Well, you could transfer to Yosemite in the spring. We'll be sending in a couple of battalions to rebuild."

"Yeah," sighed Dreyfus. "I *like* trees."

Caldwell shook his head. The conversation was getting hard to follow. His assumptions about the situation shifted beneath him like dune sand as he tried to make sense out of it.

Admiral Halleck signed off, then and turned her attention to Krasnik and his machine. "Show and tell time, Mr. Krasnik," she said.

In response, the officer touched an instrument panel on one side of the machine's black base. The column of muted light became a colorful multi-leveled sea of three-dimensional images, flowing in stately waves—advancing, retreating.

They reminded Hilyard of the "plasma clouds" he used to generate as a kid, using fractal equations on the family computer.

Krasnik tapped and keyed and adjusted and the images settled into patterns that almost made sense. Vibrant green formed hills and vales below wisps and billows of subtly changing hues.

Hilyard frowned, bemused, then felt the patterns click into sudden clarity. His mouth twitched as he turned his eyes to the ogling Caldwell.

"And who have we here?" asked the Admiral, nodding at the 3D display.

"This is Mariella." Krasnik indicated a violently eddying orange area high in one corner. "And this,"—he indicated the rolling greens— "is the coastal area we're afraid will be hardest hit when she rolls ashore."

Halleck frowned. "Poor Cuba. That's twice in three years. What's the prognosis for Florida?"

"Not so good, if this continues to gain velocity. This mass here,"—he gestured with a sweeping, circular motion—"is strengthening rapidly. We may be looking at a full-fledged blow before tomorrow morning."

Caldwell's ogle changed to a stunned scowl.

"What're the chances of seeding her to force the precipitation?"

Krasnik shrugged. "Cuba's on it. Along with a wing of storm bombers from Mexico. We can but pray and send troops to help Florida batten down."

Admiral Halleck nodded. "Too bad we can't get Mariella to dump her load on Yosemite. Coax Nature to put out her own fires. Wouldn't that be poetic justice?"

"We're working on it," said Krasnik soberly.

Caldwell's fists tightened on the catwalk rail. Confusion and anger swept up from his gut in a hot spray, warring with something blasphemously like relief.

"I've seen enough," he whispered and went to the Grid.

"What the hell was that place? Where the hell did they send us?" Caldwell turned on Hilyard the moment he stepped off the Grid. "It sure as hell wasn't a War Room!"

Hilyard blinked at him, feeling only slightly disoriented. "No sir, of course not. It was a Tactical Center."

"That was no Tactical Center like *I've* ever seen, Major."

"No sir. I don't imagine anyone else has ever seen one like it either."

"And that-and that *machine*—some sort of-of-"

"It was an atmospheric model, sir."

"A what?"

"An atmospheric model. A three dimensional projection of-"

"Yeah, yeah- Doctor!" Caldwell launched himself at Oslovski as she stepped into the room. "Where did you send me? What was that place?"

Oslovski glanced from Caldwell to Hilyard. "We sent you to a Tactical Center, just as you requested." She spread her hands in a gesture of bemusement. "I can't tell you more than that. You were there just now, I wasn't."

Caldwell swung back to Hilyard. "Major, what do you make of it? What was that all about?"

"I'd say sir," said Hilyard, his voice soft and almost patient, "that we were sent to a military Tactical Center. I'd also say that they seemed to be fighting battles on several fronts."

"Battles? What *battles?* They weren't fighting-"

"They were fighting all right, sir," said Hilyard imperturbably. "The enemy just wasn't...people."

"What did you see?" asked Oslovski.

"A farce!" erupted Caldwell.

Hilyard ignored him. "Evidently in the future, we'll be battling forest fires and hurricanes and oil spills...or so it seems." He shrugged. "Maybe reforestation will replace demolition as a specialty—an environmental defense specialty."

"That's absurd!" snarled Caldwell. "Fighting men *fight*, dammit. They don't damn garden!"

"And what's wrong with killing forest fires instead of people?" asked Oslovski. "Or planting trees instead of land mines? Wouldn't you rather be the heroes of a constructive process instead of the villains of a destructive one?"

"Villains?"

Oslovski looked him in the eye. "Most of us don't like war, General. We hate it. We're not likely to thank anyone who perpetuates it when peace is within reach. I know you don't understand that. Nor will you likely understand that most of us look forward to a day when the military is obsolete. Well, it looks like that day isn't going to come. It looks like the future needs the military, after all—needs it for construction instead of destruction. I'd think you'd be happy about that."

Caldwell stood glaring darkly at the floor.

"Looks like our interference in history didn't accomplish anything after all," observed Hilyard. "Maybe even made Gorbachev more of a hero than he already seemed to be."

"Hell," muttered Caldwell. "What'm I supposed to tell the Chiefs?" He started toward the door. It scooted obediently out of his way.

Oslovski shrugged and watched him pass. "You could find another historical crux and try again."

"We don't have the funds. Dammit, we were so sure that was the right time and place—the right enemy."

"Sometimes it's hard to know who the enemy really is," observed Oslovski. "Or if there's even an enemy at all."

He threw her a scathing glance and passed through into the hall. She found herself eye to eye with Major Hilyard.

"We have met the Enemy and he is us?" he murmured, quirking an eyebrow.

She smothered her reaction and followed the two men into the corridor, steering them toward the Conference Room. The rest of the Team was already there, along with Colonel Ferris, but Caldwell ignored them, dropping into a chair at the far end of the table.

Hilyard seated himself next door and sat back in his chair, watching Oslovski make her way to the head of the room.

"We have evidently failed in our mission," said Caldwell. He glanced at Ferris' suddenly pale, tense face. "The military of the *future*,"—he said the word as if it was odious—"is apparently more of an environmental defense mechanism than a national security force."

"Those people were defending more than the environment, sir," said Hilyard quietly. "They were helping the people of this country defend themselves against natural disaster. They were helping devastated areas rebuild." He smiled. "I'll bet they see a lot more ticker-tape parades than we do."

Caldwell gritted his teeth. There was that unholy feeling of relief again, of something stronger. "What do we do, then? Slink on home with our tails between our legs and admit all the money we've spent went down the rat hole?"

"We could get a head start on the future," suggested Hilyard. "It looked pretty interesting to me, sir."

Caldwell glanced at him, pinning his lower lip between thumb and forefinger. "I suppose we could float some ideas around the Hill...before they sack all of us."

"May I make a suggestion?" asked Oslovski.

Caldwell nodded.

"First, let us put history back the way it was."

"How can you do that?" asked Ferris.

"By sending you back to the time of the incident and having you *not* shoot Gorbachev."

Ferris shook his head. "But then, we'd be there twice."

"Not possible," said Shiro. "If we got you there a millisecond before your initial materialization, the pattern of the first event will adjust itself to the second. Think of time as light waves. The first temporal event—your first visit—set up a waveform, if you will. If the second temporal event—the second visit—sets up its waveform just prior to the first one, it will cancel it out, engulf it, re-form it."

"Then what?" asked Caldwell.

"Well, to paraphrase Saint Francis of Assisi," said Oslovski. "Have the courage to change what you can, the serenity to accept what you cannot change and the wisdom to know the difference. Accept peace. Get used to it, and to the idea that you *do* have a peacetime role that's more than just training for the next war—the war that won't come. We can help you do that. Dr. Keller could help you set up a program to ease you into that peacetime role. The future doesn't have to be miserable just because you have no enemies." She nearly crossed her eyes at the sheer absurdity of the thought. "Judging from Major Hilyard's description of the future, I'd say you'll have lots to do...and lots of support in doing it."

Caldwell chewed his lip and thought. Then he glanced at Hilyard. "What do you think, Major?"

"I think it's worth a shot...sir."

"Ferris?"

"I-I can't say, sir. I...I don't know. This peace...it isn't real. It *can't* be."

"Only time will tell," observed Oslovski. "You know, back in the early 20th century a gentleman named Abbas Effendi said, 'Why not try peace for a while? If we find war is better, it will not be difficult to fight again.'" She spread her hands toward Caldwell, pushing the ball into his court.

"You'd be willing to set up counseling clinics, uh, reorientation, or whatever?" he asked.

"Whatever it takes," said Oslovski.

"Damn!" Caldwell slapped the table with the flat of his hand, making everyone jump. He pointed a finger at Oslovski.

"You've got my back to the wall, doctor. I've got no choice and you know it. It's either put up, or shut up and go back empty handed. I'll get the Chiefs up here. You can start your psycho-stuff on them while I package a few ideas and try to sell them on the Hill. Shouldn't have too much trouble with the environmental lobby, I suppose. Right now, I've got to lie down. I've got a hell of a headache."

He pushed himself away from the table, rose and left, Ferris trailing behind him like a woebegone pet.

Hilyard sat where he was and smiled at the tabletop. The tension in the room mounted by the second. Finally, he got up and glanced down the table at Oslovski. "I don't know how you did it," he said. "And I'm not sure I want to know. There's a part of me that wants to blow the whistle on you, even though I couldn't prove a damn thing...at least, not without implicating myself in certain matters. But there's another part of me that knows what you did was right...for everybody concerned."

He gave the circle of stunned faces a long, lingering look, then nodded and moved to the door, stopping just short of the pressure pad. He turned back. "One thing I've got to know: When did you play out that little scene Caldwell and I just saw?"

Oslovski cleared her suddenly dry throat. "Two days ago in the theatre downstairs."

He nodded, smiling. "Thank you," he said. The door slipped open to let him out, then closed silently behind him.

Less than a month later, the Joint Chiefs of Staff made a ground breaking proposal to Congress that instead of mothballing fleets, bases and men, the government embark on a military overhaul, converting whatever was convertible to peace time use.

Battleships could fight oil slicks; tanks could fight fires; troops could learn to build shelters for hurricane victims, shore up leaking levees and plant forests.

The EPA loved it, GreenPeace was ecstatic, the Red Cross was more than grateful for the offer of troops and equipment to aid in their relief efforts. The Chiefs spoke of global applications and the United Nations applauded and handed them a list of ideas as long as the Great Wall of China.

"I would love to take credit for all this," said Vance Keller, scanning the latest edition of a national news magazine, "but to tell you the truth, the counseling program hasn't been as much of a factor in the conversion process as we expected. Oh, there are the inevitable individuals who are having trouble accepting the sudden shift in orientation-"

"Ferris?" Magda glanced over the top of her coffee cup.

Vance puckered. "Actually he's doing okay. He's finding a great deal of comfort in playing Gamaliel."

Magda raised her eyebrows questioningly.

"'If this work be of men, it will come to naught,'" he quoted. "He's been studying his scriptures a lot. He's come up with some interesting alternatives to the party line interpretations of prophecy." He grinned. "Vahid is overjoyed—Ferris has been asking all sorts of questions about Muhammad and Islamic prophecy... Anyway, most of the G.I.s we've interviewed seem to be happy to be beating their swords into ploughshares. Practicing for war takes a lot out of a person. If you want my honest opinion, I'd say General Caldwell and his bunch were a lot less keen on being heroes than they imagined they were."

"Oh, but they *are* heroes." Magda fielded a folded page of flimsy newspaper nylon. A half-page color picture of a glowing General Caldwell with his young aide, Lieutenant Colonel John Hilyard, smiled up from the glossy sheet under a banner headline announcing Project Ploughshare. "At least, I'm pretty sure Saint Francis would have said so."

Any Mother's Son

A story of science fiction

Any Mother's Son was originally published in the May 2000 issue of *Analog Science Fiction* and is another in my time travel series. Chronologically, it takes place some years after HEROES and continues the dialogue about the effects of present actions on future events. As one character notes, "You can only edit the present." The story also delves into the question of how much responsibility one soul has for another.

> *Lay not on any soul a load which ye would not wish to be laid upon you, and desire not for any one the things ye would not desire for yourselves. This is My best counsel unto you, did ye but observe it.*
>
> > *Gleanings from the*
> > *Writings of Bahá'u'lláh,*
> > p. 128

Dr. Sharon Glen could set her watch to her moods. From the time she woke until noon she was eager; from lunch to dinner she was determined; from dinner to bedtime she was ambivalent. But once she had poked her head into Alec's room one last time, turned off the lights and gotten into bed herself, the ambivalence gave way to anxiety and guilt.

The anxiety was for the technology in which her career lived and moved and had being. The guilt was for Alec. If the technology failed, Alec would be alone in the world except for his grandmother, whose condition at times made her unaware she even had a grandson.

It was the shock of losing Robert that had derailed Helen Glen's fragile mental train. Her son had been the center of her universe, and when he had one day walked into the future and failed to return, Helen Glen had suffered a sudden and swift descent into Alzheimer's.

Sharon could understand that. Her own universe these days revolved very much around Alec. He was their legacy—hers and Robert's—the light of her life, the reason she put one foot in front of the other every day.

Sharon knew a certain guilty relief that her mother-in-law could have no idea what her work entailed. The Helen that had been would have told Sharon in no uncertain terms what she thought of a mother who, having lost her husband to his work in a very literal sense, was preparing to put herself at the same risk. But in those long moments of introspection between lying down and sleeping, Sharon recited Helen's lines for her: You know what could happen to you. What *are* you thinking of if not Alec?

She did know what could happen. Only too well. Ten years —he had only Shifted forward ten years—a simple mission financed by the National Weather Service. He would assess the effects on climate of several large-scale Midwestern reforestation projects. He would search electronic archives, sample NWS data. Simple. But something had gone wrong—a power drop off, the technicians called it. It had caused the Temporal Grid to pull her husband into the future where it collapsed, killing him.

That had been two years ago. Now there were more safeguards, double and triple and quadruple checks and redundancies and backup systems. Spectral Shift technology was perceived as essentially stable and would continue to be so until another anomaly surfaced and another tripper was lost.

Sharon Glen was on countdown to her first future-trip. As a QuestLabs historian, she'd gone into the past a number of times. It had been fascinating, exhilarating, sometimes unexpected. But the future—that was different. Where the past was at least forensically known, the future was *terra incognita.* It was also where Robert had died.

Now, two days before her shift, she found herself fighting the sense that she was tying up loose ends. She spent as much time as possible with Alec. They had launched model rockets, played endless board and card games, solved computer mysteries, looked at family albums. And now, she thought of Helen.

"I'd like to visit Gramma today," she told Alec at breakfast. It was Saturday and they had tentatively planned a trip to the beach with a friend. "We can drop by on our way to pick up Trevor."

"Do I have to go in?" Alec's eyes were eloquent with reluctance.

"No, you don't *have* to go in, honey, but it would be nice for Gramma if you would."

"She doesn't know who I am half the time, mom. How can it be nice for her to get visited by people she doesn't even know? Besides, I hate that place. It's creepy."

"Alec, you've never been inside. How do you know it's creepy?"

It was true that in the two years Helen Glen had been in the high-tech high-care home, Sharon had never gotten Alec further than the manicured lawn. It was also true that Gramma hadn't known him; worse, she had taken him for Robert. It had been a painful visit for everyone but Helen, who, for a brief span of hours, had been transported to her own quarter of heaven. Before the elder-care facility, she had had her own home—a place from which holidays seemed to originate and which Alec had begged to visit.

Sharon was doing the begging now. "Come on, hon. She might have a good day."

Alec shook his head emphatically, poking at his yogurt with the tip of his spoon.

"Please?"

Alec sighed as only a severely put-upon eleven-year-old can. "Mom, please don't make me go there."

She relented, of course. She visited Helen alone. It had not been a good day, after all. Helen had not known her, and when she had tried to engage her mother-in-law in news of Alec's exploits on the baseball diamond, Helen had vanished into a reality in which Robert—her precious only son—was a championship pitcher in the Bear River Little League. Sharon had salvaged what she could, absorbing facts about Robert she hadn't known, wondering how veiled they were by time and neural degradation.

Sunday, she and Alec went to their local Bahá'í Center for devotions, had pizza for lunch, played miniature golf. Sharon tried again to get Alec to visit his grandmother. He would not.

"Old people are creepy when they're like that," he said and she barely resisted the impulse to slap him.

"They can't help the way they are," she told him and did not try to keep the anger out of her voice.

He was instantly ashamed. "I know. It's just... scary." He was silent for a few minutes, then asked, "Will you get like that?"

"I'm not *that* old."

"I mean, like, when I'm grown up."

"Folks on my side of the family have always been sharp as a tack till the day they die," she reassured him. "My mom told me once that her great uncle Joseph died in the middle of a sentence in which he was expounding a theory of molecular biology." She smiled, but Alec merely nodded and stared out the car window.

All in all, he made it harder by the day for her to be a field historian—to accept missions like the one she was prepping for. She was torn. Maybe it was something she needed to take to one of the QuestLabs counselors. She knew Alec was her first responsibility; she merely had to find that elusive balance between self and selfishness.

In the end, she left it with Alec. "Do you want me to cancel my mission?" she asked him.

His brow furrowed. "Won't you get in trouble?"

"I might." Especially since QuestLabs was sponsoring the Shift on its own dime for a study in culture and ethnology in future America. It would be more than an inconvenience to have to replace the senior historian on the project. And how many times had she assured them that she really wanted this type of assignment? She realized, belatedly, that this question should have been asked some time ago.

"You don't have to do that," Alec said, still looking a bit bemused. "I'll be okay at Aunt Kathi's house. It's not like I'll be there for a long time."

True enough. A successful Temporal Shift literally took no time at all; if the retrieval was successful. Any time-lag was purely for the benefit of the staff and machinery. You seemed to return only minutes after you left, regardless of whether you had spent hours or days at your post. Preparation and debriefings usually took longer than the Shift itself. Altogether, Alec would be with Kathi only a day and a half. In subjective time, Sharon would be gone for several hours.

Sharon found wry irony in that. Human beings had been looking for ways to make extra time for centuries. This was as close as they had come.

There were unsuccessful Shifts, of course. Like Robert's.
That was the way it was with Temporal Shift Technology. Either
you came back on schedule, or you didn't come back at all.

"Huh?" Sharon glanced up into her partner's face.

"I said, 'Are you ready for this?'" Trevor Haley repeated.
"But I think you may have just answered the question. What's
getting to you?"

"Who says anything is getting to me? I was looking at our
itinerary."

"Sharon, you've been reading the same page for the past ten
minutes. Either coordinates and time stamps have become a
consuming passion for you or you're zoning. Are you nervous?"

"Now that you mention it, yes, I am nervous. This is my first
future-trip, after all."

"I know." Trevor sat down on the edge of the table where he
and Sharon were assembling their gear, and leaned toward her.
"Is it...is it because of Robert?"

Sharon wanted to deny it outright, but couldn't. She
murmured something about feeling more at home in the late 20th
Century, then caught the expression on his face. She put her
hand over his. "It's okay, Trev. You can talk about it without
throwing me into a deep pit of despair. And no, it's not because
of Robert—not directly, anyway."

"So, there is something."

He knew her too well. "It's just...Alec. I wonder sometimes if
I ought to give up field work—well, at least temporal field work
—until he's an adult."

"It's never easy to lose a parent," said Trevor. He'd lost his
seventy-year-old mother the year before to a new strain of

influenza. "Besides, I doubt you could give up field work. You thrive on it."

"I could if I had to."

Was she whistling in the dark or did she really mean that? Temporal field work was heady stuff. Hands-on history. It made you feel like Indiana Jones and James Burke all rolled into one and blurred the distinction between the historian, the anthropologist and the archaeologist. It made you feel alive, aware, vital. All things, Sharon realized in a sudden epiphany, that had been all but snuffed out when Robert failed to return from a 'routine mission.' Was she replacing that relationship with temporal euphoria? More importantly, was she showering attention on her work at Alec's expense or drawing emotional sustenance from it that mothering him should provide?

She didn't think she was doing that; she made it a point, when she was with Alec to really be *with* Alec.

"You're a great mom, Sharon," Trevor said. "The best. And I happen to know Alec thinks so, too."

"Mind reading, Trev?" she chuckled. "You're just full of unexpected talents."

"I've just known you a long time."

True, she admitted as she gathered her goods into a shoulder bag, the design of which had been 'sniffed' from the window of a sporting goods store 50 years in the future. She had known Dr. Trevor Haley since her first days on staff at QuestLabs in '78 as a junior associate. She was fresh from obtaining her Masters in History and her doctoral thesis was a biography of Magda Oslovski, the primary mind and driving force behind Spectral Shift Technology.

Sharon and Trevor had become instant pals. Robert joined QuestLabs a year later and her reaction to him instantaneous and profound. Fortunately, her feelings were reciprocated; they had married and Alec had been born a year later.

She had most often partnered with Trevor on her Shifts.
Dr. Oslovski, still QuestLabs grand-dame, had a standing rule
about allowing married couples with children Shift as a team. It
was simply not done. Sharon had thought the rule a nuisance at
first; now she could only applaud its wisdom.

At 1300 hours, she and Trevor were Shift-ready. Their
electrolytes and hydration levels were checked, their seratonin
levels elevated against post-shift depression. They were dressed
in casual clothes carefully selected from fashions sniffed at their
Shift point. Jeans and shirts—styles that had altered little for the
better part of two centuries. Their target was Washington, D.C.
50 years in the future, their purposes mixed.

This was a "peek" as opposed to a "poke"—both terms
borrowed from computer technology to indicate the scope of a
mission. A peek was the minimal mission—no planned contact
with future residents, no touching. It was little more than a
manned sniff, which was done by a Totem, or Totable
Environmental Monitor—an instrument package designed to
gather images, sounds and environmental data on the Shift
target. Sniffs, peeks, and pokes usually were run in that order,
and future-pokes—which involved interacting with people in
the future—were relatively rare. There had been only a handful
that Sharon knew of in the 25-year history of QuestLabs.

Any Shift was, brief or no, an expensive proposition, so
Sharon and Trevor would be performing a number of tasks for
QuestLabs, for Stanford University and for the North American
Parliament. It was a lot, Sharon mused, standing in place on the
Temporal Grid, like being a member of one of the early space
shuttle missions—performing a plethora of experiments in order
to maximize the cost-effectiveness of the trip. Now scientists
traveled in time and college students used the stock HTO/L
shuttles regularly.

"Ready?" The question came from Shiro Tsubaki-Manyfeather, seated at the console from which she would monitor their journey. Beside her, fellow Lab Rat George Wu got baselines on their vital signs.

They nodded, gave a thumbs-up and waited while the Temporal Grid powered up. A dancing veil of light motes shimmered in an aura around the time travelers. The last thing Sharon Glen heard in 2091 was the sound of Shiro's soft voice counting down.

"Shifting...yellow plus one...orange...plus one... red..."

The delicious tingle of the Shift cascaded down Sharon's back, colors chased vividly before her eyes—yellow, orange, red. Her heart rate climbed. All delightfully normal. Only the colors were different; the past was cool, its spectrum contained blues and violets; the future was ablaze.

They shifted in the space of perceived minutes, forward 50 years to a set of coordinates ascertained by Totem to be clear of obstacles or traffic and close to their goal—the Library of Congress. The arrival coordinates were in the basement of a parking structure one block from the Library.

It could not have been more perfect. A cloak generated by the Grid afforded them invisibility over and area of four square yards. In practical terms, it allowed Sharon and Trevor to stroll into sight of any bystanders as if they'd just come up on a nearby elevator. Blending in completely with the contemporaries, they were just another pair of students with backpacks and laundry lists of look-ups.

Sharon quickly found that the hardest piece of Shift policy to obey completely was the injunction to study the contemporaries without appearing to study them. It was hard not to gawk at things that had changed subtly or not so subtly: clothing, environment, architecture, people. Language was expectedly and subtlety different, and snatches of conversation contained colloquialisms that were familiar, but in unfamiliar contexts.

"That's so tab," said a middle-aged businessman to his female cohort as they moved purposefully down the sidewalk.

To which she replied, "Well, Erin is such a straight-jacket anyway, what other kind of investment could he make?"

"He could take a chance once in a while."

"Erin? Take a chance? Like you said, he's too tab."

All of which showed the wisdom of Rule #14 in what the Lab Rats affectionately called *Time Travel for Dummies:* Don't use slang.

Once inside the Library's main sanctuary, Sharon and Trevor checked their wrist units for time and instructions. Sharon's "specialty," such as it was, was the gathering of health and welfare data. She wasn't sure exactly how it had happened, but somehow a report on personal hygiene and health she'd generated from a poke into Regency London had earned her a solid reputation as a keen sorter of pertinent health data.

"Okay," she said, "I think you've got the lion's share of work to do. Let me know if you need a hand."

"You bet. Nobody ever accused me of taking on more work than I have to. I'm sure you'll be done long before I am."

They parted, Sharon wafting on a wave of incredulity. No matter how many times she shifted, she was always overcome at moments such as these, by the sheer paradox of it all. This was work, this traveling through the waves of time, and she was struck by the sheer banality of the conversation she and Trevor had just had. Like a couple of students setting out to prepare for oral exams. In that anomalous context, the Library of Congress was a perfect symbol of Sharon's calling. Aged stone and antique appointments contrasted with the latest in information retrieval technology.

Sharon was gratified that the technology was still recognizable. She located a VR bay, seated herself in its wraparound seat and looked for a helm and gloves. There were neither. There were only a pair of flat screens about one foot on a side, that lay at approximately a 120 degree angle to each other. It took ten minutes, but with the help of some written instructions and careful surveillance of her nearest neighbors, she discovered that the canted screen displayed two-dimensional data and the horizontal screen displayed 3D holograms and served as a control panel.

She proceeded carefully through her checklist, delving into health and census records, checking birth rates, noting how natural disasters had affected the general health of the continent. That collection effort completed, she moved on to the brave new world of medicine. It was bemusing, she realized, as her task became more yawn-inducing, that a future-trip, for all its novelty and the terrifying sense of awareness it provoked, was not nearly as exciting as a trip to a less obscure past.

Alec would be in his early sixties now, she realized, and wondered what kind of man he had become. Moved by something that was more than curiosity, she toyed with the idea of entering his name into the search engine, but her conscience bleated. She stuck to her agenda.

She was in a Who's-Who of medicine, when she found herself staring at the name Alec Glen. She hesitated momentarily, for the link was not strictly within her parameters, but in the end she followed the thread. What came up was beyond a proud mother's dreams, for the name Alec Glen had both medical and political connections. Following her own inclination, Sharon pointed to the medical connection.

He would become a doctor and a researcher in the field of genetics. He would contribute to a cure for Hodgkin's disease, would invent a supplement to stave off osteoporosis, would write a seminal paper on age-related dementia.

She was reveling in the glow of these discoveries when her watch reminded her that time was wasting. She returned swiftly to her legitimate research, downloading a sampling of medical research, trends, breakthroughs and new problems. She added to the general mix her own son's contributions, wishing that Robert could be there to share her pride.

Sharon was still downloading when Trevor came to let her know he had finished his own research. She stifled a twinge of guilt that her digression might have cost her more legitimate research some time and tried not to look at Trev's face, lest it prompt him to ask her what was taking so long.

It was as she completed a final download of information to her recorder that she dared to glance up and caught the flicker of something like worry in Trevor's eyes. He wasn't looking at her, though, just staring up through the tall front windows where a single wisp of cloud could be seen flung across the visible patches of sky—an abstract painting on three tall canvases.

She poked her head out of the pod-chair. "What's wrong," she asked, forgetting Rule #14, "the pol-scene got you jinky?"

"Ah...yeah. Yeah, you could say that. Hey, it's politics." He checked the time. "You about ready?"

"Just." She logged off, slipped her computer back into her bag and could not resist the motherly temptation to glow. "I came across something really interesting while I was searching. Alec's name."

Trevor's surprise was evident. "Really? You did? In what context?"

"As a noted researcher in genetics. He contributed to a cure for Hodgkin's and I gather, to a greater understanding of aging."

"Wow," Trevor said. "That's quite a coincidence." He took her elbow and steered her toward the door. "Time's a wasting."

"Not considering where I was peeking."

"I just mean... I didn't mean to imply you were doing a personal peek. I just meant...Alec going into medicine."

"Science. He's been around science all his life. Some of our best friends are doctors and researchers. Besides, lately it seems as if medical research of one sort or another is all I do. It's just kind of good to know... I guess I've been a little worried."

"I could tell."

She stopped just outside the library's main doors and smiled up at him. "Well, aren't you impressed?"

"Of course. I guess it shouldn't surprise me all that much. Alec's a bright child—the child of bright parents."

"I don't suppose you came across him in your virtual travels," Sharon asked.

"What?" Trevor checked the time again and started down the steps. "Why do you ask? I was pursuing a completely different line of research."

Sharon shrugged, attempting nonchalance. "I found a couple of links that suggested he had some political aspirations as well, that's all. I didn't follow it—thought maybe you'd seen something. I just wondered..."

Trevor was silent long enough to make Sharon think he hadn't heard her or had gone off on one of his internal hikes. She glanced at him, her mouth open, but he was not gazing into the distant hills of his mental outback. There was an expression on his face she had seen only once before.

Zero at the core, she stopped walking, stopping Trevor as well.

"What's the matter with you, Trevor? What did you find?"

"We need to get back to the Grid, Shar." He took her arm.

She pulled it away. A woman passerby gave them a sharp glance. Sharon lowered her voice and moved a step closer to

Trevor. "Not until you tell me what you've found. Something about Alec? What happens to him?"

Trevor lowered his head till their foreheads were touching and the woman smiled and continued on her way.

"Nothing happens to him," he murmured. "Except that he goes into politics. I thought you might be disappointed. He apparently gave up his research to become a pol. Not exactly a progression his dear mother would be happy about, am I right?"

"Good Lord, don't tell me he had a party affiliation or something like that?"

"No. No affiliation, but he was—or rather, will be—some sort of lobbyist for the medical PAC."

Sharon shrugged. "Okay. I'm not wild about lobbyists as a rule, but at least it's a good cause."

Trev shook his head, straightened and smiled. "You're no fun, Shar. You've mellowed too much with age."

"Jerk," she called him. "Let's go."

#

Sharon could not have said what made her open Trevor's files. It was more than idle curiosity, less than suspicion. But she had known Trevor Haley too long not to know when he was embarrassed or uncomfortable and today, during the Shift, he had been both. The last time she'd seen that expression on his face—that sudden skittering away of the eyes—was at a dinner party when one of their colleagues had cracked a mean-spirited, misogynistic joke about Magda Oslovski and her husband, Vance.

Sharon's own data drop was complete by the time she had changed her clothes and poured a cup of tea. She began riffling through her collection, preparing an index and overview for a morning briefing. She allowed herself a moment to linger lovingly over the information on Alec, then moved on reluctantly.

She'd spent perhaps a half-hour at this when some perverse demon drove her into Trevor's domain. Anticipation building, she made a guilty search for the name Alec Glen. The search came up dry.

Puzzled, Sharon bent to her own work, but there is nothing so insidious and pervasive as fear, and Sharon had begun to fear, because she could think of no reason Trevor would fail to download the information on Alec, unless...

And that was her imagination's stopping point. Was Alec destined to die a horrible death? Perhaps by assassination? What else could be so terrible that Trev wouldn't let anyone see it?

The thought gnawed. She countered with stern logic. When she'd brought the matter up, his tone had been light and teasing. (Yes, even as his eyes crawled away to hide and his ears reddened.) He'd said Alec was a lobbyist—maybe his political career would be too unspectacular to warrant downloading. (But he might have at least done it for her, even though it meant bending the rules a bit.)

Stern logic was powerless. Not fifteen minutes had passed before she got up from her console and headed down the hall toward Trevor's office. She would simply ask. Straight up. *What did you find out about Alec?* Just a mother's fond and proud curiosity. No hint of inner panic. No *what aren't you telling me?*

But Trevor wasn't in his office. His console was on, his chair pulled back as if he had just left it. The palm unit was still in the docking slot. Sharon stood on the doorsill, indecisively, aware of the familiar buzz and wash of sound from the offices and labs—the murmur of conversations in the hall.

She came into the room, the door swinging closed behind her. It took only a moment to slip into his chair, access the palm unit and check its contents. She found what she had been hoping not to find in a folder separated from the main index and named simply "AG." She contemplated downloading it to her own

console, but realized that in any case, Trevor would know she'd
seen the data if for no other reason than that she would confront
him with it.

She prepared herself for the worst; she could not have
prepared herself for the reality. Dr. Alec Glen, Ph.D., noted
research scientist, had indeed given up medicine to take up a
political career and crusade. He was the father of the Euthanasia
Act of 2137, a piece of legislation that put into the hands of
doctors and judges and review boards the decision as to when
an individual should die. He was the first doctor to be certified
for euthanasia; the first to practice it.

Sharon stared at the monitor for an eternity before she was
able to will her hands to move, to dig further, to try to
comprehend how her son—*her* son!—could make himself the
proponent of such a heinous law.

No, not a law, an atrocity by which elderly people
unfortunate enough to require institutionalization had their
cases placed before a review board made up of medical doctors,
judges, psychologists, clergy and ethicists. Based on a complex
set of criteria, rules, conditions and formulas, a decision was
made whether or not to euthanize. There was even a list of
terminal illnesses for which euthanasia was the *de facto*
"treatment" unless mitigating circumstances could be proven.

Sharon's tears blurred the names on the list—cold, scientific
names that said nothing of the suffering they inflicted:
Myasthenia gravis, multiple sclerosis, Huntington's disease,
Alzheimer's. Some were conditions on which Alec would
expend much time and effort during his medical career. It was as
if he were trying to literally bury his failure.

Numbly, Sharon followed another link. She found numbers,
statistics, a death roll. It numbered in the thousands.

Why?

"I was hoping you wouldn't see that." Trevor watched from the doorway, face grave. Gravity was something he didn't do well under normal circumstances, but there was no hidden levity in his gaze now. "I guess I should have destroyed it. But, um, it's a development the analysts will want to know about. *Should* know about."

"You offlined it."

He reddened. "Like I said, I considered destroying it."

"For me."

He shrugged.

"How?" She shook her head.

"How does it happen or how does it happen to be Alec?"

"Both. Either."

"People live longer, but in the end they still deteriorate. People continue to have children. Population demographics indicate a glut of elderly people, inflicted with certain diseases and too few facilities to care for them. It apparently reached a crisis—*will* reach a crisis—in the mid '30's."

"Fine—a crisis. But how does a humane society justify this? How does a man with Alec's background justify it? Here, it says he was supported by the religious right. Back at the turn of this century, that same lobby fought abortion, the death penalty *and* the right to die."

"Ah, interesting, that." He came into the room. "The new sensibility will hold that since death is reunion with God, and therefore not to be feared, it's something to anticipate, not avoid."

"'I have made Death a messenger of joy,'" Sharon quoted. "Yes, but a *forced* reunion? Decided by-by committee? This...this is shades of Logan's Run. *Fiction.* My God, Trev, you can't justify that by scripture."

"No."

Sharon glanced at the screen where an image of Alec-to-be gazed back at her, soberly. There was, in the handsome, but severe middle-aged man, a great deal of the boy.

"What do I do, Trev?" she asked.

He moved to lay a hand on her shoulder. "What *can* you do?"

"Go back—forward—again and try to-"

"Sharon, come on. You know that's not possible. It takes a team of Lab Rats to run the Grid, and Magda would never send you. Besides, what could you do there as you *now* that you couldn't as you then besides create an anomaly?"

"Where will I be then, Trev, that I can't convince him that what he's doing is wrong?"

He shook his head. "I don't know the answer to that one."

"Then I have to do something here. Maybe I need to spend more time with him. Maybe—God, maybe it's my fault."

Trevor grasped her by both shoulders and swung her around to face him. "Shar, that's ridiculous. You're a great mom. And Alec knows you love him."

"Maybe that's not enough. *Obviously* that's not enough."

"Sharon..."

She glanced up directly into his eyes, capturing them. "Are you going to share this data with the Board?"

"I have to."

She knew that. Of course, she knew that. "Trevor, what do I do," she asked again. "My son is going to grow up to commit an atrocity that-" She lost her words, her thoughts, her direction and hiccuped on the horrid tightness in her throat.

"Let's look at it carefully. Let's let other analysts look at it."

"He's my son, Trevor."

"What do you think you should do? Go home and tell him his future? What would you say? Sweetheart, I hate to tell you this, but you're going to turn into a monster?"

She could only shake her head. He reached out to her again, laying a firm hand on her shoulder. "Go home, Sharon. Let me— let us get a handle on this. We'll talk about it tomorrow. Go home."

The thought terrified her. "How can I go home? How can I see him knowing what I know?"

"You said it yourself: he's your son."

Her son. The son she couldn't face. The son she no longer knew how to relate to. In the end, she called her sister and asked if she would mind keeping Alec overnight. A migraine, she said. She was desperate to see him—to hold him—but she couldn't. Not yet.

She went home—thought about going for a swim. She always worked things out swimming—the soft, cool touch of water gliding over skin, the rhythm of arms, legs, and breath. But on her way out the door to the gym, she got sucked into Alec's room and spent an hour sitting on his bed, holding a stuffed Tigger in her arms, staring at shelves covered with models of space shuttles, starships, the space station, the first commercial Delta Clipper. A child's room; a simple boyhood jumble.

He had never shown the slightest sign of cruelty toward animals or people. He was kind, gentle, thoughtful of others. How did someone like Alec grow up to believe a committee of experts should determine the end of a person's life?

Don't grow up to be a monster. If it were only that simple, she would tell him that. But if she did and it was discovered, her career would be forfeit. *Worth it*, she told herself fiercely. Yes, but there would be no way to know if the words would alter anything short of future-tripping, and QuestLabs would never allow a follow-up visit.

What if he didn't grow up?

The thought came stealthily, leaving a slimy trail of disgust. She recoiled from it, a torrent of icy horror pouring through her. Dear God, what kind of mother could conjure such an idea?

She experienced, for only the second time in her life, a complete cessation of thought and feeling. The first time was when she knew, without hope, that Robert was not coming back.

When her brain began to process thoughts again, it occurred to her to wonder if she would be sitting here now, having these thoughts if Robert were alive. Her heart came back online then, and she wept until she had no tears left. Then she slept, draped across Alec's bed.

She did not sleep well. Her mind refused to shut down, now, when she so desperately wanted it to. Trevor's call woke her, derailing the runaway train. He asked if he should come over; she told him "no." He repeated the things he had told her earlier in his office. She listened and tried to believe.

She was not surprised to be summoned to Magda Oslovski's office the next morning. She was exhausted, a prisoner of guilt, dread and confusion. Some of the dread evaporated when she saw that Dr. Oslovski was not alone. Her husband, staff psychologist Vance Keller, was there as well. Both wore expressions of compassion. Tears swam in Sharon's eyes.

Magda rose and rounded her desk to enfold Sharon in a motherly embrace. She seated the younger woman almost gently at a table by her office window and took a seat opposite her, their knees nearly touching. She reached across and took Sharon's hands.

"Trev gave us a full account of the situation," she said. "I'm sorry, Sharon. I realize this must be hellish for you. There's no way to prepare for something like this. The important thing now is that you not let this affect your relationship with your son."

"*How?*" It was the mew of a lost kitten. "How can I not let it affect our relationship? I *failed* him, Magda. I *will* fail him."

"No." Vance Keller came to stand by his wife's chair. His eyes were kind, his expression firm. "A human life is far too complex, both in nature and nurture, to assign cause to one factor—even one as critical as a mother."

"Or the loss of a father?" Sharon asked. She couldn't look at Vance. A surge of mixed guilt and resentment made her gaze too heavy to lift. "He knows how his father died. He knows I'm continuing in the same work. Maybe, deep down inside, he thinks that means I don't care."

"There's no way to know what factors could contribute to...Alec's future actions," said Vance.

Sharon tried to smile. "I don't suppose you could just send Alec and me back a few years. I'm sure I could talk Rob out of that last future-trip."

Magda squeezed her hand. "Sharon, there's no way to know what to adjust or edit in the past to change the present and future. That's why we don't do it. You can only edit the present."

"What you need to understand," Vance added, "is that there is only one thing you can do for Alec that we know will have positive effects—love him. And raise him the best way you can."

They spoke some more, let her cry, comforted her, then let her go home to get Alec—to spend the rest of the day with him. She drove slowly to her sister's house, trying to fathom what she had done—or would do—that her son would grow up so lacking in compassion and empathy.

As hard as it was for her to face, she could not deny that she saw the seed of that deficit already, saw it in his avoidance of his grandmother, his inability to comprehend her loneliness and alienation from the life she had known. He had never even been to see her in the place she was kept, safe from her own faltering faculties. He saw her only when she came out, and then, he was usually shy and aloof.

Vance had told her to do her best. So far she had failed to do that, afraid of stressing Alec too much in the wake of Robert's loss. That would change.

She pulled into her sister's car park and sat for several minutes gathering herself, afraid she'd be unable to respond to Alec. She needn't have worried. At the sight of him, smiling at her from beneath a milk mustache, the strain of uncertainty fled. She hugged him extravagantly—a thing he seemed to relish— and drank him in, her son, the light of her life.

"Is your head okay, Mom?" he asked her when she finally released him. His concern seemed sincere.

She could only nod.

They had lunch at his favorite restaurant, a place crowded with baseball memorabilia, and which served dishes named for major league greats. She bought him a Russ Ortiz Mocha Freeze; they talked about the Giant's season; they named their favorite players and tried to match them with their numbers.

They were walking back out to the car when she said, "Let's go visit Gramma."

He just looked at her.

"Okay?" she prodded.

"Can you take me home first? I got homework."

"On a Friday?"

"I got behind this week—it's make up."

"You got behind."

"My game last night went long."

Oh, God, she'd forgotten he had a Little League game. "Oh," she said weakly. "How'd you do?"

He shrugged as if it were of no importance. "We won... I pitched," he added, damning her further.

She nearly groaned. "You can do your homework when we get home. I thought I'd invite Trev over for dinner. Would you like that?"

His face lit up. "Sure!"

"Good. Then we'll go see Gramma, then go home so you can do your homework and I'll call Trev-"

"Mom, *please.*"

"She's lonely, Alec. She loves it when we visit her."

"She doesn't even know who I am. She asked if I was her neighbor's grandson last time."

"She's sick, Alec. She can't help what's happened to her. She needs us."

He subsided, but she recognized the mutinous set of his jaw.

It was one of Helen Glen's better days. She remembered who Alec was. She even remembered that Robert was gone. She didn't ask where he was. She asked about baseball and Alec thawed. He talked about baseball, school, his beloved lizard, Skinky. He thawed, warmed to her, smiled, laughed and promised to come again, soon.

Sharon felt a glow of warmth and accomplishment rise up to envelope her. For the first time since she had moved her mother-in-law here, she was not affected by the atmosphere of the place, which had always seemed to her almost a silent, ambient moan of loss and pain. It was hard to be here, but Alec had done it.

He had grown quiet again by the time they reached the car, and gazed around at his surroundings, seeming to notice the sun on the grass, the leaves glittering in the trees, the birds singing, the quiet walkways along which strolled or glided inmates with their visiting loved ones.

He was silent as they negotiated the wooded streets and headed home.

"Gramma had a really good day today, didn't she?" Sharon asked rhetorically. "You could see she really loved visiting with us."

"But we can't be there every day. We can only go there sometimes, and in between, she doesn't have anybody."

Encouraging. He was empathizing. Feeling for his grandmother. "Well, she has friends there, honey, and her nurses and doctors."

"That's not the same thing. They get paid to be there. And sometimes I'll bet her friends don't even remember her--don't even know she's there."

Sharon smiled. "Then I suppose we'll just have to visit more often, huh?"

"Yeah." While she congratulated herself, he turned his face up to her, his eyes troubled. "But it's not fair, mom. Gramma shouldn't have to live like that." He blinked as if tears were threatening to come and turned his head away so she wouldn't see them. Sunlight spattered his face, making him squint. "No one should *ever* have to live like that."

Home Is Where...

A story of science fiction

Home Is Where ... was originally published in *Analog Science Fiction* in 1991 and was the second story in my time travel series, though in the chronology of my fictional world, the action occurs many years after the time of the original story. The technology is mature and the ethical issues perhaps more mundane. This tale involves a family of time-traveling Bahá'ís, the Joneses, who find that even in their line of work, a family is a family.

Anastasia Jones viewed her new town with little interest from the crest of a maple-shaded hill. It was a fresh-washed picture postcard of a town; all green and white and brick red under a rain-dark sky. An equally fresh-washed breeze rolled up the hill, carrying with it the smell of...popcorn.

Anastasia smiled. Now that was interesting. She scanned the buildings along the cobbled main street. Ah, yes, there it was—a theater. She could see the ornate marquee peeking up at her between elm sentinels.

"Looks like they've picked another homespun backwater," said a voice over her shoulder.

She turned, noting that her brother's face looked just as dour as it had the last time she'd seen it. "What'd you expect?" she asked. "They do this every time we start whining."

"I don't whine, Stasi."

"No, you pout. The twins whine. I sulk."

She swept moist strands of deep burgundy hair from her forehead with one hand and brushed her wind-climbing skirts down with the other. Her eyes searched the trees.

"There's the school," she said finally and pointed.

"Oh, royal. Another one-roomer?"

"No... It looks kind of nice. All brick and white-washed and a green roof."

"Don't get too attached to that green roof, sis. We won't be here that long."

"I wish-"

"If wishes were wheels, gramma would've been a trolley car."

Anastasia giggled. "Where'd you dig that up?"

He shrugged. "I dunno. Somewhere about three stops ago."

"What does it mean?"

"Who knows. Does it matter?"

"Anastasia! Tamujin! Dinner!"

Tamujin Jones made a goofy face. "Sounds real down home, don't she?"

His sister giggled again. "Well, at least she didn't ring that stupid triangle she got in Armadillo or wherever that was."

"Amarillo." Tamujin snorted. "Armadillo! Geezumminy, Stasi, no wonder you're having so much trouble with geography. You've gotten it mixed up with zoology!"

The new school was okay, Anastasia decided. It was old and neat and smelled of ancient wood varnish, fresh wood oil and cedar. Their parents had done the obligatory first-day-in-a-new school thing and delivered them to the Admin office all smiles and pride. They'd filled out the paperwork, kissed their children and gone off for a day of getting-to-know-Papillion.

"Have fun," they'd said, but their parting message, as ever was, "Do try to fit in." So much for fun.

Now they sat on a wooden bench in the Admin office waiting for the vice-principal, Mrs. Thorpe, to escort them to their classes. She arrived in due process, wreathed in smiles, flourishing four fresh, new file folders. A pair of spectacles dangled from a cord around her neck.

The twins stared at her, making Anastasia wish she could reach across Tam's lap and pinch them.

"Well!" The apple-cheeked face beamed its freshness at them. She even smelled like apples. "What a lovely family! Your parents are such lucky people. So..." She set the spectacles on her nose and flipped open the top file folder. "Your names are...very unusual. Anastasia?" Her eyes bounced kinetically back and forth between the two girls.

"That's me," said Stasi. "Please, call me Stasi."

"Oh." She pulled a pencil from behind one ear (the twins fairly ogled) and made a note, then went on to the next folder. "Tamu-?"

"Tamujin," he said. "I go by Tam."

"That is unusual. What nationality is that?"

"Mongolian."

"It's Genghis Kahn's first name," offered the staring, blonde gamine next to him.

"Oh, my! How did they ever settle on that?"

Tam turned beet red and threw his little sister a get-even glance. "Dad's a...a historian. He's fascinated with that period."

"I see...well...." She made a note, then glanced at the twins. "Now, you'd be Constantine, I'll bet."

"Connie," said Tam.

"Con," said Constantine. "Connie is a girl's name, here."

"And Tahireh...my, that's pretty."

"It's Persian," explained Tahireh proudly, then announced, "Tahireh was a martyr in the cause of women's suffrage."

Mrs. Thorpe's face froze, whether because the vocabulary was bit precocious for an eight year old or because either martyrdom or suffrage was an unusual topic of conversation for a child that age Stasi couldn't guess. Mrs. Thorpe wriggled her lips back into a smile.

"Really? How interesting."

"They strangled her with her wedding scarf and threw her body down a well. Just before she died she said, 'You can kill me as soon as you like, but you cannot stop the emancipation of women.'"

Mrs. Thorpe let out a nervous giggle. "How precocious!" she burbled, then whisked them away to their classes.

Stasi thought she'd like her teacher. Her name was Mildred Tindall and she was young, pretty and quick to praise. She exclaimed over what a pretty name Anastasia was and said she thought Stasi's dress was strikingly beautiful and that she liked the unusual color of her hair.

Stasi was not so sure she was going to like her classmates.

She overheard one of them say her dress was "antique" and her hair was "weird" and her name was "foreign."

This is a learning experience, she told herself and ignored the whispers and the fact that she really did look dreadfully out of place among these wearers of plaid and poodle skirts, saddle shoes and natural-colored pony tails.

By lunchtime she had acquired a reputation as a Brain and heard the words "teacher's pet" whiffle softly through the air over her head. She thought briefly about playing dumb, but Dad said never to stifle your natural abilities to suit anyone else's expectations and besides, it rubbed her the wrong way.

She was on her way to the cafeteria when she felt someone lift her ankle-length skirt from behind. She skittered sideways, nearly colliding with a group of loitering boys and turned to find herself confronting three of her female classmates. They peered at her archly, their notebooks clasped to their chests like battle shields.

"Why do you wear such weird clothes?" asked one of them. "Beth says it's because you're a Quaker or something. Are you a Qu-a-a-a-ker?"

Her voice wavered and cracked on the last word and the two girls flanking her giggled.

"No. I'm a Bahá'í," Stasi told them.

"What's that?"

"It's a religion. Excuse me. I'm going to be late for lunch."

She started to turn away, but the tallest of the three moved to cut off her path of retreat.

"So why *do* you wear such weird clothes?"

Stasi muzzled her considerable temper and said, "I just haven't had a chance to get any new clothes since we got here. This was the height of fashion the last place we lived."

"Oh, yeah? And where was that, Mars?"

Stasi drew herself to her full height. "Paris, actually. France."

The girls exchanged glances. "Prove it," said the first one, truculently. "Speak some French, if you can."

"*Mais, bien sur. Je pense que vous parlez tres follement. Maintenant, exusez-moi. J'ai faim.*" And she slipped quickly away.

"What'd she say? What did you say?" They were on her heels.

"I said, 'I'm hungry.'"

"All that, just to say you're hungry?"

She kept moving.

"You didn't really speak French! You just made that up!"

"I'll bet you got in trouble for doing that to your hair!"

She escaped into the cafeteria.

She was standing in the chow line craning her neck to see where Tam and the twins might be when she felt someone jiggle her elbow. *Oh, God, please!* she thought. Not again. She turned to find a pair of pale, spectacled eyes peering owlishly at her from beneath a fringe of overly curly dishwater blonde hair.

"Hi, I'm Elaine. I sat behind you in class today."

"Oh, yeah. Hi."

"You just have to ignore them, you know." She tilted her head toward where Stasi's tormenters flirted with some male students. "They really do say the silliest things. I like your hair," she added, eyeing the deep red bob. "It's different."

"Thanks." Anastasia managed to turn her ogle into a shy smile. "Would you like to eat lunch with us? My brothers and little sister should be around somewhere."

The smile bounced back from Elaine's silver-clad teeth with increased amplitude and Stasi felt a sharp twinge of precognitive agony. For any member of the Jones family, a friend gained was a friend lost.

After suffering Tam's disapproving glances, Constantine's moping and Tahireh's constant chatter on the shuffle home, Anastasia was ready to explode. Her mother's half-cheery, half-anxious, "Well, how was the first day?" was like a match to a short fuse.

"Oh, Mom, it was awful! They teased me about my name, my clothes, my hair...everything! Mom, when can I get some new clothes?"

Helen Jones went for the obvious out like a hunted vixen through a privet hedge. "Why, sweetie, all you had to do was ask. How's tomorrow after school?"

Stasi rolled her eyes. "I may swoon!"

"It's a date. Maybe you should wear something a little less...conspicuous tomorrow. Okay?"

"No problem. I'll go see what I can dig out." Stasi disappeared up the stairs.

Helen Jones scanned her remaining children's faces warily.

"So, how about the rest of you?"

"It was terrible," grumbled Constantine. "Everybody called me 'Smarty-pants.' Nobody would play with me at recess because they thought I was showing off for the teacher."

"Were you showing off for the teacher?"

"Mo-om! All I did was add a column of figures."

"Six digit figures," inserted Tahireh. "In his head."

"Well, what'm I s'posed to do—play dumb?"

Helen grimaced slightly. "Of course, you shouldn't play dumb, but you could pretend to be working it out on the black board."

Con glowered and stuffed small fists into his pockets. "I s'pose."

Unprompted, Tahireh announced, "I had fun. I told the whole class about my namesake. They thought it was so dramatic. I'm going to like it here." And she took herself off to the backyard. Con followed like a glowering shadow.

"Well?" Helen swung away from her roll-top desk and regarded her remaining child with some trepidation. He still hung back in the archway between the entry hall and the parlor, looking sullen and rebellious.

"What happened to you?"

"Nothing," he said dully, and turned to head for the stairs. He paused in mid-turn and looked back over his shoulder. "Stasi made a friend today." His eyes accused her.

She smiled weakly. "That's nice."

"No, Mom, it's not nice. She does this every time. I've learned not to, but she just keeps doing it."

"Then, she obviously needs to do it. She's fifteen. That's a critical time for friends."

"Oh? Well, how long are we going to be here then, Mom? Is Stasi going to graduate from this school with her friends? Am I?"

His mother's smile strained at the eyes and slipped at the corners of her mouth. "I don't know, dear. It depends."

"On what, Mom? On what, this time?"

"The book your father is researching-"

"The Book. The Project. The Grand Theory. The Curiosity. Jesus, Mom, are we ever going to have a real home with real friends that we can invite into the house?"

Helen's expression changed radically from Mom-on-the-run to Mom reproachful. "We do not use that Name as an expletive, Tamujin Jones. And this is a real home. Home isn't a place, you know. It's people. Family."

"Yeah, I know. But sometimes family's not enough. Sometimes we need friends, too. You and Dad get so caught up in your work sometimes."

"I know. I know. But why can't you make real friends here?"

"C'mon, Mom. You know why."

"Lots of people move around—military personnel, field scientists like your father and I-"

"But they can at least write to the friends they leave behind. Call them. Visit them. We can't do any of those things, Mom. We just keep leaving little bits of ourselves all over the place while we get smaller and smaller."

He turned away from her then, and bounded up the stairs. She sat for a moment, thinking, then dropped her notes into the drawer of her desk, shutting and locking it. Then, she went to call her husband.

✦ ✦ ✦

They were halfway through a semi-glum dinner, when the elder Joneses started glancing at each other the way parents do when they've been plotting behind their children's backs. After several minutes of this, Troy Jones made an announcement.

"Mom and I have been talking," he said, and Anastasia tried not to recall the last announcement that had been so prefaced.

"Congratulations," returned Tam, and asked for the mashed potatoes.

His father ignored him. "We realize our existence is rather ...Bohemian."

"Is that what it is?" mumbled Tam.

"We know you get a little lonely and sometimes feel a bit out of place."

"Try all the time," said Tam.

His mother interceded. "Tamujin, quit behaving like a verbal sniper and let your father finish what he's trying to say."

"Yeah," agreed Tahireh. "This could be good."

Troy Jones bowed his head to his youngest daughter. "Thank you, Tar. Now. what I'm trying to get to is this: We know how hard it is on you to have to keep your friends at arm's length, so we've decided you don't have to do that anymore."

"Excuse me?" said Stasi, not sure she'd heard him right. Helen smiled at her children brightly. "We've decided you can bring your friends over. Isn't that great?"

Four pairs of young eyes stared at her.

"Seriously, Mom?" asked Stasi.

"Seriously."

"*Magnifique!*" exclaimed Tahireh.

"Of course," her father cautioned, "there will have to be some new house rules to accommodate this. We can't have people wandering into restricted areas, and we can't mark them

as restricted areas without arousing too much curiosity. So, we'll
have to disguise those areas. You'll also have to be careful with
your personal belongings. Okay? You won't be able to leave
stuff out where your friends can stumble over it."

Constantine's nose wrinkled in consternation. "You mean
we have to put all our stuff away?"

"That would be best."

"But if we don't have toys or anything our friends will think
we're fanatics. You know what the Book says about fanaticism."

Troy Jones spent a solid five seconds looking completely
confounded. He knew very well what the Book said about
fanaticism and was trying to work out how he could not have it
apply to this situation.

"It's okay, Dad," Tam interjected. "Stasi and I will go
through their stuff and pick out what's okay for public
consumption."

Troy smiled. "Thanks. Now, you can't all bring friends
home at once, so we'll have to set up a system."

"How about first ask, first come?" asked Tahireh.

Her father considered that. "Sounds reasonable."

She immediately raised her hand, waving it energetically in
the air over the casserole. "Me! Me! I'm first! Can I bring my new
friend Frog home for dinner tomorrow?"

"Frog?" echoed Tam. "Is that a friend or a pet?"

"His eyes are kind of buggy," Tahireh explained, "so the
other kids call him 'Frog.' Can he come?"

Helen glanced at her husband. "How about Friday? We'll
need some time to police the household."

Tahireh nodded. "Friday's good."

Dinner was a little more companionable after that, but Stasi
couldn't help wondering if they'd just opened themselves up to
a whole new order of agony.

"It's just going to make things worse," said Tam stonily. He kicked at a puffball toadstool and was satisfied when it burst, scattering its powder of spores everywhere.

"Must you abuse the local flora?" asked Tahireh, then charged away from him down the path into town.

"I know," said Stasi.

She admired the way the grass along the path lay over in the wind like soft, green seaweed in a lazy current. She leaned over and ran her fingers across the undulating tendrils.

Tam stopped beside her on the trail and watched her. "You're going to make friends with that Elaine, aren't you?"

Stasi straightened. "I suppose so."

"Why? You know what'll happen. It's just going to hurt."

"I know. But I can't shut everybody out the way you can."

"You could learn. I did." He turned and walked on down the path, leaving her alone under the maples.

She felt suddenly morose, and followed him lethargically to school where everybody she saw stared at her. Really stared, as if she was still wearing her pajamas. It was even worse than the day before. She glanced down at herself. Her jeans were zipped; her shoes were tied. She tilted a glance over her shoulder and down her back. There were no rips, no stains, no signs that said, "Kick me!"

It must be my earrings, she thought and settled at a desk next to Elaine in the second row.

Everything seemed normal after that until Miss Tindall asked a question and Stasi rose to answer it. She'd barely gotten two words out of her mouth before she became aware of a sudden shift in the level of tension in the room. She heard a gasp, a murmured "uh-oh," and glanced down at Elaine, who was staring at her incredulously.

Miss Tindall, hearing the sudden silence behind her, turned from the blackboard.

"Now, I know-"

The class was never to hear what she knew. Her eyes widened. Her next utterance was, "Anastasia-!"

Anastasia blinked and stared back into her teacher's face. Had the world chosen this morning to go completely mad? She suddenly felt like Alice facing a pack of ogling playing cards and the Red Queen.

Miss Tindall set her chalk in the tray and dusted her fingers on the neat piece of gingham flannel she kept on a hook by the board.

"Anastasia," she said, "please go out into the hall and wait for me."

"Why? What's wrong?" She heard "What's wrong?" echoed derisively by several muffled voices.

"In the hall, please. Class, you may start your reading assignment on page five in the history text while I'm gone."

Stasi let the door fall shut and waited, miserably, in the silent hallway. What was wrong with her? Had she suddenly sprouted a moustache and glasses? She explored her face gingerly. Did she have spots? She was supposed to be inoculated against just about every known disease. Had one of her siblings played a joke on her?

The classroom door swung open and Miss Tindall appeared, looking very serious.

"Anastasia, can you explain yourself?"

No, Miss Tindall, I can't, she thought. Aloud, she said, "Explain what? What've I done? Why is everyone staring at me?"

"Are you serious? Young lady, what do you expect, when you come to school dressed in such completely inappropriate attire?"

Stasi did a quick mental inventory of her person. The simple white shirt, canvas shoes. Her hand flew to the huge black and white zebra earrings that dangled from her ears.

"I'm sorry. Is there some rule about earrings?"

"Earrings? Young lady, you are stretching both my credulity and my patience. What ever possessed you to think you could get away with wearing pants to school? Blue jeans, no less!"

Completely taken aback, Stasi answered honestly. "They made fun of my good clothes. Mom told me to wear these until we could go shopping for something that would...fit in better."

"Your mother told you to wear blue jeans? I find that difficult to believe. Anastasia, are you sure you're telling me the truth? I don't know of a single school in this country that will tolerate girls wearing pants to class."

"Oh. I'm sure Mom didn't realize that. The last place we lived, you could wear just about anything you wanted."

Miss Tindall looked entirely skeptical. "Oh? And where was this—Mars?"

Stasi blinked and licked her lips, feeling a giggle forming in her throat. "Paris," she said. "Paris, France."

Miss Tindall sighed. "I see. Well, I'm sorry, Stasi, but I really have no choice but to send you home for the rest of the day. When you come in tomorrow, make sure you're wearing a dress. I'll send your assignments home with your brother. And I'm afraid I'm going to have to have a word with your mother about this. It's school policy."

"Good," Stasi murmured.

"What?"

"I said, 'Good,'" she repeated, her eyes feeling tight with tears. "Maybe then they'll see that we don't belong here."

She darted away, then, down the corridor, out the back door of the Secondary wing and home.

Helen Jones heard the slam of the front door and the rapid pounding of feet up the stairs to the second floor. She left her husband, who was oblivious to both the pounding and his wife's departure from their shared laboratory/office, and went upstairs to find her daughter flung across her bed glaring at the ceiling.

"Well, young lady, can you tell me what you're doing home at 0900 hours?"

"I was inappropriately attired. And if one more person calls me 'young lady' in that tone of voice, I'll scream bloody murder."

Frowning, Helen moved to sit on the edge of the bed. "You were what?"

Stasi sat up and looked her mother in the eye, a mutinous expression on her face. "Girls are not allowed to wear pants to school here, Mom. They think it's immoral or something."

Helen blinked. "Oh. Oh, dear. Honey, I'm sorry. I didn't check. It didn't even occur to me that-"

"I know, I know.... She wants to talk to you and Dad."

"Who?"

Stasi grimaced. "Miss Tindall. My teacher."

"I'll go in tomorrow morning and talk to her," Helen decided.

"And say what, Mom? What can you tell her that will make her understand why I don't fit in?"

"Don't worry about it, honey. I'll make her understand." She patted her daughter's knee and left.

Already writing the speech, Stasi thought, and flopped back onto the bed with a groan.

They went clothes shopping after lunch, and Stasi spent the remainder of the afternoon wrinkling her nose at her new skirts and dresses as she hung them up and shortening the hemlines of a few of her old ones. That task also required a modicum of facial contortions.

Tam brought her homework in as soon as he got home. She was reading and he dropped the schoolbooks on the foot of her bed.

"What happened?"

Stasi put down her book. "Girls don't wear blue jeans to school in the United States."

Tam whistled. "And Mom and Dad didn't know that? Jeez, they must be slipping. They used to have all that stuff iced."

"Why should they care? They're too busy researching books and digging up artifacts to care about what's acceptable fashion in some little pie-dink town in Nebraska."

"Podunk," he corrected. "If we were home-"

"Home? What's that?"

Tam stared at the book lying between them, ran his fingers over the smooth plastic covering. That was from Home.

"Do you remember Danice Patten?"

Stasi shot him a dark glance. "Of course, I remember Danice. She was my best friend."

"Do you wish we could go back?"

"Stupid question, Tam. What good does it do to wish? What was it you said—if wishes were wheels-"

"What if we did more than wish?"

Stasi looked at her younger brother doubtfully. "Like what? Talking to them doesn't help. They don't listen. You should have heard Mom this morning—all hot-fizz to explain to Miss Tindall why her daughter is such a social misfit. 'I'll make her understand, honey,'" she mimicked.

Tam snorted. "That means they're going to do their Richard and Mary Leakey routine."

"Right, and trot out that tired old 'Helen of Troy' line. They love this, Tam. They're home for each other. They didn't have that many friends when we were home. Just books and artifacts and colleagues in the field."

"And us. C'mon, Sis, let's not dive off the pier," he added when she pulled a sour face.

"Okay. All right. And us. But they never hear us, Tam. Then we say we're miserable or lonely or homesick, they just tune it out, or pretend we're going through a phase or having a bad day."

"Then maybe we can do something to make them tune us in. You know—actions that speak louder than words, et cetera."

Stasi picked up the book again, fingering it almost reverently—a memento from another life. Home. Suddenly, she was angry at Tam for even making her think about it.

"What actions, Tam?" she asked, bitter. "What actions could we possibly take that would show them what they can't see? You know what we can do? Nothing. We could all commit suicide tomorrow and they'd think it came out of nowhere."

Tam glanced at her sharply. "You wouldn't-"

"No, of course not. But sometimes I do think about mutiny. About tying them up and making them take us Home."

"Anastasia!" Their mother's voice floated up the stairs. "Stasi?"

Stasi got up and went out onto the landing. "Yeah, Mom?"

"There's someone down here to see you. Elaine?"

Stasi froze for a moment, suddenly loathe to carry on what she had started.

"Um, okay," she said finally. "I'll be right down." She padded downstairs with Tam on her heels and met her Mom and Elaine in the front hall. "Hi, Elaine. What's-what's up?" The last word came out a little too brightly.

"I just wanted to see if you were okay."

"Yeah. I'm all right." She looked at her Mom. "Can Elaine come up to my room?"

Helen smiled, her eyes anxious. "As long as it's clean, dear."

Stasi remembered the book. "Oh, I-"

"It's clean," Tam averred. "Of course, all the embarrassing stuff is under the pillows." He favored his sister with a secret glance.

"Thanks," she told him, and led her new friend upstairs.

Troy and Helen Jones appeared in the offices of the Papillion Community School just before classes were to start the morning after Stasi's run-in with school regulations.

Miss Tindall was obviously surprised to see them— surprised and a little nervous. That they were both dressed in the khaki uniform of field anthropologists might have contributed to that unease. She was determined not to let it show.

"Hello, Miss Tindall, isn't it?" Troy Jones shook her hand. "I'm Troy Jones and this is my wife, Helen."

Helen smiled. "That's me—Helen of Troy."

Miss Tindall smiled in return. "Yes, of course. How amusing." She seated them in a conference cubicle and moved to barricade herself behind a wooden desk. "Frankly, I'm surprised to see you. I didn't expect Anastasia to tell you much about our little misunderstanding."

"Our children tell us everything, Miss Tindall," Troy assured her. "We have a very open relationship."

Miss Tindall looked doubtful. "Did she tell you why I sent her home?"

"Yes, inappropriate dress, wasn't it? You know, I really don't understand that. With the weather being so nippy these days, I'd think blue jeans would be just what the meteorologist ordered."

Miss Tindall blinked. "I... There are rules, Mr. Jones."

"*Doctor* Jones."

"Excuse me. Doctor Jones. There are rules that govern how our young ladies dress. We expect them to be obeyed."

"Why? Good God, surely you don't want your young ladies freezing to death at their bus stops in the winter?"

"Of course not. They're free to wear nice pants to school as long as they remove them and put them in their lockers during class."

Dr. Jones ogled. "They run around in their underwear?"

Helen giggled into her hand.

Miss Tindall did not giggle. She didn't even smile. She fixed him with a cool gaze and said, "They wear the pants under their skirts, Dr. Jones."

"But that's redundant."

"It's the rule, Doctor. I didn't make the rule. I only enforce it. Do you honestly want your daughter parading around dressed like a boy?"

"Miss Tindall, who defines which clothes are male and which are female? Medieval gentlemen (such as they were) wore leggings and skirts. Scotsmen wear kilts to this day. And in Egypt, at this very moment, men stroll the avenues wearing what you would call dresses while their wives do the shopping in what you would call pants."

"This is America, Dr. Jones, not Egypt. And it's 1950, not the Middle Ages."

"Miss Tindall," said Helen quietly, "our children have led a much less sheltered life than their classmates. They've accumulated a vast library of diverse experiences. Anastasia's spent most of her life in jeans and khaki field trousers, digging up history your students here have only read about. It's going to take while for her to make the adjustment to this more restrictive lifestyle. All we're asking is that you try to understand that what seems bizarre or out of place to you is normal to Stasi."

"Normal," repeated Miss Tindall. "Maroon hair, dresses that look like ankle-length sacks and earrings made from giant fishing lures?"

"Her hair is burgundy, Miss Tindall," said Helen, "and all of those things you just mentioned were quite normal the last place we lived."

Miss Tindall pursed her lips. "Paris, she said."

"Paris," agreed Helen.

"Mrs. Jones-"

"*Doctor* Jones."

"Doctor Jones, I'm aware that Paris is the birth place of modern fashion, but I find it hard to believe that young ladies there wear such outlandish styles."

"Well, they wore them while we were there."

"I see."

"Do you?" asked Helen. "You see that Stasi is different, but do you see that there's nothing wrong with that?"

Miss Tindall sighed. "Dr. Jones-"

"There *is* nothing wrong with that, Miss Tindall. Stasi is an excellent student. A model teenager—honest, caring, mature beyond her years. Stasi is an individual. That individuality, that diversity, is very precious to her and to us. If you try to make her over in the image of some narrow ideal, if you try to squelch that individuality, we will have no choice but to withdraw our children from this school."

Miss Tindall's face went crimson. "That's illegal, Mrs. Jones."

"*Doctor* Jones," Helen corrected her. "And we'll worry about the legality of it. This is not a threat; please don't take it that way. We simply want you to understand that we are willing to go to great lengths to protect our children's individual rights.

Stasi's qualities, Miss Tindall, are on the inside; they are not woven into her clothing." She looked at her husband, who was nodding thoughtfully. "I think we've done all we can here, dear. Shall we go?"

"Certainly." He rose and reached across the desk/barricade for Miss Tindall's hand. "Thank you for your time, Miss Tindall."

They left the cubicle, drawing the gazes of the office staff after them.

Royalty in khaki, thought Mildred Tindall, and wondered where they'd come from.

Constantine Jones had a problem. He had come to school without his book bag. He had no pencils, no pens, no paper and, worst of all, no textbooks. When the teacher asked the class to take out paper and a pencil, he sat, frozen inside, glancing nervously around the room.

Two rows to the right, Tahireh caught his eye.

"What?" she mouthed.

He shrugged and signed that he had forgotten the sacred bag.

She looked thoughtful for a second, then pointedly lifted her desktop and put her own pencil in. Then she withdrew it.

Constantine knew what she was suggesting. He tried to swallow the lump of panic in his throat, but it wouldn't budge.

"Here?" he mouthed.

"Constantine, paper and pencil, please," said Mr. Matthews.

"Yes, sir."

Constantine lifted the top of his desk, reached inside and, after a moment of eye clenched hesitation, pulled out a pencil and a piece of lined paper.

Mr. Matthews smiled pleasantly and proceeded to hand out in-class assignments.

Everything was fine until he asked them to take out their history readers. Constantine panicked again. He could just say he'd forgotten his books, but that would mean a mandatory after school session, an extra assignment and utter humiliation before a council of his peers. His eyes cast about, clutching the boy next to him who had withdrawn the little textbook from his desk. It was covered in a crisp, brown paper bag.

Constantine echoed the movement, pulling out his own smartly attired book. His neighbor opened his book. He opened his, frowned in consternation, and quickly curved his arms around it.

"Page fifteen, please," said Mr. Matthews. "I want you all to take a moment to read page fifteen, then we'll talk about the New World."

Constantine put his head down and sweated. He could feel his sister's concern wash around and over him, felt it intensify to matching panic when Mr. Matthews took a bad turn and strolled up the aisle behind him.

Seeing a child hunkered so low over a textbook raises immediate suspicions in the mind of a teacher, and Mr. Matthews teacherly instincts were about as fully developed as they could be. He stopped right over Constantine and looked down. Then, he tapped Constantine on the shoulder.

"How are we doing, Mr. Jones?"

"Fine."

"And what are we reading about?"

"The New World."

"Isn't it a little difficult to read about the New World all hunched over like that?"

"No, sir."

"Well, straighten up, please. We don't want you to ruin your eyes."

Constantine stared at him for a moment, a wrinkle of pure anguish between his brows. Then he straightened up.

Mr. Matthews reached over his shoulder and nudged the book out of his protective embrace. After a moment of silence, during which Constantine was certain the entire Cosmos had collapsed, Mr. Matthews drew in a long breath and said, "Mr. Jones, can you explain to me why the pages of this book are empty?"

Constantine, clutching his older brother's hand, cowered tearfully in the principal's office. The offending volume was in the hands of the enemy and all was lost. He had no true conception of the magnitude of his crime, but he was certain it would mean the end of the world as he knew it.

Beside him, Tamujin breathed confidence and comfort into the ether.

"It's really very simple, sir," Tam said. "Connie just picked up the wrong book."

"The wrong book?"

"Yes, sir. That's mine."

"Yours? But it has blank pages."

"Yes, sir. It's a writer's journal. You know, a thought book. I got it just before we left Paris. Connie must have mistaken it for his history book. He'd wrapped that in a paper bag too, and they're about the same size." He smiled engagingly. "I guess I should've put my name on it. Sorry, sir. I feel real bad about putting Constantine through this."

He squeezed his little brother's trembling shoulder and turned the smile down into his tear-streaked face.

Mr. Benoit looked at Tam for a moment, then turned his spectacled gaze to Constantine. "Well, no harm done, I suppose. Be more careful next time, young man. Check the contents of a book before you carry it to school."

Outside in the corridor, Constantine's gratitude was effusive.

"Whatever possessed you to do that?" Tam asked, completely ignoring his worshipful elegy.

"Tahireh."

Tam looked down and shook Con's shoulder. "Try again."

"I forgot my book bag and the rule says if you forget your books, you have to do detention."

"Oh, yeah," Tam conceded. "I do recall that, now that you mention it. So, you just thought you'd go for a lesser penalty?"

Constantine glowered. "I didn't mean to get caught."

"Who does?"

"Do you think they'll tell Mom and Dad?"

Tam shook his head and rolled his eyes. "You'd better hope not. You know the rules about 'importing technologies across cultural boundaries.' Dad would have a fit."

Constantine stared down the empty corridor toward the distant classroom. "Yeah, he sure would."

"Miss Tindall hates me," said Stasi. "What did you say to her?"

Helen blinked. Next to her, her husband echoed the movement, staring at his eldest child as if she was an anthropological specimen that had suddenly risen up to protest being dug out of the ground.

"We just spoke to her about how important your individuality is," said Helen. "That's all."

"Well, now she's treating me like—like a pariah. She won't call on me unless I'm the only one with my hand raised, and even then she won't look at me or smile at me or anything."

Helen glanced at Troy, who was glancing at his notes as if he was preparing to dive back into them. She caught his eye pre-- dive and he shrugged.

"If it gets too bad, we'll talk to her again," he promised.

"Oh, great!"

"Now, Anastasia, your father and I were only trying to help."

Stasi had the grace to look contrite. "I know, but I'm afraid she'll flunk me or something."

Her mother laughed. "Good heavens! Why worry about something as trivial as that? It's not like she's actually teaching you anything. A local educator's arbitrary marks aren't going to affect your degree, honey."

"I know, but you can get black marks for failure to acculturate. She might make Professor Amadiyeh think I have a bad attitude."

"We'll tell him otherwise."

Stasi was silent for a moment, feeling incredibly freighted down and lonely. Thinking about Professor Amadiyeh made her think of Home and Danice Patten and all the other friends that now seemed light years away. Friends she couldn't reach by land or by sea.

"Can't we please go home?"

Her mother looked sympathetic (she always looked sympathetic) and said, "Stasi, honey, your father and I are in the middle of a Project."

"Can't you finish it at home?"

"How can we study the culture in and around military installations in Post World War Two America without having access to those installations?"

"Couldn't you use QuestLabs as a home base and just pop into a military base when you need to look at one?"

Her father laughed. "Stasi, you crack my mind! Do you have any idea how prohibitively expensive that would be? We blow over a hundred grand every time we power up the Grid, hon. Just settle down and enjoy Papillion, okay? It's not such a bad little town. When we're done here at Offutt, I'll see if we can't cut straight to the Pentagon. You kids'll love Washington D.C. Now, why don't you go study before dinner?"

She stared at him, at her mother, already bending over the thin plate display in her hands, scanning faux-3D pictures of military personnel in their monotone uniforms.

They're so happy, she thought. *Like two kids in a sand box.*

She went upstairs. On the second floor landing, Tam met her.

"Secret meeting of the Jones Gang," he said out of the side of his mouth. "My room. Five minutes."

"Thank you, Bugsy Malone," she said.

Tam deflated. "That was my best John Wayne."

"John who?"

"God, a cultural illiterate. You'd better bone up on your Twentieth Century films."

"Yeah, yeah. What's the meeting?"

Tam pointed at her nose. "It's a secret. Be there or be a rhombus." He turned and headed downstairs.

Five minutes later, they shared soda pop and greasy potato chips on the floor of Tam's room. Of the four, only Tahireh seemed disinclined to glower.

"I guess you're wondering why I've called you here," said Tam, munching.

"Get on with it," growled Stasi.

"I have an idea about how we might just possibly get Home before Mom and Dad retire."

Stasi snorted. "Oh, this should be good. We're gonna mutiny and take over the Grid Controller, right? Tie up Mom and Dad and slam this baby into reverse."

"Close." Tam took a swig of soda, looking arch.

"Well?" prompted Constantine. "C'mon, Tam. I could be out catching bugs, y'know."

"Mutiny," said Tam deliciously, dangerously.

"Mutiny," repeated Stasi. "Where'd you get a fuzz-brained idea like that?"

"Actually, I got it from you and Connie."

"Con."

Tam toyed with a chip crumb on the hardwood floor, scooting it around and around with his finger. "Have you ever wondered what would happen if we didn't try so hard to fit in wherever we go—if we sort of, oh, had trouble blending into the landscape?"

Stasi looked at him—hard. "Go on."

"What would Mom and Dad do if these little settling-in problems kept happening—maybe even got worse?"

"Ignore them?" suggested Constantine.

"They might try." Tam shrugged. "But if it got really bad and the teachers all got in an uproar and the Education Council got wind of it-"

Stasi's face finally lit up. "Professor Amadiyeh! If we all flunked out of school or started upsetting the local golf cart-"

"Apple cart."

"I can have any kind of cart I want, thank you. He'd have to get involved, wouldn't he? I mean, after all, it's his responsibility to see that our educational environment is sound."

"Yeah." Tam agreed pleasantly.

Constantine just folded his arms and smiled.

Between them, Tahireh, clutching a favored doll, stared at her siblings in horror. "Oh, you can't! You can't do something like that. Why, Mom and Dad would be... Well, they'd think there was something wrong with us."

"There *is* something wrong with us, Tahireh," said Stasi. "We're from another century, another world, almost. We don't belong here. We're...an anachronism."

"But Mom and Dad are so happy here!"

"Mom and Dad are happy anywhere they can dig up something or write papers," said Tam.

"But, it's not fair for us to ask them to give up their work."

"We're not asking them to give up their work, Tar. We're just asking them to reorganize it a little."

"Reorganize?" repeated Tahireh dubiously.

"Yeah," said Tam and munched another handful of chips.

No one in Papillion, Nebraska had ever seen an outfit like the one Anastasia Jones wore on a particular Monday. The ankle length jumper was a deep shade of burgundy that rivaled its wearer's hair. That hair was caught up in a fluorescing green clip on one side of her head, forming a stiffened fan. From her ears dangled the most amazing set of orange and green "giant fishing lures" imaginable, and the shirt she wore was of a shade of orange almost never found in nature.

Heads turned the moment she took off her jacket and stuffed it into her locker. They kept turning as she paraded the halls on her way to class. She smiled at Miss Tindall's ogling first glance and ignored the whispered wisecracks of her classmates. When, during a morning study break, Miss Tindall called her into the hall again, she was calm, smiling, amiable.

"Yes, Miss Tindall?" she said sweetly.

"I thought your mother bought some new clothes for you."

"She did."

The teacher made an uncertain gesture. "Well, then-"

"I like these clothes, Miss Tindall. They...suit me." Her smile widened. "Don't you think?"

"I'm not sure they're suitable for school." Miss Tindall was making a gallant attempt to sound kind and wise.

Stasi looked bemused. "Why not? Is there a rule against them?"

"Well...no, but they are distracting to the other students."

"That's not my fault, is it? Besides, I think they'll get used to it."

Miss Tindall frowned. "That's a poor attitude, young lady."

"Why? I'm not breaking any rules and I'm not hurting anybody. I'm just being myself. What's wrong with that?"

Miss Tindall sucked in her lips and fixed Stasi with a look that might have frozen a lesser fifteen-year-old on the spot.

Stasi smiled.

Miss Tindall tried another tack. "Stasi, dear, can't you hear them laughing at you? Don't you care if you become a laughing stock?"

Stasi thought about that. "No," she said.

"No," repeated Miss Tindall.

Stasi shook her head. "I'd rather be a laughing stock and be different than look just like everyone else."

"I see."

"May I go study now, please?"

Speechless, Miss Tindall opened the door and ushered her in.

Tahireh stood before her class with total aplomb, dressed in an azure linen sari that, with the lime green shirt she'd elected to wear under it, made her look like an elongated peacock. Her blonde hair cascaded in a fountain from a tiny topless blue fez.

"*When I Grow Up*—an essay by Tahireh Jones. Ahem. When I grow up I plan to be a scientist like my mother. And, like my mother, I would like to have my first Master's degree by the time I'm fifteen and my first Ph.D. at twenty—in Physics, I think, Quantum Physics...or maybe Particle Physics. I think I'd like to get my degree at Stanford—that's in California. Then, I would like to go to Juliard and study drama and voice. It is my dream to someday portray the fearless saint, Tahireh, for whom I am named, in the play about her commissioned by the immortal Sarah Bernhardt. I also plan to write several novels, books of inspirational poetry and academic volumes on travel in space and time."

She paused and thought for a moment, ignoring the titters of her classmates, then added, "I would also like to be one of the first full time field scientists on Mars."

Now the class cackled in unabashed glee. Mr. Matthews stood and clapped his hands.

"Class! Class! Please! I think we should applaud Tahireh for a very interesting and imaginative presentation. Now, seriously, young lady, tell us what you really want to do when you grown up."

"Everything I just said, although, I might like to study acting first."

Mr. Matthews smiled tolerantly. "But, Miss Jones, half those things are...just make-believe—going to Mars, time travel. And the other are not very realistic goals for a young lady. Don't you want a family? Children?"

"Oh, sure. If I fall in love with somebody, then I'll have that too."

The indulgent smile deepened. "Young lady, you can't do both."

"Why not? My Mom did. She says you can be whatever you want. She's got three Ph.D.s and her teaching credentials. She's written three books, too. One of them won the Nobel Peace Prize. I think I'd like to be the first author to win a Nobel prize for a science fiction novel."

"Science fiction," Mr. Matthews repeated. "I see." He looked around the room. "Who would like to go next?"

Pamela Harris wanted to go next. Pamela had been going to talk about being a beautician like her big sister, she said, and marrying someone who looked like Clarke Gable and moving to Omaha, but she was having second thoughts. She decided she really wanted to be a cruise ship captain like her Uncle Jerry, or maybe even an Air Force pilot like her father. She wasn't really sure she wanted a family at all. At least, not until she was very old. She thought she'd rather travel all over the world and decide about a family later.

Out of Mr. Matthew's eleven female students, seven suddenly opted to grow up differently than they'd previously planned. The word "homemaker" came up only twice as a lifetime goal. Tahireh Jones suddenly had the young ladies in Mr. Matthew's third grade class talking about careers, degrees and the equality of the sexes.

"About this paper, Mr. Jones." Mr. Schiflin pushed the three-page essay across his desk.

"Yes, sir?"

"I didn't grade it, because I wasn't sure what to make of it. I asked for an essay on the future of relations between the U.S. and Europe and you gave me science fiction."

"Excuse me, sir?"

"You can't honestly believe what you wrote here. Why did you write it?"

"Of course I believe it, sir."

Mr. Schiflin rustled the top page. "A unified Germany? The U.S. and the Soviet Union the closest of allies? A world government? English as a universal language?"

"Yes, sir."

"What makes you think the U.S. will lose its super-power status?"

Tam shrugged. "It's inevitable, isn't it? If we're to achieve world unity, there really can't be any so-called super-powers—at least, not the way we're used to thinking of them. We have to give up some sense of sovereignty to become a working member of a community made up of equal nations."

"There are those who would find that view unpatriotic or un-American. I just find it absurd. I'd like you to rewrite this essay, Mr. Jones, from a more realistic point of view."

"I can't, sir."

Mr. Schiflin fixed him with a positively deadly over-the-bifocals stare.

"This is the way it's going to be...I believe. If I wrote something else, I'd be lying. You don't want me to lie, do you, sir?"

The stare waxed more deadly. "Perhaps I need to have a word with your parents about this, young man."

"Perhaps you do, sir," returned Tam agreeably.

Tuesday, Constantine forgot his pencil bag. He stared at the empty paper before him on the desk, arms folded, stoic.

He could ask the teacher for a pencil, but that would lay him open to ridicule and perhaps even discipline. He could signal

Tahireh to toss him one of hers, but she'd probably get caught doing it and made to stand against the wall for throwing things in class. He could ask Bobby Truman to lend him one, but then he'd get caught whispering. That drew a stiff oral presentation on a randomly selected subject.

Then, again, he could always manifest a pencil—they were easy and non-descript—but he'd promised Mom and Dad he wouldn't. When he and Tam had told their parents about the blank book incident, a definite rule was established: no manifesting of books, pencils, or paper. Period.

Constantine had mumbled something about stifling the development of his God-given talents, but the rule stood— Constantine was not to manifest so much as a paper clip.

But I don't need a paper clip, he thought, *I need-*

"Constantine, begin working on the problems, please."

He glanced up toward the front of the class. Mr. Matthews gazed back, pointedly tapping his wristwatch. Constantine dropped his eyes and glanced quickly around the room, taking in the hunched figures of the other children—scribbling madly, eraser chewing, pencil tapping.

A slow smile tugged at the corners of his mouth. He glanced at his open math book, then set his gaze purposefully on the empty paper beside it, the first set of figures indelibly impressed on his mind.

Mr. Matthews started wandering several minutes later, weaving his way along and through the rows of struggling students, checking their progress or lack thereof. One of them sat unnaturally straight, eyes on his paper, smiling, hands folded inactively in his lap.

Matthews worked his way quietly toward the immobile child, snuck up behind him and peered expectantly over his shoulder, mouth open to utter a terrifying, "And what are we doing, Mr. Jones?" But the words did not form. Mr. Matthews ogled in silent disbelief as a series of mathematical problems scrawled themselves across the sheet of paper as if by an invisible pencil.

He gasped.

Constantine felt a chill of mixed terror and elation as he heard Mr. Matthews breath catch in his throat, sensed his blood cool suddenly in his veins.

The child-smile deepened.

"He hasn't told anybody," said Constantine. "I know he hasn't. And it's been three days."

Tam wrinkled his forehead. "Well, Mr. Schiflin talked to Dad about my essay. Dad said I should be less direct in my revelation of future events. He assured Mr. Schiflin that I wasn't un-American, just unusually perceptive and cosmopolitan. I'm not sure Schiflin even knows what cosmopolitan means. How're you girls doing?"

Tahireh drew herself up and smiled, tossing a thick blonde braid over her shoulder. "I've got almost every girl in our class thinking about what college they want to go to and what degrees they want to get." She exchanged the smile for a puzzled frown. "But I don't really understand how that's supposed to upset anybody."

"Oh, it will, Tar," Tam told her. "You'll see."

"I'm not so sure," said Stasi dourly. "I think maybe Mom and Dad awed the administration so much, they're just gonna grin and bear it. Miss Tindall hasn't batted more than an eyelash since our last talk. Elaine and a couple of the other girls have even started to dress like me and Beth Silverberg did something weird to her hair and Tindall just said, 'My, that's unique.'"

"Yeah, but Schiflin-"

"You handed in an essay that offended the man's sensitivities. That's not enough to get you in trouble."

"Then we need to bolster our offense."

Stasi shook her head. "We can't do anything really bad, Tam. At least, I won't."

"Me neither," vowed Tahireh.

"I wasn't even going to suggest it. I just think we need to give them something they can't ignore."

Tamujin Jones handled his fluorescent orange and blue gravi-pack with cheerful confidence, showing everyone who cocked an eye at the bright satchel that it was light as a feather despite the fact that it obviously contained every textbook he owned. He stopped to let this one touch the sleek, shiny material; grinned as that one hefted it, finding it to be much lighter than it appeared to be; laughed outright when one especially curious young citizen removed a book to find that the single volume weighed more than the entire pack full he had just taken it from.

"It's what they make parachutes out of," Tam told anyone who asked. "And astronaut's uniforms."

"Astro-what?" asked one freckled peer.

"Space suits," Tam said and grinned.

"So what else do you carry around in that 'space bag' besides books?" asked the boy who sat behind him in class.

He tried to look coy, secretive. Stasi was better at that than he was.

"Oh, not much," he said, and floated the pack into his lap.

His classmates' curiosity was suitably whetted. They watched the pack as if it might hold a football autographed by the Cornhusker's starting quarterback. They were forced to take their eyes from it as class progressed, but Tam brought their attention back from time to time by rummaging in it, extracting a pencil, a notebook, his English text.

When Mr. Schiflin began to lecture on their English assignment, Tam set his pencil down in the midst of note-taking and glanced furtively around. Then he opened the pack and extracted, with the air of a veteran safecracker, something small and black and mechanical; something that drew the eyes of his circle of watchers like a magnet.

He played it like a tiny piano—one handed—then scribbled, then listened, then played, then scribbled again. A whisper of curiosity rippled out from Tam's cast pebble, cresting within earshot of the lecturer. Schiflin, interest engaged, took his show on the road, wandering the depth and breadth of the classroom.

Tam let him come within two rows before he slipped the enticing object back into his pack. The teacher covered the distance between them in two strides, every eye in the class following him.

"What was that, Mr. Jones?"

Tam looked up, wide-eyed, and smiled affably. "What was what, sir?"

Schiflin pointed. "You just hid something in that bag."

"I didn't hide anything."

"I saw him, Mr. Schiflin," volunteered Greg Rollins from across the aisle. "He was playing with something. A puzzle, I think."

"What was it, Mr. Jones?"

Tam shook his head. "The only thing I put away just now was my pocket dictionary."

Mr. Schiflin's pointing hand turned palm up. "Give it to me, please."

"I was just taking notes and needed to look up a word-"

"Hand it over. Now."

Tam hesitated just long enough to make Schiflin's face turn red, then he withdrew the curiosity from the satchel and laid it across the teacher's outstretched palm.

Schiflin turned the thing over, frowning at it. "What is this, Mr. Jones?"

"I told you, sir. It's a dictionary. I was looking up words from your lecture."

Schiflin stared at him. "A dictionary... If you don't mind, Mr. Jones, I think I'll just hold onto this 'dictionary.' And I'll expect you to deliver a note from me to your parents."

"Yes, sir."

Mr. Schiflin started to turn away, then glanced back. "How does this work?"

"You just turn it on—the little red switch at the top. Press it; it turns green to show the unit is on. You press it again to turn it off. To look up a word, you can either enter it from the keypad or just tell it."

"Tell it?"

Tam nodded, enjoying himself much more than he knew he should. He'd always wondered what it would be like to take Jules Verne for a ride in a hover-lite or show Edgar Alan Poe a computer. This had to be almost as good.

"Just say the word," he said.

Schiflin frowned, then reddened. He glanced around the room as if he'd only just realized how big an audience they had.

"C'mon, Mr. Schiflin!" urged Greg. "Try it. I'll bet he's full of it!"

Schiflin didn't even censure the outburst. "It would serve you right, young man, to be caught with your pants down."

"I'm not lying, sir. I promise. Give it a word."

Scowling, Schiflin pressed the red button. It turned green and a tiny, flat, black screen the size of a business card displayed the words: "Dictionary Mode." Below that was: "Input Word?"

He held the thing close to his mouth and said, "Outrageous."

The screen filled with text. "Outrageous," echoed his own voice. "Grossly offensive, disgraceful, shameful, extravagant, immoderate. Shall I spell it?"

Face white with small patches of intense red at the cheeks, Schiflin stared at the tiny machine. "Shall I spell it?" asked the pleasantly aqua text.

"No, thank you," he answered, and felt immediately stupid. Tam sensed his anger warring with wonder, with curiosity...with fear.

The bell rang, jolting everyone out of the shared stupor.

Still, no one moved. Mr. Schiflin cleared his throat. "Class dismissed for lunch. Mr. Jones, you may go home."

"Why, sir? I haven't done anything wrong. It's all right to look up words—you said so."

"In a book not-"

"It's just a dictionary, sir."

"It's more than a dictionary, Mr. Jones. Even I can see that. What you've done is lied boldly and outrageously. You have disrupted my classroom. And I can only assume, you've stolen this obviously valuable piece of equipment. Now, go home. I'll speak to your parents at their earliest convenience."

"I didn't steal it."

"We'll see about that."

Tam nodded. "Yes, sir. Whatever you say, sir." He gathered his books into the mysterious pack and left the campus.

He managed to get into the house without being seen by either parent. That wasn't difficult. Troy Jones was at the Air Base posing as a scientist of some sort and his wife was cheerfully working on the text of their research somewhere in the Lab/Office.

When the others came in at 1630 hours, Stasi had her friend Elaine and two other giggling girls in tow. Tam came out to the landing, giving his sister the thumbs up sign as she entered the front hall. She returned it, looking purposefully intense and sporting a twisted, half-manic grin.

"Hi, Mom! I'm home!" she called through the front parlor. "I've got some friends with me. We're going up to my room to do some homework, okay?"

There was a moment of silence, then Helen Jones's voice came back to them from the "restricted area." "Is your room clean?"

Stasi's grin widened. "Yes, Ma'am."

"Well...okay, then, I guess."

"Thanks, Mom!"

The girls loped up the stairs, school books in arms, looking, Tam realized, like Anastasia Jones Clones. Their hair was tugged off to one side in fans or sprays; their Mary Jane shoes mimicked her astrolon flats. They wore what looked like their big sister's hand-me-down skirts and from every earlobe dangled earrings made of gaudy goo-gaws home-mounted on scavenged clips and wires.

All in all, a most up-to-date group of young ladies—if the date was 2112.

Tam said, "Hi," and returned to his room.

"Your little brother's awful cute," observed Trudy Wessa, "for a kid," she added.

"I heard he got in trouble today," said Elaine. "Do you know why?"

Stasi dumped her books on her desk and flopped into her study chair, a fulsome papasan they'd picked up in Japan.

"Gosh, no," she said, wide-eyed. "I didn't see him at lunch, though."

"I heard he got caught with some kind of Air Force secret weapon," offered Beth.

Elaine glared at her. "I heard it was just a toy."

Stasi laughed. "Sure. What's my little brother doing with an Air Force secret weapon?"

"Well, your dad works at Offutt, doesn't he?" asked Beth. "Maybe he brought something home and Tam just...borrowed it."

"Tam wouldn't do that."

"Well, Mr. Schiflin was real mad," Trudy interjected. "I saw him talking to Mr. Benoit about it while I was in the Administration Office this afternoon."

"Sounds like you heard him, too. Eavesdropping, were we?"

Trudy figured Elaine's smirk warranted retaliation. She grabbed a pillow from under Elaine's elbow and smacked her with it, sending her on a giggling roll against the headboard.

"Ow!"

Elaine sat up again, rubbing her elbow and glowering at the two very hard objects it had connected with. Her expression changed immediately.

"Oooh, wow! What are these?" She abandoned the wounded elbow in favor of checking out her find. "*Dune,* by Frank Herbert," she read. "Winner of the Nebula Award." She looked at the other one. "*Studies in Physics and Metaphysics* by Dr. Jamal Am-a-di-yeh." She glanced over at Stasi. "Those sound like book titles."

Stasi pretended embarrassment and leapt (belatedly) to collect her property. "Uh, they are."

Elaine swept them out of her way only to have Trudy grab one. "What are these? Some kind of ritzy slip covers?"

"Slip covers!" snorted Elaine. She tapped the one she held with her fingernail. "They feel like metal or plastic or something. What's this red button do?"

Of course, she pushed it, and the book opened and presented her with a full-page menu that enquired politely if she wished to go to the last bookmark and, if so, would she like a summary of what had happened in the story so far, or would she rather start at the beginning? Would she like the book in black on white or white on black or would she rather select colors from a palette? Did she want pictures as well as text? Did she want audio output in addition to visual? Would she like to print hard copy?

"Wow!" she said. "Wow! What is this? Did you get this in Paris?"

Stasi scratched her nose, hiding a grin. "San Francisco."

Trudy gaped at her.

"Who are these guys?" asked Beth. "Herbert and Ama-Ama-"

"Amadiyeh. Herbert's a science fiction writer. Dr. Amadiyeh is my educational counselor."

"Your what?"

"I thought Mrs. Hester was your Counselor," said Elaine, "same as me."

"Well, this is different. This is for my, uh, home study program. You know, supplemental education."

Beth nodded. "'Cause you're a brain, right?"

"Something like that."

Stasi reached for the books again.

"2100 edition," Elaine read. "Another Cyber-Book from-"

Stasi snatched the volume from her hands. "We'd better start on our skit." She tossed the books into a drawer of her dresser. Three pairs of eyes locked on the drawer.

Elaine giggled. "Are you from Mars?"

"Any idea what this parent-teacher conference is all about?" Troy Jones asked the general assembly, since there was nothing in the usual "to discuss (your child's name and infraction here)" blank.

Four innocent stares met him over the edge of the paper. He waved it in the air over his dinner plate.

"Anyone care to claim this?"

The four innocent stares converged over the tofu loaf in a hasty, silent conference. Then, Stasi spoke, which was, in itself, was enough to give both Doctors Jones pause. A speech by the eldest child generally meant she had been elected ringleader, which, of course, meant there was a ring to lead, which could only lead to parental aggravation.

The Doctors Jones simultaneously recalled the last such occurrence, which had centered around the appearance of an unauthorized mongoose on the house manifest after a Shift to colonial India. The resulting furor in their quiet, well-modulated environment had gotten them and the mongoose evicted from their inner city condominium to a rambling house in the Berkeley hills.

"It's probably just further repercussions from Tam's disagreement with Mr. Schiflin," Stasi said sagely, then added, "although, Miss Tindall did talk to me the other day about my clothes."

"What's wrong with them?" asked Helen warily.

Stasi shrugged. "She thought they were a little, um, bright ...different—you know, too individualistic."

"But, I bought you some new skirts and blouses."

"I like my old clothes better sometimes. They remind of who I am. Where I'm from...really."

"Are there some problems here we're not aware of?" asked their father.

Stasi and Tam shrugged in unison and glanced at each other.

"I got reprimanded for looking up some words during one of Mr. Schiflin's lectures the other day," offered Tam.

"Mr. Matthews didn't like the way I did my math problems," added Constantine.

Both Joneses Senior moved their eyes to Tahireh.

"I'm fine!" she said and smiled.

Tahireh Jones was not fine. Not according to Mr. Matthews and a sampling of mothers. She was a fomenter of discord, a libertine, a Bad Influence. Parents had complained that the daughters they'd assumed would work at the library until they married and settled nearby, now showed a sudden interest in brother's college fund. Some even showed an interest in his toys and books. Others played at being Sarah Bernhardt or Katherine Hepburn; their dolls gathered in audiences so entranced as to be left unblinkingly wide-eyed and speechless.

While Helen and Troy Jones, seated in the principal's office with that gentleman and a delegation of three teachers, pondered their response to those charges, Miss Tindall fired her volley. Their eldest daughter was an equally negative influence, encouraging the most ridiculous extremes in dress and hairstyles. Distressed mothers wondered why their daughters had suddenly taken to ripping the hems out of their dresses and twisting their hair into shapes reminiscent of ornamental shrubbery.

Mr. Schiflin observed darkly that excesses in clothing were nothing compared to the sort of un-American, irreligious philosophy expounded by Tamujin Jones in his treatise on the future role of America in the free world.

"And then," he said, pausing dramatically, "there's this." He reached into his pocket and withdrew-

"My God!" Troy Jones gasped. "Where did you-?"

"You recognize it, I see," said Schiflin mildly.

"Ah...that is, well...yes. It belongs to- That is, it's ...a piece of my lab equipment."

"Really? Your son said it was his dictionary. May I ask how this obviously sophisticated piece of equipment came to be in the hands of a fourteen-year-old boy?"

"And how your daughter, Anastasia, came to be in possession of equally sophisticated readers written by unknown authors with no record in the Library of Congress?" added Miss Tindall.

"And how Constantine appears to be able to write without a pencil?"

"What?" said Mr. Benoit, and the other teachers stared at him.

"I saw him," Matthews said, his voice low. "I did not imagine it."

Helen tried to dart in before a panic ensued. "The children weren't supposed to-" she began and stopped. Weren't supposed to what—unleash future developments on this poor, unprepared, narrow environment? She glanced at her husband, who cleared his throat.

"In our line of work, Helen and I are...privileged to make use of many rather startling new technologies."

"Your line of work?" repeated Mr. Benoit. "And what would that be? Espionage?"

"Good Lord, no. We're research scientists—archaeologists, anthropologists, sociologists, historians."

"Come now, Dr. Jones. We've seen enough to know that you and your family are digging up more than bones. This equipment, what Beth Silverberg and the others saw in your daughter's room, the things your children have said and done, all lead to the obvious suspicion. You are Communist spies, Doctor Jones." Benoit sat back in his principalian throne, looking quite pleased.

"Absurd!" said Troy irritably. His eyes followed on Tam's dictionary to the principal's desk, wondering how to get it back.

"Ridiculous," added Helen, and wondered the same thing.

"Is it? Even your children's names are foreign. Tamujin-that was Genghis Kahn, if I'm not mistaken; Anastasia—a member of the Russian aristocracy; Tahireh—the name of a Mohammedan suffragette-"

"That's Muslim," Troy corrected absently. "And she wasn't. She was a Báb'í."

"You beg the issue, Doctor. I suspect that what Mr. Schiflin has confiscated from your son is a top-secret invention. The question is: Whose top secret is it? Ours or theirs? Did you steal it from SAC Headquarters or did you bring it with you as a tool of the trade?"

"If we'd stolen it," reasoned Helen, "we'd hardly let our son take it to school."

Benoit looked unconvinced. "Oh, but boys will be boys. Your son can't be expected to ignore such a curiosity. Or maybe..." He rose dramatically and paced around his desk to perch against the front of it, looming over them like a clumsy, cliché movie cop. "Maybe Tamujin *wanted* to get caught. Maybe he wanted you to get caught—to end the years of subterfuge and pretence, the years of lonely, trackless wandering."

He gazed down at them soulfully, and was rewarded by their sudden, startled exchange of glances.

"Do you think-?" asked Troy.

"I didn't realize-" murmured Helen.

"They must be more miserable-"

"Than we had any conception."

"I feel like such an ignoramus."

"And selfish."

"And sorry?" asked Benoit eagerly.

"Well, of course," said Troy. "Those kids must be desperate."

"We've got to do something, Troy," said Helen.

"Sign a confession," urged Benoit, leaning over them.

Troy waved at him as if he were a buzzing insect. "Helen, have we been that-"

"Self-absorbed?" She nodded emphatically. "We owe those poor kids an apology."

"You owe this *country* an apology!"

"Maybe, but what they did was completely out of tune— underhanded. They could have said something."

"They *did*. They blew your cover!"

"They did, honey. They said a lot of somethings. We didn't listen. We were too busy being...."

"Spies?"

"Academicians. That's what that mongoose was all about. They wanted a real home, not an antiseptic holding pen. They were happy at the Farm."

"Mongoose? Farm? What's that—code?"

Helen nodded, grimacing. "The Farm." She put her hand on his khaki covered knee. "We need to talk this out with them. Listen to them. Compromise."

"You're already compromised," said Benoit.

"There's only one problem, Helen. We haven't finished our research in this time zone."

"Oh, you're finished in this time zone, all right, Doctor. And when Colonel Powers gets here-"

"Who?" Both Joneses turned their heads, speaking in perfect, two-part harmony.

"Colonel Powers from Strategic Air Command, the Little Pentagon, the place you've been spying on." Benoit was obviously pleased to have finally gotten their attention. "I called when this all began to come together. He'll be here any minute to question you and to see this." He patted the dictionary.

"And do you suppose we'll actually stay around to meet him?" asked Troy.

Benoit looked as if he'd believed it up until that very moment.

"You're right about this," Troy continued, nodding at the dictionary. "It is, as you suspected, a highly sophisticated piece of equipment. It's not only a Russian-English translator; it's a communications device, which you have activated, signaling our operatives as to our exact location. And-" He snatched up the little machine, activated it, and turned the glowing green button atop it on the gaping principal. "-it's also a weapon—a laser beam gun, to be exact."

He rose, taking his wife's hand. "Come, my dear. The submarine is waiting."

They backed toward the door of the office, keeping the startled teachers covered with the dictionary.

Troy opened the door and ushered Helen through. "*Za mir,*" he said. "Oh, and *pazhaloosta.*"

"Here they come," said Tam urgently.

He let the curtain fall back across the front window and headed for the kitchen.

"Wow, they're really trekkin'!" said Constantine, impressed with his parent's speed.

"They keep looking behind them," observed Tahireh. "I wonder if there's a mob after them like that time in Salem."

Stasi shook her head. "I don't see anybody. I think I hear sirens, though."

"Hey, you guys!" shouted Tam from the direction of the kitchen. "Stations!"

Children flew in all directions, assuming nonchalant, relaxed poses; looking studious, looking bored, looking in the refrigerator for leftovers.

The front door slammed open, then shut again, admitting two gasping, giggling adults.

"Stations, everybody!" Helen wheezed. "We're powering up!"

Galvanized, the kids followed their parents' trail as far as the dining room. There, they stopped to exchange bug-eyed glances, clicking invisible glasses over success beyond their wildest dreams. They heard the soft hum of the Grid coming on line and bolted as a unit for the Lab.

Their parents stood at the console; Father checking settings, Mother clearing an emergency Shift through the QuestLabs Controller. The hum grew to a flute-tone—a warm wave of pure sound. The walls of the two story brick house began to glow softly violet, to tremble, to run and change and remold themselves to vapor.

"We're on our way," murmured Helen.

"On our way?" asked Stasi. "On our way where, Mama?"

"Home," Helen said and turned to give her children a fierce grin. "Home, where you four will do some stiff penance."

"Penance?" asked Tam warily. "What penance?"

"Your father and I gave it some serious thought while we were galloping up that hill tonight."

"Serious," agreed Troy, eyes on his monitor.

"And?" Four children held their breath.

"When we get back to the Farm...."

Their mother keyed a last sequence, depressed a final button. The walls melted into a glorious violet spray, ran to red, to sunset, to Sun itself. Colors exploded in the walls; splashed and crested, then imploded, becoming solid, opaque, mundane.

Helen Jones turned back to her children with a terrifying glare.

"You're all grounded."

The four pairs of eyes got wider.

"Grounded?"

"Grounded. No Temporal Shifting, no terrorizing small midwestern towns, no anachronistic dabblings."

"Never, ever again?" asked Tahireh, her brow furrowing.

"Well," the Doctors Jones traded glances.

"Maybe...." began Helen.

"...during vacation," finished Troy.

Tam was troubled. Now that he had what he wanted, he wasn't sure he should have gotten it. "But Dad, what about your work?"

"We'll just have to adapt, compromise. But we will not compromise on your...discipline. You heard your mother. You're grounded. Right here, in Twenty-one—um," he checked his chronometer, "twelve."

The four pairs of eyes blinked. The taciturn Constantine let out a jubilant whoop. Tahireh giggled. Stasi hugged both her parents.

"Thanks, Dad! Thanks, Mom!" said Tam. "C'mon, you guys, let's go check out the old neighborhood."

The noisy rabble rolled out of the Lab, through the house and out the front door. The elder Joneses followed their progress with the delicate sonar of parenthood.

"Extraordinary," said Troy. "We've spent our lives studying history, but today was the first time we've actually *made* history.

Do you realize that for the first time since the birth of the Universe, children were grounded and liked it?"

Helen looked thoughtful. "An interesting phenomenon. We'd be delinquent not to record it for posterity."

"A research paper?"

"Why not a book? 'The Effects of Temporal Shift on Adolescent and Pre-Adolescent Development.'"

Troy Jones nodded, experiencing that peculiar, warm, fuzzy feeling he always associated with love and new projects. "I like the sound of that," he said.

Out under the autumn trees, Stasi and Tam surveyed the familiar and found it wonderful. Not far off, Tahireh and Constantine rolled in the grass of Home, giggling.

Tam took a deep breath. "Dad got the dictionary back," he said. "I saw it on the Console. It's kinda weird, thinking how close we came to making an indelible mark on history. It'll be a relief when QuestLabs perfects that Anachron Object Recall System."

Stasi's mouth did funny things at the corners. "I hope they perfect it soon."

"Huh? Why? I just said Dad got the dictionary back."

"Yeah. Well, I did something sort of...dumb." She glanced at him out of the tail of one eye. "I lent Elaine a book."

Marsh Mallow

A story of science fiction by

Marsh Mallow originally appeared in *Analog Science Fiction* in 1996. I link it here with the time travel stories simply because the technology that allows my universe-trotting archaeologist, Rhys Llewellyn, to move freely through space is the same technology developed by QuestLabs to allow its operatives to move through time.

Marsh Mallow poses the question: "What makes a human human?" This is one of a series of stories about a team of xeno-archaeologists whose activities give me a forum for exploring other worlds of God.

> *Know thou that every fixed star hath its own planets,*
> *and every planet its own creatures, whose number no*
> *man can compute.*
>
> *Gleanings from the*
> *Writings of Bahá'u'lláh,*
> p. 163

They called the planet Bog for lack of anything nicer to say about it. The name was certainly appropriate if not one hundred percent accurate. The entire planet was *not* a bog, but anyone set down in its narrow "temperate zone," would find that hard to believe. The planet's abundant supply of surface water brought to mind words like "tarn" and "bracken"—even "bilge." Not a drop of the stuff was drinkable. It contained salts and minerals in such concentration that, in some of the smaller bodies of water, you could float objects that would have sunk to the bottom on Earth or Pa-Loana or just about any other habitable planet Rhys Llewellyn could name.

Take that gently bobbing field lamp, for example. Rhys gazed at it in consternation as it was carried away on the sludgy currents of Brown Salt Lake, gliding serenely just out of his reach.

"See what I mean?" Roderick Halfax lobbed a flat rock at the lamp. It struck the metal casing with a muffled *ping!* and plopped into the water where it began the tedious and protracted process of sinking. A tiny cloud of native "fireflies," already visible in the twilight, eddied above the flotsam, apparently attracted by the gleam of alien metal.

"I'd rather not have demonstrated it at the expense of our field supplies," Rhys admitted, "but yes, I do see."

Rick peered at the sludgy liquid. "You could probably walk out and get it...but I wouldn't recommend it." He turned back from the water to make his way up the newly constructed pier laid just last week by Tanaka Corp's advance team of engineers.

After a last glance at the lost field lamp, Rhys fell into step beside his assistant. "I'll bet you can build a boat out of just about anything here—wood, metal, stone..."

"Ah, but sir," Rick countered, a frown puckering his brow, "the natives here don't build boats, nor do they work wood, make metal or carve stone...sir."

Rhys laughed; the younger man's impersonation of his very earnest female assistant, Yoshi Umeki, was humorously accurate. And, of course, what he said was also true. The "natives" of Bog did none of those things, which posed the question of whether they were "natives" at all in the anthropological sense. There was nothing like alien/human contact to blur the lines between man and intelligent animal.

Rhys could recall particular Humans whose behavior blurred the lines even further. It was that sticky question of sentience that Rhys Llewellyn had been brought to Bog to answer.

"Ah, Yoshi!" He looked up and saw the girl making her way toward them through the stacks of tarp-covered trading goods and camp supplies that sat upon what passed for terra firma in this neck of the swamp. She was pecking at a notepad with one finger and frowning earnestly over the results of her work. Seeing Rhys and Rick, she paused and waved, oblivious to the admiring glances of a handful of Tanaka engineers who'd gathered around the mobile cantina.

Rhys lengthened his stride and covered the distance between them to give the girl a hearty hug. "So, Yoshi—any candidates for sentience among our Bogies?"

"Well, there appear to be several at this location." She consulted her notepad. "The top candidates are a bipedal, brachiating mammalian reminiscent of a lemur, a burrowing reptilian form not unlike an iguana, and an amphibian that builds mud lodges in the swamp."

"Ah, now *that* sounds promising."

"I'm glad you think so, Professor. Personally, I find it all rather depressing."

The voice, sporting a decidedly British accent, came from over Rhys's shoulder, making him turn. He found himself face to face with an inappropriately well-dressed man of perhaps middle age. He was average in height, bland in coloring, and wore an expression of annoyed boredom. "And you are?" Rhys asked.

Yoshi jumped into the conversation. "I'm sorry, sir—I mean, Rhys. This is Raymond Godwin. From, um, Acquisitions."

Godwin extended his hand in Rhys's direction, his eyes sweeping the younger man with urbane horror before lingering pointedly on his McCrae tartan kilt. "Director of Acquisitions, this sector." His upper lip twitched minutely.

Rhys, suddenly conscious of how itchy the woolen kilt was in the marsh's thick sauna of an atmosphere, tried to make his smile sincere. "Rhys Llewellyn, acting Director of Trade and Cultural Directions. Exactly what is it you hope to acquire, Mr. Godwin?"

"Mineral rights to this entire planet. And first shot at its other resources."

Rhys frowned, trying not to twitch under the combined attack of wool, perspiration, and sudden unreasoning dislike. "I don't understand..."

"The advance reports on Bog came into Corporate Acquisitions just over a week ago. I was immediately dispatched to make known to the powers that be that Tanaka Corporation wishes to possess mineral rights on Bog."

"Did Acquisitions also receive the advance reports on the native lifeforms?"

Godwin nodded. "No signs of civilization." The idea obviously delighted him.

"No sign of civilization as we know it," Rhys cautioned. "Any of the creatures on Bog might be sentient."

Godwin shrugged. "Fine. You find the sentients, I'll negotiate for mineral rights."

Oh, so simple. "Have you ever done anything like this before?" Rhys asked, keeping his voice carefully neutral.

"Dr. Llewellyn, Acquisitions is my *career*. Of course, I've done this before."

"What I meant, Mr. Godwin, is have you ever pursued an acquisition this early on—before a trade partner's even been identified? Before a language has even been determined in which the parties can negotiate?"

"No. But *you're* the expert in that department, Dr. Llewellyn. I'm counting on *you* to find the trade partners and their language." He smiled. "After all, that's what Tanaka pays you for, is it not?"

Rhys glanced sideways at Yoshi, whose expression, for once in her life, was blank. "It is. I'm merely surprised that the company is acting so precipitously."

Godwin shrugged. "Bog is a mineralogically wealthy, if miserable, planet. We surely don't want that wealth falling into someone else's pockets...Bristol-Benz, for example." He favored Rhys with a lopsided smile. "Frankly, I'm surprised Vladimir Zarber isn't here already, breathing down your neck."

At the mention of his archrival, Rhys grimaced. "Like you, Vladimir Zarber is used to working more...established prospects."

"Well, Professor, I'm told that establishing prospects is your forté. I'm looking forward to seeing you in action." He glanced about at the pallets of goods. "Now, I see you have a variety of merchandise. How do you plan to determine to whom it should be offered?"

"Shotgun, Mr. Godwin. We open up our little marketplace and see who shows up to shop."

"And how long do you expect this process to take?"

Rhys smiled. "Why there's no telling about that. Could take days...months...."

"Years," murmured Yoshi.

Godwin threw her a subtly horrified glance. "You'd willingly spend that much time to determine sentience? Months in this godforsaken cow wallow?"

Yoshi's mouth twitched. "Or years," she repeated.

"That's ridiculous. Tanaka doesn't have that kind of time to invest in such a pursuit."

"You're always free to leave," Rhys told him. "We'd gladly contact you when and if we had something positive to report."

"What, and allow Bristol-Benz to sneak in and snap up resources? I assure you, what their advance teams lack in scientific method, they make up for in expediency."

"I'd hardly allow that to happen," Rhys assured him. "I've a few negotiations to my credit as well."

"Commodities. You negotiate *commodities*. I'm talking about planetary *rights*, Professor, not trinkets." He shook his head emphatically. "No, sir. You will simply have to determine the existence or non-existence of sentient beings in a reasonable length of time. Whether I deal with those sentients or deal with the Collective, I have a charter from Tanaka to acquire the mineral rights to Bog. As depressing as this ball of mud is, that sickening stew of elements" —he gestured toward the lake— "is worth its weight in platinum. Now, if you'll excuse me?"

"What an obnoxious character!" Rick Halfax exclaimed to Godwin's receding back.

Rhys followed his gaze. "Hmm. And impatient. Well, let's see if we can't get Mr. Godwin his stew."

"Do we have to?" Yoshi was watching the Acquisitions director with undisguised distaste.

Rhys glanced at her in surprise. In their several years together, he had rarely known her to express personal dislike for anyone. Yoshi reacted to causes rather than personalities and she had obviously decided that Mr. Raymond Godwin was inimical to the cause of Bog.

The next several weeks Rhys and his colleagues spent ferrying their wares to different parts of the local marsh. Within the habitat of each of their candidates they created what they hoped were attractive displays of goods. The arboreal simians hid from them, the reptilians ignored them and the amphibians wrecked the "marketplace" and incorporated the wreckage into their gloppy constructions.

"Interesting," Rhys enthused, studying a particularly elaborate mound that now sported strips of bright, Human-made fabric and squares of therma-plast and metal.

"You're not actually *encouraged* by this random destruction are you?" Wearing a crisp, new camouflage coverall and a small helmet, Raymond Godwin gaped at him from the midst of their decimated cache.

"There's nothing random about it. They needed material for their constructs—they took it." Rhys returned to where Yoshi waited at the cache with his field kit and began to rummage in it.

Godwin pursued him, stepping over the litter of left-behind objects. "Yes, indeed they did. They took fabric, food, tools, baubles—anything and everything—and used it indiscriminately. Surely you can't argue sentience based on that? Beavers do *that*, Pekulan treemunks do *that*, yet I doubt even *you* would attempt to open trade relations with them... What *are* you doing?"

Rhys ignored him, continuing to describe a circle on the soggy forest floor with a fluorescing powder. Within the circle, he placed a group of objects taken from the rear deck of their enclosed swamp buggy.

"Oh, I get it," Godwin said. "You're attempting to communicate, aren't you? You're trying to tell our amphibian friends that this stuff didn't get here by accident."

"Something like that," Rhys admitted. "I'm also trying to determine if they've a preference for certain materials."

Godwin glanced back across the glade to where the Bogies' mud lodges poked in misshapen domes from the water. "Shiny or bright stuff. They seem to like...ornamentation."

Rhys acknowledged the observation with some surprise. "Yes. The question is, is it a *cultural* affinity for ornamentation, as you call it, or is it merely an animal's attraction to shiny objects?"

Godwin seemed to show a little more interest in their mission after that and even helped set up their surveillance net. With vidicams focused on the cache and on the arm of ooze (a lagoon, technically) that poked into the glade from the marshy lake, they took their swamp buggy and withdrew to watch and wait.

Before they'd gone even a handful of meters from the spot, the amphibians came ashore to explore the cache. They were bashful at first, skirting the display of goods and sipping condensation from the broad, glossy fronds of a low-growing plant—for all the world like a band of burglars trying to look nonchalant as they case a prospective target. When they finally moved, they ignored the bright chalk circle—except to spread it about with their flat, webbed feet—and went straight for the shiniest or most brightly colored objects they could find, carrying them back to the water in their wide mouths.

Other creatures appeared as well—some large, colorful avians the size of small Macaws fluttered down to pick at anything fibrous; a small mammal of some sort shuffled among the food stuffs; a shapeless, lumpy thing like a headless, legless armadillo scuttled here and there, its only remarkable feature the irregular patches of bright color that decorated its otherwise drab hide. It trailed a cloud of the gnat-sized fireflies, recognizable in daylight only by their iridescent green wings. Everything got thoroughly pawed over, but except for the bright building materials and the food, nothing was taken. All in all, a disappointing episode.

They moved their 'trade center' north after that, determined to give the bashful simians more study. The lemuresque creatures seemed to have some promising social habits. They built tree houses—or at least elaborate nests—they lived in family groups, and formed communities made up of a number of families.

"I'm actually quite hopeful," Rhys said when they'd completed setting up shop in the fringes of one of the arboreal 'villages.' "They exhibit a number of distinguishing social characteristics that could indicate sentience."

"Doesn't the mere fact that they build those little tree-houses mean they're sentient?" asked Godwin. "That makes them tool-users, doesn't it?"

"There are any number of animals that weave nests at least that elaborate," said Rhys. "That doesn't mean they're people."

"What would make you consider them...people?"

"Observing trade would incline me to hopefulness. As would the use of a discernible language—or some other observable system of communication."

"Ah...the operative term being 'system.'"

Rhys nodded. "Another bit of evidence might be the cultivation of food or the domestication of animals."

Yoshi, peering at the monitor, glanced up. "You mean like the birds? They seem to be all over the village here. And what about those big arthropods?"

Rhys, Rick and Godwin all moved to look over her shoulder at the large flat display. In the clearing central to the simians' tree houses, several of the lumpy, waddling creatures milled like legless, armored sheep. The simians sat peacefully among them, feeding on the seed-cones of the lacy coniferous trees, tossing the used-up cores at the native 'armadillos' which snuffled up whatever the swift avians didn't nab, occasionally using some well-concealed body part to fling one back toward its point of origin.

Yoshi chewed her lip. "Pets? Livestock?"

Rhys nodded. "Could be. Could also be simple scavenging. Only time will tell."

They watched their cache of goods with great anticipation, but the simians' interaction, when it came, had more in common with pillaging than with shopping. Accordingly, Rhys took the next step. Over a period of days, they moved their observation station closer to the village perimeter, insinuating themselves into the landscape. When the simians no longer ran squealing for the trees the moment the Humans twitched a toe, they staged what Raymond Godwin snidely referred to as their "inane little skits." Rhys and Rick went through the motions of trade, playing merchant and customer, making a performance of the exchange of goods. Their performances drew a furry crowd of onlookers; the lemur-like creatures became bolder, even going so far as to touch some of the wares displayed behind each actor.

During the third or fourth skit came the break-through that Rhys had been hoping for; one of the simians picked up a piece of off-world fruit and made an attempt to interest one of his comrades in it. In a matter of minutes the creatures were picking up food and playing at exchange. Eventually, the trade broadened to include sticks, rocks, seedpods from the trees, anything they could find. Some courageous individuals even offered pilfered foodstuffs to the Humans.

But Rhys Llewellyn watched with increasing disappointment; there was no method to the madness, no pattern. The simians weren't trading; they were merely mimicking observed behavior. Even as he looked on, still searching for signs that the Bogies comprehended their actions, they began flinging stuff about and the 'trading' degenerated into a food fight. The Humans withdrew.

"I don't think they get it," Godwin said. "Pet armadillos or no, I think they're animals, not people."

"Give it some time, Godwin," Rhys told him, trying to be optimistic.

But the next day's trade went no better. Upon seeing the Humans, the simians began to caper and playfully exchange random items, which were forgotten as soon as they left the traders' hand-like paws. As before, the episode ended in a hail of badly aimed projectiles, which pelted Humans, simians and their 'pets' indiscriminately.

Rhys's only reason for hopefulness was that the simians were observed to sip water from the same broad-leaf fronds he'd seen growing in the lake environs. Since the fronds didn't grow near the tree village, he could only suppose that meant the simians had transported them. But observing that more advanced behavior was denied the Humans. The simians were never seen retrieving the fronds; they simply seemed to appear during the night. How, even Yoshi's nocturnal video records failed to show.

Rhys was disappointed. "I suppose," he told Rick and Yoshi, "that we ought to pick a new target and start again." He shook his head. "I would have bet credits that the presence of both birds and arthropods indicated nascent domestication. Evidently, it only indicated a symbiosis."

Yoshi nodded. "The lemurs leave refuse and the—the bogdillos and birds scavenge it."

"Bogdillos?" Rick repeated.

Yoshi shrugged and glanced at her notes. "I get tired of saying 'arthropods.' There are some reptiles at a sight about fifteen klicks from here that have been observed in a bipedal stance. It seems they also use sticks to pry food out of crevasses between rocks and have been observed carrying articles about what the advance team described as a village."

"We'll visit them tomorrow then," Rhys said absently.

"You seem unhappy, professor," Raymond Godwin observed.

"Unhappy?" Rhys shook his head. "No. A bit disappointed, perhaps."

"Whatever for? Surely if you find no sentient beings on Bog it makes your job just that much easier...and your departure that much sooner." He glanced around at the explosion of damp foliage that surrounded them, every leaf and stalk glistening with Bog's dank perspiration. "I've never in my life been in a place that sweats like this. My hair clings to my head, my clothing clings to my body. It makes Florida seem positively arid. I don't know how you can stand it." He gave Rhys's kilt a disparaging glance. "*I'll* certainly be glad to leave."

"I will admit," Rhys told him, "that Bog's temperate zone seems to be poorly named, but...I would like to have found some new neighbors to talk to."

"Well, speaking on behalf of Tanaka, whose interests you also claim to serve, new neighbors are a pain. They require the expenditure of time and energy that would be more profitably spent in negotiating with the Collective for planetary resources. There are probably hundreds or even thousands of candidates for sentience planet-wide. While your people interview every one of them, the mineral resources of Bog lie here untapped. If you find no one, you've spent months or even years doing it, only to find that Bog has no masters and the minerals might have been at our disposal all along. If you *do* find someone, then time and energy must be put into learning their language, studying their culture, understanding their point of view—and *still* the resources of Bog lie there untapped. I'm sure you can see that the best case scenario as far as our employer is concerned is for Bog to be completely without sentient life."

He had stopped just short of suggesting that Rhys come to that conclusion regardless of the circumstances. Rhys wondered if the thought had been in mind. He glanced forward to where Yoshi sat beside Rick in the front passenger seat of the buggy. Even in profile, he could see that her brow was knit and her jaw clenched mutinously. In the four years or so he had known her, Rhys had seen a thousand expressions cross Yoshi Umeki's face. He had never seen this one.

"Have you an alternative to suggest that will not contravene Collective law?" he asked carefully.

"It seems to me we might simply set up our mining operations —in a way calculated to make a minimum impact on the ecosystem, of course—and then if, in later years, a sentient species makes itself known, we can deal with it as necessary."

Yoshi snorted. "That's what they said about the Aborigines."

Godwin glanced at her, eyebrows raised. "Excuse me?"

She spoke without turning to face him. "That's what every conqueror has said about every conquered people since the dawn of Human civilization—'we'll deal with them as necessary.' Usually, the native peoples end up with their culture destroyed and their numbers seriously depleted."

"My dear girl," said Godwin dryly, "we are not barbarians who have failed to learn from our own history. Rest assured, should any intelligence rear its unlikely head on this sodden ball of earth, Tanaka Corp will honor both its culture and its physical well-being. You know Danetta Price better than I do, but whatever her merits or demerits as a CEO, she is not known for a conquistadorial attitude. But there are resources here—" He broke off, turning to address his argument to Rhys. "There are, for example, significant quantities of a *natural* organometallic in the water at this latitude that has *tremendous* potential. A *natural* organometallic. And then there are the ores—did you know that there are caves about 200 klicks south of here that contain incredibly pure deposits of copper? And the surface water—all of it—contains an alchemist's laboratory stew of minerals."

His eyes gleamed. A zealot. Rhys smiled. He recognized the look. He'd seen it often enough on Yoshi's face, on Rick's...in the mirror. Godwin might have been him describing an assemblage of objects dug out of someone's two thousand year old refuse bin or burial mound. And, little as he liked to admit it, there was controversy over the ethics of making use of *those* resources too.

The reptiles lived in an area that was as close to a desert as was likely to be found on Bog. The soil was sandy, merely damp, and sparsely foliated (at least more sparsely than 75 percent of Bog). In cleared areas the reptilians had built structures not unlike the giant termite mounds of Earthen Africa, pasting them together with clay from the bottom of small, stagnant red pools that dotted the landscape. Taken together with the jewel-bright green of the mounds' inhabitants, the whole area looked as if Santa's interstellar sleigh had jettisoned a cargo of Christmas ornaments.

From the cover afforded them by a tufted dune, the Humans watched the activity around the mounds. Rhys was just puzzling over a group of empty and collapsed "huts" to the north of the inhabited group when Yoshi jiggled his elbow.

"Look, sir. Tool-use."

He nodded, watching a pair of the iguana-like creatures poking about a rotting tree stump with a stick. Another teetered across the clearing on his hind legs, his arms full of water-smoothed rocks. These he deposited next to one of the mounds in a heap, shoving away one of the ubiquitous 'bogdillos', which had come along to snuffle at the collection. When the creature failed to move away, the reptile chittered at it, finally picking up one of the rocks and dealing the arthropod a sharp *thwack*. A second reptile scurried over to snag the rock and skitter away with it, eventually pressing it into the wall of a mound.

"Now *there's* Human behavior," said Rick.

"That too." Yoshi pointed to where a clutch of immature reptiles was attempting to feed one of the bogdillos a large, decimated leaf. The animal seemed completely uninterested which, in turn, caused the 'children' to lose interest in it. They next offered their wizened frond to a flock of avians with more success.

Godwin, checking the soles of his boots for unmentionables, said, "Well, doctor. I'll bet you're just in seventh heaven. There's more Humanoid behavior going on out there than I've seen in most spaceport cantinas. Shall we make an appearance and ask to be taken to their leader?"

"Perhaps," Rhys told him, "if we can determine who that leader is."

They watched the reptiles for three days without making a single move. In that time, they collected a plethora of data on community life and interaction, noted the hierarchy among the 'lizards,' and chased away nosy arthropods and avians. On day three, Godwin, whose patience was apparently not a virtue that got much exercise, returned to the base camp complaining of sand fleas and insomnia. The sands around their mobile cabin made a peculiar sucking noise at night, which Godwin found unbearable. Rhys silently (and guiltily) thanked the sands.

Their observations did indeed yield the identification of a dominant member of the reptile community. It was a female, judging from physiological and behavioral cues, who ruled the reptile roost. It was to this noble creature that Rhys at last decided to make himself known.

At first he merely let them see him at the edge of the village laying out his merchandise and making observations to his notepad. After a while he moved in closer. The reptiles watched him with their golden, saucer-round eyes, occasionally opening and closing their wide mouths; Rhys expected to hear the clack of castanets. The elder female watched him most carefully as she went about her business, which consisted largely of scolding the younger members of her group who brought her food and occasionally rocks for her mound.

By the time he was face to face with the matriarch, she accepted him without tremor or outrage, merely observing his every move through her extraordinary eyes. He proffered her a piece of glazed azure tile. She looked at it, reached out a scaly digit and touched it, then scratched her neck. He rose and pressed the tile into the earthen wall of the mound she basked beside; she watched him with vague interest. Carefully, he took a rock from the pile her young cohorts had brought her and placed it among his wares; she blinked and scratched her neck again.

He repeated the exercise a few more times, drawing a small crowd of the reptilian Bogies. Finally, one of the creatures came forward and gingerly poked at another piece of tile. Rhys held his breath, affording a quick glance over his shoulder to where Yoshi and Rick observed and recorded the goings on. The reptile handled the tile, turning it this way and that so the bright, glazed surface caught the sun, then he picked it up in one long-fingered hand and scuttled away with it to place it in his own pile of building materials some yards away. He did not return with an offering.

Rhys let out a long breath and tried not to let his hope go with it. But twenty or so pilfered tiles later, he admitted momentary defeat and retired to the camp.

"It seems," he sighed some days later with no further progress to show, "that all we've accomplished is to leave our reptilian friends with gaudier houses."

"Houses they may not even live in that much longer," Yoshi added. "I explored the other side of that little knoll." She indicated a nearby hillock covered with sand and some wispy bushes. "It seems that what these fellows do is build up their little mud igloos until the inner passages are all clogged with rocks and bits of wood or the roofs cave in. From what I can tell, they just abandon the villages little by little and start new mounds right next door."

Rhys nodded. "Which explains the trail of mud huts we followed to get here."

"Professor..." Rick was watching a playback of Rhys's interaction with the reptiles. "This is probably irrelevant, but does it seem to anyone else that those mud huts bear a more than passing resemblance to Yoshi's bogdillos?"

Both Yoshi and Rhys brought their attention to the video. "Roddy's right," Rhys murmured thoughtfully. "Although that could just as easily be by accident as by design."

Rick selected another time index, presenting them with a view of their encounter with the lake dwellers. It escaped no one that the water-bound lodges of the amphibians, with their anarchic polka-dots of bright stuff, looked much like submerged bogdillos.

Rhys exhaled explosively. "Worship? Art? Coincidence?"

"Do we stick around or move on?" Rick asked.

"I guess we'd best move on," Rhys decided. "But we'll be back. Maybe I just need some fresh ideas."

Raymond Godwin greeted their return to base camp with ill-concealed relief. "No luck, eh? Will you be giving up then?"

"Yes," Rhys said mildly, "we're going to move the base camp to the next location."

Godwin grimaced. "And may I ask how many 'locations' there are?"

"About a dozen, all told. The habitable zone on Bog is rather small, after all."

"A dozen." Godwin glanced from Rhys to his two assistants. "And I suppose you're going to check out every one of them, aren't you?"

Rhys smiled. "Until we find sentience or determine it's not to be found. That's our job this time out."

"Professor Llewellyn, you obviously have very little business acumen. I don't know how you managed to impress Ms. Price as a negotiator." Godwin turned on his heel, narrowly avoiding doing the splits on the ever-soggy turf, and made a most dignified exit.

Putting Godwin's ill temper out of his mind, Rhys visited the logistics chief next to arrange for the camp move. Unlike Raymond Godwin, Chief Pinski was thrilled with the prospect of some action. "My people have been going stir crazy," he told Rhys. "While you folks're out doing the jungle, all they've got to do is read and play VR games. You want to see how bored people can get?" He beckoned Rhys to the door of his portable office and nodded toward the cargo area where a quartet of bright blue, tarp-covered pallets stood awaiting dispersal. At the edge of the area, a handful of men and women in vari-colored coveralls lobbed the local version of pinecones into the forest.

"What are they aiming at?" Rhys asked.

"Oh, anything and everything. Leaves, seed cones on stumps, the blossoms on those big, droopy trees, the critters that skulk around the edge of camp."

Rhys smiled wanly. "I see. Well, do you think you could ask them not to target anything that moves? I'd hate to annoy the neighbors."

Pinski chuckled. "I see your point. Sure, Doc. Now, when would you like to bug out?"

"Tomorrow morning will do fine. I'll have the coordinates for you by supper time."

Leaving Pinski's office he heard a rousing cheer go up along the edge of the cargo dump. He sighed, praying the site crew hadn't hit anyone who would hold a grudge.

They were up by Bog's green early light. Forest denizens strove to outdo each other in song and a legitimately cool breeze rustled the rampant foliage. Rhys took his morning shower— essential to starting a day on Bog—and realized he couldn't face putting on his kilt. The humid atmosphere made the wool itch and cling, and he was damn tired of smelling like a wet sheep. Nattily attired in a jump suit of jungle green, he was walking cross camp when Yoshi fell into step with him.

"Good morning, sir," she said.

"Yoshi, how long have we been working together?"

"Four years, three and one half months," she said as if she'd been calculating that very thing the moment he'd asked.

"And during those four years, three and one half months, how many times do you suppose you've agreed to stop calling me 'sir?'"

She gave him a sheepish look from beneath the black silk that fell across her forehead. "Oops. Sorry, Rhys. Sometimes it just slips out. Blame it on my family—small town, Shinto-Buddhist-Bahá'í values. Every time I forget to use a term of respect for an elder or a teacher, I see my aunt Mineko shaking her finger at me and saying, 'Yoshiko, *honor* those to whom honor is due.'"

"Godwin's an elder; you never call *him* 'sir.'"

She glanced at him out of the tail of eyes that somehow blended contrition and impishness. "Your point being?"

"My point being that after four years—"

"And three and one half months," she added, and smiled. "I'm trying, but old habits die hard, and sometimes you're such a curmudgeon..."

Rhys snorted. "Curmudgeon, your Aunt Mineko!" They'd come to the mess tent and he'd pulled back the waterproof cowling over the door when he heard someone shouting for him. He turned. Rick Halfax was hurrying toward them from the direction they'd just come, waving his arms.

"You aren't going to believe this!" he panted when he reached them. "Something...I mean some*one* left us a pile of goodies during the night."

It was indeed a pile of goodies. The jumble of rocks, flowers and conifer seed-cones had been left between a pair of tarp-covered pallets at the eastern fringe of their supply yard. The rocks formed the bottom-most layer; the Bogish pinecones tumbled atop those; the flowers were sprinkled over all like brown sugar on oatmeal. Some of the Tanaka site crew were standing nearby looking on with mild interest.

A young woman pointed at the heap of stuff and said, "This is just the way we found it, professor. We haven't touched a thing."

Rhys knelt by the knee-high mound and picked up one of the large, purplish blossoms. "Interesting," he murmured. "All of the same variety."

"The botany team was really interested in those," the young woman told him and smiled. "I think the fragrance was a hit."

Rhys nodded. "There's a lot of money in perfume on just about any world."

"Mimicry?" The one word question came from Rick, who was sampling one of the rocks with a field scanner. "They've seen us pile stuff up like this. Maybe they're just aping us."

Rhys shook his head. "Possibly, but the young lady is right
—these flowers are ones the botany team was particularly
interested in." He sniffed at the bloom. "Tantalizing. They
collected scores of them."

"And you think one of the native species noticed that?"

In answer, Rhys nodded at the rock in Rick's hand.
"What've you got there?"

"Ore-bearing. Barium...." He gestured at another,
lighter-colored specimen on the ground at his feet. "Gold. Also
heavily sampled by the advance team."

Yoshi nudged a seed-cone with her toe. "Dr. Gallioni says
these are a storehouse of natural antibiotics... I guess we've been
noticed."

"Hmmm." Rhys was examining the spongy ground around
the cache, looking for tracks. "But by whom?"

"Oh, dear God, it's true." Raymond Godwin stood at the
corner of the nearest pallet, looking aghast at the collection of
native wares. "Someone or something has actually made an
overture. And I thought this was going to be a simple matter of a
corporate claim. Well, which one of our lovely natives left this
little offering?"

Rhys turned one of the native plants in his hands, feeling a
heady wash of exhilaration. "I don't know, Mr. Godwin, but I
intend to find out."

"I take it this means our move is canceled."

Rhys nodded absently, already pondering his next step.

It was easy enough to talk about finding the would-be
traders, harder to do. After a long night of sleepless reflection,
Rhys still hadn't decided where to begin or what he could do
that he hadn't already done to flush Bog's sentients out of the
swamp. He reviewed behaviors—leaf sipping, rock carrying,
tree-house building...icon making? Any and all could be
significant.

He rose the next morning, showered, dressed and literally flipped a coin. The ancient British ha'penny came up heads, and Rhys took his crew off to the reptile village. Three days later, he was ready to give up. Aside from building houses that possibly paid tribute to the bogdillo, the reptiles showed no sign of abstract thought.

"Perhaps," Yoshi said the morning they moved their remote camp to the arboreal village, "we're not going about this the right way."

Rick Halfax snorted. "Obviously not."

Yoshi ignored him. "I mean, maybe there's some sort of protocol we're missing."

Rhys raised his tired eyes to her face. "I'm all ears."

"Well, they brought their goods to our camp and left them where we'd be sure to find them."

"Which is precisely what we've been doing. For all we know this could just be a case of mimicry."

"Or," Yoshi continued, "it could be a step in some sort of trading ritual. Like the Pa-Kai dances or the Garulin processionals."

She had his attention now and he waved her on.

"We left our goods at their doors—"

"Whose doors?" Rick asked. "We left our goods at *several* doors."

Yoshi nudged him aside with a preemptory flick of her fingers. "I don't know yet, but what if they took that as the first step in the protocol? A bid to establish the trading ground, let's say. To them, what we're saying is, 'We elect your village to be the trading ground.' So they take the next step; they elect *our* 'village.' Now we've put the ball back in their bailiwick. But maybe that's not the polite thing to do, maybe we're supposed to accept their offer to let us host the trading."

"So you're suggesting we lay our goods out where we picked theirs up—in the middle of the supply dump?"

Yoshi nodded. "We make a gesture of accepting the goods they brought and place our own on the exact spot where they were delivered."

Rhys glanced at Rick, whose nose was buried in his coffee mug. "What do you think, Roddy?"

The other man shrugged. "I say anything's worth a try. If we can't prove any of the Bogies are sentient, this planet is going to become a big, soupy rock quarry." He leaned closer to Rhys across the table and lowered his voice. "I've seen the geological reports Godwin's been salivating over. There are so many rare-elsewhere minerals in the so-called crust of this mud ball that there's virtually no place you can dig that you won't unearth something marketable. And if you don't think Godwin would cheerfully tear up every tree, siphon off every drop of standing water and dispossess every native lifeform to get it..."

"Danetta would never allow that," Rhys protested. "And she's in the driver's seat at Tanaka."

Rick gave him a wry glance. "Come on, professor. You know big business better than that. Even Danetta Price has to listen to the Board of Directors. And the Board of Directors listens to the shareholders and a lot of shareholders listen to the siren song of the almighty credit."

"You're right," Rhys admitted, guiltily recalling that they, too, worked for Tanaka. "And Godwin's been singing that song since we met him. He has a vested interest in our failure because our success would mean a substantial investment of time. And Tanaka Corp has traditionally favored investing financial resources over investing time. Whatever we determine about the lifeforms on Bog, we've got to be damn certain."

They pursued Yoshi's idea, making a studied ritual out of accepting the native collection of goods and replacing the stash with one of their own. Then they settled down to watch. When no one and nothing put in an appearance by nightfall, they turned in for the evening and turned on the brace of monitoring vidicams around the site.

The pile of goodies was still there in the weak morning light. But something else was missing. All four of the stockpiles near the cache had been relieved of their bright blue coverings.

While Pinski had his crew replaced the tarps with extras from their shuttle's supplies, Rhys and company checked the recordings. It had been a foggy night, which is to say a normal one, and shapeless wings of mist trailed across the camera eye or rolled along the ground. Rhys began to realize that virtually anything could be concealed in that.

"What's that?" Rick asked, pointing a finger to what looked like a field of tiny stars in a slowly swirling nebula. "Fireflies?"

Rhys squinted at them. "Or the local equivalent. We've seen them before."

"Sure. Over the bog. Never in camp."

"They may travel at night. They're certainly not our traders."

Rick grinned. "Oh, I don't know. Maybe if a whole bunch of them teamed up..."

Rhys gave him a mock severe glare. "I suppose you'd like your signature to be on the report that identifies a local insect as the species Tanaka has to do business with?"

Rick turned his attention back to the monitor screen. "Not a chance."

'Not a chance' pretty much described their attempt to ferret any new visual evidence out of the video. There was darkness, fog, more darkness and a flotilla of brightly lit insects. Rick hit on the idea of turning off the picture and focusing on the sound. That yielded little more—only the sound of plastic clips being sprung and tarpaulins being tugged from their mounts and dragged away through the primordial ooze.

There was nothing for it but to attempt tracking the missing tarps. Under normal circumstances, following a drag trail would have been a simple task, but Bog's springy soil and general sogginess made it a hit or miss game. There was nothing like a discernible spore, but only broken fern fronds and irregularly depressed patches of earth. They found the trail; they lost it; they found it again. Then they found a place where it appeared to fork.

"It looks like they split up," Rick observed. "One tarp was dragged off that way,"—he pointed northeast—"another toward the lake. And from the look of that..." He broke off to examine a third swathe of disturbed ground and foliage. "Two toward the eastern plateau."

Rhys straightened from his own perusal of the trails. "Roughly, one deeper into the forest, one toward the amphibian population and two toward the reptile village."

"Coincidence?" asked Yoshi.

"Let's find out. The simian tree houses are closest. Let's try that direction first." Rhys led on, following the on-again, off-again trail until they came within sight of the nearest tree village. He was scanning the foliage above and before when Rick gave a shout.

"Pay dirt!"

Rhys, Yoshi, and the several members of the site crew who had joined them, hurried in the direction of his voice. He had found one of the missing tarpaulins snagged over a small sapling and a couple of ferns. A handful of small avians bathed themselves in the water that had pooled in its draped folds.

One of the site crew made a move to reclaim the tarp; the birds fled, chittering. Rhys put a hand up to stop the man. "Leave it. They paid for it, after all."

"But it's just sitting here, gathering water."

Rhys dabbled a finger in the pool vacated by the birds, then glanced toward the village where a group of the simian inhabitants watched with mild interest. "Indeed. Yoshi...set up a monitor pack to take in the tarp and its immediate area. Then we'll be on to the next site."

"Why bother, Doc?" Rick asked. "Doesn't this pretty much prove that the simians are our sentients?"

"There are two other trails to follow, Roddy. Trails that may lead to other conclusions entirely."

They took a couple of swamp buggies to the reptile colony next. Both of the missing tarps were located with ease sheerly by contrast to the earth-toned surroundings. Like the first one, these had been draped in deceptive abandon over protruding objects so that fresh water from the humid atmosphere pooled in the low points. They found the first of the two roughly two-thirds of the way between their base camp and the reptile colony. The other was just outside the village at which Rhys had attempted to barter some time before. And this one was in use—a group of the reptilians were gathered about it sipping in turns from the vivid puddles while one or two avian friends showered beneath drops of spillage. Rhys took notes, Yoshi made a video record, then they continued to the third site.

It took longer to find the fourth tarp. Blazing blue not-with-standing, the lusher colors and foliage around the lake made spotting difficult. But spot it they did, near sunset. Once again it appeared to have been set up to collect fresh water. The five-person team from the site crew took their buggy and returned to camp immediately, having no particular desire to bivouac in a true swamp overnight. Rhys hardly noticed their absence. Nor did he particularly notice the presence of Raymond Godwin, who, realizing the importance of recent events, thought it in his best interests to stay close by.

By the time Rhys and his cohorts had set up camp, the rude water collection system had been in use several times by both amphibians and avians. Review of the monitor packs Yoshi had set up at the other tarpaulin sites showed similar use by both simians and reptiles.

"Are they *all* sentient?" asked Godwin irritably as they sat in the twilight and watched the activity over the lake. "Have we stumbled onto some sort of...of alien co-op?"

Rhys, watching the movements of aquatic life in and around of one of the waterlogged lodges, shook his head absently. "So it would seem. Damn! They communicate with each other—how do we get them to communicate with us?" Rhys fell silent, gazing out over the lake as the alien sun pulled in its green-tinted skirts, plunging the swampy glade into sudden dim twilight. He reached for a camp-light. Yoshi's hand fell on his arm, sending an inexplicable army of goose bumps marching up and down its length.

"Rhys, look at this."

"This" proved to be billows of the tiny Boggian fireflies that, though nearly invisible by day were anything but at dusk. It was as if someone had released a cloud of willful sparks; the fireflies danced over the face of the thick water and the water's surface gleamed in reply. It was a rare and remarkable sight. The mass of insects was so bright the camp-light seemed superfluous.

Rhys, unable to withdraw his arm, glanced at Yoshi's face in the spectral glow. Her eyes were bright mirrors of wonder. His, suddenly captive, watched the glow of alien fire in them.

"Bioluminescents," she murmured, "never cease to amaze me. I've never seen so many all in one place."

"Oh, and here come a few more," said Godwin dryly.

A few more was a gross understatement. A small, compact fleet of the fireflies was flitting through the tall grasses and ferns that bordered the lake. They moved at a leisurely pace, taking time to spiral skyward now and again before coalescing into a puff of green-gold brightness.

"That's odd..."

Yoshi's sudden tension broke the odd spell that had momentarily held Rhys in thrall. As the hand that had lain across his forearm went to her field scanner, he blinked and followed her gaze. Below the cloud of approaching fireflies, the grasses waved and bobbed as if the beating of those tiny wings was creating a massive down draft. At the water's edge, no more than thirty feet from where the Humans sat, the reeds parted.

"Huh!" snorted Rick. "Mystery solved. I didn't think those little sprites could create that much commotion."

Yoshi nodded, watching as two bogdillos slid into the water, their escort of fireflies commingling with the brilliant mist that hovered over the lake. "I forgot they were parasites."

Rhys stared at the bright water. "Parasites? Or pets?"

"What?"

Rhys was on his feet, keeping his voice low with an effort. "What was the one thing we *did* see on the security monitor the night the tarps were taken?"

Yoshi had risen too. "Fireflies."

"And what do fireflies have in common with every one of our potentially sentient species?"

Yoshi's brow knit. "Bogdillos?"

"*Bogdillos?*" Rick repeated. "But they're scavengers. They sponge off everybody. They even horn in on the houses the amphibians build."

"They've got symbiotic relationships with not just one other species," argued Rhys, making emphatic gestures with both hands, "but with three or more. They get fed, petted, and scratched—"

"And in return" said Godwin, "they provide house plans?"

"No. They provide *water!*"

"Water?" echoed Rick. "I don't—"

"Remember the broad-leaf plants we couldn't account for near the simian village? Good God, they were all over the ground in the reptile colony too, I only just realized. What if those are the bogdillo's attempts to provide water to the other species? We came into town with a better system of trapping water, and the bogdillos—having observed what *we* found interesting—traded some of it for what *they* found interesting. Namely, big, blue 'leaves' that could be used to trap precious water in larger quantities."

"They're a diurnal species," added Yoshi, "yet they have adapted to nocturnal activity by—possibly—harnessing another lifeform to provide light."

"And just how do you propose to prove this marvelous construct?" Godwin asked, blinking up at them through the eerie faux-twilight. "We've heard not murmur one from those bug-dillos of yours."

"That doesn't mean anything," Rick objected. "They could communicate via species-specific telepathy for all we know."

"We'll offer further trade," said Rhys decisively.

Bearing another tarpaulin along with plant and mineral samples Tanaka had found most interesting, Rhys and Rick approached the shore of Brown Salt Lake. Yoshi monitored while Godwin stood by like bored royalty. With Rick behind him holding a tarp, Rhys hunkered at the water's edge and smacked the surface lightly with the flat of his hand. He repeated this several times, then paused and glanced back over his shoulder to where he could see Yoshi with her vidicam. She was nodding.

"They're there. Just out beyond that near lodge."

Glancing to where Yoshi had directed, Rhys could see them too, looking like nothing so much as a clump of giant chocolate marshmallows bobbing in a cup of hot cocoa.

And there, for all of Rhys's ministrations, they stayed. He had Rick wave the tarp. He laid out the samples of the goods the bogdillos (presumably) had brought them, trying to demonstrate that he would trade one thing for the other. He even left the tarpaulin on the shore and retreated. The marshmallows stayed right where they were, bobbing beneath their radiant canopy.

"I think," said Godwin, "that I am going to run, screaming, into the jungle. How *do* you manage to have so bloody much patience? If I didn't know better, I'd think you were all brain-addled." He snorted. "Hell, I'm not sure I *do* know better. *Are* you all brain-addled?"

"I was beginning to wonder, myself," yawned Rick, gazing at the motionless dumplings.

"They're waiting for something," murmured Yoshi. "I can *feel* it."

"Oh, now *that's* scientific!" Godwin got up and went out to the shore to stare at the flotilla of bogdillos. "I say," he addressed them. "Are you in the mood for a spot of tea? Eh? How about some anchovy wine or something equally tasty?" He bent over then, and before Rhys could guess his intention, he had tossed a rock out into the water. It landed with a squishy *smack!* right in front of his alien audience. They dispersed immediately.

Rhys was on his feet in an instant. "Godwin! What the hell do you think you're doing?"

The other man turned on him, face red with frustration. "Trying to communicate."

"Communicate? You frightened them away!"

"At least, *my* way got *some* result."

Rhys took a step toward the other man forcing him to withdraw to the other side of the swamp buggy.

Twilight lingered for perhaps an hour. True darkness fell. Now no fireflies brightened the lake's murky surface, no bogdillos plowed through the waist-high reeds. Rhys was thoroughly depressed and disgusted, convinced Godwin had ruined their chances of communicating with the Bogian denizens.

He was sitting in the stygian darkness between an equally glum Yoshi and a dozing Rick when something thudded to the ground just out of reach. Startled, he leapt to his feet and reached for a palm torch, flipping on the diffuse beam. Yoshi echoed both movements, adding her light to his. Barely an arm's length from where they had sat was a rock.

"Are they attacking?" Yoshi whispered.

"I don't know. Kill your beam." He matched action to word, flicking off his own torch and plunging them into darkness. When nothing else happened, he stepped to where the rock had fallen and knelt to examine it, switching on his torch again to do so. Almost immediately, a second object plopped to earth another three feet or so ahead of him. As he rose to find it with his eyes, the entire lagoon was lit up like the Christmas trees of yore.

Rhys extinguished his torch. The alien insects went dark a heartbeat later. He felt Yoshi at his side and gave her a quick glance before stepping to the second projectile. It proved to be a large, soggy seedpod of some sort.

"Your torch," Yoshi whispered.

He turned it on. The fireflies blazed in reply. Another missile fell midway between Rhys and the shoreline. He heard a soft exclamation from behind him, and realized Rick was awake. A fraction of his mind wondered what Godwin was doing just about now. He stepped to the next marker without turning off his torch.

Yoshi flicked hers on as well. "I'll get the goods." She was gone for a moment, during which time Rhys responded to another invitation to come closer. He was now a mere foot from the waterline and could see the lumpy shapes of the bogdillos out in the water. He waited, but they came no closer. When a full minute had elapsed, he bent, picked up the rock at his feet and tossed it out into the little lagoon, so that it fell midway between shore and watchers. After a moment of hesitation the bogdillos drew closer, moving as one.

Rhys felt a chill sail up his spine. There was a moment in every first contact Rhys had known when he wondered if the other party would suddenly prove to be fanatically carnivorous xenophobes. In this case, the possibility presented itself that the bogdillos viewed the visiting Humans as a potential addition to their petting zoo.

He cursed the forefathers of science fiction, chased the ridiculous thought away, and tossed out another rock, this time bringing the arthropods to just over a yard from where he stood. Signaling Yoshi to attend him, he squatted on the shore and began playing charades. He showed the bogdillos the tarpaulin, describing it ("tarp") in case they could hear him, and demonstrating with a flask of water that he understood what they used it for. Then he displayed the several most valuable of the items they had left in the base camp cargo dump, and lastly, laid the tarpaulin on the shore and stepped back.

During the brief wait, he was witness to what he could only call a conversation between the various members of the bogdillian group. There were dolphin-like squeaks, watery gargling sounds, a gamut of muted tones, and tiny, rhythmic slapping patterns executed with a foot or tentacle (he couldn't see which) upon the stiff surface of the water. Most incredibly of all, the fireflies dancing above each bogdillo—for he could now see that each entity had its separate tribe—winked on and off and subtly altered color and direction during the exchange.

"My God." The exclamation was in starchily accented English. Raymond Godwin had come down to the shore to watch.

"Don't you dare," growled Rhys, "throw anything."

"Wouldn't think of it."

The bogdillos had obviously come to some sort of decision, for some of their number dispersed, some withdrawing to the shore and into the tall grasses, others disappearing into the amphibian lodges, still others seeming to dive beneath the water —an amazing feat considering its native buoyancy. Two of the remaining individuals glided right to Rhys's feet and emerged to face him.

After each had appraised him via a trio of eye stalks, they proceeded to handle the tarpaulin with what appeared to be fins...or tentacles...or flabby pincers, depending on the use to which they were put—lifting, poking or pulling.

Rhys sucked in a long awful breath. Now, *that* was adaptability. Even so, he noticed that one of the bogdillos was having a little trouble folding back a corner of the thin but durable fabric. Noticed, too, how it kept changing the shape of its pseudo-hand to gain a better purchase. On a whim, Rhys lowered his own hand to where the bogdillo could see it and slowly, carefully peeled the corner back. He left his hand in plain view—the eye stalks took note. After a few permutations, the bogdillo had approximated a hand (albeit, without digits it looked like a hand in a sleek, shiny mitten) and had satisfactorily manipulated the thin folds. Rhys sat back in amazement.

In short order, the missing bogdillos returned and, after a very brief and bright consultation with their confreres, deposited an array of goods on the silty squelch of beach. Rhys heard a scanner's metallic purr to his right.

"Lord," said Godwin. "What a treasure trove."

The two arthropods in possession of the tarp made a show of removing it from the beach, then returned to gesture very pointedly at their own pile of offerings, now at Godwin's feet.

Rhys glanced at the Acquisitions director. "Fair trade?" he asked.

"Oh, I'd say so."

"Then make a show of picking it up."

"Me? You want me to take part in this...negotiation?"

"It seems you may have started it. What could be more appropriate than for you to close it?"

Godwin bent and picked up an armful of ores and plant-stuffs. He stepped back a stride for good measure. The bogdillos seemed satisfied. They took their tarpaulin and departed, fireflies blazing. The lagoon returned to a deep green sort of twilight as the alien light receded further into the lake.

"Well," breathed Godwin. "That was something, wasn't it? Did I really start all that, do you think?"

"I'm pretty sure of it." Rhys chuckled. "When I think of all the clues we got—lakeside foliage turning up in relatively faraway places, bogdillo-shaped constructs, the simians tossing food at them...." He trailed off, a strange expression flitting across his face.

"They were aping the bogdillo trading methods, you mean?"

Rhys nodded, his eyes apparently on some fourth dimension only he could see. "So it would seem. And while we were being pleased with ourselves for all our neat efforts toward trade in the villages, what probably convinced the bogdillos to give us that first cache of goods was the cargo crew lobbing seed cones at them."

Yoshi waggled her palm torch. "Now they know we can harness light...just like they do." She grinned. "I guess that makes us bogdillos too."

"I'm willing to bet they'll suspend coming to any firm decision until they've known us longer, but *this*," said Rhys, "is where we step out, Mr. Godwin."

The Englishman did a double take. "I beg pardon?"

"We have found you a sentient lifeform. I will even recommend the experts necessary to continue working with them. But *they* will have to determine if the bogdillos can lay claim to the mineral resources of this planet on a scale necessary to cede them wholesale to Tanaka."

"Now wait just a moment. You've found a sentient, now you're supposed to recommend that I negotiate with them for Bog's resources."

"A sentient, yes, but I've not proven them to be the representatives of a civilization. All I've shown you is a race of clever natives, which you wish to deal with as necessary, or so you said. The Collective takes a dim view of people—or even major corporations—dealing with native populations according to expediency. This is a culture, Godwin. There is potential for trade, potential for communication. But are these people in a position to barter away the mineral rights for their entire world? Would they even understand what they were bartering away? Until we know those things, we can do more than deal with them on a purely local basis."

"Like this, you mean?" asked Godwin incredulously. "Beads and trinkets for ores and botanicals?"

"Not trinkets. An exchange of useful commodities. But yes, just like what we did here. A little at a time—while we establish communications...and search for other possible contacts."

"Ah. Other contacts which *could* negotiate mineral rights for Bog."

Rhys shook his head. "You're forgetting a fine point of Collective law, Mr. Godwin. If the bogdillos are not the only race of men on Bog, neither party would be allowed to barter away planetary resources. I believe you have jumped the gun. There is nothing here for you to acquire...yet. Only trinkets, as you call them."

Godwin, crushing his armful of ores to his chest, brought himself stiffly upright. "You sir, have forgotten who pays your salary. I intend to tender a full report to Corporate as soon as I return to headquarters. I'll call in the requisite experts—"

"I'll give you my recommendations."

Godwin opened his mouth to retort, but Rhys cut him off. "They'll get the quickest results, Godwin. Don't sabotage yourself out of dislike for me."

"Take me back to the base camp."

"With pleasure."

"He'll try to find a work-around, you know," said Yoshi, her eyes following the stiff column of Godwin's back. "He'll try to find a way to get more sooner."

"Of course he will," Rhys acknowledged. "But fortunately there are saner heads at Tanaka. And there are the laws of the Collective. Until he can prove the bogdillos have the knowledge and authority to negotiate for such vast resources, those laws will force Tanaka to be content with limited commodities—still worth having, if our advance surveys are any indication."

"Until?" Yoshi turned off her palm-torch, plunging them into moist darkness. "What if he never can prove it? What if the bogdillos are not world-aware enough to negotiate and no other sentients turn up?"

She could feel his smile even in the darkness. "Oh, I think there may be other sentients here, all right. And I'm not the only one who thinks so."

"I don't get you."

"The bogdillos provide water to at lest three other species-- species capable of community existence and lodge building. Species also capable of a high degree of mimicry. After all, we saw them throw things at the bogdillos, and we saw the bogdillos throw them back."

Yoshi sucked in a deep breath. "You think the bogdillos are trying to get the other species to barter?"

"Maybe its that simple. Maybe it's not. Consider this: What if the bogdillos are trying to *teach* the other species barter? What if they're trying to help them take an evolutionary step?"

"Is that possible?" Her voice came out in an awed whisper.

"I don't know. I wasn't around when our ancestors learned these things. But I do know this—Mr. Godwin will have to acquire someone else's resources."

"Rhys, do you hear yourself? It's not just Godwin. It's Tanaka Corp. Most employers take a very dim view of an employee who feels he'd scored a moral victory in keeping them *out* of a multi-billion credit deal."

Rhys grimaced. "You're right. And one of these days I expect my scruples will catch up with me. Unless my conscience gets there first."

"Your conscience?" She shifted closer to him in the dark to peer up into his face. "What would you have to feel guilty about? You've always conducted yourself ethically. I should know. I've always been there."

He turned to look at her, realizing that she had, indeed, always been there. He could just see the pale moon of her face, the glitter of her eyes. "Have you ever wondered what it would be like," he asked, "not to serve a corporate master? To be a scientist, pure and simple?"

"I know what it's like. So do you. When we were on sabbatical—"

"Not just when we're on sabbatical, Yoshi. But every day. You saw what happened on this assignment. The same thing that always happens. We serve two masters—Tanaka and science, in that order. And sometimes, like *this* time, their aims are mutually opposed. Science doesn't care if it takes a century to establish meaningful contact with the denizens of Bog. Tanaka most certainly does. And that puts us in an untenable position."

"You've thought about resigning before." It was a bald statement of fact.

"Aye, but I don't recall discussing it with you."

He could see the flash of white as she smiled. "I know things."

"Ah, now don't go all inscrutable on me, Yosh. In this frame of mind, I don't think I can take it." He put his arm around her shoulders. "Come on. We'd best get Godwin back to his tidy corporate shuttle before he starts throwing things again. I'd be dreadfully embarrassed if he accidentally started another round of negotiations and us with nothing to trade."

"You do have to give him credit for that," Yoshi acknowledged as they picked their way back to the swamp buggy, leaving their torches dark in silent mutual consent.

"I do? Well, I suppose you're right. After all, he's leaving. I can afford to be charitable."

"Aren't we leaving too? I thought you were going to recommend some experts to take the post."

Rhys scratched his cheek. "Yes, well. Actually, I thought I'd recommend us. After all, we're already here, aren't we? Godwin wants expediency—how much more expedient can you get? Besides, if what I think's going on here is going on here, I surely don't want to miss it."

"And your resignation?"

"Can wait. A wee bit longer."

They had reached the swamp buggy by now and could hear Godwin, already within, haranguing Rick Halfax about his superior's complete lack of company loyalty. Rhys sighed. *Well, perhaps a very wee bit.*

A Tear in the Mind's Eye

A story of science fiction

A Tear in the Mind's Eye was originally published in *Analog Science Fiction* in 1993 and is a psychological study dealing with the relationship between body, mind, and spirit as it is strained by mood disorders such as manic depression. It was inspired by the brave souls I have known who are coping with this disease, and by these words of Bahá'u'lláh, Who likened such impediments to a cloud:

> *Neither the presence of the cloud nor its absence can,*
> *in any way, affect the inherent splendor of the sun.*
> *The soul of man is the sun by which his body is*
> *illumined, and from which it draweth its sustenance,*
> *and should be so regarded.*
>
> Gleanings from the
> Writings of Bahá'u'lláh,
> p. 155

They had cured his diabetes. They could do that these days with their clever balancing-act drugs. And they had corrected his vision with their intelligent nano-surgeons and their organic plastics. But they had not cured his desire to die.

He held it at bay uneasily. Always had. Not without the help of his therapists—a veritable battalion, he sometimes imagined, of psychologists and psychiatrists and neurologists.

In his near-sleeping moments, he could see them marching, rank upon rank, a blur of multi-colored faces above white lab coats and smart suits. So many people, he thought. All to keep one insignificant soul from surrendering to depression.

His life recently had centered around the battle to keep from being institutionalized. That, more than anything, had come between him and the urge to overdose on something. Adversity was good for him. The psychologists fancied they kept him limping along with their archaeologist's curiosity about the buried.

They dug and they dusted and they put everything they found in boxes with neat labels and they bit back their frustration and uttered mild, milky words about "making progress." They had been "making progress" for nearly a decade but were no closer to understanding what made Brooke Burchard sink into increasingly viscous bogs of depression.

It must be frustrating for them, he often thought, and wondered how many of them succumbed to their own depression or to ulcers. He wondered how many of them had therapists of their own.

He wondered that anew as he watched his current healer, Dr. Annette Geller, patter away at her notebook, her usually attractive mouth twisted into a peculiar grimace. Computers, Brooke decided, were a bad idea. At least in the past psychiatrists had had their pencil caps or erasers to chew on in moments of professional angst. Now they could only smack at the compact keyboards with staccato strokes. Heaven help them when the new sub-vocal triggering technology became widely available.

They'd not even have the keypads to abuse. He thought of Dr. Geller chewing on the plastic cover of her notebook and smiled.

"What?" she asked. "What strikes you as funny?" Her hand poised over the notebook, ready to note it.

Brooke blushed slightly. "Oh, nothing, really, just...wondering about the effects of technology on psychology."

Her dark brows rippled. "How so?"

He gestured at her computerized tablet. "My first shrink was a pencil chewer," he said. "I was just wondering how you exorcised your frustrations."

"Exorcised," she repeated, fingers jigging tunelessly over the keypad. "What an interesting way of putting it. What makes you think I have frustrations to exorcise?"

"You're human, aren't you?"

She smiled and nodded. "Very. I swim. I go to a spa every night when I leave here and swim myself into a nice, tired blob of protoplasm."

"Beats gnawing on your machinery, I'll bet."

She looked down at the notebook. "Yes, that it does."

He took a deep breath, exhaled it. "How'm I doing?"

"I think we're making progress," she said.

He smiled again. "Are we really? And where are we headed?"

"Excuse me?"

"Progress implies motion. It also implies a goal. My goal is not to be at war with myself just about every waking moment.

How much closer to that goal am I today?"

She crossed her legs and leaned forward in her seat. "What do you think, Mr. Burchard?"

"Brooke—and please don't do that. I've already told you what I think. I told all of your predecessors what I think. I have nothing to gain and everything to lose by not being absolutely

honest with you. I think I am a sick man. I hear voices that aren't
there. I see things that don't exist. I want to kill myself. My
father killed himself. My mother never recovered from the loss.
My grandfather killed himself. I don't want to do that to what's
left of my family. I want to be... unified. Completely and
irrevocably unified. I want control of my own thoughts and
feelings."

"Meaning that right now, you think someone else has
control of them?" Her fingers were at work again.

*Stop that. Please stop that. While you're doing that, you can't be
listening to me.* "No, not someone else. That's not what I meant,
just...that they're out of control."

"You spoke of exorcism a moment ago. Do you think you
might be possessed?"

He sat back in the too-comfortable chair and gave her a long
look. "Did I say that?"

"Not in so many words, but-"

"I didn't say that." He kept his voice gentle, firm,
reasonable. Heaven forbid she should decide he was hiding
some cock-eyed belief in ghosts or something.

She tapped at her keypad and eyed the results on the tiny
screen. "Do you have hallucinations, Mr. Burchard...Brooke?"

"You know I do. You've got my whole file right in front of
you. And no, I don't think they're the result of any outside
agency. I know I...occasionally see the world through a warped
window, but I don't think I'm possessed or anything like that."

"Does the idea of possession frighten you very much?"

"No, because I don't believe in it." Calm. That sounded very
calm. Maybe she'd respect that. *Come on, doc. Don't go off on some
idiotic tangent.*

"What do you believe in, Brooke?" she asked him. "Do you
believe in God?"

"Yes."

Her eyes came up from the little computer. "That was a very ready answer."

"I suppose because it's a very ready belief."

She sat back in her chair, uncrossed and recrossed her legs the other way. "Do you ever feel that God is punishing you for something?"

He almost chuckled. "I used to wonder. I used to think, when I had these terrible black moods, blue moods—whatever you want to call them—that I must have unconsciously done something wrong and God was trying to alert me to it."

"Used to?"

"I've grown up. That was twenty years ago."

"Dr. Furillo said you mentioned something to him about a family curse."

Brooke threw his head back and rolled his eyes. "Lordy, Lordy, Lordy! That's the biggest problem with being a mental case, you know? You can't just *say* things like 'normal' people. You don't dare be sarcastic or flip or ironic or just...make a joke of something."

"Is that what you were doing? Making a joke of your family curse?"

"My family isn't cursed, Dr. Geller, but we do seem to have more than our share of troubles. I suppose that might seem like a curse to some...superstitious individuals. Do you think it's a curse, Doctor?" He gazed at her expressionlessly, letting his gray eyes go blank and opaque.

She gazed back, intently. "What might your ancestors have done to deserve such a curse?" she asked in return.

Damn. He knew that look. The "I think we may have something here" look. He shouldn't have joked about a curse, of course, but sometimes he just got so damned tired of the endless, groping questions.

"My grandfather was an ordinary man. He was a diabetic and, in those days, that was a pretty damned tragic thing to be. I suppose he drank too much. I suppose that exacerbated the situation. But he was just an ordinary guy. My father was an ordinary guy, too. Nice. A nice man. A nice man who hated himself for no apparent reason and decided he wasn't worthy of living. But he was just an ordinary man. Like me. Ordinary."

"And self-destructive." She was leaning forward again, intent, like a cat, like an eagle. That was it—she reminded him of an eagle. "Let's talk about the feelings, Brooke. Why do you feel unworthy?"

"I don't know, Dr. Geller. If I knew that, I wouldn't be sitting here now reeling out my insides for your personal inspection."

"My professional inspection," she amended. "You sound resentful."

"That's even worse," he mumbled, then pulled himself to his feet. "I'm just frustrated, doctor. I want, more than anything in the world, just to be ordinary. Plain. Unremarkable in every way. I want to be able to say something—anything—and not have you or someone just like you worry each word ragged." *With your sharp little beak.* "I've been in therapy now for ten years. I've seen four different mental health specialists in that time. And they have all asked me the same set of questions. None of them have presented me with any answers. I have a mental disorder that seems to be hereditary. Unfortunately, neither my grandfather nor my father lived to be studied sufficiently. I realize I make a dandy guinea pig-"

Geller came to her feet. "Mr. Burchard, please. You are not a guinea pig. And as to your condition being hereditary—I really don't think that's verifiable. Given that your grandfather committed suicide when your father was fourteen, it isn't really surprising that your father was affected."

"Ah, I see. The old death-wish theory. My father came unpegged because his father killed himself at a critical juncture in his young life. He developed a keen sense of guilt; guilt made him begin to obsess; he developed his own sense of unworthiness and failure and killed himself, in turn, when I was twenty-two. Now I'm a candidate because I didn't make it into Stanford like daddy wanted me to."

"The suicide of a loved one is a traumatic event, Mr. Burchard. The survivors often wonder if something they did or didn't do may have...contributed."

"Of course they do. And of course I did and my mother did. But in the final analysis, we had no effect one way or another. Dad was too far sunk in his own misery to care about us. That's one of the most frightening things about this...disorder, Dr. Geller—it's stronger than love or loyalty."

She was looking at the little notebook screen again. "Your grandfather's business folded just before he died; your father had just been denied a loan that would have put you through college-"

"Excuses. Those so-called 'contributing events' are just excuses. Don't you understand that? I came close to taking my own life three times over the years. Once after my father's funeral, once when my wife lost our first child, the last time when I was passed over for promotion due to my erratic performance at work. And in between those attempts, I contemplated death incessantly. Those weren't reasons; they were excuses. Excuses to act on feelings I carry with me constantly. They weren't causes. Hell, you know that! Why'm I telling you?"

Why, indeed, she wondered when he had gone. Why did he even bother to visit her when he so obviously felt he knew more about his problem than she did? Unfair, Annette chided herself.

He wants help. He needs help. It isn't his fault he's put four good psychologists on the ropes.

Annette rubbed her eyes in frustration, then swore as she remembered her eye make up. She'd wanted this case. Wanted it because she thought she could handle it. Wanted it because she thought it would be a matter of applying her unique intuition to Brooke Burchard's problem and spotting something that no one else had seen, drawing from him a revelation no one else had been able to call out of hiding. She hadn't expected him to be so... self-aware. It was disconcerting.

She went over her notes again, pixel by pixel, line by line. Jesus-Buddha! That question about exorcism! Where the hell did I think I was going with that?

A moment later, she checked herself. No, that was a valid question. After all, he might have been starting to think it was inevitable. Fate, doom or destiny—God's will—any or all of the above. She could not let him fall into that trap. He had to believe he could control it. Had to. She thought, absurdly, of a childhood cartoon she'd seen about mentally superior rats—a cartoon that had subtly influenced her choice of careers. There had been a magic amulet with an epigrammatic inscription: You can open any door, it said, if you only have the key.

The adult woman believed in that epigram with the same faith the little girl had vested in the amulet it was inscribed upon.

"You look tired."

Annette grinned ruefully and smote her companion on the nose with her menu. It was card-stock parchment, not a DataSlate, so it left no lasting marks there. "Is that anything to say to your beloved when she's gone out of her way to look gorgeous for you?"

"If you care about your beloved, it is."

She watched him seat himself across from her in the intimate booth and contemplated the pale blond lock of hair that nodded over his forehead. It stood out from its darker fellows like the crest of a wave.

"Well? Care to talk about it?"

"What? Oh—I'm sorry, Elliot. It's just a little melting at both ends of my candle. Nothing serious. No—I don't mean that. It is serious, it's just not...my problem."

He nodded. "A case. Patient-doctor privilege, then. I'll stand down and merely lecture about emotional distance and attachment, et cetera."

"Please don't. I've heard it all—in my own voice, as it happens. I don't need to hear it in yours, too. I needed to hear that I was beautiful."

"You are beautiful," he said dutifully. "And tired-looking. Maybe we should cut our evening short. The film will still be there on Saturday."

"No, I want to see it tonight. Why do you insist on calling it a film? Movies haven't been on film for years."

"I was trying to differentiate. We access CD's, we listen to CD's, we watch CD's at home...film is a nice, venerable term."

"So's 'movie.'"

"Oh, all right, then. The movie will still be there on Saturday. Or we could just wait for it to come out on CD."

She smiled, but lacked the energy to push the expression all the way up to her eyes. "Elly, what's your professional opinion of hereditary mental disease?"

It might have been her imagination that he was suddenly wary, but she didn't think so.

"Why do you ask?"

"Because I'm interested in the answer."

He paused long enough to allow the waiter to get to them. He placed his order, she placed hers, and the waiter hovered a moment before leaving them alone. There was silence in the booth.

"Hereditary mental disorders, Elliot. What do you think?" She put a little steel into her voice. Don't play secretive scientist with me, boy.

He shrugged. "I think they're a real possibility."

"But what's the mechanism? How the hell does it get passed on? Is there a gene for insanity?"

His lips compressed. "Would this have anything to do with that case we weren't discussing a minute ago?"

"It might."

"There could be a gene that...affects the mental processes. Other diseases are genetic—why not mental ones?"

She shook her head. "No. I don't buy it. If that were the case, the drugs we've been prescribing lo, these many years would be having more of an effect and psychology and psychiatry less of one."

"I didn't say all mental disfunction was caused by...genetic predisposition. Just some. Maybe the kind we see when entire families are dysfunctional."

"That could just as easily be environmental."

He shrugged. "Could be. Doesn't have to be. Imagine, Annette. Imagine being able to treat schizophrenia or manic depression the way we treat MS or Alzheimer's. Repair the cells, 'teach' them to replicate healthy replacements, unkink the DNA —quite a feat. Quite a future."

"If it were that easy," she murmured.

"Not easy," he said. "But simple. Plain. Straightforward. The human mind is a maze—so's the human body, but it's a clinically observable maze. What would you say to that,

Annette? What would you say to a physical treatment for mental disorders?"

"We tried that—lithium, anti-depressants. Works in some cases, has devastating results in others."

"Not drugs. Actual repair of aberrant physiological processes."

She laughed. It fell short of her eyes. "Trying to put me out of a job, Dr. Hamlin?"

"Isn't that the point of what we do? Aren't we all trying to put ourselves out of a job?"

This time the rueful smile was complete. "I suppose it is, at the core. You just said a mouthful, Mister Genetics." She raised her water glass and toasted him.

Brooke Burchard called in to cancel their next appointment —voice mode, only. Annette didn't know whether to be encouraged or worried. She tried to gauge the sound of his voice and found it did not encourage her. He sounded evasive, wary, in a hurry to get off the phone. Trying to draw him out, she asked when he'd like to reschedule. He said he'd call her back.

She used the free hour to go over his case files again and noticed they'd been accessed in the last four hours by another Med-Net node. She was immediately suspicious that he'd jumped to another therapist. The thought was wounding. Burchard was male, older than she was by some fifteen years, and while Hollywood still made bad movies about sex-starved men who developed mental and emotional disorders just to obtain a young, good-looking female "shrink," life did not imitate art. In her brief but successful career, Annette had had more than one male patient quit on her because she did not fit the image of a lady psychologist. She'd even tried wearing a lab coat. It hadn't helped.

Burchard, though...no, she couldn't accept that of him. He was intelligent, rational. Oh, yes—and suicidal. He was a victim of his own mind—how had he described it? Disunified. Inwardly divided. How rational could he be, under those circumstances?

She was still poring over his files when the phone peeped, calling her to her desk terminal. "Dr. Geller," she said, distracted still, and only just realized that the caller was Elliot Hamlin when he started to speak.

"Hello, Annette, I, um, need to ask a favor of you. A professional favor."

She smiled, relief flowing through her. "Sure. Ask away. Need to borrow a tongue depressor? I'm fresh out."

"This is serious, 'Nette. It's about a patient. I'd like to have you in as a consultant."

She was pleased and let herself glow a little with the pleasure his professional approval brought. "I'd be honored, Dr. Hamlin. If you could just link me to the files, I'll be happy to have a look at them."

He glanced to one side, cleared his throat before looking back at her. "You seem to have them open already. The patient is Brooke Burchard."

"You knew last week, didn't you?" she asked, struggling to keep her voice calm. "You knew when we were pointedly not discussing his case that he was going to come in to see you."

"Yes, of course I knew. What was I supposed to do? I couldn't tell you that any more than you could tell me who you were thinking of when you asked me about hereditary mental disorders. He hadn't agreed to have you consult, then. That happened this morning."

"Your idea, I suppose."

"No, actually, it was his. He says you're fresh. Might bring some insights to the battle. I agree whole-heartedly, of course. We need some gauge of his improvement, if he makes any. You're the individual best qualified to do that."

"Improvement? Aren't you getting ahead of yourself? You don't even have a clue what to look for, do you?"

He nodded. "The Wolfram gene."

"What? Wolfram causes physical disorders-"

"Diabetes and severe vision problems, both of which our Mr. Burchard had as a child." He was excited, the skin over his cheeks flushing rose with pioneer pride. "The research team at Chapel Hill has developed an RNA 'enzyme' to isolate the gene. A beautiful, shiny, new, patented enzyme. They've identified Wolfram's physiological effects—it plays havoc with insulin production and blood sugar assimilation, among other things— and it has a similarly negative effect on the brain's endorphin balance. We don't know how, yet, but we can now test for Wolfram's. I've already done a panel on Brooke Burchard."

"All right, so you can isolate the gene. Then what? You can't cure a genetic defect, can you?"

"We've got an enzyme that can isolate the Wolfram gene. We've got enzymes that help the body break down sucrose. Maybe we can create enzymes to restore the mental balance."

"Are you serious? Enzymes to cure depression?"

"If Brooke Burchard's depression and dementia is a consequence of having the Wolfram gene—and his profile is certainly consistent with its presence—then I don't see any reason why we couldn't use enzymes to effect a cure." He grinned suddenly and unabashedly. "What do you think of that, Dr. Geller?"

"I...I think it's a fascinating theory. I hope you can prove it," she added and realized she only half meant it. Her emotional reserve shocked her wordless, draining the blood out of her face.

"You don't look happy at the prospect."

Dear God. She felt his eyes on her, probing. Could he see that horrid, selfish thought, doing a slow neon-fade from the darkness inside her head. Dear God, what kind of doctor am I?

"Of course, I'm happy!" she retorted belatedly. "If you can take this from the realm of theory into reality, Brooke Burchard will be a free man."

"This is not just about Brooke Burchard, Annette. It's about his children and his children's children. It's about an estimated eight percent of the people in this country who've seriously contemplated taking their own lives."

"Yes. Yes, of course. But what about Brooke? When will you know if he has the Wolfram gene?"

"He's already been sampled for genetic material. The report, I'm expecting literally any moment."

"But they've already cured the diabetes, the loss of visual acuity. Burchard had both taken care of years ago. If the mental disorder has a physiological cause, wouldn't the treatment he underwent for those problems have cured that, as well?"

"Why should it have? He wasn't being treated for the results of a genetic disorder—specifically, he wasn't being treated for Wolfram's Syndrome. Bad genes can cause alteration or even absence of critical enzymes. The doctors who treated Brooke weren't looking for bad enzymes; their patient had diabetes. They didn't think they needed to look any further. They treated the symptoms, Annette, not the disease. This was—what—ten, fifteen years ago, remember."

"Treated the symptoms," she murmured. "And that's what you think I've been doing, too—just treating the symptoms?"

He looked suddenly uncomfortable, caught between his colleague, Dr. Geller, and fiancée, Annette. After a moment of juggling the two, he nodded. "A distinct possibility."

"And just how do you propose to treat the disease?"

"There are several procedures being reviewed right now. First, we want to try to balance the endorphins—to affect some measure of mental stability. There are several methods of doing that. Some hold out more hope of permanence and reliability than others. You've heard of chromaffin grafts?" He didn't wait for her to answer. "One method of treatment involves a similar transplant of pineal gland cells-"

"Wait. Wait. That's a treatment for mutliple-sclerosis."

"Ah! A successful treatment for multiple-sclerosis. Pineal transplants involve a different set of endorphins. But that's just the beginning." He was glowing again. "I believe the answer is in the enzymes. Follow me, okay? If the Wolfram gene can cause an aberration of sucrase enzymes—enzymes that work at metabolizing sucrose—then why not any other enzyme in the body? If we can only determine which enzymes are being effected, Annette-"

"But these aren't proven procedures."

He blinked at her as if she had mumbled to him in an alien tongue. "The procedures are new, but not untried. The pineal transplant has been used successfully in other cases of depression and the Chapel Hill enzyme does isolate the Wolfram gene. What more do you want? None of your procedures have ever been tested in a laboratory—you went directly to human subjects."

She ignored that. "You're relegating Brooke Burchard to the status of guinea pig! You can't hold out any real hope of improvement to him. You're just going to get his hopes up, get him believing in a simple solution to a complex problem, then leave him high and dry."

"The problem is chemical, Annette. And we could be this close-" He made a pinching gesture.

"This close? Elliot, this man has tried to commit suicide three times! He sees things that aren't there. He hears voices in his head. He goes from being as rational as you and I—and, I'd swear, more self-aware—to being a raving basket case. He and his wife calmly discuss institutionalizing him. If he comes to believe this sickness of his is written in his genes it could literally kill him!"

"I don't follow."

"Fatalism, Elliot. As long as he can look at his disorder in terms of-of finding the key, he may keep looking for the key. If you tell him there is no key, that there's nothing he can do for himself, that he's helpless, he'll also be hopeless."

He seemed to consider that for a moment. "Hopeless? To be told you're not crazy, that you've just got something wrong with your chemicals?"

"But you're saying that crazy, as you call it, is chemicals! Just sort out the chemicals and, voila!—you've effected a cure."

"There's something wrong with that?"

"What if it's not true?"

"What if it is, Annette? What then?"

She waved her hands fiercely, fending off the idea. "Veracity is not the point, Elliot. The point is what effect this is going to have on my patient?"

"My patient. He put himself in my hands. You're consulting, yes, and I will hear your opinions, yes, but you're not running the show."

"The show, Elliot? Is that what this is? A circus act where the handsome, young doctor in his shining, white lab coat, waves his magic amulet and saves the day?"

"That is not what I meant. Brooke Burchard is a human being. I care about him. I want to see him and the millions of others like him free of this debilitating disease. I'm offering a medical solution, Annette. A solution I know is there. That's hardly a magic amulet. And I think it's ironic that a member of your profession should accuse anyone else of mumbo-jumbo."

He might just as easily have slapped her. She almost wished he had. "That was low."

He had the good graces to look ashamed. "Yes, it was—but then so was that crack about my shining white lab coat." He pawed at the clean black and white tiles underfoot with the toe of his shoe. "Was it Clarke who said that any sufficiently advanced technology looks like magic?"

Annette grimaced. "I'm not sure technology is the answer to Brooke Burchard's problem. If you determine the presence of Wolfram's gene, then what? Doesn't that basically manacle him to his sickness?"

"Or does it free him from guilt and self-loathing? If we find Wolfram's, at least he'll know there's nothing wrong with his head."

Don't think of a white horse. Brooke grimaced and pulled his mind back to his computer screen. Hard to wait. Hard not to imagine that right this moment (every single moment) the report was downloading to Dr. Hamlin's computer. That all his genetic code was scrolling across another monitor, miles away. He looked at his own screen and wondered if genetic code looked anything like Delta-RPL.

Coffee. He wanted coffee. Badly. Couldn't have any though. It would only make an anxiety attack more likely and that could roll over into something else.

It had been relatively easy not to think of hospital reports when the office had been full of chatter and purposeful activity.

It was after hours now—just—and the Development Room was quiet as a church.

I should go home, he thought. But he didn't want to go. Neither Debbie nor Valerie would be there and somehow an empty house was worse than an empty office. He checked the time again. Twenty minutes. They'd be home in twenty minutes. If he left now and drove very slowly, maybe went around the park, he might only beat them by a minute or two.

He glanced at the phone. It was a simple act—a mere shifting of the eyes and attention—but it brought a stab of unease. Why hadn't Elliot called? He'd said there was progress, that he expected a report from the lab at any time. What if they had the data and it was negative? What if he didn't carry the Wolfram gene? What if he was just another manic-depressive? Would Elliot put off telling him that?

Brooke realized he was worrying his stylus—wrapping its light, slender cord around and around one finger. He dropped the thing and rubbed suddenly sweaty palms on his pants. Ridiculous. Even if Elliot had the data, he'd still have to interpret it, consider the implications—decide on a course of action. It could be a whole day before he called...either way.

Brooke shut down his computer and got up. Senseless. *Senseless to sit here and fume.* He left, carefully laying out his homeward course and shifting his thoughts to wife and child.

Better. That was better.

The car garage was dark and eerily quiet and Brooke felt a creeping unease. The smell of oil rose in eddies from the cool concrete. The sharp sound of his heels slapped back from wall and roof. A frisson shivered up his spine, then down again and he jumped as a *hum-click!* rolled at him from all sides.

The core-lift opened and three women stepped out, arguing about which of two football teams really deserved to win the divisional playoffs. Their high-heels punctuated the dialogue with arrhythmic staccato.

"The Forty-*clackity*-Niners-*clack* are def-*clack*-initely *clack-clack* superior this-*clackity*-season."

"But Sac-*clack*-ramento's-*clackity* defense-*clack* has *clackity-clack* dismantled-*clack*-"

"Sacramento *clack-clack-clack* is playing above itself."

Clack-click-thunk-thud! The conversation moved into the silver Lexus and became too muted to hear.

Brooke sighed and settled into the front seat of his car. He'd loved football, but it got him so wound up he had nowhere to go but down.

He was surprised at how dark it was outside. Dark and cold. The streets were shiny-wet and reflective, spitting the glare of headlights and street lamps back into the darkness. He felt suddenly and completely separate from the rest of the universe —gliding through a corridor of grey cotton and black nothing in a silent capsule. The tires hissed delicately on the wet asphalt and sealed his isolation.

Stop it, he told himself, and did for a moment. He peered up through the windshield—misting now—into a creeping 3-D night.

I hate this weather. ...No, not hate. Hate's too strong a word. Too strong a feeling... Dread? He turned on the windshield wipers.

Headlights sped by—vanguards of other silent, hissing capsules, each bearing its separate occupants. But no, some would hold families, chattering happily on their way to dinner, a show, death.

He shook himself. Dad died on a day like this.

His mind skittered sideways and he thought of Debbie and Valerie coming home together from across town. Hurrying to meet him.

A car in the westbound lanes skidded suddenly and shot toward him in a long scream of brakes. He reacted quickly, expertly, automatically, pulling his own car to the right, bumping his front tire up over the curbing. The other car swept by with a wriggle of taillights, dragged itself straight in a few yards, and passed anonymously on—as did he.

Lucky. That could have been-

Yes. It could have been fatal and it could just as easily have been Deb and Valerie. They have further to drive.

The adrenaline really hit him, then, forcing its icy fist up through his solar plexus, driving the terrified blood up into his head. His hands shook on the wheel. Rain began to batter the windshield, pitting its chaos against the staid rhythm of the wipers.

I should pull over for a moment.

Oh, but not in this. He could make it home. He could.

The shaking was not subsiding. The hissing lights and rush of outside slid too quickly past his windows. And neon. Neon with its cold glare. Even red neon was cold.

What if Deb and Valerie were killed on their way home? What then? It could be happening now—right now. Now. He had to get home. He had to know.

Bad. It was a bad, heavy, horrid feeling. Like a premonition. Oh, right now—right this very moment, their car skidding out of control into the dark, sudden impact, metal bending, tearing. Sudden. Death was sudden. Home.

Sweating, he put his foot down harder on the accelerator. The car surged forward—it had good acceleration for an electri-- and picked up speed, fishtailing only a little on the curve of road that cut, now, through tailored lawns.

The radio. There must be news on, a voice to talk to him, to keep him from talking to himself. He reached for the dash unit.

They're dead.

The voice was audible only inside Brooke's head. It seemed to exit his ears rather than enter into them—a waking-from-a-dream voice. The kind that makes you jump and shiver. He did both. His skin crept.

"Brooke." It was a man's voice, dark as the roadway beyond his headlights. His father's voice. "Brooke, can't you feel it? They're gone. They aren't here anymore."

He reached out frantically with straining senses, not even questioning the voice. Not questioning his credulity. Were they still there? Surely if they'd died he would know it—would feel the loss. Hadn't he felt something when his father died? Hadn't something made him call home and say, "Is everything all right?"

Nothing was all right, but his mother didn't know that.

"Yes," she said. "Everything's fine, honey. Just fine."

"Let me talk to dad," he'd said. Dad was in the garage, she'd said and went to get him. But he could no longer be reached.

Anger spitted him. How does a man do that? How does he kill himself and leave his wife alone to find the body? How does a man get that selfish?

"Selfish, selfish bastard," he muttered. And I'm your son, you know. So obsessed with my own dark thoughts and my black moods, you'd think I was the only person in the universe.

Guilt mounted his anger and spurred it. Stupid, he called himself. Stupid, selfish bastard. You and all your problems. How does Deb put up with it, year after year? Why does she put up with it?

"She loves me," he said aloud. "She loves me."

Laughter. He heard it, rolling up from the darkened back seat. He went hot and cold simultaneously; the skin of his face twitched. Someone was there! Someone had hidden in the back of his car and had heard him muttering non-sequiturs to himself and had now given themselves away.

He could feel it now, a Presence, like a field of static electricity rising from the carpeted floorboards behind him. Like a tingling ball of malevolence. He thought of peeking. He thought of reaching a hand back to feel it. To prove himself wrong, he thought. To prove just how crazy he really was.

He heard the whisper of movement as he rounded a corner, as his unseen passenger coiled to spring. Game over. Serious stuff now. Deadly stuff.

He cranked the wheel over violently, banked against a curb, and rode the brakes to a loud stop. He shoved out of the car, tumbling in wet grass and was soaked by rain and an unseasonable sprinkler system. He lay there for long seconds, waiting.

Waiting for God-knows-what. When it didn't happen, he got up and peeked into the back seat. In the pinkish glow of street lamps, he saw nothing. No one.

Mind grinding, pulse still shrieking, he shivered his way back into the car, abashed, ashamed, embarrassed. He felt blank, but for that. He was blank. Black hole man. He tried to laugh and couldn't, though his teeth chattered. He started the car. It whined and hummed along with his adrenaline. Far from being spent, it was building up a fresh charge, swept along on a current peculiar to Brooke Burchard.

His sixth sense stage-whispered that there was danger. That perhaps the malevolence had been in the back of Deborah's car. Was in the back of her car. Now. Right this moment.

His foot came down on the accelerator. He wove like a drunk--like a madman. He wound his way home, powered by frantic fantasy. The house came in sight (*Dear God, no car!*), its porch light automatically on in welcome. (*They aren't home-*) He glanced for a second at the clock in the console (-*and they should be home by now!*) before he dragged the car, screeching, into the driveway, hydro-planing, shooting water skyward.

He took the long drive much too fast and when a small white blur danced into his headlights, he wasn't ready for it—had forgotten about it. He slammed on the brakes, skidded, and overshot the place he always stopped. Always. He hit it, the small white blur, caught it in mid-scamper and flung it against the garage door.

The car came to a stop. Brooke sat, still, but not silent. His brain and body shrieked at him in strident voices.

What've you done-what've you done-what've you done?

He stared at the great arcs of light on the garage door, watched the wipers shake long, accusing fingers at him, whispering hatefully. He got out of the car and moved forward into the light to see what he had done.

The kitten was dead. Living things did not twist this way and that like wire dolls. Rain pattered gently on the tiny heap of white fur and bone and red, red blood. It fell into the open blue eyes and gave them tears.

Brooke Burchard sat down in the rain beside the little body, caught in the public glare of his headlights, and wept.

"You have the Wolfram gene." Elliot Hamlin gripped the high-impact plastic of the guardrail and watched for some sign he'd been heard.

Brooke Burchard lay silently, his head and shoulders elevated, staring at a blank TV screen. He twitched, grimaced, squeezed his eyes shut, shuddered. But that was not a reaction, Elliot knew. That was what he'd been doing for nearly twenty-four hours straight—awake or asleep—reliving the moment, flagellating himself, rubbing his conscience in the memory. That was what Brooke Burchard and people like him did. It was the snowball effect—guilt upon guilt, shame upon shame, misery upon misery, until there was only one Exit.

And through no fault of his own, Elliot thought. No karma aws at work here, but only a tweaked gene and its obedient flotilla of enzymes, doing what it programmed them to do. *But which enzymes?*

Elliot took a deep breath, exhaled it. His voice would be warm, calm, cheerful. "Brooke, did you hear me? You have the Wolfram gene. We can begin now. We can..." He wanted to say, 'We can lick this thing. Control it. We can cure you. We can give you normal guilt, average shame, reasonable misery.' He couldn't say that, or promise to do it. "We can procede now." Safe words. "We'll start with the pineal graft..." He stalled. And then, what? Take months, years maybe, to determine what enzymes were being affected by the gene?

He glanced sideways at Annette. Her eyes were on Burchard, professional dispassion overcome by compassion, anxiety. She clutched her DataSlate to her chest and met his eyes. Now what?

"She loved that kitten."

Both doctors swiveled their attention back to the hospital bed. Brooke Burchard's eyes were focused now, on them.

"She loves you more," said Annette.

"I don't know what I can say to her."

"Whatever it is, she'll be happy just to hear you say it."

He shook his head. "I put them through so much. So much suffering..."

"They're waiting in the lounge," said Elliot. "You can put an end to their suffering right now. Talk to them."

Brooke licked his lips. They were pale, bluish. He nodded. "Yeah. Okay... Have you told them about the gene?"

"I told your wife."

"Doctor..." His eyes squinted as if at sudden pain. "My daughter...couldn't she carry the gene too?"

Elliot sucked in air. It wasn't an unexpected question, but somehow he was unprepared, nonetheless. "It's a possibility, Brooke. Although, she's shown no indications of it so far. Her blood sugars are normal, her eyesight, likewise. She seems like a happy child."

Burchard grimaced. "No thanks to me. But she could still develop Type II, couldn't she? She could still become diabetic."

Elliot nodded. "She could. But that's not what you're really worried about is it?"

He didn't answer. "You can isolate the gene now, right? If she's carrying it..."

"Yes."

Burchard nodded, looking miserable. "I'd like to see them now, please."

Elliot nodded and escorted Annette from the room.

"His daughter." Annette smacked the wall of Elliot's office with the flat of her hand. "I was so busy concentrating on how this would affect Brooke, I forgot about how it would affect his daughter."

"Could affect her," corrected Elliot, sliding into his chair. "She may not have inherited the gene."

"And if she has?" Annette felt heat building behind her cheeks, pressure behind her eyes. "What if she has?"

Elliot blinked at her. "Then she has."

"Jesus Christ, you can be cold-blooded!"

Elliot leaned back in his chair and closed his eyes. Too damn long without sleep, he thought. He was on the verge of saying something regrettable. "Don't shoot the messenger, Annette. I didn't give Valerie Burchard that bum gene—if she's even got it. I just diagnosed her father. I think you're losing your objectivity."

"To hell with my objectivity!" she snapped. "You're so intent on coming up with a medical coup, you've lost sight of the human reality here."

"Oh? And what is that, Dr. Geller?"

Annette came to sit opposite him, across the desk. "You saw what Brooke went through just to find out he had the gene. The tests, the procedures, the waiting. Now you're saying you want to put Valerie through it, too. She's twelve years old, Elliot. Twelve!"

"But she's not a manic depressive. And she may never be one."

"May not. You can't guarantee that. All you can do is raise the specter. Look, little girl, you might be just like your daddy someday. Someday you may hear voices and jump at your own shadow and scare the people you love half to death."

Elliot threw up his hands. "What was I supposed to do, Annette, lie? No, Brooke, your daughter couldn't possibly have that gene; let's not even bother to look. Or maybe you think I should have refused him treatment when he first came to me."

"He came to you?"

"I didn't recruit him. He said he'd been doing some reading about mental disorders and had come across the Wolfram's connection. He came to me and asked if there was any way we could find out if he had the gene."

"And you said, you could, of course."

"It is my field, Annette. What would you have told him?"

"That the connection between Wolfram's and mental disorder is not universally accepted. That even if he had the gene, there was no conclusive proof that it was responsible for his depression."

"And that his best option was still talk-therapy?"

"I'm not just trying to save my job, dammit!"

"No? Then what? Why are you resisting the idea that Brooke's problems could be physiological?"

"That's not it at all. That's not what I'm resisting."

He leaned toward her, eyes open, now. "Then what, Annette? What are you resisting?"

"Nothing," she'd said. "I'm not resisting anything. I'm just cautious."

She fooled no one with that dodge, least of all Elliot. No, least of all *herself*. And so the question, like Brooke's eyes, like Valerie's stricken face, like Deborah's fraying determination, came back to haunt her.

What am I resisiting? Change?

She mouthed a tuna salad sandwich and pondered that. It wasn't impossible, she supposed. There were those, she knew, who treated the theories of behavioral psychology as if they were a body of religious law. Law that somehow was at variance with technology. She wasn't one of them. Or at least she hadn't thought she was.

She sipped coffee and meditated on the steam, imagining herself a sylph buoyed upward in its draft. Was she a secret devotee of the status quo? Or was she just afraid of being put out of work by a rapidly expanding technology?

She grimaced. Stupid. The whole point of psychiatry was to help people control their impulses—control their Selves. Graduation day, for Annette Geller, was any day any patient stood up and looked her straight in the eye and said, "I don't need you anymore."

She tossed the coffee cup into the WASH bin and wandered out into a dazzling, dew-spackled day. She stood in front of the cafeteria on a herringbone tweed of sunny, red brick, and stared up between immense cedars.

I am afraid, she admitted. There. Now. She took a deep breath. Afraid of what? The cedars declined to respond. She looked past them. "You," she said to a fleeting patch of azure framed by silver billows, "You, he believes in. Me? Why should he believe in me?"

There, but for the grace of God/Goddess go I.

Patient/doctor trust. Was that at issue? Did she feel distrusted? Yes. Yes, she did. And she reacted. Humanly. And protested out of hurt?

No. But I protest without conviction.

She began a slow walk back toward her office across campus. She had no real conviction, she realized. Nothing but a strong desire to prove that Brooke Burchard's disease was psychogenic, not physiological. She dug for the root of the desire, but it eluded her.

Probably, she thought, because I want it to.

"Physician, heal thyself," she muttered and scurried for cover as rain began to fall.

"Your husband has explained the situation to you?" Annette watched Deborah Burchard's face carefully, for what, she wasn't quite certain. It was a composed face. Yes, that was what Deborah Burchard had—composure. Annette supposed one developed composure after fifteen years with a man like Brooke. One did that or one left.

Deborah Burchard was nodding. "And I talked to Dr. Hamlin at some length. I...I wanted to try to understand the full implications of this. I wanted to understand what they're going to try to do."

"And do you understand?"

"No. Do you?"

"In part. They're going to try to control the depression first, using a type of cell grafting. It works very well in the treatment of Ms. Elliot—Dr. Hamlin—thinks it can be applied to your husband's condition as well."

"I don't see how, but then, I have no medical background whatsoever." The woman's gaze sharpened and dug into Annette's composure. "You're a doctor, Ms. Geller. More to the point, you're his doctor. What do you think of this?"

Don't ask me that. "I'm...neutral, I suppose." Liar. "My first duty is to your husband's welfare. He voluntarily applied to Dr. Hamlin to take part in his research-"

"In the hope that it meant a cure." Deborah slid forward in her chair. "You have don't know what it means to him to believe this is genetic and not...emotional." She looked suddenly embarrassed. "That was stupid thing to say. Of course, you know—you're his psychiatrist."

Annette raised her hand. "No, please. You're right. I don't know what it means to him, because he's never discussed it with me. I had no idea he was following developments in neurobiology. My degree in psychology doesn't make me omniscient, Deborah. You...you think this an important development, then. That his expectations are high?"

"Oh, yes. Oh, yes, of course. He can handle the idea that there's something wrong with his body. But to think there's something wrong with his mind—that's terrifying."

Annette glanced down at her hands. Her fingers were knotted together like a bundle of jointed snakes, strangling each other in a white-knuckled death grip. She made them slip apart and lie benignly in her lap. "Deborah, Brooke needs to be aware that this could be a false trail. That he could find himself right back where he started—fighting depression from the inside. In fact, I want him to remain in counseling during the treatments."

"Oh, of course. Dr. Hamlin said it was essential that he have counseling during the treatment process. For patience. He'll have to have so much patience."

Patience. More than she seemed to have. Annette wanted to storm Elliot's office and demand results. *Miracles, Dr. Hamlin. Give us miracles. And give them now.*

She swam that evening until she was exhausted, sat in the hot tub until she was limp, and went home too tired to contemplate resistance or patience or anything else. Elliot called to see if she wanted to go out to a movie. No, she said, she'd just read the book. She didn't want to see someone else's conceptions of *The Land Between Two Rivers.* That would ruin it for her.

She went to bed early instead, and dreamed of driving a car too fast on a rain-slick road. Of not being able to find the brake pedal. All night long she swerved drunkenly through her own backcountry. By morning she was exhausted.

"How do you feel?"

Brooke sat back in the overstuffed chair and smiled. "Good. Tired. Good."

Annette nodded encouragingly. "Good?"

"Yeah. I feel..." Brooke rolled his eyes up to the ceiling and laughed. "This is going to sound silly, but I asked Deb that just after she had Valerie. 'How do you feel?' She came up with tired, cozy, spent, fuzzy and radiantly exhausted. That's how I feel, I guess. Like I've just had a baby. Radiantly exhausted."

"It's too early to feel any effects from the graft," Annette observed, cautious.

"Oh, I know. It's just knowing. You know—knowing that it's just a cocked-up gene not a-a ghost."

"A-"

He raised his hand. "Not literally. You know what I mean. Something...supernatural in the sense that you can't make it go away. There's no medicine for it, no remedy. You can't even pin it down, put a name on it. These enzyme's of Dr. Hamlin's—they have names. And they have jobs. Now, we just have to find out who's loafing."

Oh, how easy that sounds. "It's not that simple, Brooke. I think you know that...don't you?" She turned the statement quickly into a question.

"It's simpler," he said, "than sifting through complexes and compulsions and..." He grimaced. "Ghosts. Chimeras."

And what does that make me—a witch doctor? "What if they never isolate the enzyme?"

"Oh, they will. I might not be alive to benefit from it, but Dr. Hamlin or someone like him will isolate it."

Annette spread her hands. "So you're willing to resign yourself to it, then?"

"Resign myself?" He read the ceiling for a moment. "I hadn't really looked at it that way. I guess I feel like I have a point of reference now. When I feel that...pumping start in the back of my head—the Nightmare Generator, I call it—I can at least say I know what's going on. I can...isolate it. Deal with it."

"And that helps?"

"Yes. God, of course it helps! Doesn't it always help to know what you're fighting?"

"But it's out of your control, doesn't that bother you?"

"Doctor, it's always been out of my control. I just didn't know it. Didn't want to admit it." He leaned forward in the chair, hands clasped between his knees. "Do you have any idea what it feels like to fail yourself over and over again? That's what it was like all those years I spent in therapy, knowing I had this disease, not knowing where the hell it came from or why. All my doctors led me to believe I could control it. You led me to believe it. And every time I lost control and the Nightmare Generator went off on one of its maniac jaunts, I felt like a total and complete failure. A traitor...to myself and to the people who depend on me. I started wondering if deep down inside I wasn't just like one of those little nested dolls. The kind you open up and find another, smaller doll inside? Selves within selves, complexes within complexes. Maybe, I thought, I want to fail. I want pity. I like guilt. I'm punishing myself for... not being able to save my father's life."

She started to leap on that and caught herself. "Do you think that's a possibility?" she asked neutrally.

He chuckled. "Sure. I did feel guilty about my father's death. If I'd been a better son, he wouldn't have killed himself. I don't believe that, of course, especially not now. But the thought does occur. But don't you see? Anyone would feel like that under the circumstances. *Anyone.* But because of the gene, what might have been just an occasional, nagging doubt became...a nightmare. All my doubts, all my fears, all my unhappinesses ran away with me." He paused and looked down at his interlaced fingers. "Run away with me."

"But you think you can control it—the Nightmare Generator?"

He shook his head. "No. But now I know where it lives."

"I can't help him, anymore, Elliot."

She might have been a bit of data that had refused to behave itself, the way he looked at her. "That's absurd. Of course, you can help him."

"This isn't my field. This is your field. I don't know what I'm doing here."

"This isn't a competition, Annette. Brooke needs both of us. He needs me to isolate the problem and you to help him deal with waiting. He's still a manic-depressive. He still hallucinates. His brain is still overwhelmed by the impulses that cause both disorders. It doesn't matter that the cause is physiological rather than psychogenic. The effects are psychological."

"I might as well resort to beads and rattles."

"Don't knock beads and rattles. If that helps Brooke stay in control-"

"He can't stay in control, dammit! There's nothing for him to do but wait."

"Then, for God's sake, help him wait. You're a psychiatrist, Annette. You have a degree in behavioral psych. Use it."

"How? *How*, use it?" What was that look? Was that pity? Frustration? She couldn't tell, but it unraveled the last of her objectivity and she felt like hitting him. Or crying.

Too close. We're too close for this to work. She opened her mouth to say that, but he was talking.

"You've counseled terminal patients, haven't you?"

The question disoriented her. She spent a dazed moment trying to see the connection. She shook her head. "No. No I haven't."

Elliot pulled his eyes away and began toying with a paperweight on his desk. "Out of choice or never been called upon?"

"I...I have been approached, but..." She felt in her pockets for lint. "I've usually referred them to other doctors. Specialists."

"Why?"

"I'm...not...a specialist in that area."

"Don't you mean you don't *want* to be a specialist in that area?"

She stared at the blond forelock that shielded his eyes from hers. "Switching fields, Elliot?"

"What is it about terminals you don't like?"

"I didn't say-"

"I know what you didn't say. What is it about terminals that...disturbs you?"

"I'm not disturbed by-"

"Why don't you want to deal with them, Annette? Why do you avoid dealing with them?"

She crossed her arms tight over her chest. "All right, Dr. Hamlin. Since you seem to know me better than I know myself, you tell me why I avoid dealing with terminal patients."

"Because you can't control what happens to them."

Outrage flooded her ears with hot, stinging blood. "I can't- I can't control what happens to them? God Almighty, Elliot, you make me sound like some kind of control freak! Annette, who would be God!"

He was shaking his head.

"Is that really what you think of me? As a professional? As a person?"

"Well, you are just the tiniest bit of a control freak. But that's not really what this is about, I don't think." He smiled, which only poured fuel on her fire.

"You don't believe in what I do, do you? You don't believe in psychiatry as a valid science."

He waggled his head. "Belief? It's not a religion, 'Nette. It is a science and an art, but like any other methodology, it has its domain. I think in this case psychiatry has to share a kingdom with neurobiology. I can deal with the concrete business of irregular molecular ferries and genetic disorder. Slowly, surely, we're learning more and more about what makes the human animal tick. But, I need someone like you to handle the human consequences. Brooke needs someone like you."

"Someone like me, maybe, but not me. I can't do anything for him but sit and listen. I don't even know what questions to ask him anymore."

"Ask him how he feels."

Annette took a deep breath and felt her face cool. "I'm going to turn Brooke's case over to another therapist."

Elliot hung his head and she believed for a moment it was in contrition. But when he looked at her again what she saw in his eyes was disappointment. "I never thought you were a quitter, 'Nette," he said.

She turned Brooke over to a resident psychologist who dealt, largely, with terminal cancer patients and AIDS victims. She saw him only rarely and in passing, and saw Elliot less. She heard about both of them, though. She had a girlfriend on Elliot's staff who kept her abreast of developments, and she spent her lunch hours in the cafeteria where she would be sure to hear any talk among the residents.

"Were you listening?"

Annette pulled her eyes away from the row of French doors that opened onto the patio. Suzanne Murphy gazed up at her over a turkey sandwich dripping with alfalfa sprouts.

"I'm sorry, Suz. I guess I wasn't. You were, um, saying something about dopamine?"

Suzanne nodded. "That's what they thought it was at first, dopamine flooding the neural network. Elly was proceeding on that idea, but..." She shrugged. "False track. Dopamine levels were normal even during critical episodes."

She'd captured Annette's full attention. "He's had... critical episodes? Bad ones?"

"There's such a thing as a good one?" Suzanne shrugged again. "It's been difficult for him. Difficult for his family."

"How is he responding to Dr. Faizi?"

"He likes her, well enough, but I think he feels more comfortable with you. You've been with him longer." She glanced at the rising pile of sprouts on her plate. "It was hard for him to have to switch therapists at such a critical juncture."

Damn. "I'm sorry. I just didn't feel like I was doing him any good."

"I think you underestimate yourself."

Annette ignored that. "So what's the current line of attack? If it's not dopamine, then what is it?"

"Well, we're all pretty sure Elliot's right about the flooding. The indications are all there. Brooke gets a shot of adrenaline, a charge of emotion and, where the charge should normally shut off and dilute, it keeps snowballing until he's completely overwhelmed. That points to at least one enzyme that's not doing its job. It's getting the emotional messages out into the neural junction, but its not picking up after itself... Reminds me of my eldest son."

Annette glanced up at her. She was grinning lopsidedly, turkey dangling from the half-eaten sandwich. Annette had to smile. "That simple, huh? An adolescent enzyme?"

"Well, more or less. Transporter proteins, to be more specific. Well, we've eliminated dopamine as the offender. It could be...any number of other neurotransmitters. GABA, nrepinephrine, serotonin. It's a matter of trial and error at this point."

"So let's say you find the guilty party. Then what?"

"You ought to have Elliot explain this to you. He'd do a much better job of it."

"Yes, well. I haven't spoken to Elliot for a while."

"I thought as much. You ought to, you know...speak to him. It's been hard on him, too. The stress, having you...disappear on him."

"I haven't disappeared."

"Might as well have."

"Besides, he's got to be loving this. This is his passion—neurobiology, genetics. This is what he lives for."

"Huh. Man does not live by neurobiology alone." Suzanne studied her for a moment, making her feel naked and transparent.

"Look, I don't know what's gone haywire between the two of you, but I really think you ought to talk about it."

Annette started to issue a defense, but Suzanne waved the sandwich to forestall her. "Ignore me. I'm just a nosy, backseat-driving yenta. It's your life, hon. You're drivin' the car."

Driving the car. Funny she should say that. It reminded Annette forcibly of her nightmares. Of cars without brakes. Cars with steering wheels that broke off in her hands. She was driving the car. Brooke couldn't drive his.

Something had made of his waking moments what she only encountered in nightmares—forced him to live what "normal" people like Annette Geller only dreamed. A Nightmare Generator.

And Elliot might—just might—be able to pull the plug.

When Elliot paged her that afternoon, she was already on her way to his office. She surprised him by appearing within ten seconds of his page.

"That was fast."

"I was already on my way," she admitted. "I wanted to apologize for my behavior and to say...that if you still need my help, I'll gladly offer it."

He swept a hand through his hair, making the pale forelock stand almost on end. "Not a moment too soon. Brooke...is

I Loved Thy Creation

having a very difficult time just now. We've been tracking transporter molecules for eons of weeks and it's getting harder and harder for him to wait it out."

"The pineal grafts-?"

He made a dismissive gesture. "Limited effectiveness. It takes more to kick him into a manic episode, but when he goes, he goes just as deep."

"Suzanne tried to explain to me about the neurotransmitters and the flooding."

His expression changed. "Yeah. Yeah." He stood up and came around his desk, hands gesturing. "We're on the right track here, I just know it. I can feel it. It's just a matter of isolating the neurotransmitters that are flooding, then backtracking to the transporter molecules responsible for cleaning them up."

Annette sat down in his patient chair and folded her hands in her lap. "Enlighten me, doctor. What's the mechanism?"

Elliot perched on the edge of his desk. Lecture pose, thought Annette, and realized how much she'd missed him.

"Okay, look. In response to stimulus, neurotransmitters deliver a chemical message from one nerve cell to another. Be sad. Be happy. Get your hand off the stove. That sort of thing. So far so good?"

She nodded.

"When the stimulus ends, the transporter proteins or molecules, which are enzymes by the way, are supposed to ferry the neurotransmitters back to the cell of origin."

"Clean up committee."

"Exactly. Only in Brooke's case, there is no clean up committee. The synapses stay flooded with the neurotransmitter and the system is overwhelmed."

"Assuming you isolate the lazy transporter, then what?"

"Then, the serious work starts. We isolate, from Brooke's brain, the DNA sequences that create the transporter proteins, which, in turn, target the problem neurotransmitter or transmitters. We should be able to insert those sequences into lab grown cells and cause them to produce the needed transporters. Then, we'll re-introduce the healthy, productive cells back into Brooke's body."

"That probably means more grafting, then. And what, bone marrow transplants?"

"Possibly. But we're close, Annette. Really close."

Annette nodded. "So, suddenly Brooke is having trouble waiting? Now, when you're so close to a solution?"

"Not exactly, doc. Don't fly off looking for self-immolation complexes. He's running true to form. It's guilt."

"Guilt? Oh, Valerie-"

Elliot shook his head. "No. Valerie doesn't have the gene. Brooke feels guilty that so many people are putting so much time and money and effort into solving his little, insignificant, if-I-die-it-will-go-away problem. He doesn't think he's worth it."

"Doesn't think he's worth it? Does he realize what's riding on this research for other depressives?"

Elliot gestured at the door. "Go give him hell, doc."

"What about Dr. Faizi? Hasn't she been able to help? She's so good with the terminal patients-"

He was shaking his head. "Annette, Brooke isn't terminal. He's a relatively young man, with a young family and a lot of living to do. A totally different scenario. Brooke isn't dealing with a biological fact that will affect the way he dies—unless commits suicide. He's dealing with a biological fact that will affect the way he lives. He's not surrendering control. He's fighting to achieve it for the first time in his life."

"A faceless enemy," murmured Annette. "That's what he's been fighting. Only your work could give the enemy a face."

"It's easier to fight what you can see."

"And understand," she added. "And control." She got up and smoothed her jacket. "Where's Brooke now? I'd like to see him."

"In Observation."

She nodded and moved to the door. "You were right, you know. About the control issue. I was terrified of not being able to stay in control of Brooke's progress. I was terrified for him and for me."

"Because you care," said Elliot. "That's what you didn't wait around to hear that day two months and seven days ago when you stormed out of here in a high dudgeon. You wanted to control Brooke's progress because you care about him. I knew that."

Annette grimaced and waggled her head. "So much for my professional objectivity."

"Oh, to hell with your objectivity. I like you this way."

"Enough to marry me?"

"I never took the wedding off my calendar." The tone of his voice caused much dancing among her own neurotransmitters. She didn't care if the clean-up crew took the rest of eternity off.

"Dinner tonight?" she asked.

He nodded. "And a movie?" His eyes glinted.

"What's playing?"

"The Land Between Two Rivers."

"But I just read the book and-" She made a wry face. "Ah. The control freak strikes again. The movie sounds great. Right now, I'm going to go do my job. I'm going to tell Brooke Burchard just what I think he's worth."

Brooke Burchard sat at a window table, a book open in front of him, his eyes on something outside. He was haggard, lost-looking. It was enough to make Annette want to cry out, "Unfair!" Unfair to booby trap someone's body. Unfair to fill it with miniature terrorists that could hold an entire life hostage. Especially unfair to such a remarkable man as Brooke Burchard.

Who might not be so remarkable, Annette realized, without his particular torment to shape him. Is there really no such thing as complete darkness?

She stirred slightly in the doorway of his room, folding her arms over her chest in a reproving pose. "Elliot tells me you've been causing trouble."

He glanced up at her—a quick parry of the eyes, followed by a downward feint. He dog-eared the page of his book, worrying it.

She entered the room, allowing the door to close behind her, and took the seat opposite him at the little table. "I owe you an apology," she said. "A heartfelt apology. I'm sorry, Brooke. I'm sorry I let you down."

His eyes swung upward again, gauging, reading. He shook his head. "You don't owe me anything. I'm the one who should apologize. I've been so much trouble."

"No. I'm the problem, here, not you. I want to try to explain to you why I quit on you."

"I understand-"

"No. I don't think so. Brooke, you could do me a big favor, if you would."

"What could I do for you?"

"Listen to me. You've told me about your nightmares. I'd like to tell you about mine."

He nodded, wariness covering his eyes like a shield.

"Just before I...abandoned you to Dr. Faizi-" He started to protest, and she raised her hand. "No. I did abandon you. No excuse for that, but I want you to understand why. Just before that, I started having nightmares. Nightmares about driving a car with no brakes over an icy road. About losing control of the car and crashing. I failed, Brooke. I failed to control the car. And it scared me.

"I quit because I couldn't control what was happening to you. I wanted to cure you, I guess, with my bare hands. I thought, somehow, that when Elliot found a biological determinant in your case, it took you out of my control. And that if I wasn't in control, I couldn't help. But you never were in my control to begin with."

She glanced down at her hands, folded on the table. "The truth is, we're more complex creatures than I realized and more...integrated, I guess. Somehow, I saw Elliot's province as the body and mine as the mind, and I couldn't see that those provinces are not as separate as I would have them be. I can't do anything about that gene. Elliot can. But I can help you through the process of dealing with it...if you'll have me back."

He looked doubtful. "You're sure you want to do that? I've been so much trouble. You people are trying so hard to cure me and I'm hardly worth-"

She grasped both his hands, curtailing their torture of the book. "That's our job, Brooke. It's what we do. But before you write yourself off as a waste of time, let me admit something to you. I told your wife once that a Ph.D. in psychology doesn't make someone omniscient. Truth is, it doesn't necessarily give them clear insights into their own workings. You've done that, though. You've given me insights I've never had."

He almost smiled, his mouth tugging tentatively upward at the corners. "I've helped you?"

She nodded. "Everybody has a Nightmare Generator, Brooke. You're not alone in that. You helped me recognize mine...and control it. I owe you one. And a lot of other people are going to owe you, too, once Elliot comes through with his part in this."

"How do you figure that? I won't have done anything."

"You'll have stayed alive. You'll have shown other people with this disorder that the search for a cure is worth wading through the nightmares and exorcising the ghosts. Maybe that will give them the courage to do what you've done. You can be...a role model."

He laughed outright at that. "Me? A role model?"

"You've been that for me. You know yourself well, Brooke, because you've had to. That's more than a lot of us so-called 'normal' people can claim. We who do not have to fight for sanity may take it a bit too lightly."

He ducked his head—an odd, bashful gesture. "That thought had occurred to me." He looked up at her, smile complete and roguish.

She laughed. "Somehow, Brooke, that doesn't surprise me.... So, do I have my old job back?"

He nodded.

"Thank you," she said.

"Thank you." He extended his hand to her over the table.

She took it, shook it, and rose to leave. "I'd better check in at my office. See what other lessons I can learn today."

"Dr. Geller..."

"Annette."

He nodded diffidently. "Annette. Thank you for sharing your nightmares with me. Somehow a nightmare shared is...just a bad dream."

Warmth. She looked at him sitting there in his hospital blues, weary and vulnerable and hopeful, and felt it flood from core to extremities. *So much for my objectivity.* "We'll share some good ones, too," she told him, "I can feel it in my synapses."

Pipe Dreams

A story of science fiction

Pipe Dreams was originally published in *Analog Science Fiction* in 1997 and is the result of a challenge between myself and two other writers: the first one of us to use the phrase "Ambush two tangerines" in a published story would be treated to dinner by the other two. The source of that phrase is alluded to in the story itself. That the main character, a defense programmer, is a Bahá'í is revealed only subtly, largely through the contents of his subconscious, which conditions even the symbols he embeds in his computer code.

It was a normal day for Beckett Hodge. Which is to say an extraordinary day, for Beckett Hodge attracted extraordinary situations, things, and people the way black pants attract white cat hair.

Beckett—'Beck' to wife and friends—was, to outward appearances, an archetype—the mild-mannered and somewhat nerdish professor of Computer Science, habitually forgetful and distracted, his mind engaged in a never-ending background computation. He did not drink; he did not swear; he forgot his own birthday and resorted to electronic wizardry to remember his wife's. He was a renowned lecturer and an author, too, of thick, arcane tomes about AI, nano-tech and enviro-programming, every one written in what his wife, Marian, called 'technese.'

In Beckett's head, he was a fictioneer—a storyteller—though no one had ever read a word of his fiction. The clutter of scientific and academic accomplishments was merely a source of income, something he just *did,* the same way that he breathed, ate, slept, and performed other necessary functions.

Beckett Hodge wanted people to be as impressed with his fiction as they were with the rest of the things he did, but as he approached his thirty-sixth birthday, that goal seemed no closer than it had the day he first opened a word processor file to write about something other than neural nets, bio-computing, and self-policing AI security systems.

He was bemused by his academic publisher's lack of interest in seeing a work of fiction with his name on it. "You write like a programmer," Terrence Lance had said, upon reading Beck's synopsis for a novel. When Beckett failed to see the problem with that, he'd added, "Write what you know, Beck."

Beck disregarded the commentary. After all, the fellow edited and published textbooks, not novels. He had downloaded the synopsis to three publishers anyway, using his academic credits to get a foot in the electronic door. Nearly six months later, he was still waiting for the door to budge.

He put that out of mind now and assembled his lecture notes, penned neatly on yellow legal paper. He loved the feel of paper between his fingers, the smell of it when he flipped a page. It was a soothing touch of realism for a mind that habitually courted the abstract. He loved the smell of magazines and books, too. In his vivid imagination, the pages that held his own fiction were especially savory.

He brought his mind firmly back to the here and now—not usually so difficult a thing for a man who lived for the nano-second—and began his lecture on the dynamics of programming the mood-sensitive entertainment system.

The hall was packed; students stood along the walls and in every nook and cranny that would hold a body. Beck knew his peers speculated about his popularity—was it the subject matter or the fact that he reminded his students of a Disney character who might any moment begin lecturing on "flubber" instead of silicon?

When the lecture was over, Beck had a series of appointments: One with the head of the Life-Science department, one with the board of directors of a major financial institution, the third with his government liaison, Colonel Traynor. The department head wanted him to consider teaching another class in nano-programming, the bankers wanted to commission him to design one of his patented security systems for their customers' valuables, Traynor was negotiating enhancements to a security and defense system Beck had put in place the year before for the Department of Defense.

He didn't want to teach another class in nano-tech, and said as much. He found it difficult to concentrate during the meeting with the contingent from First Continental Finance. He accepted the job with his mind on how he might punch up the opening of his latest attempt at a novel, saw the bankers out of his office, and settled in to grab half an hour of writing time before his military escort arrived to take him to his next meeting.

He wasn't certain he really wanted the First Continental job —it would distract him just that much more from his writing-- but he supposed Marian would think him foolish to turn it down. And as to the military contract, he disliked working with the government in a vague, abstract way. They were an incredibly paranoid group of people. He had difficulty thinking the way they did, but Marian said that was because he was naive.

The thought brought a smile to his wide lips. Marian could say things like that and mean them as compliments.

To Beck, the DOD was a paradox: Having determined never to use their deadly arsenal of nuclear weaponry, they must now make certain no one else could use it either. It was as if a man had purchased a gun to protect his home and family, only to decide he couldn't bring himself to point it at anyone and pull the trigger. It was therefore necessary to go to great lengths to hide the gun, to lock it away in a series of increasingly forbidding vaults, complete with booby traps. The whole idea seemed absurd, and despite the fact that the contract would bring him several million dollars by completion, he would have still cheerfully advised the government to simply get rid of the gun—or at the very least to unload it and throw the bullets away. Instead they had opted for a vault. Now, they wanted it strengthened and enlarged.

The meeting with Traynor was cordial and orderly and Beck could hardly wait to get away. Specs in hand, he had the driver take him straight home. He was in a hurry to get into his office to get to work. The notes on the first chapter of his novel were burning a hole in his briefcase.

Marian was already home. "Took off early," she said, handing him a glass of orange juice. "Had a lunch meeting with Liz Harris. Lord, that woman gives me a headache. Acts like she's our only account. You have e-mail from a publisher."

It took him a full five seconds to catch that, even though he'd had ten years of practice sorting through the diverse information his wife could layer into her dialogue.

"I what?"

"I checked the mail." He was already on his way into the office, orange juice sloshing; she raised her voice. "Some guy named Bourbon—Seton House, I think."

The name was Laurence Bourbon. The publisher was Sefton House. The message made a sharp, shrill tingle of anticipation vibrate up Beck's spine: *I'm going to be in Boston next week and I'd like to meet you and discuss your manuscript. You have some very interesting ideas and I think we can work together. Lunch Tuesday at the Sheraton? Please let me know if this is agreeable.* His Internet address followed. There was a 3-D scan with the message, showing a smiling man, probably above middle age, with sparkling dark eyes and distinguished streaks of gray in his dark hair and beard.

Shaking, Beck dropped into his chair and logged onto the Net. *I find it very agreeable,* he sent back. *Around one? I have classes until noon.* He sent back a canned scan of himself so Bourbon would be able to recognize him.

The reply came while he was sitting there staring at the original e-mail, sipping but not tasting his orange juice. "You have mail," the computer informed him.

One is fine. Meet you in the main lobby. I look forward to it.

Beck felt a hand on his shoulder, followed almost immediately by warm lips at his ear. "You're shaking," Marian murmured. "I used to do that to you, once."

Beck was not so much the absent-minded professor as to miss that cue. "Why don't we go into town tonight? We'll have dinner and go for a long walk in the Commons."

She was watching his hand where it lay atop the keyboard, fingers just caressing the keys. "We'll grab a quick bite at Giovanni's and come home. That'll give you about three hours to work on chapter one. Be in bed by eleven." She left him alone to save his precious messages and read the rest of his mail then, swaggering out of the room swirling her orange juice in the rounded glass as if it were expensive brandy in a snifter. He noticed—he always did notice—how lithe she was, how long and catlike. She walked like a gunslinger. He, nerd, wondered how he had ever managed to snare a Marian.

The rest of the week was a blur of lectures and programming and anticipation. He got a lot of work done on the Pentagon Piece, as he called it, adding subtle and not so subtle nuances to his existing system. And he actually made a decent

start on the Bank Vault program as well. Surprising, considering
that in every spare moment he was noodling with the novel.

Marian's business partner, Ruby, thought that was silly,
"Considering," she said, "that someone's shown interest in the
book as is."

"He may want changes," Beck told her.

"Mm-hmm, but will he want the ones you're making?"

That disconcerted him so much he spent Saturday and
Sunday fully engaged in his programming with only half an
afternoon out to go bike riding with Marian (his concession to
her insistence on regular exercise) and start work on a short
story which would no doubt end up in the same electronic file
folder all his other unpublished short stories ended up in. He'd
never had the temerity to publish even one of them on the Net. It
wasn't anonymous enough.

The Sheraton was corporately bland in its ostentatiousness;
it's foyer gleamed with brass that reflected only muted beiges
and peaches. The potted foliage that decorated the place wasn't
real, nor was it intended to look real. It was intended to look
alien. It didn't. It looked like naked, airbrushed manzanita and
cinchona spangled with tiny faux seed pearls or draped with
locks of gold and peach silk that gave the impression of
poodle-dyed Spanish Moss.

Beck eyed it with vague queasiness as he waited for the
concierge to check him through to the elevator to the Tower
suites. He was impressed in the extreme. He'd thought that the
wealth in the publishing industry was invested in those who
wrote, published, or owned the movie rights to the latest
multi-generational saga, horror classic, or mucus-making
romance. That Laurence Bourbon could afford such

accommodation set him to musing about the differences between academic and commercial publishing. No textbook editor he knew could afford such luxury.

Bourbon was a tall man, Beck's height or better, dapperly dressed in a suit with gleaming white shirt and red silk tie—an Ascot, not a Windsor. He was polished, urbane, even suave, yet his face seemed open, friendly. Humor sparkled in his dark eyes. Beck liked him immediately and allowed his hopes to rise. More so, when he saw a printed copy of his manuscript sitting in the middle of the round, glass-topped table at which Bourbon bid him seat himself.

"Dr. Hodge," the publisher said expansively, sitting opposite him.

"Uh, Beckett, please...or Beck...whichever."

There was a carafe of coffee on the table; Bourbon spoke as he poured. "Beckett, then. I'm very glad we could meet like this. And on such short notice." He put down the carafe and laid both hands flat on the manuscript. "I don't mind telling you, this is quite a book."

Beck could feel his skin flushing. "I don't mind hearing it. I'm surprised you actually wasted the paper to print it. Surely, a cyber-reader..."

"False modesty, Beckett, seldom impresses an editor. This is a good book. Very solid. Exciting plot. Interesting characters. Especially Martin, your programmer/mage. Your knowledge of programming certainly comes through."

Beck chuckled. "My textbook editor says I write like a programmer. He's suggested to me that I should stick to academics and leave fiction to people with imagination."

Bourbon shook his head. "I can only think he's afraid of losing you to fiction. This novel shows a *vivid* imagination. At the same time, you apply your science extremely well. I'm impressed...obviously, or I wouldn't be here. I hope you don't mind my idle chatter, but I like to get to know my writers."

His writers. Beck had the absurd desire to grin. He gave in to it and hid the grin in his coffee.

"Now, as to possible contracts," Bourbon continued, then shot a glance at his watch. "I've an appointment shortly—could you drop by this evening...oh, around seven-ish? We could discuss terms..?" He spread his hands, leaving the ball in Beck's court.

Beck was ready to jump at that but remembered before he'd opened his mouth to accept, that Marian had no idea what was going on. "Can we do it tomorrow? My wife and I have a rule. We never make last minute, solo plans without consulting each other—especially after hours."

Bourbon's brows twitched. "There's the phone."

"She's on a buying expedition today. It...it wouldn't be fair to her to spring this on her. She might have—er—plans for us this evening." He flushed, hoping Bourbon wouldn't inquire as to what kind of plans.

"A possessive woman, your wife?"

Beck had the impression the questioning tone was tacked on as an after thought. "No, she's not really. Well, I mean, she *is*—but we *both* are. It's hard to explain, but we both have such hectic schedules and put in such long days; our time together is very precious to both of us. Tomorrow, maybe..." He trailed off, feeling vaguely idiotic—like a man who's won the lottery only to balk at having to go down to the bank to pick up the check.

Bourbon's smile was quick and bright. "Tomorrow's fine. Some more coffee?"

Beck relaxed into the depths of his chair as they discussed some changes to the manuscript—all of which seemed impossibly minor. He left the Sheraton riding the crest of an adrenaline wave, eager to bring Bourbon a slightly reworked first chapter. He got home, had the house play an entire library of Vivaldi and Blue Oyster Cult, and worked on the book for what only seemed like minutes before Marian's appearance at his office door interrupted him.

"What're you doing home?" she asked, brow wrinkling. "Don't you have classes this afternoon?"

He stared at her for a full two seconds before he realized she was right. He *did* have classes this afternoon—or rather, he would have, if he'd remembered to go to them. Swift heat suffused his skin. "I..."

"Lost all track of time," Marian finished for him. She laughed, leaned over and kissed his forehead. "Beck, honey, I think you're halfway to discovering the secret of time travel."

"What's up?" The female voice came over Marian's shoulder from the doorway.

Beck mumbled, "Hi, Ruby," and tried to decide whether he should get up and race down to the campus in an attempt to retrieve his last class of the day, or to just call in and plead that he'd felt ill (cough, cough), taken a nap and...lost all track of time.

Marian's partner, Ruby Wilson sauntered into his office, arms folded across her substantial chest and said, "You're not supposed to be here."

"Save file," he told the computer. He looked up at her. "Are you having a secret meeting?"

The two women glanced at each other. "Yes," said Ruby, "we're part of a coven of cyber-witches and we're having a ritual sacrifice this afternoon in your backyard."

"No, no." Marian shook her head. "That's Tuesday. Today is the secret swearing-in ceremony for the new members...and, of course—"

"The orgy," finished Ruby, nodding. "How could I forget?"

"So are you just going to sit there?" Marian had folded her arms across her chest, too, and was glancing between him and the antique walnut wall clock that hung over the mantelpiece. "Shouldn't you go over and catch the fallout?"

"I could call..."

"You could," agreed Marian, "but then again, you *could* still catch your last class."

Beck glanced at his computer screen—longingly. His sense of responsibility kicked in hard. He saved the file a second time, idled the machine, popped out the memory core, pocketed it and headed for his car.

The two women watched him from the *lanai* at the front of the house, side by side, waving at him. *Like conspirators,* he thought, then wondered where the hell that had come from. It came to him as a surprise that he hadn't told Marian about his book deal. It came to him as an even greater surprise that he was reluctant to tell her. He was a man who often dealt in secrets, and, because of this, he shared everything he could with Marian. It was odd, he thought, that this secret was one he rather relished keeping.

He was just able to salvage his last class, then logged onto the school Net to apologize to the students he had stranded, promising not to let it happen again. Then he went home. Ruby was gone when he got there, and Marian, fresh from a shower, was sipping orange juice on the *lanai* while the house audio system gave forth the sylvan sounds of a Northwest Coast rain forest.

"So, talk to me," she said, when he'd kissed her forehead and folded himself into the seat across from her at the bistro table. "How was the appointment this morning?"

He hesitated, but the secret refused to remain a secret. He grinned. "It was terrific, Marian. Absolutely terrific. This guy really likes my book. *Really* likes it. He had some suggestions for improving the first couple of chapters-"

"Did you sign a contract?"

"Not yet, but-"

"You shouldn't really make changes until you see the whites of President Grant's eyes."

He stared at her, bemused. "He *wants* the book, Marian. He just wants to see if I can correct a few things."

She nodded. "What was the name of the publisher again? I told Ruby it was Seton. She said I must've meant Sefton. It isn't Sefton, is it?"

"It's..." He broke off and looked at her. That question had an agenda behind it; he could tell by the tone of her voice and the fact that she was gazing into the bottom of her OJ glass, not into his eyes. "It's Sefton. Why?"

"Do you know what their last big publication was?"

"Not right off hand."

"*Voice from a Burning Bush* by Ibrahim X."

Beck shook his head.

Marian leaned forward and grasped a handful of the hair at the back of his head. "Sometimes, my beloved husband, you are too much of a nerd to live. Ibrahim X was the self-proclaimed ringleader of the Shalom/Salaam terrorist group. You might have heard of them if you read the news we subscribe to. Sefton made a killing on his book, which is basically a 'how-to' manual for wannabe terrorists and a self-serving justification for mass murder. It generated a heated first amendment debate in Congress and all sorts of bad press for Sefton, the net effect of which was record book sales and handsome royalties for one and all." She stopped talking and just looked at him.

He waited a beat. "And?"

Her grip on his hair tightened. "You're going to deal with these people? People who've figured out a legal way to make a buck from terrorism?"

Beck did not swear. Marian did occasionally, and he had no doubt she would be doing it shortly if he did not answer her questions in the appropriate manner. Beck, mounted on the horns of a dilemma that was at once clear and impenetrable, wished he did swear. A good solid, 'hell' or 'damn' would feel somehow purging. Instead he asked, "Are you sure?"

"I'm sure about the book and the author. Ruby's sure about the publisher." She let go of his hair. "Seriously, Beck. How can you do business with people like that?"

"Sefton is a big company. I'm sure their fiction department-"

"Cop out." She got up from the table, chair sliding back with a metallic groan.

"Marian..."

"Cop out, cop out, *cop out.*" She disappeared into the house, the door sliding behind her with a slight popping sound. The rain forest fell silent. Some of Marian's exits, Beck thought, really ought to be followed by the sound of a door slamming.

They argued about it further over dinner. He refused to make commitments of either feeling or intellect and she refused to see what a rejection of Bourbon's offer (or potential offer) meant to him.

He was not good at verbalizing emotion, but in the eleventh hour, he gave it a good shot. "Look, Marian. Try to understand. I see the bigger moral issues, really I do. But they're not my issues. I just want to publish some science fiction. It has nothing to do with Mr. X or his book. I may be a hot shot when it comes to AI systems, but I'm nobody when it comes to fiction. Bourbon could change that. This is something I've dreamed about for years. For decades. My fiction in print, Marian. My name on a book."

"And what about principles, Beckett? *Your* principles."

He shook his head.

She went to see Ruby. He removed himself to his office and pecked at his manuscript, all the while imagining the two of them, hunched in a booth in their favorite latté bar, dissecting his character as if he were a piece of bad fiction. In the backwash of angst, his POV character took on a decidedly cynical bent.

Marian didn't get home until after eleven, making a mockery, Beck thought, of everything he'd said to Laurence Bourbon about their "rules." He was lying in bed, feeling a little betrayed, when she lowered herself into bed next to him. They drifted into sleep without touching.

By morning, Marian was curled in Beck's arms and he had a hazy memory of hot sex during which he had played a decidedly non-aggressive role. He thought he'd dreamed of Marian riding through a stormy sea dolphin-back. It was a strangely erotic image. He wondered if he might make use of it fictionally.

She fixed breakfast for him. That was an unspoken apology, but she was still nettled by the whole terrorist thing. "You know, it's possible that your publisher friend even knows who Ibrahim X is—and where he is."

"I doubt it."

"Well, think of it, Beck. Money has to change hands, manuscripts have to be delivered. Even if it's all done through an agent of some sort, *somebody* must know *something*."

He glanced up at her over the rim of his coffee cup. "And?"

"He's wanted by the World Tribunal, for godsake. He's a criminal. If somebody knows where he is, they should turn him in."

"Look, Marian. 'Somebody' knew where Salman Rushdie was for years, but his enemies were kept in the dark until their regime fell. These people are obviously clever."

"So are you."

Hair stood up on the back of his neck. "You want me to spy? What—vigilante espionage? I'm not a spy, Marian. I'm a programmer."

"A programmer whose business is to *thwart* spies."

"Not even in the same *county*, Marian." He got up and collected his briefcase. "I'm a nerd. A nerd who writes science fiction. If I wrote spy novels, I could see how you might get the idea that I could do counter-espionage. But I don't write spy novels, and I'm not even going to be working with the editor who handled the *Burning Bush* manuscript."

"Are you sure?" she asked.

He wasn't sure, but he pretended to be. What would a science fiction editor be doing with a controversial non-fiction manuscript? "Here's another thought for you and Ruby to toss around," Beck said as he headed for the door. "What if the whole thing's a hoax? What if they got some ghost writer to make all this up based on news files and just promoted it as the real terrorist?"

"That's dishonest. You're telling me you'd work with a publisher you knew was dishonest?"

He left without answering the question.

He had only morning classes today and spent the afternoon until nearly 3:00 working on his commercial programming contract. The bank routines were proving problematic. Continental wanted some of the same safeguards he had incorporated into the DOD software, but national security dictated against his using the same code or anything remotely like it. As a result, he had to come up with new approaches to old problems—a nice enough challenge, but Beck was soon frustrated with the number of times he had to pull himself up short, realizing he was on too familiar ground.

At 3:15, he kept an appointment with Bourbon in his Sheraton suite, bringing along his edited pages to show. Bourbon read them in complete silence—not so much as a 'hmm' or a nod or a throat clearing to mark his progress. Beck sipped a virgin daiquiri and wriggled like a middle-school kid at his first dance.

In the end, the editor raised his head and smiled. "Good edits, Beckett. I especially like the rougher edges you've put on Martin James." He paused, nodded. "I think we can work together." He rubbed his palms together in some sort of symbolic gesture, then reached out to shake Beck's hand. "Now, about contracts. I'll have them downloaded from Sefton so you can go over them tonight, review the terms and sign them at your leisure. I'm going to be in town a few more days, as it happens."

Beck nodded. "Uh. Terms?"

"Well, in view of your other work—your scientific publications, et al, I've been authorized to offer you an advance of twenty thousand against royalties."

Beck was still nodding. "Twenty that's...that's great." *Damn Marian, anyway,* he swore silently. He should have been savoring this but wasn't because she and Ruby had raised the shade of Conscience. "Um, I was curious. Sefton published *Voice from a Burning Bush* didn't they?"

Bourbon's eyebrows rose delicately. "Yes, we did."

"You wouldn't have been the editor to handle that property, would you?"

"Why do you ask?"

"My wife was...curious about how that sort of thing is handled. I mean with the author being...who he is and all." He offered up a half-hearted smile. "I think she fancies I might get into writing spy novels or something."

Bourbon's mouth tilted wryly. "I'm afraid I'm just a science fiction editor. Mr. X did not enter Sefton through the servant's quarters, I assure you. He had an editor from the non-fiction side of the aisle."

Beck shook his head. "Servant's quarters? I don't get it."

"Inside joke of the genre ghetto, Beckett. Finish your drink. I'll get those contracts going."

Beck glanced at his watch. "How long will it take to download them? My wife..." He broke off, clearing his throat. He was relieved when Bourbon didn't react.

"I understand. It will take but a moment."

During that moment, Bourbon came back to the table and seated himself, pouring Beck a fresh, cold refill of creamy, pink crushed ice. "You know, Beckett, I really hoped we'd have an opportunity to talk programming. I've got this little AI project I'm working on for Sefton—" He broke off with a self-deprecatory smile. "Well, I'm only coordinating it, actually. I'll probably hire a real programmer to do it, but I'd like to at least help design it."

Beck was immediately interested. "Oh? A maintenance system, security—which?"

"A little of both, actually. You'd be surprised at the type of security problems we have in the publishing industry. Especially a house like Sefton that has a number of celebrity clients."

Beck sipped at the daiquiri, trying to hide behind it. "Like Ibrahim X?"

"Yes, like that. Like J. R. Koenig. I can't tell you the number of times our system has been hacked into and his manuscripts downloaded and distributed over the Net before we can get them to press. There's a lot of money lost there for our cyber-press division, as you can imagine. Koenig even tried downloading a manuscript to us under his wife's name and e-mail account. The hackers still got to it before we could publish it."

"Sounds like it could be an inside job," Beck said. "Are you sure you can trust everyone who's working for you?"

Bourbon grimaced. "You may be right. And no, I'm not certain of everyone in our employ. But I thought, perhaps with your advice... I'm, em, not above taking advantage of this situation. I hope you don't mind." His smile betrayed embarrassment.

Beck flushed, smiling. "Of course not. I'd be happy to talk shop with you."

"Tomorrow night, perhaps? A late dinner here?"

"Ah...how late?"

"Ninish?"

"I don't know if I can, on such short notice, but I'll try." For the first time, Beck felt a spark of resentment for Marian's possessiveness. It was embarrassing to seem so...well, hen-pecked. He had the absurd desire to puff out his chest and proclaim adamantly that he most certainly would be there for dinner the next evening. He opened his mouth, but nothing came out.

"I'd appreciate it," said Bourbon. "I'm really quite stumped by our hacker/thief."

When Beckett left the Sheraton, he was surprised to find himself standing on a lamp lit street. Somehow it had grown dark while he chatted with Laurence Bourbon. Puzzling, but not distractingly so. He drove home in a haze of buoyant cheer, ready to reconcile with Marian. But, though her car was parked in the curving drive when he arrived home, the house was dark.

Out with Ruby, no doubt, who would commiserate with her about having a husband who stood her up for dinner without notice. The aroma of Kung Pao still hung in the kitchen, making Beck salivate. Guilt warred with irritation and hunger. He grabbed a white carton from the refrigerator and headed for his office, deciding he'd work on the First Continental program while he waited Marian out. He would save the contracts for later, when he could savor them.

He slipped the memory core into the computer, put on VR half-helm and gloves, and let himself into the program. It was a bigger mess than he remembered—a crazy quilt of mismatched security failsafes. He was deep into it, working on a lock for one of the bank's massive data vaults when a blinding flash of light all but knocked him from his chair. His head felt suddenly cool and light, as if—

"Beckett Hodge, what the *hell* are you doing?" Marian emerged from the haze of light wearing a rumpled, over-large Red Sox t-shirt, her short hair an auburn riot. She held his half-helm in one white knuckled hand.

"I...was waiting for you."

"To do what? Take up sleepwalking? Do you have any idea how worried I've been? First I thought you'd mutated into a jerk, and then I thought maybe you'd been kidnapped by corporate spies or aliens or something, and then I started having these visions of you lying in a ditch somewhere. *Where were you?*"

"I had a meeting with Laurence Bourbon—you knew that. He's given me a contract to sign."

"And that took until one a.m.?"

Beck felt as if all the air had been squeezed out of the room. "One..? That's impossible."

"You wear a watch. Use it."

He did wear a watch, when he remembered to put it on. He pulled up his sleeve. Evidently this morning he had not remembered. He tilted the naked wrist so Marian could see it.

"The world is full of clocks, Beckett. Your car has a clock. Your computer has a clock. Your pager has a clock. This office has a clock, although it's damned hard to see in the dark. Are you telling me you didn't glance at any of them?"

"No. I didn't." How had time slipped away from him like that? How could he possibly have gone into the Sheraton at 3:15 in the afternoon and come out at—he hastily back-tracked, trying to calculate how long he'd been working on the First Continental project—10:30 p.m.?

Marian threw his half-helm into his lap. "I'm going back to bed. Now that I know you're not dead or kidnapped, I don't particularly care what you do." She turned and made a patented Marian exit.

"Marian..."

"You could have called," she slung over her shoulder.

"I'm *sorry*."

"You could have left a message on my pager." She was heading up the stairs into the loft. The trapdoor door slammed.

The house was silent. Beck sat in the semi-darkness of his office, half-helm in his gloved hands, feeling singularly confused.

By morning he had a plan of action. He would make it up to Marian. He would woo her. He would win her back. It was Saturday and Beck took full advantage of it. He had the bakery deliver scones. He made strong Arabicus coffee. He cut roses from a convenient bush that hung over the wall from their neighbor's prize-winning garden.

Marian was surprised, pleased, and appeased. So much that when Ruby called to see if she wanted to go antique store hopping, Marian turned her down in favor of a weekend with Beck at a resort north of Marblehead. He effectively forgot about First Continental, Laurence Bourbon and his contracts until late Sunday evening.

There were three messages for him from Bourbon when he finally got back to his computer again. They all said the same thing: *Hope everything is all right. Have to return to New York Tuesday. Tied up all day Monday. Must meet Monday evening if you're interested in a book deal. Around eight, my hotel. Bring contracts; hope you'll stay late to talk revisions and programming. My apologies to your wife.*

Beck pondered his options, which were exactly one—he had to meet with Bourbon and complete the deal. Marian would just have to understand.

She did not understand. "His apologies? Why didn't he just include me in? Doesn't he want to meet your fabulous wife? What've you been telling him about me?"

"I haven't told him anything about you. I mean, nothing *negative.* He wants to pick my brain a little about programming. Something I know you find incredibly boring."

"Not boring, just mystifying. Programming is like...invoking ancient gods. You know—mumbo-jumbo, hoodoo-voodoo, open sesame, and a partridge in a pear tree."

"Fine, mystifying then. At any rate it's not something you'd-"

"And why do you let people take advantage of you that way?"

"Take advantage of me? Marian, the man wants to publish my book. He even wants to *pay* me for it. How in heaven's name could he take advantage of me? He has a little security problem, that's all. Some hacker's been into his e-mail, seems to know whenever J. R. Koenig turns in a novel; he snags it and publishes in on the Internet before it can get to press."

She whistled. She could do that. It was something he vastly admired, but just now he found it annoying. "And you're so fascinated, you're going to give this guy free advice."

"We hardly need the money."

She shrugged and he read into the shrug all sorts of censure. "Did you ask about Ibrahim X?"

"He had nothing to do with that, personally."

"His house still published the book."

Beck got up from the sofa they shared and headed for his office. "I have some work to do."

"Avoidance tactic," she called after him. "That's cheap, Beckett. Really cheap. Ruby says-"

"I'm getting damn tired of what Ruby says," he muttered.

"I heard that." She got up and followed him from the room, something she never did during their rare arguments. But then, *he* never swore. "You *never* swear," she accused him. "What's gotten into you? And why this sudden antipathy toward Ruby?"

Beck flopped down in the chair behind his desk and rubbed the bridge of his nose. "I don't know what's gotten into me. I'm tired. I'm keyed up. I'm on the verge of maybe publishing something..."

"Well, hell, if publishing something's going to make you behave like a witch with sore tits, I'm not sure I *want* you to get published."

He looked at her, balefully, he hoped. He'd never looked at anyone balefully before, so his face wasn't quite sure what it felt like. "Maybe that's the problem, Marian. Maybe you don't want me to get published...for reasons known only to yourself."

She turned and left the room, leaving him free to make whatever late night dinner plans he desired. He dropped

Bourbon an e-mail at the Sheraton confirming the engagement,
and dove into his government project files.

It was very late when he finally crawled into bed—or very
early, depending on how one looked at it. He was frustrated. He
wanted to be writing fiction, not noodling computer code, and
the effort to keep his mind on his work left him irritable and
sapped. Yet, when he'd switched to a piece of short fiction
around one a.m., he'd quickly discovered that guilt was just as
debilitating a disease as frustration.

He gave up at about 1:30 and rolled onto his side of the bed,
perching there horizontally as if he were sleeping on the edge of
a cliff. Marian did not, as was her habit, trespass onto his dream
turf and he did not trespass onto hers. They slept the entire night
on either side of an imaginary line that bisected their mattress
with perfect parity.

She was gone when he awoke in the morning, having
evidently risen before the alarm went off and disabled the
system. It was a cheap and childish thing to do and made Beck
ten minutes late for his first class. He was determined to get
even, which was strange. Halfway through the afternoon, he
realized he'd left his computer's memory core at home. That was
also strange. He swore he'd put it into his briefcase just as he'd
done every morning for the last five years, but it wasn't there
when he opened the case, and in its place was a copy of *Voice
from a Burning Bush*. Obviously Marian's work. Fuming further,
he went home to get the core.

Ruby's car was in front of the house when he got there. His
lip curled in distaste. He had always liked Marian's business
partner, but lately he'd come to realize how much she reminded
him of a pit bull in a Christian Dior suit. The image was funny.
He was almost laughing by the time he entered the house
through the kitchen door. The women were nowhere in sight,
but he could hear their voices. Probably haggling over some

piece of wallpaper—should the Feinmans have a nice rose pattern or Navajo white with a holographic life-scene?

He slipped into his office and got the core from where Marian had left it in a potted plant; he caught the obvious symbology. God, but she was unsubtle.

Core in hand, he headed back out into the kitchen, reaching it just as Marian and Ruby did. The two women were lounging along side-by-side, arms about each other, eyes locked in an intimate smile. He stopped and stared at them staring back at him. Marian started to pull away from Ruby, but the other woman held her fast. Beck's blood felt like liquid nitrogen. This could not possibly be happening. Marian was completely and unrepentantly heterosexual. He'd have bet his life on it.

"Hi, Beck," said Ruby, her brown eyes amused. "Fancy meeting you here."

"Oh, dear," said Marian, and put her hands to her mouth. Marian never said, 'Oh, dear.' 'Oh, damn,' maybe. But never 'Oh, dear.' What had this woman done to his wife?

"Wh-wh-what..?" he stammered.

Ruby shrugged, glanced at Marian, then smiled—no, grinned—at Beck. "Caught in the act," she said. "Or nearly so."

Marian giggled and shrugged. "Sorry, Beck."

The tableau froze just like that—hung, like a bad piece of spaghetti code. *Reality.sys corrupted,* read a tiny monitor in Beck's head. *Reboot universe, Y/N?* Somewhere in the room, a persistent, rhythmic beeping started. *The microwave,* he thought. *Who turned on the microwave?*

Marian opened her mouth. "The time is seven a.m.," she said. "The time is seven a.m. Coffee has been brewed. Instructions?"

The scene dissolved in a foggy special effect and Beck found himself staring at sunlight filtering in through the sliding glass door that gave onto the loft's balcony. "The time is seven a.m.," the house repeated. "Coffee has been brewed. Instructions?"

Beck sat up, the dream clinging to the inside of his head like mildew. He shook it. A futile gesture. "Where's Marian?" he asked.

"Marian has left the house," said the house.

Which meant she was still mad at him. He thought about calling her, but did not. He got up, showered, dressed, ate a meager breakfast and went to school. After his second lecture, when he realized he had forgotten to bring his computer core, his stomach tied itself in a double granny. He would *not* go home. Instead, he called the house from a terminal in his office at the school and asked it to turn on his desktop and download the files he needed. On the verge of breaking the connection, he hesitated. Skin clammy, stomach protesting, he asked, "House, where is Marian?"

"Marian is home," said the house.

He hesitated long enough to have the house computer prompt him. "Instructions?"

"Is she alone?"

"No. Ruby Marsalis is also in the house."

He cut the connection, checked the time and left the campus. Obviously his dream was, if not prophetic, at least a subliminal message from himself to himself about the state of Marian's relationship with Ruby. He, who confronted nothing that could be avoided, would confront them.

Marian's minivan sat in the driveway, its nether regions full of carpet and drapery samples. He rounded the house and cut through the garden, gliding up the back steps and noiselessly opening the kitchen door.

"I don't believe it," he said.

The two women were seated at the kitchen table, coffee in hand, poring over the flat display of an electronic drafting pad. Their heads came up in unison.

Marian frowned. "What's wrong, Beck?"

"How can you ask me that?" He gestured with both hands. "The two of you...together...here."

They exchanged a look. "And?" prompted Ruby. "What's unusual about that?"

"Nothing, now that I think of it. Dear God, you're always together like this. Why didn't I see it?"

"See what?" asked Marian.

"You two are lovers."

The two of them gaped at him, then Ruby threw back her head and laughed. When Marian joined her, Beckett turned and let himself out the way he'd come.

Beck very pointedly did not answer any communication from Marian for the rest of the day. He went downtown well in advance of his dinner appointment with Bourbon. To while away the hours, he availed himself of the hotel bar, got out a borrowed notebook computer and tried to write.

He began drinking lattés around six and had had four of them by the time Laurence Bourbon spotted him and came over to say hello. There was another man with him, a tall, thin fellow with an amazing tan and gleaming black hair, who he introduced as Zev Darren—an art director at Sefton.

They dined in Bourbon's suite, and Darren captivated Beckett with talk of book covers. After dinner, the art director was called to his computer to answer some urgent e-mail. Beck turned over his signed contracts to Laurence Bourbon.

"No questions?" Bourbon asked.

Beck, lounging in a futurist's idea of a recliner with a cup of cappuccino in hand, wagged his head, feeling remarkably relaxed considering the stress of the day and the sheer amount of caffeine he had consumed. "But I believe you had something to ask me."

Bourbon smiled. "Indeed." He leaned forward on his sofa. "This cyber-crook really has me baffled. Are there any traps I could lay for him—any lockouts I could devise—that would keep him from breaking and entering?"

Beck nodded and yawned. "I don't know if I can explain them to you, though."

Bourbon frowned. "Well, I am somewhat of a hacker, myself —an amateur, certainly, but I think I might understand. Still...could I record our conversation? What I don't understand, I'm sure one of our programmers could."

Beck agreed, and Bourbon got his recorder and popped in a tiny optical disk. He grinned in a way that belied his sophistication, a telltale hacker-gleam in his eye and said, "I really appreciate this, Beckett."

In that moment they achieved rapport. Laurence Bourbon asked questions, and Beck answered them enthusiastically. It was easy stuff, but it got Larry (Beck found it easy to think of him as "Larry" suddenly) sitting on the edge of his seat. Beck felt like doing the same, but no matter how much internal enthusiasm he generated for the subject matter, he couldn't seem to get his body to reflect it.

Zev Darren, he noticed, had no interest in hacker-babble. He had evidently finished with his e-mail and was immersed in a computer game, his face half hidden by a VR helm. Not unlike Marian, Beck thought, Darren obviously saw the computer as an entertainer. He leaned back in his chair and chattered on.

✦ ✦ ✦

When he left the Sheraton sometime after midnight, Beck was tired but exhilarated. He had a contract in his pocket; his novel would be published within the next year. In the elevator, he paused to savor the signing, but found the memory imprecise and hazy. Despite the virgin daiquiris and cappuccinos, he'd come close to dozing several times during the evening; exhaustion had robbed him of his moment of glory. He blamed Marian, who, after all, had caused him to lose sleep.

Well, he'd sleep tonight—or rather, this morning. He checked his watch as he crossed the lobby: 12:22. Small wonder the place was subdued. He glanced toward the concierge. There was no one in attendance. There was no one in the lobby at all, in fact.

He shrugged as the brass and glass doors slid open before him, and stepped out onto the sidewalk. It clacked back at him as if he wore taps on the heels of his shoes. He glanced down at his feet; the concrete gleamed a grooved black, like obsidian scored with a fine-toothed comb. He looked up. Gone was the city street, the cars, the buildings, the street lamps, the painted curbing, the traffic signals. There were, in fact, no intersections for traffic signals to preside over. The glossy surface beneath him curved away to the right and left in a flat arc and, while the Sheraton's bulk still loomed comfortingly behind him, the rest of Boston had vanished.

Beck could have fled back into the hotel, but he didn't; curiosity had gotten the better of more sensible fear. He moved forward, toward the center of the curving track and a circular red patch with a tall steel pole in the middle of it. As he crossed the odd tarmac toward the shaft, it occurred to him to wonder what light source allowed him to see either color or form. He could see none. The sky was an unrelieved, light-sucking black with not so much as a star to brighten it. Despite that, the shiny spindle gleamed softly in its field of bright, unambiguous red.

Heels in the black, toes in the red, Beck put hands on his knees and peered down. Letters stared back at him. The letters formed words and the words formed a recognizable phrase: THE PLANETS—Holst. The score, directionless, ambient, now oozed out at him from some unseen source.

Beckett Hodge straightened and gazed right and left. He was standing, he realized, on an immense record album. Not a CD or an OD, but a titanic, archaic, vinyl platter. He turned and made his way toward the outer edge of the record, discovering the source of the light. At the turntable's rim, softly glowing walls rose into a haze of ambient light. As Beck tried to decide whether he should have noticed this feature of the place before, the turntable began to move.

He allowed it to carry him along away from the familiarity of the hotel. He had come to the inevitable conclusion than he was asleep and dreaming, and that, dreaming, he was exploring his own subconscious. He knew a moment of intense embarrassment at the realization that wherever his mind was, his body was still in Larry Bourbon's suite in a shameful state of repose.

He was hearing "Mars," now and hummed along tunelessly, watching the glowing, featureless walls move imperceptibly by. *Curious. How can one know one is in motion if one cannot observe the evidence of motion?*

As "Mars" continued to play, Beck noticed changes in his environment. The album beneath his feet was now carrying him toward a golden hoop that protruded from the glowing wall some yards ahead at a height of about twenty feet. The hoop, like the walls, seemed to gleam with its own light. It was turned on edge, its open circle facing him. He thought of brass rings and carousels, which were not unlike turntables in their basic design.

It was a consistency that both delighted and comforted him. Approaching the hoop, he wondered if he could manipulate the dream plane.

That train of thought derailed when he noticed a mist gathering around the golden circle. It seemed to issue from nowhere, surrounding the ring, flowing through it, then lowering itself toward the turntable. Obvious symbology. His particular brass ring was the book contract he had just signed; the mist was something that attempted to obscure it from him.

As he was pondering the mist, the turntable slowed perceptibly and a wire basket filled with soccer balls appeared to his right along the wall. Beck started to analyze exactly how the basket had appeared and what it might mean, then decided, instead, to accept the playful nature of the dream. He reached into the basket as he passed by it, fished out one of the balls, and lobbed it through the hoop, expecting to miss.

As this was a dream, he did not miss; the shot was perfect, soaring through the ring without touching any part of its gleaming rim. If only he might have done that in high school.

Beck laughed and turned to get another ball. The basket was gone. A tone sounded—like a crystal goblet struck with a mallet. Overhead, the mist sucked away into the noplace it had come from and the hoop went dark. The turntable picked up speed. Beck knew this without knowing how he knew it. There was no breeze, the walls gave up nothing but diffuse light; he simply knew.

Another ring appeared high on the curving wall ahead. A basket of balls awaited his approach. This time, the turntable didn't slow, but continued on at a leisurely pace. Beck snagged a soccer ball and put it through the hoop with pinpoint accuracy.

Perhaps it was the sixth hoop or the seventh at which Beck decided he no longer wanted to play. He was bored and the turntable was moving more briskly; he wasn't convinced he could make the shot. He wasn't convinced he cared enough to try.

He approached the hoop, lazily dribbling the soccer ball off the grooved surface beneath his feet. When he had by-passed the point at which he usually threw, the turntable slowed. He continued to dribble the ball, glancing toward the center of the record. The cut was "Uranus." He could no longer see the spindle.

Movement above him drew his eyes back to the great golden ring. The vapor that had surrounded it seconds before was sinking toward him.

An icy cold prickled over his skin. The vapor was malevolent; he was absolutely certain of it. Not poisonous, not toxic, but *malevolent.* In the instant it touched his face, he loosed the soccer ball, hurling it in a soaring arc through the golden hoop. The vapor was gone in a breath, leaving behind the irrational conviction that it had almost sucked his soul out of his body.

He did not tempt the vapor at the next hoop or the next. He sent the soccer ball through unerringly, still uncertain how a man for whom sport was torture was able to do such sporty things. As the bright ball cleared the ninth hoop accompanied by the strains of "Pluto," the world around Beck changed. The turntable glided to a halt and to his right, in the curving wall, a doorway spilled light out onto the grooved, black plane.

Beck glanced around. *Pluto.* Unlike the others, this cut was oddly disturbing. Beck had little time to decide why. As he hovered in the open door, all light disappeared from the turntable as if sucked up by a vacuum. He stepped through the door.

He stood in a corridor, at the end of which he could vaguely make out a staircase. If he recalled his Freud correctly, climbing that would be symbolic of having sex. He wondered if the nights without a willing Marian were beginning to take its toll. He chuckled. The hoops and balls would no doubt also count as expressions of sexual desire in Freud's book. How wonderful and complex was the language of dreams.

Before him the floor of the corridor lit up. It was a simple pattern of blue and white tiles that seemed to be pulsing in a random sequence. He stared at the checkerboard momentarily. It brought to mind his grandmother's kitchen floor. A floor on which he used to play his own peculiar version of hopscotch. As he recalled, grandma's kitchen floor hadn't blinked on and off.

Another memory was invoked, oddly, of an episode of *Dr. Who* in which the good Doctor(s) (five of them, as he recalled) was confronted by such a puzzle. It had been booby-trapped with a laser beam that would zap anyone unwary enough as to wander onto the wrong square.

Beck crouched to watch the play of light across the tiles. The Doctor's solution to the puzzle had lain in computing the value of *pi*. He rose. *Pi*. There were nine rows of tiles. 3.14159... The digits couldn't stand for *rows* of tiles, but they might stand for *columns*.

In the first row of tiles, a white lit up, three tiles from the left edge of the checkerboard. Beck moved to stand in front of the tile and waited. When it lit up again, he stepped on it. A tone sounded, the tile blinked several times in rapid succession and then stayed on. He looked down at his feet. There was just enough room for both of them on the tile.

"Okay," he said aloud. "I'll play your silly game."

He watched the first tile in the next row for a flash of light. When it came, he missed it, because the tile was a deep blue. He waited nearly a full minute (or so he thought) until the square lit up again. He stepped on it this time and was rewarded as before with the tone. As the first, the tile stayed lit.

It was easy after that—merely a game of waiting and leaping. In due time, he found himself in the very center of the corridor. There the pattern made an abrupt change. Both feet on a tile of blazing white, Beck stared in consternation at the floor ahead of him. From where he stood to the suddenly distant staircase, the tiles formed an expanse of strangely patterned brown and muted gold. Here was a group of three gold tiles, here a group of two, here a single tile. The squares themselves were smaller, too, leaving room for only one foot at a time to occupy them.

Recognition made Beck chuckle. He'd viewed similar patterns of tiles in myriad public men's rooms. He waited, but none of the tiles before him lit up. After a moment of study, it seemed to him that the gold tiles did form an irregular, but navigable path from here to there, if one had a reasonably long stride and was willing to play hopscotch. The only problem was the size of the squares. Dreamer's instinct told him that stepping over the edge of one was a Bad Thing.

He was contemplating his first move when he noticed a slight dimming in the corridor. A glance over his shoulder revealed the reason—behind him, the lighted tiles were winking out, darkness marching toward him. He had the creeping feeling that it would not be very pleasant to find out what happened when the square he was standing on went dark. He glanced ahead. About three feet away was a set of two gold tiles set about two feet apart. Not a bad split. He leapt.

When he landed, the 'reward' tone sounded and the gold squares beneath his feet blazed with brilliance. At that moment, he realized he was wearing sneakers instead of the black leather ankle boots he'd started out with. His dream was nothing if not accommodating.

Pleased with himself, he made another selection and hopped again. The third leap was harder, leaving him teetering on one foot. In searching for his next landing pad, he lost his balance and toppled forward, only barely managing to land with his left foot on one square and his right hand on another, his opposite arm and leg flailing for balance. Gingerly, he moved his free foot to the square where his hand rested. He came close to falling again, but somehow managed to keep his balance and work his way upright.

He now saw the wisdom of plotting his moves in advance. He negotiated the remainder of the corridor in carefully planned hops, skips, and jumps. The pattern took an interminable amount of time to complete. Beck was glad he was dreaming; in real life, he'd be close to collapse.

From the bottom of the staircase, he took a look back at the field of tiles he'd traversed. The golden tiles, now ablaze, seemed to form a stylized question mark. As he watched, the tiles began to dim, just as the previous set had done. He turned his attention to the next obstacle—the staircase.

It was of aged-looking wood—mahogany, Beck guessed. It even smelled of age, the incense of mildew and ancient varnish. It was a pleasant odor and it reminded him forcefully of his childhood. A wash of reminiscence came, giving the staircase a time and place in Beck's existence. Like the checkered kitchen floor, this came from his grandparents' house in Swampscott.

Finding his grandparents' staircase in a dream tickled him. He'd loved that staircase. It had given him hours of pleasure as he practiced climbing it without making a sound. This was difficult at best, for the stair was full of the creaks and moans and complaints of advancing age. He paused a moment to savor the memory, trying to recall the formula that would take him safely to the second floor landing, for to call forth sound from the venerable beast was to loose gremlins in the house that would swarm the stair and carry little boys off to "bedlam."

Grinning, Beck began the climb. Center tread, far left, far right, step on the knot hole, skip two by climbing the banister, right of center, center, leap to the landing.

"Ha!" Beck exulted and turned back to give the staircase a triumphant glance. It had been replaced by a slick expanse of oily-looking metal. A slide. A means of escape? A pitfall? Bemused, Beck checked his forward trail, which opened up, not into the second floor of his grandparents' house, but into a sunny meadow of waving ultra-green grass, teeming flowers, and chirping, Disney-esque bluebirds. The sky was at once pink and blue, the sun literally smiled down at him, and clouds looked very much like cotton candy. Such scenes populated uncounted refrigerator doors.

A circle of woodlands surrounded the place, tiny, bright orange fruit fairly glowing amid the dark foliage of hip-high bushes. *Clown noses,* Beck thought, and was struck with the absurd image of clowns skipping through the woods picking baskets full of noses. *Picking their noses.* The pun doubled him over with laughter.

And Marian said he had no sense of the absurd.

He wondered if he could bring her here, tried, and was rewarded with a "moo." He straightened. Aside from the overly cheerful birds, the meadow was populated by exactly one black and white cow that munched the terrifyingly green grass ruminatively as it gazed at him through immense, chocolaty bovine eyes. A bright golden cowbell hung from a blue cord around its neck. This was not Marian. There was nothing remotely bovine about Marian.

Okay, Beck thought. *I'll bite.*

He walked over to the cow, scaring up a score of the bluebirds. They circled and chirped like something out of an old Warner Brothers cartoon.

"Hello," he said to the cow, because after all, dreaming is no excuse for discourtesy.

The cow gazed back, opened her mouth and said, "Watch this." She proceeded to rise up on her hind legs, produce three of the outrageously orange fruit and juggle them. She was actually quite good, Beck thought.

After about thirty seconds of juggling, the cow caught one orange globe between her front hooves, then snapped the other two out of mid-air and gulped them down whole. She came back to all fours, belched and shook her head, ringing the golden bell.

"What did I just do?" she asked. "You have thirty seconds or four guesses, whichever comes first."

"Isn't that supposed to be three guesses?"

"That's wishes. Three *wishes*. Do I look like a genie?" She didn't give him time to answer. "First guess."

"You...juggled clown noses?"

"Wrong. Three more guesses. Fifteen seconds."

"Oh, sorry. Tangerines. You juggled tangerines."

"Is that your answer? *Juggle tangerines?*" She rolled her eyes. "Wrong again. But you're getting warmer." In the cotton-candy clouds over the cow's piebald head, a slot machine face appeared, its rollers spinning like crazy. The one furthest to the right stopped, showing the word "tangerines." He assumed that he'd score a jackpot if he got the right answer. It occurred to him to wonder what he'd score if he *didn't*.

"What happens if I don't guess the riddle?"

"You lose."

"And then what?"

"You're out."

"Out. Out of the dream, you mean? I wake up?"

"What makes you think you're asleep?"

"The fact that I don't usually hold conversations with spotted cows in Technicolor meadows or watch them juggle clown noses."

The cow sighed. It was a deep sound and seemed to issue from her voluminous belly. "Do you need a clue? I'm allowed to give one more clue."

Beck nodded.

"Watch." The cow turned her brown eyes on the fringe of woodlands where a man in a pith helmet and bush outfit carefully stalked something among the foliage with a large, cartoon butterfly net. Beck couldn't see what he was pursuing so raptly. He started to ask the cow, but she shushed him.

The hunter tiptoed up to one of the bushes, then leapt forward with a cry and took a swipe at it with his net. Two of the orange globes fell into the webbing. He swiftly scampered away with them.

The cow turned her increasingly mournful eyes back to Beck. "Well?"

"He, um. Shoot. Ah, capture...net...um..." Beck opted for the literal approach. "*Bush-whack* two tangerines?"

In the slot machine another window braked to display the number '2.'

"Ooh," said the cow. "Close, but no cigar."

"What's close?" Beck asked, but the cow merely looked away across the meadow, toward the bushes. "Bush-whacked was close?"

She sighed again, jiggling her udder.

The answer came to Beck with the sudden recollection of a story a colleague had told him about the strange combinations of words her students would produce during classroom exercises in a Vietnamese language class she had taught. He knew it was the answer—it was his dream, and his own memory had provided it.

"Ambush two tangerines," he said. Overhead, the final bar rolled into place and a loud bell sounded.

"Foqit ai qwit." The cow repeated the phrase in flawless Vietnamese, and disappeared along with the pink/blue sky, cotton candy clouds and clown-nose bushes. In their place the violently green sward sprouted a graveyard complete with ravens, crows, ornate, listing headstones, and a gleaming white mortuary.

Beck was momentarily taken aback. Why a graveyard? He'd answered the riddle correctly; why this presentiment of doom? The place was eerie, but familiar, and he felt more memories pressing for release. He made his way to the mortuary.

The foyer was empty. He moved into a display room where a fleet of new caskets was arrayed, tops open like convertibles in a car lot. On the opposite side of the display room, he could see the steel and glass doors that led to the nether realms. He certainly hoped his dream journey wouldn't take him there.

He turned and peered across the foyer. A chapel—the carved wooden doors bore a representation of the solar system—nine planets arranged around the central Orb. Each planet was engraved with a religious symbol: a Star of David, a bowl of fire, a lotus, a cross, an Evam, a yin-yang, a five-pointed star, a star and crescent, a nine-pointed star.

He moved to the door, put his hand on the handle and pulled. It was locked. He glanced at the solar system again. The planets, with their religious symbols, were out of order. Another puzzle.

After a moment of thought, Beck rearranged the planets in their engraved orbits—beginning with Mercury and its nine-pointed star, and ending with Pluto, bearing the Evam. *Pluto*. The ninth planet was Pluto. But it hadn't been discovered when Holst wrote *The Planets*—the music he had heard on the turntable, he suddenly realized, was a symphonic rendition of

the Mickey Mouse Club theme, music Beck had always
associated with the immortal rodent and his dog. Nine planets,
nine religious symbols, nine hoops, nine everything.

Teetering on the verge of recognition, Beck entered the now
unlocked chapel. At the altar in front of a closed and locked
casket, stood a clown in a black suit. He had blue hair, a
tangerine nose, and a pair of red, floppy shoes that looked
incongruous with the natty attire. His face bore a half-mournful,
half-manic expression. When he saw Beck, his bright red lips
stretched into something that bore a closer resemblance to rigor
mortis than a smile. He produced a clipboard out of the ether.

A manic depressive clown, Beck thought. Oh great.

Clowns had never amused him as a child. They had given
him the willies. He now realized they *still* gave him the willies.
He'd often thought they'd make ideal scarecrows—or rather
'scarekids'—for people who had flower beds or pools they
wanted to keep the neighbors progeny out of.

He steeled himself and went to the altar to confront the
clown-mortician.

"You are...?" the clown asked lugubriously.

"Beckett Hodge."

"Beckett Hodge, you must answer four questions for me,
before you may proceed."

Beck nodded, not at all sure he wanted to proceed. Right
now what he really wanted was to wake up, even if it meant
having to go through the embarrassment of explaining to
Laurence Bourbon and Zev Darren why he'd fallen asleep in the
middle of a conversation.

"Listen carefully," said the clown, "and finish this sentence."
He glanced down at the clipboard and read: "Touch not the
cat..."

"But with a glove," said Beck automatically.

The clown smiled and checked off something on his clipboard. At the foot of the casket, a latch popped open. Beck jumped.

"Now," said the clown, "complete this: He was like a giant on dry land..."

"And...and like a selkie in the sea." Another check mark was drawn, another latch popped open, and an icy shaft of recognition speared Beck's brain. He knew these sequences. And he knew them for reasons other than their association with childhood games or television shows he had watched.

"By the prickling of my thumbs," the clown read.

Beck backed away from him. Memories had been converted to binary expressions and coded into a targeting series and eight pattern-matching sequences.

"By the prickling of my thumbs," the clown repeated.

Memories had built a nine level security system for the DOD. Beck turned and fled.

Behind him the clown said tonelessly: "Abort. Restart sequence. Touch not the cat..."

The graveyard metamorphosed as Beck crossed it, back into a meadow full of bluebirds, butterflies, and tangerine bushes. The cow did not look up as he flew past her, but he thought he heard her say, "Abort. Reset."

The meadow had faded by the time he reached the top of the staircase/slide. It was still a slide. He threw himself down it, landing at the bottom on his behind. Scrambling to his feet, he confronted the corridor of tiles. Both sections of the course were now just ordinary-looking floors. He took them without so much as a hop, skip, or jump and came out onto the giant turntable. It rolled away and to his right, inexorably.

If he was where he thought he was, the situation demanded that he exit this scene just as he had entered it. While the eight pattern-matching segments of the program were reset upon completion or exit, the initial nine layer "hacker trap" was not. It could be tripped as easily by a clumsy exit as it was by a clumsy entrance. Beck had no desire to find out what it meant to be caught by his own failsafes.

He stepped out onto the turntable. Not content to let it simply carry him along, he trotted along with the rotation, eyes open for the hoops. His mind churned. How the hell could he be here? Was this a drug-induced dream, or was it more real than that? Was it being monitored?

The image of Zev Darren playing a VR game in the corner of Bourbon's suite came to him with the force of a blow. Could that be it? Could he literally be *inside* the DOD program? He had constructed the DOD scenes with specialized programming Gear —had seen them as programming objects. But interpreted by a VR system—provided one could be made compatible—with his own imagination in control...

He shook his head as if that might rattle some answers loose from the inside of his virtual skull. The Who and the Why were obvious, the How conceivable. The question was what would prompt a fiction editor and an art director from a major publishing house to get involved in terrorism and espionage?

He hurried to the first basket of soccer balls and hurled one through a hoop before the Ghost routine could intercept him.

Timing. This part of the program was all timing. He worried that he might do better if he didn't know what those bright hoops and balls represented: clever traps and one-way viruses that would backwash into the inept hacker's system—in this case, his mind.

Beck chafed as he negotiated the nine hoop stations, returning at last to where he had entered the program.

The "Sheraton" stood alone on a barren corner, symbol of Beck's connection with the real world—a world where Laurence

Bourbon and Zev Darren waited for him to unlock the gates to hell.

He stood inside his own creation—a place where virtual cows juggled tangerines and where manic clowns presided over coffins full of death—and pondered explosive things. What he needed was a break program that would shatter the external connection—a virtual bomb.

He floundered for a moment, trying to decide how to create a bomb in this impossible universe. Then he laughed at himself. Impossible it might be, but it was *his* universe and ultimately obeyed his divine decree.

He patted the breast pocket of his suit. His wallet, a pen, his pager. He took out the pager and examined it. It was as much a computer input/output device as his keyboard or Gear. He thumbed it on and started to speak into it. But wait—what if his words were audible to those who had put him here? He had to take the chance, he supposed.

He held the pager to his lips and whispered. "Break routine...uh, 'Sheraton.' Delay fifteen seconds from activation. Activate on command 'destruct.' Routine: Induce general protection fault at address..." He glanced up at the corner of the hotel and almost grinned—a bronze plaque gleamed dully on the virtual wall. "Address 008D:0015."

Fine, but that might not be enough. The system had three overt inputs, two covert ones. Five in all. Two of these were set up for Gear protocols. His vicarious hackers could be using either, but if he shut down both, the system alarm would engage, which could cause...well, panic for one thing. A military panic was not a pretty thing.

He'd have to make a choice. The covert link made the most sense. It would be accessed at the installation only in an emergency, so the hacker/spies could expect little chance of interruption. Beck completed the routine with a fatal interrupt to the covert Gear device, wondering how long he'd been here and if Marian had tried to reach him.

He entered the virtual hotel lobby cautiously, as if Bourbon or Darren could be expected to pop out of nowhere to intercept him. He didn't think they had the technology to do that—to enter this dream world completely—and doubted they could even monitor him precisely.

He wondered which of them was the programmer. Maybe they both were. He doubted either of them had anything to do with publishing. But then how they had intercepted his manuscript? He remembered what Bourbon had said about novels being lifted electronically off editor's desks. Had that happened to his?

He moved directly to the elevator core, chose the center shaft and punched the 'up' button. The doors slid apart.

"Destruct," he told the pager, lobbed it into the elevator car and ran, thinking of Marian. He was still thinking of her when a flash of blinding light enveloped him and lifted him into the non-existent sky.

"I thought you weren't speaking to him," Ruby said.

Sometimes, Marian thought, Ruby could be impossibly dense. "Not speaking isn't a synonym for not caring, Rube. It's two a.m. He hasn't answered his pager and Mr. Bourbon hasn't answered his phone."

"So, they're out celebrating the book deal."

"Until two a.m.?"

Ruby shrugged. "Why not? We're commiserating over his thick-headedness until two a.m."

"You don't know Beck the way I do. He would *never* stay out so late without calling me. Even when I know his schedule and he *knows* I know his schedule, he calls."

"Uh-huh." Ruby sipped coffee, steam coating her glasses. "Even if he's not speaking to you?"

"*Especially* if he's not speaking to me. Then guilt takes over. He *has* to call." She got up and headed for the kitchen, leaving Ruby camped in front of the fireplace.

Ruby sighed volubly. "Shall I lock up?"

"Whatever." Mentally, Marian was already on the road, already pulling up to the Sheraton, already leaving her car in the hands of a bleary-eyed valet. Already on her way through the lobby to the elevators.

Fifteen minutes later, when she actually entered the Sheraton's spacious lobby, she had to take a detour to the concierge—she had absolutely no idea which room Laurence Bourbon was in. As it turned out, he was in one of the Tower suites and would have to issue an invitation to her if she was to go up. Marian decided a good lie was in order.

"My husband had an appointment with Mr. Bourbon this evening and he forgot his heart medicine." She scrabbled in her fanny pack and produced her own pill case, full of stress tabs, vitamin C, and Midol™. "He didn't expect to be this late. He should have had one of these hours ago." She knit her brow and let her voice sound very slightly frantic.

The concierge called a rather muscular bellman to escort her up (as if she might possibly need to be overpowered). The elevator ride was silent. Marian looked at the ceiling of the car's stained-glass ceiling, it clashed with the once-upon-a-time *moderne* decor of the lobby. The broad corridor that gave onto the Tower suites was Queen Anne.

What *could* they have been thinking?

"He's stuck."

"He's what? What do you mean, he's stuck?"

Zev Darren turned away from his monitor and pointed at the flashing cursor, which had sat for the past forty-five seconds in the same place in a crude but colorful maze. "Check his pulse rate."

Bourbon glanced at the tiny screen that displayed Beckett Hodge's vitals. "It's up."

"He's stressed over something. He may be having trouble with the last stage. Sometimes programmers put randomizers into their routines—sort of a code *du jour* thing. He may not remember all the different sequences. Damn." He watched the cursor a moment longer. Watched it until it abruptly blinked out. "Oh, hell."

It was like something out of a James Bond movie. As Marian knocked repeatedly on the door of Bourbon's suite with no result, someone within the suite howled.

Having no pass card, the beefy bellman opened the locked door with his foot. Marian flung herself through the door. She was hardly prepared for what she saw—Beckett, strapped to a chair, VR Gear on head and hands, with two men hovering over him. One had hands on his shoulders and was shaking him hard enough to make his teeth rattle.

Marian's female instincts kicked in. "You sonofabitch! Get your hands off my husband!"

Lawrence Bourbon obeyed without hesitation, while his partner reached for a gun lying holstered on the sofa. The bellman was having none of it.

+ + +

When he woke, Beck was surprised to be alive and in a hospital room. The room was under military guard and, besides Beck, held two occupants. Marian and Colonel Traynor chatted quietly in one corner. He cleared his throat, drawing their immediate attention.

"Bourbon?" he croaked.

Marian, her eyes still showing concern, afforded him a lopsided grin. "A little early for the hard stuff, isn't it?"

He shook his head; his brain wobbled. "I mean..."

"I know what you mean. He's in military custody, courtesy of your ferocious and quick-thinking wife and a burly bellman named Frank. And he'll stay there for awhile too, thanks to Colonel Traynor and his buddies in the CIA."

Beck's eyes shifted automatically to Traynor's face. The movement hurt. "They-they—" He choked, prompting Marian to give him a sip of water. Throat wetted, he ploughed on. "They linked me to the ICBM security system using some kind of specialized VR rig. They wanted me to crack it for them—my own code..."

The colonel was nodding. "Yes, we suspected as much when we saw the system. It was...tremendously sophisticated. We had no idea a high-end 'off-the-rack' system could be modified to that extent."

"But why? An editor and an art director? Why?"

"Money. But people aren't always what they seem. Oh, Mr. Bourbon is an editor, all right. A minor, poorly paid line editor. But Zev Darren is no art director. He's a computer expert lately in the employ of Shalom/Salaam and Ibrahim X. In simple terms, a terrorist."

Beck glanced at Marian. She was looking away, her face wearing the patented Marian Whaley-Hodge 'I-told-you-so' look. The blood drained out of his head. If he hadn't been lying down, he would have swooned. "Ibrahim X?"

"Bourbon line edited his best-selling manuscript," said Traynor. "Mr. X evidently felt his position in the publishing industry could be advantageous. Unfortunately, he was wrong; Bourbon was a poor choice of accomplices. Zev Darren is a professional mercenary, at least in the realm of hacking, but Larry Bourbon is only a greedy amateur. The threat of a treason charge rattled just about everything loose. Your editor friend got swept up in the romance and intrigue of it all. He simply wasn't prepared to be caught." He gave Beck a sideways glance. "Honestly, professor, how close did they come to breaking it?"

Beck wetted his lips. "Too close. I was deep inside the program, at the last security protocols, when I realized...sort of...what was going on—that someone had set me up to breach my own program."

The colonel's alarm showed as tiny white brackets on each side of his mouth. "But you stopped them. I assume you recognized your code."

Beck closed his eyes. "No. I recognized my childhood."

"Excuse me?"

Beck smiled wanly. "You would've had to be there."

Later, with Traynor gone, Marian sat next to him on the bed and held his hand. Her scent struck him softly. He opened one eye.

"You were right all along. Bourbon *was* connected to Ibrahim. In ways I couldn't have imagined. I seem to have an imagination deficiency. Not a good thing for a guy who wants to write science fiction."

"What was it like in there?"

"Weird. Like being in a dream. Or down a rabbit hole. But it was *my* rabbit hole—which is why I finally recognized the...the programming. It was all from my childhood. Games I played, shows I watched, pictures I drew, riddles I made up. Patterns in floor tiles, staircases, cow pastures. But it was the clown. The clown in the funeral chapel. That was what did it."

Marian grimaced. "Imagination deficiency, huh? Hell, I'm not even going to ask."

"Aren't you at least going to say, 'I told you so'?"

"Do I need to?"

He shook his head. A sigh, deep and silent, broke over him as a realization struck.

Somehow Marian heard it and squeezed his hand. "What?"

"The book. Sefton never really wanted the book."

"Maybe they did, and it gave Bourbon a legitimate excuse to contact you."

"Maybe. But it's more likely I got duped. I let my naiveté compromise the secrets I hold for my government." He closed his eyes again. "But the worst thing is what they led me to believe about you and Ruby. I think they must have drugged me, planted suggestions in my head that I couldn't trust you...and other things. They wanted you out of the way, I guess."

Marian's mouth curled. "So, that's what that was about. And that was worse than almost giving away the deed to Uncle Sam's farm? Sweet, but silly, Beck. There was a hell of a lot at stake in those silos. On the bright side, I think this little episode has given Colonel Traynor and his fellows reason to consider an alternative to hiding loaded guns."

Beck looked out the window where the sun had risen on a brilliant day. "Funny. I guess I turned out to be a secret agent after all. So secret, even I didn't know it. Secret agent double-oh-one, binary spy."

"You could write a book about it."

"Yeah, I could. But, who'd buy it?"

There were, in fact, several publishers standing in the electronic queue in Beck's e-mail box when news of the virtual break-in surfaced and Ibrahim X was run to ground and arrested on charges of master-minding it. Beck had his pick of offers, his shiny, new agent finally accepting the high bid from a large publisher most widely known for its techno-thrillers.

Beck was pleased, without being ecstatic. He had a book contract, but it was non-fiction—just one more real-world title on cutting-edge programming by Beckett Hodge, destined one day to reside on the shelves of universities and computer super-stores everywhere. Still, given the sensational nature of the subject matter, it would almost certainly arrive there by way of the NYT bestseller list.

At least that was the picture until the Pentagon intervened in the form of an apologetic Colonel Traynor, who appeared in the Hodge living room one evening and parked himself in Beck's favorite chair.

"I'm sorry, Professor Hodge, but we simply can't allow you to publish this book. It would reveal too much about our security system and its..."

"Vulnerability?" Marian suggested.

"I was going to say, its nature."

Beck didn't care what he had been going to say. All that registered was that the brass ring had dodged him once again.

"But if you prevent it from being published-" Marian objected.

"The public would suspect a cover-up," Traynor finished for her. "And they'd be right. That's why we're willing to allow the book to be published provided two conditions are met."

Beck raised his head. "Which are?"

"First, that it be published in a vastly altered form. You would have to fictionalize the account. Change names and circumstances, alter the order of events, make up different riddles."

Amazement settled on Beck like a woolly cloud. "But anyone who followed the news would know-"

"Ah, no. You see that's the second condition: you have to wait."

"Wait? How long?"

"Three years...or the length of time it takes for you to completely redesign your security system."

Beck sagged back into his chair. "Completely?"

"You'll have to design *two* new systems, actually—one for the warheads and one for the delivery system...which we've decided should be separated by...some distance."

"But in three years, there may not be a publisher still interested in the story."

Traynor shrugged. "I'm afraid that's the only recourse you have, Professor Hodge. We simply can't allow the story to be published now—not even as fiction."

Beck nodded. He was still nodding when Traynor was gone.

"You should be happy," Marian told him. "They're unloading the 'gun.'"

"I suppose I should be, but I just feel...exhausted...and silly. I was so taken in by Bourbon and his flattery. What made me think I could write fiction? Terry Lance was right; I should stick to what I know."

Marian made a rude noise. "Terry Lance is a textbook jockey. He wouldn't know good science fiction if he had a close encounter with it. Besides, you *did* write fiction. You just wrote it into the national defense system."

Beck had to laugh, and Marian, who didn't need to be told why he was laughing, laughed with him. The irony was delicious: He wrote fiction like a programmer and programmed like a science fiction writer.

Mentally, he was still laughing when his head touched the pillow that night. He didn't know if he could convince a publisher to wait three years for the story—especially a fictionalized version of it—but he did know he would continue to write both programs and fiction. Eventually, he would get them straight.

The White Dog

A story of magic realism

The White Dog was originally published in *Interzone* issue #142 in 1999. It is my favorite story in the collection and was a Best Short Fiction finalist for the 1999 British Science Fiction Association Award. Woven into the narrative is a brief episode from Abdu'l-Bahá's visit to New York from which the story gets its title and one of its themes.

> *"Just as physical science has shown that every*
> *particle of matter in the universe attracts and*
> *influences every other particle, no matter how*
> *minute or how distant, so psychical science is finding*
> *that every soul in the universe affects and influences*
> *every other soul."*
>
>

Esslemont,
Bahá'u'lláh and the New Era,
p. 209
>

Beauty and the Beast was the first story Mother ever read to me. I have read it myself a myriad times in a variety of forms and seen countless dramatic renditions of it. At each telling or showing or reading, I have felt, for a moment, a sense of contentment. That is, until I realize that this is a fairy tale and it has nothing whatever to do with me.

Oh, it's not *just* that it's a fairy tale—*everything* is a fairy tale from my vantage point—it's that the Beast is a man and I am a woman.

What difference? Merely this: an ugly man can be said to have character; even the most hideous of men, as the fairy tale illustrates, can be loved for his kindness and 'inner loveliness.' But an ugly woman...well, I quickly learned that by no combination of graces or talents or virtues can she be considered lovely.

Humorists make a tired point of it:

"I've fixed you up with a date," says the sitcomedian.

"Oh?" responds the object of his largesse. "What's she like?"

"She has a great personality," he is assured.

Whereupon the charm-challenged moron moans tragically, "Oh, God! She's a bow-wow!"

The media assure us that the corollary is also true—a man will put up with any amount of inanity and selfishness to adorn himself with Beauty; all stupidity can be forgiven it. Beauty can redeem a lack of character, but no amount of character can redeem a lack of good looks.

This is not to say that Gorgons cannot have friends, for there is a certain type of male who will befriend the charmless female for no other reason that, early in life, she seems almost 'guy-like' in her gracelessness. Later, of course, he will abandon her, lest someone get the idea that they are an 'item,' but by this time, she will be much sought after by other, more attractive young women merely because they look so good by comparison.

I've always thought the jealous Aphrodite was a fool not to have made Medusa her bosom buddy. How much simpler to have given the feckless Paris the choice between herself and the Gorgon—she'd have had the apple *and* the guy. Anyone stupid enough to even notice Medusa would have ended up as an ornamental coat rack in the goddess's front hall.

Am I comparing myself to Medusa, you ask? Yes, though I flatter myself that the comparison is favorable. After all, she turned men to stone for all eternity. My personal best is only five seconds.

Let me make it clear that I am not homely. (Now, *there's* a word! So old-world, so comfortable-sounding—as if the woman in question were a favored but dilapidated love seat.) Nor am I unattractive, or ugly. I am nothing short of grotesque. Hideous. I enter a room and conversations cease, heads turn and quickly return. Men turn to stone.

I was four, I think, when I became truly aware of this. My mother's and father's eyes had that myopia that is peculiar to parents. But in the eyes of strangers, teachers and family friends, I saw distress, veiled revulsion, and pity. In the eyes of other little girls lurked something like horror, while boys peeked at me with speculative amusement.

I was slow to understand this, until I came to realize how different my mirror image was from theirs. They had glossy, colorful hair, and eyes of brown or blue or gray. Their cheeks were rosy, their lips pink, their faces a balance of normal human features.

I am shrunken, and colorless, as if water runs in my veins instead of blood. My flesh is like rice paper—its fine mesh of veins clearly visible. And my hair—if that really is the word for such an anarchistic mop—has all the vibrancy of cellophane. One of my young faux-friends referred to me once as the 'visible girl.' It stuck.

Oh, and my eyes—how can I possibly describe them? They are not gray or hazel or even albino white, but are as devoid of color as a glass of water.

"Jesus Lord!" exclaimed my friend of the 'visible girl' epithet, "you've got puries!"

"Oooo-*ee*-ee-ooh," school mates would intone when they passed me in the hall.

"Spooky," the girls called me, and, "Ghost."

The boys were worse: "Pasty-face" and "Slug" were two of their less innovative offerings.

When I was about nine I realized that I looked, more or less, like the archetypal Whitley Streiber alien.

Fortunately, parents' eyes are calibrated differently than the rest of mankind's. I was my mother and father's Little Moonbeam. Mother could gaze at my alien features and tell me I was beautiful. I swear to this day, she meant it.

I believe that's where I first got the idea that I could affect the way people saw me. Yes, my parents perceived me through a filter of love and pity, but *I* also provided a filter--the desperation with which I needed and desired their love and approval. Desperation demanded that I perform for them, that I be their happy Little Moonbeam, an ethereal will-o-the-wisp.

Not quite understanding the nature of parental love, I believed that I won it by being as engaging as I was grotesque. That belief instilled in me the confidence I needed to win the regard of others who were not so impossibly blinded. Pity, sympathy—call it what you will—I learned, over the years, to milk human kindness for all it was worth.

I'm not bitter about that. Far from it. While I undoubtedly brought out the worst in those disposed toward cruelty, I brought out the best in anyone with even an ounce of compassion. I suppose in an abstract way, you could say I helped make them better human beings.

Of course, there are always those disinclined to kindness. They were harder to deal with. Their regard could wound; their words could draw blood.

Such a one was Bobby Bane (an ironic and appropriate name, if ever there was one). If there was one *bona fide* bully in our tiny neighborhood, it was Bobby, and he established himself as such from the moment his family moved in.

I heard rumor of him before we met. He had beaten up my friend Robin—who was twice my size—and taken away her bike and the Popsicle her mother had given her as an afternoon snack.

I was impressed. Robin was my own personal bully. So often did she terrorize me—leveling me with a push and taking whatever toy I happened to be playing with—that I now lay down on the sidewalk the moment I saw her coming. I considered Robin my friend solely by virtue of the fact that she did not call me names.

Robin was not the only child Bobby Bane flattened. Soon, neighborhood Moms were in turmoil. They confronted Bobby's mother without satisfaction.

"Why," I asked my own mother, "is Bobby so mean?"

"Well," she said thoughtfully, "I suspect he's very lonely. His family's moved twice in the last year. He doesn't have any friends."

That, I thought, was perfectly understandable and unlikely to change any time soon.

I met Bobby for the first time at the bottom of my driveway where I, in the floppy hat my mother tied to my head to shield my translucent skin from the Sun, was taking a group of Teddy Bears and dolls for a drive in my Radio Flyer. One moment I was alone, the next, I was facing a brush-cut, glaring terror at least twice my bulk and three years my senior.

His eyes widened when I looked into them, but the words he had prepared for me came out steady and strong. "Gimme the wagon, Spook," he said, and I was delighted that he had chosen such a gentle epithet. Still, his fists clenched and unclenched as if it were all he could do to refrain from tearing me limb from bloodless limb.

I did not lie down. Nor did I attempt to flee. Instead, I drew very close to Bobby Bane—close enough that he could count the tiny blue veins beneath my skin. Close enough that he could imagine that my transparent eyes afforded him a view of the inside of my alien skull.

I tilted my head, looked up into his face and said, "I know you don't really want to hurt me. You're a nice little boy. You just need a friend. Can I be your friend?"

Bobby Bane turned and left without uttering another word.

The next time I saw him, he invaded a small group of neighborhood children just as Robin's mom was passing out homemade cherry popsicles speared on little plastic forks. From that moment, he was just another neighborhood kid. The Moms figured his parents must have 'had a little talk' with him, but I knew, as our eyes met over our bright cherry ice cubes, that his transformation had not arisen from anything his parents had said.

Mother also knew this, having witnessed my confrontation with him from our kitchen window.

"Meg," she said when I told her how Bobby had joined our play group, "you have a way about you."

A way about me. In my young mind, Way translated to 'power' or 'magic.' The fairy tales I read were full of such things, and they inspired hope. An ugly princess might possess such goodness as would grant her the gift of Beauty. I was certain my powers, such as they were, did not run to literally making myself beautiful, but I now knew that they would allow me to wring compassion out of the kind, and tolerance out of the surly.

Perhaps, in some sense, my Way was a veil behind which I could hide my repulsiveness, and if I could not transform *myself*, perhaps I could transform the way others saw me.

As I grew older, I discarded the idea of magical powers, of course, but I still recognized that what Mother had said was true —I did have a way about me.

By the time I was in junior high school, I had concocted the theory that what I had exercised on Bobby Bane and countless others since, was a shrewd understanding of the human psyche. Everyone needed acceptance, even the seemingly needless.

The history of my religion provided me with a totem for my ability to parry the mindless, visceral hostility toward the alien: The White Dog.

It is recorded of the Son of the Founder of my faith that when He, in His twilight years, journeyed through the United States, He would travel the neighborhoods of New York in a carriage accompanied by a handful of believers. In one of the affluent neighborhoods on His accustomed route lived an elderly woman who had shown such hostility for the Master (as He was called), that the believers avoided her at all costs, finding other paths for Him to take to His appointments.

The Master, on the other hand, would seek her out, making certain that His carriage passed her house every morning where she could be seen taking the Sun on her front porch.

While the believers cringed and probably prayed, the Master would smile and wave at the dowager, who would only glare at this Persian 'mystic,' then avert her gaze, her hands stroking and smoothing the silky fur of the small, white dog in her lap.

One morning, after He had been rebuffed repeatedly by the hostile old woman, the Master bid the driver stop before her home. Over the protests of His companions, He debarked and strolled up the path to the front porch. Seating himself across from His enemy, He noted how very beautiful was the little white dog and inquired as to what kind of dog it was.

Well, the woman loved that dog above all things, as the Master obviously knew. His praise of the animal unleashed such a flood of delight from her that she regaled her unwelcome guest with tales of the little animal's cleverness.

The Master was late for His appointments that day, but He had made a great friend. When the believers begged to know how He had transformed the forbidding harpy into a welcoming angel, He told them about her beloved pet.

"Everyone," He said, and I imagined a twinkle in the deep azure eyes, "has a White Dog."

They did. And I learned to find those favored pets unerringly and parlay them into, if not friendship, at least acceptance. When a first meeting threatened to be hurtful to me, I invoked the White Dog and diffused the potential for injury. Sometimes with a smile, sometimes with a word, sometimes with (I swear) a mere thought. 'Spook' became an endearment or, at least, a good-natured tease on the tongues of my agreeable conquests. I fit safely in.

When I reached high school, things changed. Fitting safely in was no longer enough. My male 'buddies' had become single-minded automatons powered by testosterone and failure fear, and my girlfriends were beginning to disappear into the nether realm of dating and hushed, giggle-punctuated conversations about the relative merits of this or that hormone-flushed, peach-faced 'stud.'

For a while it seemed as if my only role in all of this would be as a shill when my merely plain companions toured the local mall. (As I said, Doraverage, it pays to take Dorugly with you when shopping for potential princes.)

I was alone so often, so suddenly, cloistered with my books, my parents were alarmed.

"What's the matter, Moonbeam?" Daddy asked me one solitary Saturday night. "Did you and Cora have a falling out? You're usually inseparable."

"Cora," I said, pretending not to care, "has a date."

"Cora?" Daddy repeated, and the corner of his mouth curled.

Cora, it should be noted, was overly plump, horribly myopic and tended to bray like a mule when surprised into laughter. Her round face was shiny with adolescence and her eyes behind her thick lenses had the naked, strained look of a perpetual squinter. She was my best friend and I adored her. Until now, we had done everything together.

"Cora," I affirmed, and felt a swift stab of betrayal. I had as good as gotten her that date. I'd been with her when she met *him* in the yogurt shop at the mall. I got Frozen Raspberry Truffle all over my best sweater and she got the *klutz* who put it there.

Maybe, I thought, I could rent myself to other dateless high school girls. I could just see my billboard ad: *Getting late—no prom date? Call 1-800-OGRE. We guarantee speedy results.* I could call the business Rent-a-Wretch.

Daddy patted one knobby knee, then ruffled my lately close-cropped thatch of cellophane, which Mother (bless her heart) had attempted to dye strawberry blonde. I so resembled a peach-colored dandelion that I expected to see the fuzz float and scatter to the four corners of my room.

"Don't let it get you down, Megan," Daddy told me. "I expect you'll be dating any day now—and way too soon for your old man. You have a way about you," he reminded me with a smile, and left me alone with Charlotte Brontë.

I did have a way about me, and up till now, I had employed it only in the interest of survival. But might it do more? Just how powerful, I wondered, as my mind returned to the gothic, was the White Dog?

While I no longer believed in magic, I had also discarded the idea that I was a natural psychologist. I now was leaning toward the belief that I had psychic powers for which the White Dog was a focus. Then too, I had read much of tribal cultures, totems

and animal guides. There was certainly a healthy dose of that in
my adolescent philosophy.

I lay awake that night in a moral stew. I had invoked my
totem purely in self-defense, never for self-aggrandizement. I
had used it to dissuade attack, to promote tolerance and never to
inveigle or seduce. I had never used it selfishly—had I?

When I went to sleep the situation was black and white—
self-defense was acceptable, coercion was not. When I awoke,
black and white had merged into a pleasant shade of gray.
Self-defense and coercion were all but indistinguishable. And
equally innocent, I assured myself. After all, I intended no harm
to anyone. I only wanted a date. My manipulation would be
guiltless because my motive was pure—salvation through right
motivation.

I set to my task shyly at first—prodding, probing, the way I
have seen chimps poke at a log full of ants. There was no one
boy I doted on—quite frankly, I had considered forming such
attachments ridiculous and futile. So, I issued a general appeal,
replacing my habitual mental suggestion (*I'm average, just
average, ignore me*) with a new one (*I'm pretty, I'm charming, please
notice me.*)

You expect to hear that it didn't work, don't you? That I
discovered it was mere winsomeness and warm-heartedness
that made people befriend me. You're wrong. It *did* work. I got,
not just one offer of a date, but two.

By the time my senior prom rolled around, I was dating
even more steadily than Cora, who had lost weight and gotten
contact lenses. But after the senior prom, I put this more
powerful manifestation of my totem aside. I no longer suggested
to all and sundry that I was anything more than someone they
should feel amiably disposed toward.

Why?—you're no doubt asking. Hadn't I virtually assured
myself a normal life?

No. That was a chimera. Certainly, I could suggest to someone that I was a princess, win their regard, perhaps even enter into a relationship with them. But the thought of creating such a fairy tale and then having to live in it terrified me utterly.

What if I should attract someone so much he should ask me to marry him? And what if I were to fall in love with him and that love were to make me so stupid as to say 'yes?' Would there not come a time when I would let the veil fall in the desperate hope that my husband would play Roxanne to my Cyrano and love me for me and not because of the White Dog? How would he feel when he realized that his princess was really a frog? How would *you* feel?

That prospect numbed me so much that I spent my entire post high school summer sequestered with the first fruits of the Sarpy County library system.

I left home in the fall to attend a college in upstate New York, where a fine arts program allowed me to surround myself with beauty both natural and man made. I had a few friends, mostly female. To men I was more than transparent; I was invisible.

This was fine for most of my first semester. For another half semester I hung on in diligent self-denial, feeling noble and self-sacrificing, the real power of the White Dog lying untapped.

It was a lonely existence, the life of a perpetual witness—observer of everything, participant in nothing.

Finally, I succumbed. I gave in to the lure of being at least a fringe participant. I'd be fine, I reasoned, as long as I understood that this was a fairy tale and that at intervals I would be obliged to awaken myself, whisk a wrist across my brow and exclaim, "It was only a dream! Only a dream!"

I was content to haunt the fringes, at first, but of course that didn't last. Life is addictive. I could not resist the temptation to imbibe.

I started my fall by merely suggesting that I was not only vivacious and winsome, but cute. That garnered me friends of both sexes and a role in one of those lighthearted groupings of young people that are the perpetual stuff of sitcoms.

It was a happy association, a cozy rabble of art students who did nearly everything together, who saw each other through thick and thin, and who did not begin to pair off in earnest until the middle of their senior year.

The first pairing was within the group and hardly changed the dynamic at all, but the second brought a new face into the crowd, left only three singles and sounded the death knell of our carefree band.

I was saddened by it all, but also profoundly and painfully relieved. It meant I would never face the post-graduation good-byes, the empty promises to write, to call, to reunite once a year at that special place.

When I graduated, I shared tearful good-byes with no one. My parents were all smiles as they watched me accept my diploma and helped me move my belongings to an apartment in Queens. I had already gotten a job at a respected art gallery in Manhattan, which was where I met Simon Bruce and fell irretrievably in love.

He was one of the gallery's clients, a talented, prolific artist with a broad range that somehow still managed to embody unique style. You could not see one of Simon's paintings and mistake it for anyone else's work. He used primaries as well as pastels, he rendered the dark and atmospheric as convincingly as he did the light and airy. His paintings were sharply realistic or they were whimsically surreal. He painted landscapes with as much conviction as he did portraits, but he did not consider them landscapes.

All his work, he pointed out to me, was about people. And it was, I realized. Even in the most overwhelming work of natural or sur-natural beauty, there was a person. And that person, in Simon's eyes, was the focus of the painting.

He was as vivid as his work, with hair the color of old gold and sea green eyes that could melt me at thirty paces. I was smitten, both with Simon and with his art. And, in that fragile and exalted state, I considered the unthinkable—pursuing the chimera. Then, I did more than consider it; I did it.

I no longer had any *beliefs* about my 'powers,' other than that they existed. I exploited the White Dog shamelessly—no, untrue, there was shame and I felt every morsel of it. But not enough—not nearly enough—to make me hesitate or halt. As we spoke of painting, I impressed upon him that I was, myself, a work of art—not merely pretty, but ravishingly, heart-breakingly beautiful. I knew I could attract him, of course, but could I make him fall in love with me?

Mornings: He dropped by the gallery with coffee and muffins. Afternoons: He happened by more and more often just in time for my lunch break.

Finally, one night, he came by and asked me out to dinner.

Three months after our first official date, he took me on a carriage ride through Central Park. It was a crisp autumn evening and the moon hung over the Chrysler building like an errant balloon whose string had tangled with the spire.

It occurred to me as we drove through the silky night that I must be nearly invisible beneath the moon—colorless light on colorless hair and skin. If he painted it, the work would be called *The Courting of the Ghost Maiden*. The thought nearly made me giggle and then it made me pause and wonder how he saw me this night—how he saw me any night. I had no idea, you see, how I looked to the people I used my Way with. I never held in my mind an exact image when I 'broadcast' my suggestions. They were amorphous, never specific.

As we drew to the end of our ride, to a place near the restaurant where he had made dinner reservations, I suddenly felt the evening groan under the weight of moment.

"Megan," he said, and took my hand and turned his face to me.

My heart stopped in my breast. Oh, dear God. Here it was—the moment of truth. I was suddenly terrified and practiced the word 'no' mentally over and over.

"Megan, marry me?"

I opened my mouth and the word 'yes' fell out into his hands. I tried to make myself take it back, but I could not, so I cried what he took for tears of joy and cursed my own weakness.

I lived out the night in a state of siege, held hostage by my love for him and horror at what I had allowed to happen. It was no use saying that only I would be hurt by my deception. If he ever discovered the truth about me, *he* would be hurt.

I considered dropping my façade. Several times that evening and all the evenings that followed, I came close to doing it, but I couldn't bear the thought of how he might react.

Finally, one morning, I awoke with a suitable plan. I would let the veils drop gradually. That way there would be, for Simon, no sudden shock of revulsion, but merely a gradual cooling of ardor and the puzzled sensation of having just arrived someplace without knowing how he had gotten there. It would be no less painful for me, perhaps, and would only prolong the inevitable, but he would be spared me breaking off the engagement while he yet thought himself in love with me.

Having made this sensible decision, I did not pursue it as sanguinely as I might have daydreamed. Did you imagine I would? Any number of things stood between me and the detachment I aspired to.

First and foremost, I loved Simon. And I wanted to believe that he loved me—*me*, not the phantasm. Sometimes, I would tell myself that, of *course* he really loved *me* because he was, after all, a man of great spiritual insight and maturity. And then I would find myself raging at him, for naturally, being a man, his physical attraction to me was the cornerstone of the relationship and the originating impulse for anything else he might feel. And that being the case, the removal of that cornerstone would cause the immediate collapse of *everything*.

That was the war waged daily in my heart: Simon, Good and True versus Simon, Frail and Male. That was the $64,000 question which, thanks to inflation, had increased tenfold in value: *Confronted with my grotesque reality, Roxanne, will you yet love me?*

Really, after being so betrayed, would he even *like* me?

In the weeks leading up to our wedding—a legendary thing I believed in with the same certainty that I believed in Avalon—I began to wish I had never called upon the White Dog to win Simon. And I waffled. Oh, how I waffled. Every time we met, I was going to begin dropping the veils. And every time we met I thought of a reason I should wait until the *next* time we met.

Ultimately, it was Simon who provided what was at once the most perfect and painful reason to put off the inevitable. He asked to paint my portrait.

Well, you can imagine (or perhaps you can't) the gamut of emotions that stampeded through me then. Terror—of what, I have no idea. Pleasure—it was, after all, a loving gesture. Curiosity—my ultimate undoing.

As I said, I had no idea how others saw me. I knew only that I could make myself attractive to them. I'd heard my hair compared to moonlight, my skin to milk, my eyes to a misty pool. (Yes, even I had the occasional male friend who considered himself a poet. I have the hastily scribbled napkin-verse to prove it.) I knew my physical self only from mirrors and rare photographs. Both of these are unrelentingly cruel in their honesty.

I wanted to see the portrait and I did *not* want to see it. Want won. I would not withdraw my veils until after it was complete, I told myself, so I could know just how strong were my powers of suggestion.

I sat for him in the evenings in his studio where he could manage the waning light so that it did not cover me with carnival colors. The light was gold and it was silver and it lasted for perhaps twenty minutes in the state he required. He would not let me see the painting, I knew, until it was finished. Simon never showed unfinished work to anyone.

After about two weeks of nightly sitting, my patience began to wane as my curiosity waxed.

"Isn't it nearly done?" I asked.

"Nearly," he said. "Just a few more evenings."

But a few more evenings stretched into a week of evenings, then a week and a half. I have *some* self-control. In this case, it was abetted by my knowledge that my unveiling must begin the very moment the portrait's did. As much as I thirsted to see myself through Simon's eyes, I dreaded it. Not only would it end us (unless Simon were, indeed, the saintly Simon of my fairy tale), but it would, once and for all, establish the exact width of the gulf between Megan the Real and Megan the Imagined.

I have *some* self-control, I say, but not nearly enough to counterbalance either my curiosity or my penchant for flirting with pain. I still had not decided, as I surreptitiously entered Simon's darkened studio one night after a sitting, whether I would drop my veils one by one or all at once.

Do it gently, bid one voice. *Let it fade naturally.*

Get it over with, prodded another. *Cut the cord and get on with life and don't ever do anything this idiotic again.* (There's a promise I could never make in good conscience.)

I slipped into the studio as silently as a shaft of moonlight and took care to close the door behind me before touching the dimmer on the wall. The lights rose, revealing the easel with its draped canvas.

I was resolute, and made my steps to it certain. I stood facing it for only a moment before reaching up and flipping aside the linen drape.

I have no words to describe the sight or the feelings it evoked. Thunderstruck. Overwhelmed. Numbed. None of these things come close to that paralyzed, chaotic, silent shriek of emotion. Cold and heat struck me in turns—my cheeks burned and were bloodlessly icy. I raised my hands to them, but my numb fingers felt nothing.

Caught on the canvas in a wash of silver-gold, was the same pathetic creature that inhabited my mirror. And yes, I reminded myself, the real world. Simon had painted me as I was—a Spielbergian alien with stick arms, huge bottomless eyes, fright-pale shock wig and see-through flesh.

In my struggle for meaning, I didn't hear the studio door open.

"Do you like it?" he asked from behind me.

I half turned, then stopped myself. "I'm...overwhelmed," I said, honestly. My voice shook.

"You didn't answer my question." He moved to stand beside me. "I think it's a very good likeness. Do you?"

"Too good," I quipped, then, "Is that really the way you see me?"

"I suppose it must be."

I let go of the White Dog, let it escape—lick, bark, and howl.

"It's the way my *eyes* see you, at any rate. But it has to be filtered through the heart, doesn't it? That," he added, stepping around to face me, "was what I wanted to get on canvas. I tried, but I think I failed."

I have never wanted to cover my face so badly in my entire life. I started to raise my hands to do it, but he stopped me.

"What's wrong, Meg?"

Did I try to explain the White Dog? Did I try to make him believe I had these powers that had worked on everyone but him?

"I had no idea," I finally managed to say, "that I was so grotesque to you."

"Grotesque?" His eyes went past me to the painting. "No, Megan. Unusual. Exotic. Other-worldly. Never grotesque. Look again."

I did. And I saw that I—the painted I—was part of a landscape that was not, Simon would have reminded me, really a landscape at all. The eyes were not just eyes, they were mirrors, and the image that repeated in them was a cloud-draped moon. The pale hair faded into snow-covered hills. The mouth had a Mona Lisa tilt to it and lips that seemed poised to speak or laugh.

The only real color in the picture, which was almost stark in its Sun, Moon, and midnight palette, was in a rose held breast high, cradled in the bloodless hands as if being offered to the viewer. It was a red rose and at its center was a tiny, semi-circular hearth in which a fire blazed welcome.

I realized something about Simon in that moment. Simon did not paint people into landscapes, he painted the landscapes *within* people—landscapes in which they moved and lived as surely as they moved and lived in the world outside.

I realized something about my own internal landscape too, of course, but such things are best left unsaid. What I will say is that I was forced to abandon my cynicism. What the Prophets have said is true after all, that what is in a person's heart—their inner landscape—is more important in life and love and loyalty than the outer one, at least among those who are aware of such things.

With Simon's arms around me I leaned to look more closely at the hearthside scene. At the foot of the chair...

"Is that a white dog?"

He chuckled. "I don't know why I put that there. Pure whimsy, I guess. It just seemed...homey. Welcoming. Is it silly?"

"No, not silly. Not silly at all," I said, and began to wonder about the existence of Avalon.

www.ingramcontent.com/pod-product-compliance
Lightning Source LLC
Chambersburg PA
CBHW031212050726
47495CB00017B/234